If I Remember Him

If I Remember Him

Book 1 of
The Croy Cycle

Louis Flint Ceci

les croyens press

Published by Les Croyens Press
An imprint of Beautiful Dreamer Press
309 Cross Street
Nevada City, CA 95959
U.S.A.
lescroyenspress@BeautifulDreamerPress.com
www.BeautifulDreamerPress.com

This is a work of fiction. All characters, places, and incidents are the products of the author's imagination. Although some names, places, and events are referred to for historical context, all are used fictitiously. Any resemblance to actual events, locales, or persons, living or dead, is entirely coincidental.

An earlier version of Chapter 5, "Christ Lag in Todesbanden," first appeared in *Trikone Magazine*, Vol. 22, No. 1 (June 2008).

Paperback Edition
10 9 8 7 6 5 4 3 2
Printed in the United States of America

ISBN: 978-0-9708310-8-8
Library of Congress Control Number: 2020935349

Cover design by Tom Schmidt
Cover art, *The Tornado*, by John Steuart Curry. Used by permission of Kiechel Fine Art, John Steuart Curry Estate
Author photo by Dot

for Wade Dowdell,
who listened to every word,

and

Ruth Bader Ginsburg,
"Dissents speak to a future age."

CONTENTS

Part 1

Part 2

Part 3

Part 4

Part 5

Part 1

Since with all my soul I behold the face of my beloved, therefore all the beauty of his form is seen in me.

—Gregory of Nissa

Chapter 1

AN ARK

The tornado that scoured more than half the town of Croy off the face of Oklahoma passed into legend even before its dying tendrils coiled back into the sky. It was given many names: The TriCounty Twister, the Cyclone of '35, the Wild Horse Tornado—so named by some for a herd of horses said to have been scooped up by the winds and flung down upon the hapless citizens of Pesogi moments before the settlement itself was flattened. Others said "Wild Horse" was a mishearing of "White Horse" since most of the towns leveled by the twister were along that river: Vasoma, Nelson, Croy, Hoche, and the western half of Tyrola, where the White Horse empties into the South Canadian. Residents of Croy itself called it the Digger Twister and swore that Lower Pond was carved into the municipal park by the cyclone itself as it stalled in its southeastern path through town before turning northeast and following the river.

The editors of *The Croy Evening Call*, who eschewed the appellation "Digger Twister," reported local Chickasaws were calling it Crazy Woman Weather. The *Call*'s readers, however, were quick to point out that that was a common native expression. Anyone who lived any amount of time in their state knew the weather had a tendency to turn everything inside out on a moment's notice.

The debris trail sliced through the cross timbers country of Oklahoma, that rolling landscape renowned for its dense, shrubby woods where a single tree could take more than a day to fell and wear out ten men and two axes in the process. Even decades later there was enough damage to determine there had been a single, continuous vortex on the ground for fifty miles, at times stretching over a mile wide, with winds that stripped the bark off trees. No one who survived the events of that afternoon was ever comforted by these findings. They already knew, deep in their blood and their bones, the extent of the damage. Their escape had had nothing to do with facts on the ground. They had been lucky, that's all.

For many, a life of hard-won prosperity lay scattered in crazed heaps across fields and city blocks. Bewildered residents got lost in their own neighborhoods for lack of landmarks. Most of the city was reduced to rubble, something to be disposed of, hauled off to dump-pits constructed for that purpose by the Army Corps of Engineers and manned by troops from the 45th Infantry, many of them local boys with relatives of their own to bury. The bonfires burned for ten weeks, consuming uprooted trees, slabs of roofing, kitchen cabinets and bedroom walls; unclaimed mattresses, shattered wardrobes with the clothes still in them, photo albums and sea chests; farm wagons, hymnals, mangled livestock.

Some towns never recovered; their foundations have disappeared into the Oklahoma red clay. But the town of Croy held on. Peculiarly, the Negro quarter, shabby and flimsy on the east side of the White Horse, was untouched by the storm, its salvation an irritating puzzlement most folks didn't care to think about. Aid came from there first, traveling by cart over the footbridge near the Oldfield farm on the south end of town. On the west side of the river, the town's main brick and stone buildings escaped mostly intact. The county courthouse was still there, though its belvedere was gone. The Alquist mansion, with its stylish carved lintels and limestone walls, rose like a beached ship among the flotsam of its shattered neighbors. The steeple of St. Elizabeth's, the Catholic church, was stripped to the timbers, but its cross remained affixed, bent northeastward, pointing the way ruination had gone. The Santa Fe depot, a squat Romanesque fortress in native sandstone, reminded survivors there was still an outside world not overwhelmed by the sheer mess and sorrow of it all. People took comfort in these markers. They stood above the rubble like sentinel stones, promising that Croy would rise again to fill the valley of the White Horse with farms and ranches, mercantiles and churches, straight streets and tidy homes, which, flaunting history, would mostly lack basements, though due to the times many would sport elegant Art Deco lines. As the ruined past went into the dirt or drifted away in greasy smears across the sky, the lucky survivors buried their grief and the unbearable shame of their survival and got on with their lives.

Not all the damage could be cleared away, though. For decades, the sycamore and magnolia trees lining the streets had a peculiar, sheared-off look, as if the entire town had been pollarded at once. The perceptive child who asked about this was answered with silence as his elders turned and looked away to the west, their gaze fixed and unfocused, lost in a time when the sky turned green and a wedge of black darker than pitch had boiled up out of the earth and filled the horizon, devouring the hopes and dreams of an entire generation in less time than it took to boil an egg.

And not all who survived survived whole. Lerner Alquist never did get the dirt out of his skin. Running wild through the streets of Croy at the height of the horror, shrieking the name of his already lost wife, he had been sandblasted by the frenzied sky as it overtook and nearly swallowed him. He emerged in the dead calm aftermath so thoroughly covered in mud and debris that the first person to come across him mistook him for one of the Negroes from over the river, blown clear across town by the wind. From that day forward, blue-black specks peppered his face, making it hard for people to look him in the eye. Those that did were met with a glare directed at all persons equally, as if every survivor who was not his beloved Ada was an insult, a grievance, and one he intended to settle personally.

So when he showed up at the first Town Council meeting after the devastation, they were not especially glad to see him. The basement where the Council met was damp and unheated, but it was the only public structure left intact aside from the county courthouse, which was acting as a joint command center for the city's police, the sheriff, and the 45th Infantry while the armory was being rebuilt. The basement was also the only part of a planned city library that ever got built, and the Council could well imagine what the rolled up sheets of paper tucked under Alquist's arm contained.

Bennett Pautler leaned over and hissed loudly into the Mayor's ear, "Are we going to have to go through this again?"

The Mayor sighed. "He's on the agenda, Bennett. He has a right to speak."

"We have a shit-load of work to do here, Mayor."

"I am aware—"

"I agree with Councilman Pautler," Lisle Armbruster piped up, loud enough for Lerner Alquist to hear him plainly. Nevertheless, Lerner stood patiently before them, the faintest hint of a smile creeping up the side of his face.

"Mr. Alquist is next on the agenda," the Mayor said firmly to the members on either side of him, "and Mr. Alquist has the floor." He gestured to the tall, gaunt man whose face was a map of what the town had been through.

"Thank you, Mr. Mayor," Lerner said, letting the smile drop. "I'll make this brief." He shifted the papers to his hands and looked down at them a moment, then said, "Gentlemen, where are we?"

There was a pause. The Mayor said, "I beg your pardon?"

Lerner shrugged. "Where are we?"

"You call this brief?" Pautler muttered. Even the Mayor's patience was tested. "Lerner, you know perfectly well where we are. We're in the city records store room."

"Correction, if you please, Mr. Mayor," Lerner said. "You are in what is *now* the city records store room. But that was not its original purpose."

"Oh, here we go," Pautler said.

"You all know this basement was originally dug as the foundation for the town's library," Lerner went on.

"Yes, yes," the Mayor said. "Lerner, this is old history. We all know how disappointed you were when that New York foundation decided not to fund the library after all, due to," he glanced right and left around the table, "a certain lack of financial commitment on the part of the town, and," here he leveled his gaze at Alquist himself, "what the good folks out East called 'excessive and extravagant decoration unsuited for a free library in a town of this size.'"

"You're not going to make us out like some charity case!" Pautler declared.

"Who wants to be slapped down like that again?" Armbruster chimed in.

"Gentlemen, please, order," the Mayor insisted. "Lerner, a library is a fine thing, and I suppose someday Croy will have one, but—"

"But what good is an encyclopedia if you can't eat it?" Pautler said abruptly. The Mayor raised his gavel but Pautler charged ahead. "I'm sorry, Mayor, but we've got bigger fish to fry. We can't be talking about stocking up on children's books and ladies' journals and building monuments to our great success when our own citizens, our neighbors, and, yes, even some of our family and kin are without food or water or a fit place to live. And some of them don't even know what's become of their own sons and daughters, their parents or wives." He stopped then, aware he may have crossed a line, and looked quickly at Lerner. Everyone knew what had become of Ada Alquist.

But there was not the expected outburst from the town's redoubtable citizen. Instead, he nodded calmly and said, "Exactly." The Council was silent. He had their attention now. "Food is on the way, thanks to the kind folks nearby." The councilmen did not look at each other. Victuals were showing up at church halls and the VFW on a regular basis; "nearby" was as close as anyone ever got to saying, "from the Negro quarter." Alquist continued. "The Corps has the water system nearly repaired. And bricks and plaster, walls and windows can be replaced. But people cannot."

He swept his arms around to encompass the entire room, the huge basement that was the only part of the elaborate library that was ever built, now nearly full of crates and boxes, filing cabinets, broken office furniture, and, for the moment, the Town Council.

"Gentlemen, we are in one of maybe half a dozen below-ground shelters in the entire city of Croy, perhaps the entire county, and the only one on municipal property. Look around you. How many people could have safely sheltered here? How many could have ridden out the storm and emerged unscathed to rebuild the town? And how many did?"

He looked from face to face, and now his own face darkened. "You know the answer. None. And you know why. Because the building above it was never built. Because it had been turned into a warehouse, a dumping ground for fading records and broken typewriters, commodities we deemed so precious that we locked them up lest someone creep in and steal them. For what? For scrap? I don't know. But I do know many good people in this town, those with sense enough to seek shelter, came pounding on those doors above us, and when they did, they found them chained and shut. And some of them, many of them, have not been seen since."

Pautler sat silent, his face red with fury. The Mayor wiped his mouth. "Lerner, what are you saying? How would a library—"

"An ark," Lyle Armbruster said bleakly.

Lerner grasped the metaphor and immediately saw its advantage. "Yes," he said, "an ark. To weather the storm."

"That's . . . that's preposterous," sputtered Pautler. "You couldn't fit the whole town in here."

"No," Lerner admitted, "not the whole town."

"A hundred," the Mayor said thoughtfully. "Maybe a hundred fifty."

"Closer to two," said Armbruster. "They wouldn't have to sit or lie down. Most could stand. It wouldn't be for long."

"And how are we going to pay for this?" Pautler said. "Those New York fellers ain't gonna give us a second crack."

"Who needs New York?" Lerner said. They all turned to him.

"I beg your pardon?" the Mayor said for a second time.

"Who needs New York?" Lerner said, and he stepped up to the Council table unrolled the sheets of paper before them, and with them his plan to finance the main construction with his own money. Subscriptions and fund raising would finance the rest once the building was up.

There was haggling. The original plan had stumbled on Alquist's insistence on a grand scale and elegant ornamentation: two stories of stacks and reading rooms, Ionic columns out front, a central rotunda with iron scroll work and a dome, fireplaces and mosaic floor tiles—all things that had led the eastern philanthropists to reject it as overreaching. Would Alquist accept the Council's decisions on reducing the scale? He would. Would he hire only local workers for the construction? He would. Could he guarantee an independent foundation with sufficient funds to see the project through to completion? He could, if he had to mortgage his own home to do it.

In the end, the Council was satisfied.

"So," Bennett Pautler said, "instead of an Andrew Carnegie Library, we get the Lerner Alquist Library."

"No!" The vehemence of Alquist's denial took them by surprise. "Not mine! Not with my name!" He looked at each of them furiously, but saw only bewilderment and incomprehension. "Not mine," he repeated again, softer. Surely they could see why. When they still said nothing, he said, "It's meant to be a memorial. A memorial to . . ." And suddenly, he could not go on. He had meant this to be the clinching argument, knowing what sentimental old fools these men were. But when it came to saying her name out loud, he suddenly found he had no voice.

The Mayor nodded slowly, understanding. "A memorial to all those who lost their lives in the storm. A fitting tribute that both honors their memory and looks to a brighter future. Lerner, this is just what the town needs." But Alquist shook his head; his jaw worked, but no words came out. "Is that not what you meant, Lerner?" Bennett Pautler asked. "A memorial for all the town?"

And then the Council saw something remarkable: they saw doubt on the face of Lerner Alquist, and when he spoke, there was a hollowness in his eyes and voice as if he weren't speaking to them at all. "If that is what you wish," he said, and then nodded as if hearing a reply, though none of them had spoken.

The Council proceeded with what other business was urgent, but Lerner Alquist left, gathering up his plans and walking up the stairs to the devastated world outside without saying another word. As soon as the closing of the outside doors echoed down the stairwell to the basement, the council members ceased their talking and looked in the direction he had gone.

"I don't think that man is long for this world," the Mayor said.

"He's losing it," Pautler agreed. "We'd better be sure that foundation is established before there's a single contract signed or a single brick laid."

Lisle Armbruster giggled. "'Who needs New York?' I guess no one does. Not if you're Lerner Alquist, you don't. He's New York enough for anyone."

From then on, Lerner Alquist was known as "New York" Alquist—though never to his face.

Outside, the chill evening air filled Lerner's lungs and brought him back to life, as if upon emerging from that cellar he inhaled for the first time in weeks. The air was unusually cold. The day after the tornado, the temperature dropped so rapidly the rubble was dusted with snow. It felt that cold again tonight.

But that was not what brought him back to life. For one brief instant, as he was about to beat it into their thick skulls that it was Ada's Memorial—Ada's, not the whole sorry town's—she was suddenly there before him. Her face was as real and palpable as the last day he had seen her alive. And he had spoken to her, and she had nodded. For that moment, while her face still hung before him, he was not alone.

The damp that cooled his cheeks now must be more snow. He wiped it away savagely. He would complete this project. The Council could do what it damned well pleased, but the town would see her in what he built. He would make sure of it.

Construction went in fits and starts. Men eager for work poured in to rebuild the town and start erecting the library. But there were interruptions—the Second World War and the Korean Conflict and a shortage of men and materials. There was constant meddling by the Council as it cut corners and chipped away at the design with all the tact and ruthlessness of a committee. Lerner kept his end of the bargain with a stream of public subscription drives and personal donations, which he used to cajole, glad-hand, and shame his fellow businessmen into matching. All the while, the land deals that funded his contribution made evictees and tenant farmers of the town's rural neighbors. The steel in Alquist's eyes reflected the iron of his will, which inevitably and relentlessly replaced what was left of his heart.

In the process, he lost sight of his daughter, Virginia, who was not yet two years old when her mother was borne off by the wind. Left much to herself, she grew up with just as strong a will as her father, but pointed in a very different direction. The library project dragged on as she grew from neglected childhood, through overlooked adolescence, and into headstrong young womanhood. If Alquist noticed at all he had resources other than his county-wide holdings to protect and projects other than the library to oversee, he noticed too late.

In the spring of 1952, almost seventeen years to the day that the Tri-County Twister tore the heart out of Croy, a second funnel cloud touched down. It did only minor damage, and most of that to the Negro quarter (leading some folks to feel a misplaced sense of "natural balance"). And true to New York Alquist's prophetic vision, seventy-three citizens took shelter in the basement of the nearly finished Memorial Library, most of them getting a look at the interior for the first time. They were suitably impressed. Knowing the town was buoyed on a crest of civic elation at having escaped a second scourging, Alquist mounted one final fund-raising campaign, this time to restore an ornament that had disappeared early under the Council's artless knife. It would be a fitting crown on what for him had always been and would always be Ada's Memorial.

Chapter 2

YOU'LL NEED THE INDIAN

Andy Simms shuffled the music on the piano as he watched Pastor Jacobs approach down the aisle of Mt. Hermon Bible Church. Simms had been the music minister at Mt. Hermon since arriving in Croy two months earlier. A recent graduate of the Conservatory of Music at Wheaton College, he still felt like an outsider, a Northern elm among Southern magnolias. He hoped to take a step toward ending that tonight, but he would need Jacobs's permission first.

"Everything ready for Sunday, Andy?" Jacobs asked, smiling.

"Ah, yes, Pastor." His hands, usually so quick and sure on the keyboard, suddenly didn't know where to go. He sat on them. "There's one or two hymns I'm not certain of." One hand flew out of its own accord and slid the music uselessly back and forth on the stand. "That is, which one would fit best."

Jacobs smiled. "We don't want to be too set, now, do we? That leaves no room for the Holy Spirit. I'm sure He'll send you the proper hymn at the proper time."

Andy smiled but cringed inwardly. The Holy Spirit had left him high and dry a few times in the past.

"Was there anything else?" Jacobs asked.

"Well—"

"Pastor Jacobs?" Mrs. Oldfield, the church secretary, walked toward them across the sanctuary.

"Yes, Mrs. Oldfield?"

Andy looked down, smothering his impatience.

"Harry Edom's here with the invoice." Mrs. Oldfield lowered her voice. "I looked it over but I think you should double-check it. I don't believe all the work's been done."

"It ain't been," a voice boomed from the pastor's office. "That's what I come to see the Reverend for."

Andy turned to see a figure in the doorway. He was medium height and broad-shouldered, dressed in blue jeans and a loose-fitting plaid shirt. Straight black hair framed a face with high cheekbones and a smiling mouth.

"Come on in, Harry," Jacobs called out and Harry Edom advanced. Mrs. Oldfield avoided looking him in the eye as she left. "Harry, this is Andy Simms, our new music minister," Jacobs said.

Harry's smile broadened to a grin, white teeth flashing against smooth dark skin. "So, you're the miracle worker," he said and reached out a hand. "Glad to meet you."

Andy felt a sudden thud in his chest and stumbled to his feet. "Thanks," he said, extending his hand. He caught a whiff of fresh-sawn pine as he leaned in. Harry's grip swallowed his, the calluses making Andy's palm tingle. "I'm hardly a miracle worker."

"Naw, I've heard you. Heard the choir and the music these past Wednesdays. You've done wonders."

"Well," Andy looked to his pastor, who simply smiled his usual smile. Andy turned back to Harry, but as soon as he made eye contact he felt that thud in his chest again. *Not here*, he thought. *I am safe here, I am sealed.* He raised his eyes to the man's forehead. "I don't remember seeing you in church."

Harry turned to the pastor with a wink. Jacobs responded, "Ah, Harry is of a . . . different persuasion."

"Which is to say, none," Harry added happily.

"Then how . . . ?"

"Oh," Jacobs said, "I suspect one can hear our voices rising up pretty well from outside. From across the street, even. From a porch swing, say, on a certain porch," and here it was the pastor's turn to wink at Harry.

"Guilty as charged," Harry admitted. "Though a little less so lately. Lerner's on the warpath again. Got Ginny bottled up tight."

Jacobs nodded. "Susan's said as much."

Andy's ears pricked up at the mention of his pastor's daughter. Here was a chance to get back to his original question.

"Lerner Alquist has a powerful temper," Jacobs was saying. "That happens sometimes with wealthy men. The Good Lord has said as much."

"Yeah, eye of the camel and all that," Harry said.

"Well, something like that. They have no practice with patience, no reason to take responsibility for their moods. You need forbearance with the very rich."

"Or the very handsome," Andy added. They both looked at him. "Sorry," he said and busied himself with his music.

"The point is," Jacobs went on, "you and Virginia had better stay on his good side if you want things to go aright."

Harry's face went blank. "Things? Can't think what you might mean, there, Reverend. So, maybe we'd better take a look at that invoice."

"Yes, maybe we'd better."

Listening in, Andy learned that Harry had been working on long-delayed maintenance the recent storm had made more urgent. There was talk of joists and flashing and drainage, all of it beyond him. But near the end, Harry said something that caught his ear. Both men were looking at a corner of the ceiling nearest Andy when Harry said, "Nope, plaster work's not my strong suit. You'll need The Indian for that."

That's how Andy heard it: The Indian, capitalized and pronounced like some kind of title. But Harry's smile held a half-smirk when he said it, undercutting the honor.

When Harry left—yelling a loud "See ya, Miracle Man!"—Andy turned expectantly at Jacobs, who smiled and chuckled. "I've been preacher here nearly twenty years, but now *you're* the Miracle Man."

Andy blushed.

"I'm sorry, Andy," Jacobs said. "There was something you wanted to ask me, wasn't there?"

It's now or never, he thought. Time to grow up. "Yes, Pastor."

"You can call me Matthew, you know."

"Ah, yes." Yes, he could, but he couldn't. "I was wondering if— I was wondering if I might call on Susan this evening." He told himself to be ready for anything and expect nothing.

"Of course," Jacobs said. "What time?" Jacobs asked.

"Um . . ." He hadn't thought that far ahead.

"Sometime after supper, say?"

"Uh—"

"Say, eight o'clock?"

"Sure. Yes!" Andy wiped his hands on his trousers. "Thanks. Thanks, Matthew."

"Oh, I think we might be back to Pastor, now," he said soberly, but at Andy's panicked look he laughed. "Oh, Andy, I'm joking! I'm sorry. No, you can truly call me Matthew. God willing, we'll be working together for a long time, and I don't want there to be any sense of hierarchy between us. You should think of me as a friend, not just your pastor. That's what a good pastor is, really."

Andy nodded and felt his shoulders relax.

"Was there anything else?"

"No. That was it." Andy laughed. "That was the big one, at any rate."

"Was there a little one?"

"Well, I noticed Harry called someone 'The Indian.' But Harry's an Indian, too, isn't he?"

"Yes, he is. Chickasaw. But you heard right. Not *an* Indian. *The* Indian. Harry was talking about Sundar Singh Sohi, who most people hereabouts call 'Sunny.' Sometimes they also call him 'The Indian' on account of his heritage. It isn't always meant kindly, but he and Harry are old friends."

"Is he a Sikh, then?"

Jacobs nodded appreciatively. "They taught you well up there at Wheaton."

"I didn't know there was a Sikh community in this part of Oklahoma."

"There isn't. Not in this part nor any other part, save those few that winter over with the circuses. Sunny's uncle and all the rest of his folks, they all settled in California. He doesn't speak of them. His father's dead, lost in the India partition riots a few years back. I don't know what became of his mother." Matthew Jacobs shook his head. "No, no community. I thought for a while he was looking for one here. Even came to a few services. But something didn't take and he drew back. He's a bit of a lost soul, I'm afraid. Cut off from his people."

Andy nodded, looking down. "I know what that feels like, having no people."

Jacobs patted him lightly on the shoulder. "You have people now, son. You have us."

Andy drove home soon after that, head full of ideas. Topmost was the need to get ready for his date—should he call it a date?—with Susan

Jacobs. He'd have to shower, iron a fresh shirt, and do something with his hair, which had been on a wild rampage since moving to Oklahoma. Would a crew cut solve the problem? Is that why so many men around here had them?

He passed the town library, scaffolding erected across the entrance. He'd heard about the library almost the day he came to Croy. It was Lerner Alquist's life's work: a memorial to his dead wife, lost years ago in a storm far worse than the ropy twister that skipped across the county last week. Through the gossip that regularly churned around choir rehearsals, he learned Alquist had poured most of his fortune into the project. It was supposed to be finished at last, to be dedicated later this summer. So why the scaffolding? Had it, too, been damaged in the recent storm? He peered at the iron pipes and wooden planks and wondered if Harry worked there, too.

He crossed the railroad tracks and headed for the small house he rented from Mrs. Oldfield. The "granny house" sat at the back of Mrs. Oldfield's property, just off the alley and at the bottom of a long lawn that sloped down from the main house. When a storm had struck shortly after his arrival in Spring, he'd known better than to try to ride it out in such a flimsy structure. A Midwestern boy, he was used to violent thunderstorms. But unlike the sturdy houses back in Illinois, most homes in Croy had no basement. They were built on bare concrete pads or cinder blocks, just begging to be scattered from here to Kansas. Mrs. Oldfield's was an old farmhouse that the town had grown up around. It, too, lacked a basement, but it had a storm cellar. He spent that thunderous evening in it with her, counting the jars of canned tomatoes and pickled okra on tidy shelves while she crocheted. He had been grateful for the refuge at first, but it grew claustrophobic after the storm passed. Nevertheless, Mrs. Oldfield insisted they stay in the dim cellar a full hour. "You never know around here," she said, looking up from her work at the cellar door with suspicion.

And here she was now, pulling something up by the roots from her garden as he pulled into the alley and parked. How had she gotten back here before he did? He had a brief image of her gliding into the yard on a broomstick. He giggled, then immediately felt a burst of shame. He lectured himself as he headed for the shower. *This isn't college. You're on your own, now. Be faithful, be sober, be chaste.* Mt. Hermon was his first ministry. Mrs. Oldfield was not just his landlady, but a coworker and fellow parishioner. He should practice charity and fellowship. This was what he had trained for. Everyone back at Wheaton had said he would be great at it. He was the best they'd seen in years and they were certain they'd hear great things from him. He wished they had been a little less certain. He wished, in fact, that no one was listening for "great things" from him at all.

Chapter 3

HERMAN'S

"Oh, Daddy, no, not tonight!" Susan Jacobs pleaded.

"I'm sorry, dear, but I've already given him permission. He'll be here shortly."

"But Ginny and I were going to—" She broke off, caught between making her desperation clear and concealing its reasons.

"You can see Virginia any day," the Reverend Jacobs went on.

Maybe not for long, she thought, but she couldn't say that, so she started to say, 'I can see Andy Simms any day, too,' but she couldn't say that, either. She knew that Andy, shy in all things except his music, had been doubly shy around her, and she thought she knew why. She was old enough to recognize a crush when she saw one, and this one was clearly coming to a head. But why tonight! "Couldn't you call him and tell him to come by tomorrow? Or Sunday, after church?"

"Well, yes, I could. Is that what you think I should do?"

Susan hated it when her father smiled at her like that, with that I-know-this-is-difficult-but-it's-an-important-lesson-for-you look, as if he were the wisest man on God's green earth and she the silliest child. "But, Daddy, it's impossible."

"How so? You do like him, don't you?"

"Well, yes. I mean, he's okay. But he's so . . ."

"So what?"

Odd, is what she meant to say, but that would be unkind. "Old. He's nearly twenty-three, at least."

"And that's old, now, is it? Good heavens, I must be downright archeological."

"Oh, of course you're not. I mean, he's been to college and everything."

"And you've been stuck here with your old Dad. I thought Andy's erudition might appeal to you, since none of the local boys have caught your eye."

Susan bit her lip. There are some things you don't tell your father, especially if he's also your pastor. Her father caught something in her hesitation. "Or perhaps I'm just being an old fool?" he asked.

"Oh, for heaven's sake, no. I mean, yes, I like him and no, you're not—" Her father openly grinned at her now. "Oh, foot! Do I have to?"

The grin vanished. "Of course not. But think a moment, Susan. He's a stranger here. He has no folks at all back in Illinois now that his mother's passed. Everyone loves his music and what he's done with the choir, but I can tell he just isn't settling in. He's hesitant, embarrassed almost, like he doesn't believe our welcome, though we've given it often enough. You could help him feel at home. Besides," her father added, the twinkle returning to his eyes, "you owe him one."

Well, he had a point there, she had to admit. Playing the same music Sunday after Sunday on their woefully tuned church piano had driven her nearly bonkers. Andy had taken over from her, and he not only tuned that old clunker but somehow managed to make it sing. She didn't want to acknowledge her father's insight, though, so she put on her best adult face and said, "Okay, Daddy. For you."

Her father smiled in a way that let her know she hadn't gotten away with anything and took his papers into the study.

She was in the front room when the doorbell rang. "I'll get it," she called out and opened the door ready to smile. She almost burst out laughing instead. There was Andy Simms with a part in his hair that looked like he'd taken an axe to it, the ends sticking up on either side. *Somebody needs to tell this boy about Brylcreem*, she thought, then quickly recomposed her face. "Andy! What a pleasure to see you."

"Susan."

He looked so hopeful. "Won't you come in?" she said. Her father emerged from the study as they entered the living room. "Daddy, Andy's here."

"So he is. Good to see you again, Andy."

"And you, too—" an awkward pause "Matthew."

Well, thought Susan, *first names. There's been some negotiating going on behind my back. Very well, let's see how far we get.* "Won't you sit down, Andy? No, here on the sofa, where we can talk. Daddy, is the sermon going well?"

"Well enough," her father said. She raised an eyebrow at him. "But perhaps it could use a little polishing. I trust you two will comport your-selves in my absence?"

"Oh, yes sir!" Andy said a bit too quickly. As soon as her father left the room she turned and smiled at Andy. He smiled back. His hands did a funny kind of flip-flop in his lap. He brought them together as if they were going to fold in prayer, but then they just sort of passed each other by and ended up on opposite thighs, then clutched together, then quickly back to where they'd started, looking kind of lost and worn out. She was mesmer-ized by the display.

He spoke first. "I want to thank you for your leadership in the choir," he said.

"Me? I don't lead. I just sing loud."

"Oh, no, you do more than that." He blushed, which Susan found both childish and kind of cute. "I mean, I don't think you sing loudly. You sing well. Very well. Your voice carries the melody effortlessly, clearly."

"Why, thank you."

"No, I mean it. You can really hear the Spirit in it. I think the whole congregation can feel it. I certainly can."

"Well, I've always enjoyed singing. And the church makes a perfect audience. Captive, you know."

"Captivated, I would say."

Now it was her turn to blush. "I've often thought of getting some pro-fessional training," she said to recover. "But there's no one here in Croy who's really qualified."

"Oh, no," he said. "Don't do that."

"Don't do what?"

"Don't over-coach your voice. Your voice is clean and clear. No af-fectation, no styling. You're fine the way you are. You're pure."

Susan looked at him, startled. He looked steadily back at her. "Well," she said, "your piano playing is certainly a gift to the congregation, espe-cially after they had to suffer through my hammering away."

"I'm sure you weren't that bad."

"Oh, no, I'm sure I was. I'm not the only one who's glad you took that burden off my hands." She laughed. He didn't. "Literally," she added.

He laughed then, too, but a bit late. They fell back into the silent hole they'd started in. She cleared her throat. "Even Ginny likes it."

"Who?"

"Ginny Alquist. She's my best friend from high school. She's not in our church, but she and her boyfriend listen from across the street."

Andy nodded slowly. "Harry Edom."

"Oh, do you know him? Oh, but of course you do. He's working on the church. How silly of me."

"No, not at all. I just met him today. I've never met—Ginny, is it?"

"Would you like to?" she asked impulsively. There might be more than one way to get through this evening, she thought. Kill two birds with one stone.

"Sure," Andy said. "If she's your best friend, I mean. I'm sure I'd be happy to meet her."

"Daddy?" Susan called over her shoulder.

"Yes, dear?" came the answer from the open study door.

"Andy and I are going to Herman's. Is that all right?"

The Reverend Jacobs appeared in the doorway. "Of course it is. It's a fine night for a drive. Just be sure you get back by the usual hour."

"Oh, I'm sure we won't be that late, sir," Andy said, rising.

Susan smiled to herself. *You don't know Ginny.*

Andy had his own reasons for wanting to go. He'd heard the kids in the choir talk about Herman's Dairy Queen drive-in, apparently the only decent place to hang out on a summer evening. He thought he might be able to connect better with them if he went there himself and got a feel for the place. Besides, he had run out of things to say in a surprisingly short time. Perhaps having another person along would take the focus off him.

They drove the short distance to the Alquist mansion, a two-story house in native stone that sat across from the church. It looked more like a fortress than a home. They found Virginia sitting on the curb outside, her back against a magnolia tree. "What took you so long?" she said and climbed into the front, squashing Susan against him. It would be difficult shifting gears without brushing her knee. Susan didn't seem to mind.

"Ginny, this is Andy Simms. He directs the choir at church."

"Yeah?" Ginny said, leaning over and smiling at him. "Pleased to meet 'cha."

Andy couldn't very well offer his hand with the three of them crammed together like that, so he just smiled and nodded.

"Oh, hey!" Ginny suddenly exclaimed. "Simms! Miracle Man!"

Andy groaned.

"What?" said Susan.

"That's what Harry calls him. Miracle Man."

Susan looked at him with raised eyebrows.

"I wish he wouldn't call me that," Andy said.

"Oh, that's just our way down here," Ginny said.

"It's a sort of nick-name," Susan explained, "a sign of acceptance, really. He doesn't mean anything by it."

"Oh, hell, no," Ginny said. "Everyone has one. Even old Lerner, God help us."

"Lerner's her father," Susan said calmly.

She didn't seem at all upset at Ginny's language. He frowned. "Well, I wish he'd just call me Andy," he said.

"You can tell him so yourself," Ginny said. "He's meeting us at the DQ."

"Oh, Ginny, is it that bad?" Susan said.

"Do *not* get me started. I've been cooped up so long I could explode. Oh, hey, Suzie-Q? I'm dying for a cig. You got one?"

"I've just come from home, remember?"

Ginny leaned forward. "How 'bout . . . ?" She leaned back when she saw Andy's thin-lipped expression. "No, I don't suppose so."

They pulled into the lot at Herman's, a small white building with bright red trim outlined in neon. On a pole high above the lot an over-sized white ball with multicolored neon tubes flaring out of it gave the DQ a modern look. Andy's eyes immediately picked out Harry, a warm dark shape lounging against a pick-up. He got that feeling in his chest again. Ginny popped out of the car almost before it came to a stop and ran up to him. Andy rounded the front of his car and reached to open Susan's door just as she emerged on her own. She murmured a soft, "Sorry."

"That's okay," he said. "Can I get you something?"

"Sure, a coke, please."

"You got it. What kind?"

"Oh, 7-Up, I suppose." She hurried over to join Ginny and Harry at the truck.

Andy walked slowly to the order window. The crowd was mostly high school kids, though a few were closer to his own age. The younger kids were segregated by sex, the girls clustered in groups near the walk-up window or crowded in the small but brightly lit interior. The boys were all outside, further off from the light and under some trees. He recognized Scott Pritchard from choir practice. He was blowing little chunks of ice through a straw at one of his friends for entertainment. The older kids were in couples, draped in or on the cars parked haphazardly around the lot.

Andy returned with their drinks, lit only by the rainbow of neon from Herman's sign. Ginny and Susan were in tight conversation. Harry lounged against the truck's side-panel, an arm casually but possessively hooked around Ginny's waist.

Andy stopped, a drink in each hand. Shadows of different hues spread out before him. He looked at Harry's easy slouch, the way he was entwined with Ginny, the way Ginny took it for granted. *Of course*, he said to himself, *of course he is*. There was a different feeling in his chest now, as if his heart had been replaced by a wooden block. He stepped forward.

Susan was speaking earnestly: "You've got to tell him, Ginny, and soon."

Ginny shook her head and shot a jet of cigarette smoke from the corner of her mouth. "Unh-unh. Harry'd lose his job, and it's the only decent one he's had all year."

The conversation dropped off as he approached but he pretended not to notice. "I'm sorry," he said, "I didn't think to ask you-all what you wanted." He handed Susan her drink.

"'Sokay." Harry patted his back pocket. "I got what I need."

"And are you just going to stand there and lean on it?" Ginny asked.

"Don't want to shock the deacon here," Harry said.

"I'm not a deacon yet," Andy said. "Besides, you're an avowed heathen, so I don't see how it makes a whit of difference."

"You got a sharp one there, Suzie-Q," Harry said.

"Are you going to answer my question?" Ginny asked.

"Maybe we should go someplace a little less well lit?"

"Oh, for God's sake!" Ginny made a dive for his back pocket.

"Whoa, Nelly!" Harry said, fending her off. He pulled a hip flask out of his pocket and handed it over, flashing a smile at Andy.

Andy turned away. He agreed to go to Herman's to get to know these people better, but now it felt like a set-up. He would never fit in with them and they were making sure he felt it. He turned back, intending to suggest coolly that they should be leaving, only to see Ginny extend the flask to Susan. "Hooch?" she said.

He froze, his mouth open.

But Susan merely shook her head and sipped her 7-Up. "I'm pure," she said.

Ginny laughed, which came out more like a snort, but Susan looked up at Andy and winked. It was as if the two of them were putting something over on Ginny. He saw Harry notice the exchange and nod his approval. It made all the difference in the world. He relaxed. He wasn't the outsider after all.

"Uh-oh," Susan said, "here's trouble." They all turned as a police car pulled into the lot. Ginny slipped the hip flask into her clutch and took a step away from Harry, who stood up straight, dropping his arm from her waist. "Big trouble," he said.

Andy watched as a tall man stepped out of the passenger side of the patrol car and approached them. There was something odd about his face. At first Andy thought it was a trick of the multi-colored lighting, or that a cloud of dancing gnats hung in the air between them. But as he got closer, he could see the man's face was dotted with bluish-black specks, some no bigger than a punctuation mark, a few the size of a small fly trapped beneath the skin.

"I expected to find you at home, Virginia. Like we agreed." He spoke directly to Ginny, not even looking at the others.

"I had a change of heart," she said.

"I don't care what you changed. You don't leave the house without my permission."

"You weren't there to ask."

"Don't get fresh with me, young lady. I haven't got time to chase you down all over town."

Ginny looked on the verge of saying something nasty, but Harry laughed softly. "It's just Herman's," he said. "It's not like she's run off to Timbuktu."

Mr. Alquist turned slowly and looked Harry in the eye. Andy would not have wanted anyone to look at him that way, nor could he have looked back as steadily as Harry did. Alquist turned back to his daughter and said, "I thought I told you to stay away from this red nigger."

Andy felt the color drain from his face. He looked at Susan, at Ginny, at Harry, but none appeared shocked by this language. Harry looked calm, indifferent. "She's way past eighteen, Mr. Alquist," he said. "She can make up her own mind."

Alquist turned to him again. "Is that alcohol I smell on your breath?" he said. He turned to the policeman hanging out by the car. "Officer Owen, I do believe this young man is intoxicated. Again." Harry's expression changed then, and it was something ugly. It looked to Andy as if he wanted to punch Alquist in the face, and it looked like Alquist just hoped he'd try.

"Come along now, Harry," the officer said, stepping forward a bit but staying out of arm's reach. "Let's you and me have a little chat down to the station, what'd'ya say?"

"You can't do that!" Ginny shouted.

Alquist turned to his daughter. "You have no idea what I can do."

"It's okay, Ginny," Harry said. "Well, Percy," he said addressing the officer, "is it going to be sirens and lights like last time?"

"Oh, I don't think there's call for all that," Officer Owen said.

"Well, that's a pity. You know how this town craves excitement." He turned back to Ginny. "I'll be back soon."

"I wouldn't count on that," Alquist said, not even looking at him. Harry shot him one more glare then walked over to the patrol car and got in. The car rolled quietly out of the lot and into the night. "I'm going to call a cab," Mr. Alquist told Ginny.

"I don't want your cab!" she shot back.

"Which will take the two of us home and then return me to the office," he continued. "I'm not losing one more minute of work over this escapade."

"Why not just go to your old office, then, and leave me out of it?"

"You are going home."

"Not in a cab with you I'm not."

"Fine! Have the cab to yourself!"

"I'll walk!"

"You most certainly will not! No daughter of mine is going to—"

"I'll take her home," Andy said. He surprised even himself.

Alquist stared at him as if he'd been addressed by a tree stump. "And just who might you be?" he asked.

"Andy Simms, sir," he said, holding his voice level as he met Alquist's gaze.

"Andy's the new music minister at my father's church," Susan said, taking his arm with a smile.

"I was the one who brought Virginia here," Andy said. "I'm sorry if I've caused any trouble. I was just taking Susan and Virginia out for a Coca-Cola, it being such a warm night." Alquist continued to glare at him. "I'll take them home now," Andy continued. It was getting harder to meet that stare. "Susan's father will be expecting her."

Alquist looked him up and down. Andy felt sure he wasn't buying it. But in the end he gave a brief snort and said, "You're new here." Then he turned and walked away, calling out without looking back, "Get it right, boy. You won't get a second chance."

Susan tried to settle Ginny on their way home but no matter what she tried, Ginny would just shake her head and mutter, "I hate that son of a bitch," and, "God damn this town." When they pulled up outside the mansion, she leapt out of the car, slamming the door behind her. When Susan called out to her, she yelled "God damn it!" and ran up the steps into the house.

Susan fell into a silence of her own then, biting the knuckle on her right thumb. As they turned the corner to her house, she noticed Andy wasn't talking either. "I'm sorry about all that," she said.

"I'll bet the language is just a front," Andy said. "She puts up a tough exterior just to keep from crying."

Susan glanced at him. *That's a rather quick sketch for someone you've just met*, she thought. She turned away. "Well, she's crying now."

"She doesn't really hate her father, does she?"

She sighed heavily. "You don't know what he's like. One word from him and Harry'd lose his job on the library project. Two words, and he wouldn't be safe to walk the streets."

"He could really do that?"

"In a heartbeat. That project is supposed to be under contract with the City Council, but Lerner's got them under his thumb. Without it, Harry's only got the work at our church for them to live on, and we pay him little enough as it is."

She wondered if she'd said too much. Or had he already guessed? He was looking intensely out the windshield, not at her.

"No one should have that much control over somebody's life."

She shook her head. "It's not just her father, throwing his weight around where he pleases. It's the whole damned town. They can't see outside their little box of set ideas. Anything grand, anything new— If it's not what they expect, it must be something wrong, something wicked. Not just different, wrong. People, houses, families, jobs. It all has to fit." She rubbed her forehead with the heel of her hand. "Ginny's right. I feel it, too. This place sucks the soul right out of you. If you have one."

They had arrived at her house. Andy parked the car and looked at her. "Everyone has one," he said.

She laughed without humor. "You can say that? Even after tonight?"

"Yes."

"Even Lerner Alquist?"

"Even Lerner Alquist."

"Well, you're new here."

"It has nothing to do with me," Andy said. "Everybody has a soul. That's true no matter how new I am."

She took a moment to regard him, this calm young man sitting in the car beside her. Was he just practicing platitudes on her? No, there was no condescension in his voice, just simple conviction. It almost cut through her anger and cynicism—almost made them look like a pose—but she wasn't ready to give them up. At least, not yet.

Chapter 4

THE INVITATION

Andy didn't know what had gotten into the choir at the next rehearsal. For starters, he could actually hear the basses; the tenors made their entrances with authority and near unanimity; the younger members weren't trying to out-sing the older ones; Mrs. Littledeer, a sturdy but wavering alto, was miraculously on pitch (or nearly); and Susan's clear, strong soprano sailed out across the sanctuary with honesty and yearning, a joy that came straight from the heart. He should tell her to hold back so she would blend more, but he didn't want to. He wanted her voice to shine out and lift his soul to that musical realm where time stops and all feelings are sacred and welcome.

Even before rehearsal, Scotty Pritchard had come up and asked him a question, a real pastoral question about dating. Could it be that he was finally fitting in? That there was a role for him as deacon in this church? Of course, he wouldn't apply for it until he was married. That was the custom and he intended to follow it.

During a break, he bounced on the balls of his feet beside the piano. Susan came up and all either of them managed to do was grin at each other. Then Susan's gaze flicked to something behind him and he turned to look. Mrs. Oldfield stood at the side door where an elderly black man stood in a pinstriped blue suit. He had removed his fedora, revealing close-cropped white hair. He spoke briefly and softly, too softly to hear, but the rumble of his voice made Andy imagine he'd make a fine bass. "Who is that?" he asked.

"Reverend Jameson," Susan said. "From Mt. Zion A.M.E., across the river."

He watched Mrs. Oldfield listen to Reverend Jameson, then head for the church office, a frown deepening on her face. "Mrs. Oldfield doesn't look too happy."

Susan waved dismissively. "That woman wouldn't be properly dressed without a scowl."

Andy laughed, but to him Mrs. Oldfield looked upset, not disapproving. Oh, but things were going too well to dwell on it, so he brushed the concern aside. In a brief spark at the back of his mind it occurred to him that he might actually be happy.

In the church office, Pastor Jacobs rose and extended a hand to his fellow minister. "Brother Cecil, so good to see you."

"And good to see you as well, Brother Matthew."

Matthew motioned to a chair and Cecil took it. "You are doing well, I hope?" Matthew asked, taking a seat himself. He chose one near the other pastor rather than his usual post behind the desk. "Your family unharmed in the storm?"

"By God's mercy, yes, though many of my parishioners were not so fortunate."

"I am very sorry to hear that. Is there anything we can do?"

"Thank you, Brother Matthew, we are taking care of our own. And how are you and yours?"

"All in good health."

"I noticed Susan as I came in. She is growing into a fine young woman."

"Ah, yes. A bit too quickly for my poor heart's sake. But every day, she looks more like her mother."

"Amelia would be proud, and proud of the job you've done in raising her."

"It is very kind of you to say so."

"No kindness at all, Brother Matthew. Simple fact." And then they just sat there a moment, two aging gentlemen, smiling and nodding in the day's heat. Cecil Jameson broke the silence first. "I see the repairs are going well."

"Yes. Well, they were. Harry Edom seems to have disappeared for the moment, but I hope to get Sunny Sohi in here to finish the job."

"Ah, yes, Sunny Sohi."

Matthew took note of the look on the other pastor's face. There was a mixture of fondness and pain there. He imagined his own face must look like that sometimes when he spoke of Susan. The thought embarrassed him and he tucked it away for examination later. "And your church?" he asked. "How is it faring?"

Now the Reverend Jameson looked genuinely pained. "Not well, I'm afraid. The roof is a total loss. I fear we cannot safely congregate there in the Father's house any longer, though so many of my flock wish it. I understand their hearts, but I'm afraid my duty as shepherd requires finding them a different pasture. At least for the while. I need to see them safe first, and settled later."

Ah, that was what Matthew Jacobs had thought. And it was instantly clear what needed to be done, if he could do it without offending the other man's dignity. "Brother Cecil," he said, "there is no need to look any further. Our church can easily accommodate your congregation any Sunday."

"We are a sizable bunch."

"We can put folding chairs in the aisles."

"You are surpassing kind, Brother Matthew, surpassing kind. But we couldn't put you through all that trouble. I thought perhaps, with your kind indulgence, we might gather here Sunday afternoons. After your own services, of course."

"Or before. Our service starts at nine."

Cecil Jameson smiled. "Most of my congregation's up at daybreak, which comes mighty early this time of year. There's all manner of things to be done in some folks's kitchens if there's any rest at all to be had on the Day of Rest. And for others, there's fields and folks's homes to tend to, even on the Sabbath. But by afternoon, those toils have been washed away and we are ready." He rose and made to leave.

"Well, of course it will be our great pleasure to accommodate you," Matthew said, accompanying him to the door. "But are you certain? Couldn't you just join us at nine o'clock?"

Cecil Jameson smiled again, examining both sides of his hat. "No, it's better as is. Some services last well into the evening."

"Ours, too, expand as the Spirit wills."

"I will set my son, Ethan, as a watchman. He will make certain your congregation has sung and celebrated before any of us arrive."

The Reverend Matthew Jacobs felt a sudden chill on this warm June day. He looked his fellow pastor in the eye and said with urgency, "Your flock is safe with us."

"Oh, it is not out of concern for *my* flock, Brother Matthew, but for yours." He put on his hat and held out his hand. "Peace be with you, Brother. We are forever in your debt."

Matthew shook his hand. "Peace be with you," he said, but it sounded hollow.

Jameson's simple acknowledgment of the gulf dividing their community bothered Matthew deeply long after he left. He sat wondering if there wasn't something he could do about it. *No, he finally decided, not something* I *can do, something* we *can do.*

It took several phone calls, but the concept was well received by most of the ministers he spoke to. However, there remained one pastor he could not just telephone, one who required a personal visit. So he made the appointment, and later that afternoon, Matthew Jacobs found himself in the nave of St. Elizabeth's, gazing at the interlaced scissor trusses.

"Ah, there you are, Matthew," a hearty voice called out. "I see you've come to your senses at last and decided to convert to Mother Church."

Matthew Jacobs smiled broadly as a short but powerfully built man in a black cassock strode towards him, his hand extended. "Not this time I'm afraid, Francis," he answered. Father Francis Herron had a presence and a voice that came from a much larger space than his body. His homilies rivaled those of his Protestant brothers in their soul-shaking authority, and St. Elizabeth's summer baseball team, which Father Francis personally coached, made even the Baptists green with envy. It was said that he had been the terror of Notre Dame's defensive line, and as he gripped his hand, Reverend Jacobs was firmly reminded of that.

"You still owe us one for Amelia, you know," Father Francis said.

"I was never happier than when she joined me in my ministry," Matthew said, "but never happy that she left your church to do so."

"Well," Francis said philosophically, "where the heart leads, the soul must follow or be torn apart." He ushered Matthew through the vestry into his office. "So, if it's not the long hoped-for conversion of apostates, to what *do* I owe the pleasure of this visit?"

Matthew recounted his disturbing talk with Reverend Jameson, Father Francis nodding and even wincing at parts of the tale. "I think I understand Cecil's concern," he said. "The Tulsa riots are well within living memory of many at Mt. Zion. It takes more than a generation to heal a wound like that. But I think I see where you're headed, Matthew. There must be some way to close the rift, or at least bridge it."

"Exactly. And I think St. Elizabeth's is the perfect place to hold it."

Francis scowled at him from across steepled hands. "Are you sure of that?" he said. "The lingering taint of bells and smells might give your people the heebie-jeebies. There's some, you know, don't even call us Christian."

"That's the whole point," Matthew said. "This town is too small for 'your people' and 'my people.' We're one people, surely, in God's eyes. And we've been through a bit of a scare lately—for some, more than a scare. I think we can get past these differences and get together long enough for a simple service of praise and thanksgiving."

"One people, eh?" Francis looked thoughtful. "I'm not so sure the Rosens would agree with you—or, rather, that the rest of the town would agree with including the Rosens. But everyone else has agreed?"

"Most everyone. A few seem to be holding back to see whether you'd throw your hand in as well."

"Holding back? For the Church of the Anti-Christ?" Father Francis guffawed. "Oh, that's a clever one, Matthew. You know right where to pitch it. Still," he looked thoughtful, "the idea has merit, and currency. Ecumenicism is a river swelling through many branches of the Church these days. And holding it here has a certain symbolic appeal. The whole town remembers the TriCounty Twister and how Saint Liz sailed right through. We hosted several protestant congregations right here while they rebuilt. We shone like a beacon back then." He slammed his palm on the desk. "By God, let's do it!"

"Won't you have to clear it with your bishop first?"

"Och," Father Francis waved his hand, "His Eminence is too busy with really big do's up in Oklahoma City to be bothered with something piddling like this. No, I've no worries in that direction. It's a more local nexus of power I'm concerned with."

Matthew nodded. "I think I know who you mean."

"No amount of sand-blasting seems to have revealed the least trace of a spiritual vein in that man. You know how he treated the Sohis. I don't know how he'll take to mixing Protestants and Catholics, coloreds and whites." A troubled look crossed his face. "Say, have you contacted them? Is there a Sikh high priest or rabbi or what-have-you to talk to?"

"Ah," Matthew said, embarrassed to know more about this than Francis, "I don't think they have that sort of thing."

"What, no episcopacy?"

"No priests."

Francis looked shocked. "You're joshing me! What a way to run a church! Oh, well," he said, "they're new at it, just like you. Give them another thousand years or so and they'll have it all sorted out. But have you contacted them?"

Matthew shrugged. "I think Sunny's the only one left."

"Oh." Francis nodded. "And he's unlikely to show. And even if he does, chances are Alquist won't. Or so we can hope." He rolled his eyes heavenward. "Father forgive me, I have just prayed that one of my own lost sheep won't come back to the fold! I'll have to confess to myself and give an appropriate penance." He smiled at Matthew. "I think a rosary or two should do it, don't you?"

Matthew raised his hands. "Don't ask me. I don't know how those things work."

Father Francis rose. "Well, we'll need to set a date and iron out the details, but for now, you can tell your brethren—tell *our* brethren—that St. Liz's is in."

Matthew rose smiling and shook his hand. He turned to leave but stopped abruptly. He had been facing Father Francis during their interview, so it was only now that he saw the crucifix hanging on the wall by the door. About four feet tall and carved in glowing mahogany, it depicted the crucified Christ in a way he had never seen before. Here was no suffering savior shown at the moment of death. This Jesus had his eyes open, looking down and to his right, his expression not that of a man in agony, dying of blood loss and shock, but one of tenderness, deeply concerned for those looking on. Most remarkable of all, the right hand was no longer nailed to the cross, but extended, still pierced, in a gesture that reached forth and beckoned, drawing you toward him with both longing and a promise of fulfillment. The Reverend Jacobs stood transfixed.

"It sort of catches at you, doesn't it?" Francis said.

"It's remarkable," Matthew said, shaking his head. "Beautiful."

"It's called 'The Invitation.'" Francis came and stood beside him. "We had it in the alcove by the statue of St. Joseph for a while, but the ladies of the altar guild would find a sudden need to fan themselves after tarrying too long in its presence. It's safer in here."

"Who did it?"

"Sunny Sohi."

Matthew nodded. He might have guessed. Father Francis continued, "I thought I had that bird snared, but when I went to look, there was nothing but net. I sometimes wonder if that crucifix wasn't some sort of apology—not that I've ever known that boy to apologize for anything."

"I think he must have sampled every taste of the Spirit he could find hereabouts," Matthew said.

Francis nodded. "Sampled, yes. But never really sat down to a proper meal."

The Reverend Jacobs stopped frequently on his walk back to the parsonage, his thoughts returning again and again to "The Invitation." The figure tugged at his heart and worried his mind. What does it mean for Christ to invite you to join Him on the Cross? To be lifted out of sin, surely, but that is merely a symbolic reading. Sunny's sculpture was shockingly literal, defying the conventional presentation that pious eyes had passed over a thousand times, making them look again at what they thought they knew. And yet the carving was symbolic, too, for a real Christ could no more have hung on a real cross by one hand than he could have by two.

Matthew recalled with a shudder that the Romans impaled their victims on a short wooden peg to keep them in place while they died. Crucifixion was meant to be not only slow and painful, but degrading and dehumanizing. Christ's cross was real and His death a horror, death by defilement. *"Accursed is every man hanged upon a tree,"* St. Paul had said. As one Bible scholar put it, "A man who is strung between heaven and earth is abandoned by both and worthy of neither." If for our sake Christ accepted being accursed, are we then relieved of the obligation to suffer at all? Or do Christians accept humiliation and scorn in the eyes of the world when they accept salvation? Many would say, "Of course," but they would be thinking abstractly, not of immediate and real consequences, not of state-sanctioned torture. And what Christian in this nation expects humiliation and death just for being Christian? *No*, Matthew thought, *we do not expect to join Jesus on the Cross in that way. We see ourselves as set apart. We expect the scorn of the world, even welcome it as a badge of honor. But do we really reject the world? No.*

What we reject is people. The Cross we mount is one from which we can look down on others.

Sunny's Jesus rejected no one. The invitation was open to all. The torment in his eyes was not from the piercing thorns and mocking crowds, or the hours spent joined to the rough wood. The only real pain He felt was the absence of someone beside him. *Does God suffer if we ignore His invitation?* Jacobs wondered. *Can this be the true cause of our own suffering, our holding back from physical and spiritual union with God?*

The Reverend Jacobs hadn't puzzled it all out by the time he reached the parsonage, but he felt he had the seeds for his Sunday sermon.

Chapter 5

CHRIST LAG IN TODESBANDEN

Summer sank into a month of smothering nights. Andy tried cooling down by taking showers, but the steam lifting from his body just thickened the air. No sooner would he dry himself off and wrap himself in a towel than his skin would begin to slick and film over. He would heat up from the inside.

After a second try, he stood before the mirror on the inside of the bedroom door and brought a comb to his hair, but his hand trembled and he could not make a straight part. Another weekend approached. Another date with Susan. He paused and took a deep breath to calm himself. It was no good; his hand would not stop shaking. His skin was alive with a million tiny sparks. He let his arm drop and stared at himself in the mirror.

The trembling had begun at church that evening as he practiced the tenor aria from Bach's Cantata No. 4, "Christ Lag in Todesbanden." The movement unfolded with a beautiful obbligato in the right hand and a continuo in the left. These he could master. But time and again when he tried to fit the aria's melody into the endlessly tumbling notes, his hands would waver and the voices would fall apart.

The choir was doing a chorale from the cantata this Sunday in an English translation, "Christ Lay in the Bonds of Death." He wished they could do the whole piece, but one practice had convinced him that the gifts of the Holy Spirit could only stretch so far. Still, the fifth movement drew him in with its geometric purity in the piano part and vast spiritual longing in the vocal. If only he could master them both—will his hands to find the unity he knew lay hidden in the notes! It was an impossible task, but he would stay here late into the gathering dark, hoping to grasp the mystery and escape the airless embrace of his small rooms.

"It's really gotten to you, hasn't it?" came a voice from above.

"What?" Andy said as if waking from a dream.

"That Bach piece." Sundar Sohi, perched atop a ladder, was applying the last of his plaster repairs. "It's really gotten under your skin. You can't let it go."

Andy looked up and saw Sunny smiling down at him. His eyes were the most remarkable color, something like the green of malachite but with flecks of gold in them. His piano's reading light caught their glint. "I'm sorry," he said. "It must be tedious to listen to. I'll stop." He reached for the keyboard cover.

"No, no!" Sunny said and began descending. "Keep playing. It's the only thing keeping my mind off the heat."

"It must be hot up there," Andy said, his heart rate increasing. "It's hot enough down here."

Sunny stepped onto the floor, his white linen work shirt soaked through and clinging to his torso. Andy could clearly see the curve of his chest and the tiny crescendo at each nipple. Sunny unscrewed the lid on a jar of water and took a deep drink. He smiled ruefully at Andy. "Should have had this up there."

"Do you need more? I can get some."

"Naw, I'm nearly done. It's getting too dark to see up there." He walked over and leaned on the piano. "What keeps you so late?"

"Oh, this piece we're doing." Andy didn't notice his lie. He tried to memorize the color of Sunny's skin. It wasn't the deep brown he had seen in some of the Negroes in town, undertones of blue and yellow seeping out, nor did it have the cinnamon cast he'd noticed in the local Indians. It was something richer, as if just beneath the smooth, dark surface were a layer of gold leaf about to shine through. He had difficulty remembering where he was in the conversation. He swallowed. "So, you'll be finishing up soon?"

Sunny looked up to where the ceiling joined the wall. "I should be done now, but this damned humidity slows everything down."

Andy silently thanked God for the damned humidity.

"Another day or two."

"Then what?"

Sunny turned and grinned broadly. "Then the really big stuff."

"Here? At Mt. Hermon?"

Sunny shook his head dismissively. "Naw, this job is finished. I'm talking about the really big job in town. The library." He walked around the piano and Andy quickly made room for him on the bench. Sunny straddled it, his face lit up. "It's more than just a restoration," he said. "Mr. Alquist wants to put back the most important feature. The sculpture!"

"Sculpture?" Andy said, dazzled.

Sunny leapt up, drawing pictures in the air with his hands. "There's this triangular space above the main entrance. But it's empty, see? The City Council cut the sculpture back when they were being stupid, when they thought Alquist couldn't raise the money and they'd be stuck with the bill. But that Alquist, he's sharper than the lot of them. Those old skinflints tried to cut the heart out of the project, but they never touched its soul. I know. I've seen the plans. And they're brilliant. Pythagorean triangles, Fibonacci series, golden ratios everywhere: in the elevations, in the layout and size of the rooms, even in the window leading! That building is a temple to the whole history of Western art, architecture, aesthetics, mathematics, geometry—all in one, all in stone and steel and tile and glass!"

Sunny's eyes shone. It took Andy's breath away. "Who did it?"

"I have no idea, but the man's a genius."

"So, you're going to work on the restoration?"

"Naw." Sunny came back and landed next to Andy. "That's Harry's thing. I'm talking about the sculpture. Alquist wants it back, but here's the thing: there's no drawing of it in the plans. So he's going to take bids. And I'm going to win it."

Andy laughed despite himself. "You seem awfully sure."

Sunny gave him a wicked smile. "I've got a secret edge."

"What is it?"

Sunny got up and headed back to the ladder. "Unh-unh-unh," he said, wagging a finger. "If I told you, it wouldn't be a secret now, would it?" He started to climb but stopped with his feet level with Andy's eyes. He muttered a soft curse and whipped his shirt off over his head, wadding it into a ball. Hanging onto the rung with his left hand, he leaned out over the piano, his right hand extended with the shirt still in it.

Andy was rooted to the spot looking up at the young man reaching down to him. The left arm tense, fingers gripping the rung, the bicep flexed in a perfect mound. The right hand held the wadded shirt, a silvery bracelet glinting on the wrist. For two breaths, Andy watched the fine black hairs on Sunny's chest and abdomen rise and fall. He could see the strong pulse of Sunny's heart quake just below the sternum. His ears buzzed. He'd been asked a question.

"Would you?"

Andy looked into Sunny's eyes. "Would I what?"

Sunny smiled. "Take my shirt, please?"

"Sure." Andy reached up and took hold of the shirt, but Sunny didn't release it right away. For a moment, they were poised, one reaching down, the other reaching up. Then Sunny smiled and let go and scrambled up the ladder.

Back home, Andy played the scene out in his mind again. There was something in Sunny's pose on the ladder, something like an invitation, but an invitation to what? The bedroom drew close around him. He abruptly felt his heart beating, pounding almost audibly in his chest. Was he having a heart attack? What should he do? Call a doctor, an ambulance? But there was no phone in the tiny house.

In a panic, he ran for the front door, then stopped. Where was he going? Up to Mrs. Oldfield? To tell her what? "My father died of a heart attack at thirty and I think I'm having one, too"? Ridiculous! But his heart was leaping as if it had somewhere to go even if he did not. And he couldn't breathe. There was no air in the house, no space, no room to move. He threw open the front door and flung himself through it.

The night was quiet, intimate. He took huge gulps of air and looked up. The sky was flecked with stars and glinting moistly. A sweet perfume like roses and watermelon wrapped around him. *Mimosa.* He could make out the shape of the tree on the lawn leading up to the main house. He remembered his first sight of it, so unlike the stolid trees of his native Illinois. It had horrified him. It tried to be too many things, its sticky pink blossoms like hairs waiting to be caressed, its leaves delicate like a fern's yet leathery and tough. But now in the tangible midnight its fragrance calmed him. It was everywhere, and he could melt into it and be everywhere at once, feel himself drift freely out on the slow and secret dark.

And somewhere out there he knew someone was breathing in the very air he was breathing out, sharing the night and the secret. And he was beginning to realize what was welling up from inside, shaking his whole body with each beat of his heart and leaking out through his pores. It was joy.

He wanted to know Sunny's secrets. All of them. And he wanted to tell him all of his.

Chapter 6

Lift Every Voice

Jonathan Robert Pautler—known as "JayRob" to his family, his friends, his fellow Elks and American Legionnaires, and his co-religionists at Mt. Hermon Bible Church; "Mr. Pautler" to his employees at Pautler's Groceries and Dry Goods; and "Mr. Mayor" only when he sat in the center seat during City Council meetings—was currently installed in the rear office of his store, scowling at three stacks of paper. One was store receipts, which Marcie had entered into the ledger in her nervous hand and which he would double-check later. One was a somewhat troubling announcement in the Mt. Hermon bulletin about an upcoming praise and worship service plus a handful of letters sent to him as church deacon concerning the same. He supposed he would have to come to some sort of understanding about that service before answering them, and the anticipated effort vexed him.

But the shortest stack vexed him the more: Lerner Alquist's latest proposal for that boondoggle of a library. It should have been finished ten years ago and would be by now if that pig-headed Yankee would quit adding gew-gaws and parapets to it. Now he wanted a dome and an "ornamental tympanum," whatever the hell that was. All free and paid for since Alquist had already raised the funds by subscription. Supposedly. But JayRob knew from what he heard around the courthouse square that Alquist had raised nowhere near enough money to cover these extravagances. And yet the construction had commenced as if all were well. The dome was nearing completion, bids were sent out for the ornamental whatsis, and the dedication date was bearing down on them relentlessly. Banners were being hung on the lampposts, for chrissakes.

He could see where this was headed. The dedication would already be upon them when Alquist (or more likely, one of his contractors) would suddenly turn to the City Council and say, "Oh, couldn't you just please spare us another ten or twenty thousand dollars to finish the job? After all, it's for the Memorial." JayRob practically spat at the thought of it. "Nothing will bankrupt you faster than something a rich man gives you for free," he growled to the canned vegetables and boxes of laundry powder. Well, if Alquist came begging, he could go whistle for it. His father may have been fool enough to approve the project, but he would by God be the one to see the end of it. And he had the Council votes to do it, too.

He put that stack of papers aside and picked up the middle one, the letters about the church service. He frowned. He'd already read through them once and for the most part found them chock full of foolishness. The one sensible comment he'd read was a concern about the church finances. Granted, it was couched in terms of giving support to a Papist conspiracy, but if Mt. Hermon was expected to front one penny for this shindig, well, he'd have something to say about that. Jacobs was a bit of a starry-eyed idealist. Fine for preaching but no head for business. Maybe he ought to go down there and talk sense to him. He'd be at the church now, most likely, since the bulletin said there'd be a mixed choir rehearsal this afternoon.

He got up from his seat and approached the swinging doors that opened into the store proper and peered through the scratches in their round plastic windows. Who was on cash register? If it was that Tibbits boy or even Marcie, he might consider going. Oh good Christ, it was Dale Longacre, lounging behind the counter picking at his teeth with his fingernails. Well, he couldn't let that stand. He entered the store with a loud *harrumph* and saw Dale straighten up with a satisfying jolt. You had to watch these kids every minute. Church would have to wait.

Mt. Hermon was alive with song. Andy had written a hymn, stirring as an anthem, and distributed to all the choirs:

> *When I think about Jesus*
>   *And the glory to be—*
> *We'll be living in Heaven*
>   *For eternity—*
> *All my troubles and worries*
>   *Have no hold upon me.*
> *I think about Jesus*
>   *And my soul flies free.*

The words and music had come to him in a flash the morning after he met Sunny, and he'd immediately written them down. The verses voice the troubles that weigh a soul down: uncertain times, loneliness, hardships, spiritual doubt in time of suffering—all things the people of Croy could relate to. Then the chorus popped in with a joyful change in mood, how just the thought of salvation could lift the heaviest burden and give wings to the soul. He'd copied out the verses by hand, added melody and some basic chords for accompaniment, and sent it around.

What he got back was surprising—and exhilarating. With his own choir, he developed simple four-part harmony that anyone familiar with shape-singing could follow. He hoped that was what the other choir directors were doing, too, those who had time to rehearse at all, that is. What he was not prepared for was the choir from Mt. Zion A.M.E. and their director, Ethan Jameson, the Reverend Cecil's son.

For one, there was the way Ethan directed his choir. Andy's conducting was precise, controlled, and gave clearly marked entrances and cut-offs. Since Mt. Hermon was the host for this rehearsal, Andy showed off his choir with a reprise of their Bach chorale piece, and followed with his version of "When I Think about Jesus," closing with a harmonious "Amen."

Then Ethan and his choir took to the risers. Ethan stood on the conductor's podium, quietly smiling at his charges as they rustled into place, then all eyes were on him. There was no reedy pipe wheezing out a pitch, no arms raised carefully and deliberately to signal the chorus to raise their folders in synchrony. There were no folders; there wasn't even a downbeat. Ethan just took a deep breath and launched them straight into a spiritual. It was "I Shall Not Be Moved," and Ethan didn't so much conduct it as channel it. There was no pattern to his gestures, but they embodied the spirit in the words and music. At times, it was his facial expression alone that signaled an entrance, and for one repeat of "I shall not, I shall not be moved," he actually stood stock still, and the chorus too, in that moment, sounded as if they had suddenly grown roots sunk deep into the banks of the White Horse.

Andy found himself on his feet at the end of it, the hairs on the back of his neck standing up. "That's it!" he said and he rushed forth and grabbed Ethan's hand and shook it. Ethan beamed down at him. "That's what our piece needs, too! Can you do that with 'When I Think about Jesus'?"

"I was hoping you'd ask," Ethan said. Andy turned to his choir. "What do you say, folks. Do you think we can do it?" The younger kids were all smiles. Mrs. Armbruster looked uncertainly from side to side and Mrs. Littledeer had a pinched look. The older men among the basses were looking at each other over the tops of their bifocals. But Susan called out, "You betcha'!" and scrambled up onto the risers among the sopranos.

There was a brief pause. Andy felt as if he were teetering on the edge of a precipice. It hadn't occurred to him what he had asked his chorus to do until Susan was already up there, one white face among a sea of black and brown. They would refuse. It would all fall apart, his chorus, the rehearsal, the pastor's dream of an ecumenical service. And it would all be his fault. He would be shown to be the fraud he was.

"What I think it needs," Ethan Jameson was saying, "is a repeat of the chorus at the end, even more up-tempo. And then the final line again, but with a soprano rising up over it all. It would take a high C, though, and I don't know . . ." Susan opened her mouth but abruptly closed it again. Andy saw the little signal Ethan had given her, then noticed there was a black woman among the Mt. Zion folk who also kept her lips tightly clamped.

"Of course, we could do without it," Ethan said.

"I can hit that note," Mrs. Armbruster said and stepped over to the chorus. "Where do you want me?"

"Stand by me," the black woman who had been silent said. The two women sized each other up as Lila Armbruster took her position.

"Can we clap?" one of the tenors asked. It was Scotty Pritchard.

"What?" Andy said.

"Can we clap, like they did? While we sing?"

"Of course!" Andy said.

"Count me in!" Scott said, and he and the rest of the teenagers took their places.

"Are you sure these risers'll hold us all?" grumbled one of the older basses as he ambled forward.

"We'll make room," Ethan said. Pretty soon Mt. Hermon's choir was interspersed with Mt. Zion's, all save one man who sat in the pews and didn't look up. Andy beamed at the mixed choir as he turned around and noticed him. He made as if to call out to him but felt a gentle touch on his shoulder. Ethan looked down at him from the conductor's podium with a kindly expression, but with the slightest movement, he shook his head.

"Now," Ethan said turning to the combined choir, "let's put some spirit into this excellent music. Can y'all keep up?"

"Don't worry about us," Lila Armbruster called out cheerfully. "Where the Spirit leads, anyone can follow."

"Right, then. Here we go!" They ran through the song three times, each time growing more cohesive and joyous as the choirs filled themselves with each other's energy—and perhaps something greater that moved between them.

No one noticed when the lone man rose up from his seat and walked up the aisle. No one, that is, except the two people at the back of the church. Mrs. Oldfield sat three rows in, stiff and alert on the edge of her pew, as if watching some riveting drama. As the man passed, she broke her reverie and crossed over to speak to him, but he spat out a single word without giving her a glance and strode out through the doors without stopping. Mrs. Oldfield's face still hadn't recovered when she turned to see Ginny Alquist grinning up at her. She gave her a withering look.

"Well, don't look at me," Ginny said. "I didn't say it."

Mrs. Oldfield was like to bust for want of slapping her. The girl had no business being here, and she was certainly not in a prayerful position, perched on a back pew and leaning against the one in front. *Forbearance*, Mrs. Oldfield reminded herself, *can be a heavy cross to bear*. She struck the wrinkles from her skirt and marched back to the church office, passing the choruses who were now disbanding amid handshakes and mutual congratulations.

Ginny rolled her eyes and leaned back in the pew. She held a small package wrapped in brown paper, and she passed it from hand to hand as she watched the rehearsal break up. She could see Andy and Susan at the front of the church. If they didn't notice her soon, she would have to go down there or call out or something, but she just didn't feel like it. They looked so happy. Susan glowed as usual, and Andy was all fumble-thumbed gathering up his music. *He's just like a puppy*, she thought. But he got all still and focused when Ethan Jacobs walked over to shake his hand. And then the Mt. Zion choir and their director left—not out the front door, like the Mt. Hermon people, but out the side. *That's probably the same door they use when they enter on Sunday*, Ginny thought. She almost swore aloud. *This town,* she fumed. *Half the time, they do it to themselves.*

She lost sight of Susan as a pack of Mt. Hermon choristers passed in happy chatter up the aisle and through the front doors. If any echo of the muttered curse still lingered there, it was dispersed. When Ginny turned around, she could no longer see Susan. It was just Andy standing at the piano. She'd have to give the package to him instead. She rose with a weary grunt. Andy looked up and waved. "Hey," she called out, but it sounded kind of feeble after all that bouncing jubilation. She started down the aisle. Andy seemed a million miles away.

"How you doing?" he said, coming toward her.

"Not so good. Got some kinda bug, maybe."

"I'm sorry to hear that." He didn't look sorry. He looked radiant. Probably from the rehearsal. Ginny tried not to take it personally. At least his energy was carrying him up the aisle faster than she was coming down it. "I got something for you," she said as he reached her.

"What is it?"

She handed him the package. "Not for you, really. For Sunny. I was supposed to give it to Harry to give to him, but as you can see, Harry isn't around so much anymore."

Andy took the package almost reverently. "Yeah, I noticed. Is everything all right?"

"Like ducks and roses," Ginny said. Andy looked at her goofily. "Aw, what the hell," she said and collapsed into the nearest pew, weeping.

Andy immediately sat beside her and put his arm around her. "Ginny! Ginny, what's wrong? Should I go get Susan?"

"Oh, no. No, I don't want her to see me like this. She was right. The little snot. Oh, why does everything have to be so screwed up!" She looked up at him. "Oh, I'm sorry. I shouldn't be saying that to you."

"It's all right. I'm not a—"

"Yeah, yeah." She waved a hand at him. "But still, not here, not to you." She wiped her nose on her sleeve and then looked at it in disgust. "Good God, what am I turning into?" Then she took a deep breath and straightened up in the pew.

"Is it something to do with you and Harry?" Andy asked helpfully.

"Well, yeah, you might could say that."

"Did he lose his job? At the library?"

Ginny laughed. "Oh, no. Lerner's no fool. Nobody but Harry could finish that job on that budget. No, he might slap a restraining order on him so he can't get within a thousand yards of our house without getting arrested—which precinct, you may have noticed, includes your little chapel here, too bad about the unfinished repairs and all that. But there's no way in hell Lerner's going to let personal feelings mess with his schedule. The dedication must go on! It is decreed! Your church be damned, if you'll pardon the expression, but Ada's Memorial comes first. It always has."

She got up from the pew. It took Andy a moment to realize she wanted to leave and he was blocking her way. He got up awkwardly, almost dropping the package. "Hey," she said, "you be careful with that. I went through a lot of trouble to get it. Now you get it to Sunny."

If anything, her admonition made him more fumble-fingered. "How?" he stammered. "I . . . I don't know where he lives."

"Oh, it's over to the . . . Oh, here, it's easier to show you," she said and tugged on his sleeve so that he followed her outside. She showed him the hill west of town and described the road that led there. "Now git," she said. "I need to lie down. All that joyful noise wears a body out."

Chapter 7

PLAYING WITH FIRE

Andy drove up to the trailer and mounted the wobbly steps but hesitated with his hand raised, ready to knock. He dropped his arm and the steps pitched left, nearly toppling him into the jimson weed's unfurling bells beside the stoop. The door swung open.

"Did you bring it?" Sunny asked, his eyes dancing. Without waiting for an answer, he grabbed Andy's arm and pulled him inside.

Andy hefted the small package in his hands. "Is this your secret weapon?" he asked.

Sunny clapped his hands in glee. "Oh, she did it! She did it!" He took the package from Andy's hands and went digging for a knife amid the clutter of his kitchen drawers.

Andy looked around the trailer. It was remarkably like his granny-house at Mrs. Oldfield's, though smaller and with a lower ceiling. There was no partition to separate the living room from the kitchen, and while Andy had actual bookshelves, Sunny had piled his books on the floor, some of them opened, some of them stacked on top of each other. Where the grannyhouse had a sofa-bed hugging the wall between the living room and bath, there was an enormous drafting table overflowing with paper, sketches, drafting tools, and more kinds of pencil than Andy had ever seen. Before he could notice anything further, Sunny let out a whoop. "What is it?" he asked.

Sunny held a photo in a silver picture frame before him with both hands, but he was dancing around so that Andy couldn't get a good look. "Who—?"

"It's Ada!" Sunny said. "Ada Alquist. The only known portrait of her. New York smashed or hid or burned all the others when she died, but Ginny knew he kept this one photo, tucked away in a drawer that's always locked. But that Ginny," he smiled up at Andy, "nothing gets by her."

Sunny's enthusiasm threw sparks in every direction. Andy was dazzled and baffled. "I don't understand," he said. "How does this help you?"

"For the sculpture, for the library." Andy responded with a confused smile and Sunny leapt to the drawing table. "Look," he said, pulling a random sheet of paper from the clutter and grabbing a pencil. "There's going to be a pediment over the entrance—well, actually there already is," he sketched the front of the library in quick bold strokes, but detailed enough that Andy could easily recognize it. "And the center space here," he circled the area above the main entrance, "that's the tympanum. Now I just knew ol' New York had plans for that space, and by God I was right. I had Harry check it out. It's all set up to hold a sculpture, not too deep and not too heavy, but something was meant to be there, and that something is going to be mine, my biggest piece ever." He grabbed the picture again and grinned at it. "And you, pretty lady, are going to help me put it there!"

Andy found himself grinning, too. "How does Ada figure in?"

Sunny looked at him slyly. "Oh, 'figure in.' That's a good one. You've already got it, haven't you?"

Andy's grin froze. "No, I'm sorry," he said. "I really don't understand a word."

Sunny scowled a moment, then his face softened and he relaxed. The energy jetting out of him dropped off, like closing the door to a furnace accidentally left open. "I'm sorry," he said. Putting the photo down, he took both of Andy's hands. "I sometimes forget that not everybody lives inside my head." He pulled Andy over to the drafting table and started leafing through the papers with one hand, still holding him by the other. Andy felt like a balloon being pulled along on a string. "Here it is," Sunny said as he pulled a sheet toward him and let go of Andy's hand. Andy continued drifting towards him until they stood hip to hip, looking down at the sketch.

"The sculpture is in three parts," Sunny said, all his attention on the drawing. "On the left are allegorical figures representing Agriculture and Ranching. On the right, Industry and Commerce. In the center, the Goddess of Prosperity reigns on a throne, flanked by Wisdom on the left and Good Governance on the right. That's where Ada comes in. She is the Goddess of Prosperity. She's the center of it all."

Almost without his feeling it, Sunny had slipped his arm around Andy's waist. He didn't move. "Is that such a good idea?" he asked. "I mean, if he's so sensitive about her picture."

Sunny gave a short laugh. "Look, everybody knows it's Ada's Memorial. It's time she made an appearance. Besides, I can put other faces in the sculpture, too. Mayor Pautler can represent Good Governance, the Superintendent of School's wife can be the Goddess of Civic Duty or the figure of Pioneering Spirit or whatever. Hell, even old New York himself can show up as Industry."

"That seems kind of vain, if you ask me."

"Of course it's vain! That's the whole point. Everybody in this sink hole thinks they're some kind of pioneering hero. Braving tornadoes, dust bowls, Indians! They'll eat it up."

"Even Alquist?" Andy said, trying not to let his spirit sag as Sunny moved away from him. "It's hard to put one over on him. That man's older than dirt."

Sunny shrugged. "Actually, parts of him *are* dirt." He picked up the photo again. "But that's where my secret weapon comes in. He'll never be able to resist her."

Andy shook his head. "I don't know, Sunny. I think you're playing with fire."

"Of course I am. How else do you get anything done?"

"I'm serious, Sunny. I wouldn't mess with him. Ask Harry. Did you know he's got some sort of court order on him?"

"Aw, Harry's fine. Gives him a chance to get away from that—" He stopped short, giving Andy an appraising look, but it quickly dissolved in delight as a new idea hit him. "Hey, do you wanna see him? Him 'n' old Stone Face ought to be up at Elephant Rock by now. Wanna come?"

"Come? Come where? Who's Stone Face?" But Sunny was already out the door and racing up the hill, and Andy could do nothing but follow.

Andy hadn't noticed much on his drive out to Sunny's trailer. He was concentrating on remembering Ginny's directions. He found the road that snaked around the shoulder of the hill west of town, passed the broken gate and its double-rutted trail leading uphill to an uncertain end, and nearly missed the turnoff onto a red dirt road that followed a dry ravine to his right. Sunny's trailer lodged nearly a mile in from there, surrounded by dried clumps of bluestem grass and bare dirt that rose in red clouds at the slightest stir. Behind it rose scrubby dark oaks Andy supposed were blackjacks.

Sunny was behind the trailer now, running up a path that followed the ravine uphill. He was whooping as he went and Andy found he had to run something fierce to catch up. The further up they went, the more signs of water there were—small brush, some wildflowers still in bloom, an occasional flycatcher on alert or swooping through the air—until the ravine showed itself to be an actual running creek. The heat of the day and the steepening grade of the path had them both panting and sweating as they rounded a corner and entered a sudden expanse of green and leafy shade surrounding a pond behind a low earthen dam.

"Yee-haw!" Sunny yelled, whipping his shirt over his head and heading for the bank.

Andy rested a moment, leaning with hands on knees, trying to get the thick summer air into his lungs. His shirt was dripping with sweat. It would be a great relief to shuck it and follow Sunny, but he was too taken by the setting to want to enter it yet. Cottonwoods and live oaks edged the pool on the south bank where it nestled into the side of the hill. The opposite bank was bordered with sedges and cattails, where red-winged black birds flashed their shoulders and sang praises about their claims. A rock jutted from the side of the hill and over the pool. Half of it was in shade and looked as cool as a cave, the other half glittered with mica baking in the sun, dazzling the eye. *That must be Elephant Rock*, Andy thought, though other than being large and gray it didn't look much like an elephant.

The dazzle kept Andy from seeing the two figures on the rock until they moved. They had been lying in the cool, deep shade, invisible until one of them stood up. Andy yelled "Hey!" to warn Sunny, but the word stuck halfway in his throat when he saw Sunny strip off the last of his clothes and plunge buck-naked into the pond. Andy stood there with his mouth hanging open, the blur of Sunny's firm and furry buttocks searing itself into his brain.

"Hey, yerself!" called the figure on the rock. Andy recognized the voice. It was Harry Edom. Of course! Sunny had said Harry and "Stone Face" would be up here. The other guy, who was now sitting up, must be Stone Face. Andy waved, and then froze again as Harry stepped into the sunlight. "What's up, Miracle Man?" Harry hollered, naked as a jay bird. The other fellow stood up, too, and Andy didn't even have to look. Taller, stockier, skin the color of cinnamon and rust, Stone Face towered over Harry.

"C'mon!" Sunny called from the pool. "Chuck your clothes and jump in."

Andy felt very thin, white, and over-dressed. He told himself it was simply a matter of removing layers of clothing that had gotten too sticky to bear. He folded and neatly stacked his shirt and pants in a tidy pile atop his shoes, into which he had tucked his socks. But when he got down to his bleached Jocky shorts, he balked.

Sunny had gotten out of the pool and was sunning himself on the rock, leaning back on his elbows to watch. Harry sat in a crouch beside Sunny, sunlight gleaming off his broad shoulders, his ballocks grazing the top of the boulder and forming a little puddle of sweat beneath him. Andy wondered how the heat of the rock felt on that sensitive skin. It gave rise to feelings his Jockys strained to conceal.

Jedediah Tucker, the one Sunny called Stone Face, was looking on with his brows knit. "You do your own laundry?" he asked.

"Huh? Uh, no. I give it to Mrs. Oldfield."

"Well, what are you going to tell Mrs. Oldfield when you come home with pink underwear?"

"What?"

Harry laughed. "That's right! She'll take you for a pinko and turn you in to the FBI!"

"Or the Senate Investigation Committee!" chimed in Sunny. "I can hear her now. 'Senator! There's a commie in my grannyhouse!'"

"I don't get it," Andy said, feeling even more defenseless standing in his underwear than he would naked.

"It's the dirt," Tucker said. "Oklahoma red dirt. It's finer than silt and thicker than blood. You take a dip in that pool and your tidy whiteys will come out pink. Ain't no amount of washing will get rid of it, neither."

"What'd'ya say?" Sunny said, curling into a sitting position. Andy watched the muscles ripple beneath the hair on his abdomen. "Are you now or have you ever been—a pinko?"

Andy looked him in the eyes. That spark of gold was dancing there. With a flourish, Andy stripped off his shorts and threw them over his head. Sunny leapt down from the rock with a whoop and grabbed him by the hand and both of them ran splashing into the pool.

Harry and Tucker stood on the rock and watched them. Harry shook his head. "You'd better rein that boy in," he said.

Tucker grunted. "When has that boy ever had reins?"

Chapter 8

ELEPHANT ROCK

Andy, Sunny, Harry, and Tucker lay sprawled on Elephant Rock in the lengthening shade. They had retreated to the cool side when Andy started turning visibly pink. He felt relaxed enough around these guys to joke about it. "I guess I come from the wrong side of the Atlantic to keep up with y'all. I'll never be dark as an Indian."

Harry guffawed. "Or as dark as The Indian."

Sunny groaned and put a hand over his eyes. Andy rolled over on his side and smiled at him. "Why do they call you 'The Indian'?" Sunny just moaned again and shook his head.

Harry chuckled. "When Sunny-boy here first showed up in school, which was, what, fourth grade?"

"Third," said Tucker.

"Anyways, the teacher, Mrs. Rottschalk, had trouble with his name. 'Son-dar'? 'Sin-guh'? 'So-high'? And with each screw-up, you could see Sunny getting madder and madder. Finally, Mrs. Rottschalk says, 'What are you, some kind of Indian?' And he shoots up from his seat and yells—" and here both Harry and Tucker stood up and bellowed out across the pond, "I'm not *an* Indian! I'm *the* Indian!"

The two of them collapsed on the blanket, Harry laughing, Stone Face chuckling softly. Sunny removed his hand. "I still don't see why you think it's so funny. You let these people call you by a name based on a stupid mistake made by some Italian guy five hundred years ago."

"'These people'?" Andy asked.

"It don't matter what they call us," Tucker said. "They still treat us like dirt. You new-comers found that out soon enough."

"How's that?" Andy asked.

"The law was on our side!" Sunny said.

"Don't tell a member of 'the civilized nations' about the law being on your side," Harry said "And what do you mean, 'our side'? Are you saying this is your land, now?"

"Well," said Sunny, "as much as it is yours. You ain't Choctaw. Or Osage."

"Um, guys—" Andy interjected.

"You can squat here all you want," Harry said, "you ain't getting that farm back. It's Alquist's now and he never gives up nothin'. Not one damned square inch."

"Well, it was my family's farm before it was his."

"And some German guy's before that, and some Indian's hunting ground before that. How far back do you wanna go?"

Sunny just growled at him.

"Sunny's pa used to own this place," Tucker said to Andy. His glance included more than just the idyllic little pond before them. "The hill, the orchard, the springs, the farm house. That cagey Arab—"

"Sikh!" Sunny yelled.

"Whatever."

"How'd you like it if I called you a Comanche?"

Stone Face gave him a stone face. "Anyways," he continued, "he's the one who drilled the well and found the springs, built the dam here to make the pond, and pumped the water up the hill."

Harry snorted. "Who'da thunk you could grow apples in Oklahoma? Only a crazy ay—"

"Sikh!"

"—Indian."

"Well, okay. Indian."

"So, what happened?" asked Andy. "I mean, how did Alquist end up with everything? If your dad owned the land, it should have gone to you."

"He made a mistake," Sunny said sullenly.

"He thought he was white," Tucker said.

"Not white. Caucasian."

"Same difference."

"No!" Sunny got up on one elbow. "The law says land can only be owned by American citizens, and only Caucasians can become naturalized American citizens."

"As opposed to Injuns, who are naturally unnatural."

"It's the American Dream," Harry said, "if you're white. Oh, begging your pardon, counselor. Caucasian."

Sunny continued unabashed, "And Indians—real Indians—or, more precisely, Punjabis, which is what Sikhs are, are Caucasians. In fact, we are probably the original Aryans on which the whole notion of Caucasian is based."

"Uh-huh," said Tucker.

"So, you're more white than me?" Andy said, dubious.

"That's not the point. The point is, only Caucasians can become citizens, and only citizens can own land. So Dad applied for citizenship."

"And he got it?"

"He should have. That's what the law says."

"Unless, of course, it says something else," said Harry. "Which it does if people like Alquist dig into it. They got enough money and muscle to make it say what they want it to say."

They were silent a while. The glow was fading from the golden afternoon. "So," Andy said at last, "what happened?"

"The court took away our land and my dad got deported," Sunny said flatly. "Because we weren't Caucasian enough."

"White enough."

"Yeah, fine, have it your way."

"And Alquist snapped it up," Harry said. "Good-bye farm, good-bye orchard, good-bye American Dream." He turned to Sunny. "Welcome to Indian Territory."

"And now you're squatting here, in that little trailer," Andy said. "Aren't you afraid he'll find out about it and kick you out?"

"Unh-unh" Sunny said, smiling up at him. "I've got Alquist wrapped around my little finger."

"Oh, now there's a disgusting picture," said Harry. He got up and stretched. "Boys, I reckon it's time to head on out. I've got shirkers to supervise." He looked down at Tucker. "What about you, Stone Face?"

Tucker grunted and got up. "Gotta head over to Pesogi, pay a visit to Uncle Crazy Head. Something my mom wants to ask him."

"Guys?" Harry said looking at Sunny and Andy. Sunny grinned up at him. "It's too fine a day for work," he said and crossed his arms behind his head and closed his eyes. Andy was lying on his stomach and said nothing. Harry looked over at Tucker, who looked away. "Okay," Harry said, "see ya," and he hopped down off the rock, grabbed his pile of clothes, and headed down the path.

Tucker stood a while looking down at Sunny and Andy lying side by side. "That's my uncle's blanket."

"I'll get it back to him," Sunny said without opening his eyes. Tucker didn't bother to respond as he shrugged into his clothes and headed over the hill.

Andy's skin burned and tingled beneath his shirt as he drove the blanket back to its owner. He and Sunny had spent the rest of the afternoon on Elephant Rock. Then back at the trailer Sunny had cooked something amazing with spices that turned everyday chicken into an eye- and mouth-watering adventure. As soon as they finished, Sunny had shooed him out, saying he had drawings to work up.

"Your prize-winning secret project?" Andy taunted.

"Yeah, yeah, now go. Oh, and don't forget Uncle Crazy Head's blanket." Sunny tossed him the surprisingly heavy cloth.

"How do I—?"

"I'll draw you a map. Pesogi's just over the hill, but if you spit, you'll miss it. We can't have you Northerners wandering through the cross timbers in the dark. Some trigger-happy fool might mistake you for a coyote. You'd better drive." Sunny drew as he spoke, quickly embellishing the map with local landmarks.

Andy looked on in amazement. "Wow, that's . . . convoluted. I can see why Stone Face walked." Sunny was busying himself around the trailer as if Andy had already left. But Andy wasn't ready to leave. "I also see why you call him Stone Face."

"Yep, it fits," Sunny said, picking up a pencil and inspecting its tip.

"So, why's his uncle called Crazy Head?"

Sunny just looked at him like he was an idiot. "Because that's his name."

Andy reddened. "Oh. I just thought—"

"Jedediah—Stone Face—he's a Crazy Head, too. On his mother's side."

Andy covered his embarrassment with a laugh. "Well, good, then. So, Uncle Crazy Head isn't really crazy."

"Oh, he's crazy all right. Don't get him talking or you'll find out."

"Is he senile or something?"

"No. He's actually younger than he looks. He was in the war with the 45th. Came back all screwed up."

"What happened?"

Sunny shrugged. "The 45th was the battalion that liberated Dachau."

Andy whistled. "That would do it, all right, seeing what those guards did to those prisoners."

"Oh, it wasn't just what the guards did to the prisoners. It was what the 45th did to the guards."

"What was that?"

"Murder them." Sunny shoved the map into his hands. "Now git!"

Andy drove the labyrinthine route that took him back to the main highway then into Pesogi, a grouping of three low houses and the ruins of a few more hidden in a grove of blackjacks. He found "Uncle Crazy Head's" place by the token Sunny had drawn for him: a carved wooden horse. The revenant of some long-forgotten carousel, the animal leaned against an unpainted wall, pierced by a pole. The horse's mouth twisted in fury, eyes wide, its tongue a slash of red thrust out between huge teeth. A dark crack wound its way through the torso, and dusty curls of white paint peeled from its side and lay like leaves beneath it. Part of the tail was missing. Before Andy had mounted the steps, the uncle appeared on the porch and took the blanket from him. There was a spark behind his eyes that looked like it might catch fire if Andy lingered, so he left quickly with just a short nod. It was dark by the time he got back to Croy.

He was bursting with excitement and ideas. New songs kept popping into his head full of images of the Garden of Eden and the beauty of God's creation:

> *God's spirit moved across the deep*
> *And with a word it woke from sleep;*
> *Let evening fall, let morning come,*
> *Let all be good that God has done.*

He wanted to go back to Sunny's to share it with him, but that would be stretching his new friend's patience. So he drove around aimlessly for a while, not wanting to go home. It was almost by accident that he found himself pulling up outside the Jacobsen' house, glad to see a light on in the living room. He rang the doorbell and Susan answered, as he hoped she would.

"Andy?" she said, then stepped out onto the porch, closing the door behind her. "Where have you been? It's late. I haven't seen you since rehearsal."

"I've had the most amazing time," he said grinning. "I'm on top of the world!"

"Yes, I can see that. And a little too close to the sun, too, if I may say so."

"What?"

"Your face," she said and reached out to touch it.

He suddenly leaned forward and kissed her. She was surprised, but she didn't recoil. "Well," she said, looking at him askance with a smile.

"I'm sorry, I—" Andy said. "It's just that— Gosh, Susan, I feel so good! And I wanted to share it with someone."

"Just someone? Would anybody do?"

"Oh, gee, I mean—"

His hands started flapping at his sides like agitated crows. She patted him on the chest to calm him down. "It's okay, Andy. I'm just teasing. Look, it's late, and it's been quite a day."

"Do you think we could—?"

"Not tonight. It really is late."

He looked down, crestfallen. "I shouldn't have come, I shouldn't have called so late, I . . . I shouldn't have kissed you."

"Hey, now, don't get ahead of yourself." She smiled and put a hand on his shoulder. "Let's just back up a bit and start over, shall we?"

"Okay." He looked up at her hopefully. "Tonight?" She raised an eyebrow at him. "Okay," he said, "not tonight. Tomorrow night, then?"

She nodded. "I'd be delighted. So long we can start sometime *before* eleven."

"Eleven?! Oh my God!" he said. "I mean, oh my gosh! I'd better get home."

"Yeah. You'd better."

"See you, Susan," he said and dashed down the stairs into his car.

"Yeah," she said, although he was long gone, "you'd better."

Andy remembered to slow the car down before entering the alley that ran behind Mrs. Oldfield's so he wouldn't kick up any dust or gravel. He was surprised to see a light on inside. He didn't remember leaving one on; it had been midday when he left, the sun pouring in through the windows facing the alley.

The pole lamp in the living room was on when he entered; only one shade was lit. Beneath its narrow cone was a brown corduroy reclining chair, and in it sat Mrs. Oldfield. "Mr. Simms," she said.

"Mrs. Oldfield," he said as the screen door snapped shut behind him. "What are you doing here?" He turned on the kitchen light.

"I have a concern I wish to talk over with you. I have been wanting to speak to you about it since this afternoon's rehearsal. I have looked and waited for you all afternoon and evening. I wanted to be certain I wouldn't miss you."

"I'm sure it must be urgent, Mrs. Oldfield, for you to put so much time and effort into it, but it is rather late, and—"

"Yes, it is rather late. That is something else I wish to talk to you about."

Andy felt his patience slipping away. "I would be happy to talk to you, and perhaps we can do it tomorrow. At your house or at the church, or wherever you'd like. But it's been a long day I'm pretty tired."

She rose from the chair. "These may be your lodgings, Mr. Simms, but I am still your landlady. And I hope I may be something more."

Andy put his hand to his forehead. Hot. Sunburn. "And what would that be, Mrs. Oldfield?" He walked into the kitchen to get a glass of water, deliberately turning his back on her.

"I hope to be a friend." He stopped short of the sink and turned to face her, puzzled. She stepped forward. "I saw what you did at the rehearsal today. Inviting all those people, coordinating the whole thing, the risers, the music stands, and that song you wrote and passed around so they all could sing it."

Andy drew a glass of water. "If this is praise, Mrs. Oldfield—"

"I'm not done." She took another step. "And then you mixed the choirs. Mt. Zion's and Mt. Hermon's. You had them up there, standing side by side."

Andy swallowed a mouthful of water. It went down like a stone. His heart thumped in his chest. He knew he would have to face this sooner or later, but he hadn't expected it here, now. "Look, Mrs. Oldfield, I know what you're going to say—"

"I think it was courageous."

He stopped and stared at her. "What?" The glass of water was still in his hand, halfway to his mouth.

"It is the single bravest thing I have ever seen in this town, and it is long overdue."

Andy smiled shyly and put down the glass. "Well, I guess the Spirit just moved me."

"Oh, don't get so full of yourself." She stepped into the kitchen. She was a small woman but it was a small kitchen. Andy felt cornered. "You did it on impulse and you did it without thinking, and that just will not do. It is too important to be handled willy-nilly like that. Do you know who that man was who didn't join the rest of the choir?"

Andy thought back to earlier this afternoon, to the rehearsal. It seemed years ago. "Mr. Swofford, you mean?"

"Jake Swofford. Have you any idea who he is?"

Jake Swofford, Andy thought. Something to do with the local feed store—or was it the sheriff's department? And with a trouble-maker for a son. But he thought that wasn't what she was asking. He shook his head.

"Klan," she said. "There hasn't been any activity around here for years, and now is not the time to start stirring it up."

Andy stared at her. "Are you asking me to cancel the service?"

"Oh, for heaven's sake!" Mrs. Oldfield said. "Haven't you been listening? No, I don't mean cancel the service. That's not my decision, or yours. That's Pastor Jacobs' and he has made it. It's the right decision, too. This town needs healing. And you, Mr. Simms, had better not be the one to mess it up! Every step you take from now on has got to be beyond reproach. That beautiful, fragile thing you created this afternoon has got to be managed with special, deliberate care. And with one whale of a lot of prayer and humility."

"I think I understand."

"I hope you do. That chorus has got to shine without blemish. Certain proprieties must be observed, certain rules followed. The merest whisper of scandal and the whole thing falls apart. I'll help you with it, but you are its center. You brought them together. It is your responsibility. The question is, are you up to it?"

"I think so."

"Be certain, Mr. Simms. As certain as God can give you the strength to be certain. I am not joking when I say lives are at stake."

"I can do it, Mrs. Oldfield. I am certain."

"Good. Then you can start by not staying out till all hours of the night."

He almost laughed in her face. Instead, he took another sip and said as calmly as he could, "It couldn't have been more proper. I was with Susan."

"Well," she said, crossing back into the living room, "all the more reason. You have her reputation to think of, too."

"And what about your reputation, Mrs. Oldfield?" She turned and scowled at him. He spread his arms to encompass the grannyhouse. "Staying up to all hours of the night in a single man's lodgings? What will the neighbors say?"

She visibly colored. "Mr. Simms! Please take me seriously."

"I do," he said, walking to the door and opening it. "And call me Andy, if you're going to take such a personal interest in me."

"It's not personal," she sniffed. "It's for the good of the church. And the town." She stepped to the door but turned and stared at his forehead. "Put some salve on that or it will blister—Andy." Then she turned and disappeared into the scented night.

He listened to her feet swishing over the lawn. He turned on the porch light but felt certain she could find her way up the slope with her eyes shut.

Was she just trying to spook a gullible Northerner with tales of bogeymen in white sheets? Or did she believe it herself? He'd almost believed it too, for a minute. But as he crawled absentmindedly into bed (first remembering the salve—that much he did believe), he found it difficult to credit, especially the warning about Susan's reputation. Susan had nothing to fear from him.

Far off in the distance, a train whistle blew. The 12:04 was beginning its south-bound rumble through town as it did every night. In a few moments, the throb of its diesel engines and the rhythm of its wheels would drum up through the floor of the grannyhouse until his body hummed. As he closed his eyes and slid into sleep he thought he could still feel the heat of the rock beneath him, and Sunny's hand moving slowly along the length of his back.

Chapter 9

GRAND PLANS

The men working on the library hooted as Sunny entered Harry's office trailer. They were used to seeing him in splattered dungarees, not a suit and tie, and carrying a plasterer's hawk, not a teapot. *These people mean nothing,* he reminded himself. When he was famous, he would have many clients, all of them rich, and these louts would be long forgotten. He entered the trailer with his head high. He had preparations to make before Alquist arrived.

As he made tea on the hot plate, he visualized the studio he would rent with money from the commission: something above one of the Main Street stores, something with northern light. In his head, he heard a warning: "Don't count your eggs before they are hatched!" He giggled. Trying to explain the proverb to Uncle Bhavjeet had led to one of their spectacular arguments. Now, it seemed oddly fitting.

He adjusted his tie. Harry had one of those portable air conditioners jammed into a window, but he felt warm. He was hot and the room was cold. Was it too cold? Would the tea cool off? In a panic, he checked under the cozy. He had a special surprise for Alquist there. Chai, made the way his mother used to. He felt the pot. Still warm. Hot even. Where the devil was Alquist?

Speak and he appears.

Alquist entered the trailer in a hurry, scarcely looking at Sunny. He flung his fedora on a table and sat down, crossing his long legs. "You've got five minutes," he said.

"Perhaps you would like some tea, sir? It is a specialty of my country—" Why was he suddenly talking with his uncle's accent?

"None of that nonsense! This is a business meeting, nothing more. No matter what's gone on between our families, that's all in the past. I don't owe you anything and you don't owe me anything. Are we clear?"

Sunny stopped pouring and put down the pot. "Absolutely."

"Good. Now I've seen three and a half designs to date. They were presented by two morons, a crazed old biddy who wants the whole thing made of corn cobs, and a high school art teacher who wouldn't know the difference between terracotta and bat crap. So far, the entire exercise has wasted two hours and fifteen minutes of my time, for which I was not paid and from which I may never recover. So unless you plan on showing me a sculpture made of tea leaves—and you by God better not be—I suggest you stop trying my temper and get on with it."

"Right." Sunny swallowed and pulled out the first of four large sheets. "The sculpture will be divided into three parts, each fired and mounted separately, but interlocking so that the seams are invisible to the viewer. You can see the—"

"Yes, I see the specs. What are the three parts?"

"They symbolically represent what holds the community of Croy together. Both in a literal sense—practical things like agriculture, ranching, and manufacturing—and in a more metaphoric sense—like pioneering spirit, hard work, honesty, and good citizenship."

"You've left out religion."

Sunny hesitated. "I wanted to avoid anything that might be divisive or too particular, favoring one group over another."

Alquist nodded. "Smart move."

Sunny felt a rush of adrenaline. "At the same time, I want the people of Croy—particular people—involved in the project. So I am going to use their faces on the figures. That's why most are only sketched in what I'm about to show you." He held up another sheet, this one done in ochers and tans with a sidebar showing how the colors harmonized with the brick exterior. "This is the left section, showing ranching, agriculture, and the contributions of indigenous peoples."

"Of what?"

"Native Americans."

Alquist snorted. "You mean Indians."

Sunny looked at him evenly. "Yes," he said. He pulled another sheet from the pile. "This is the right side: industry, the railroads, commerce."

"The train doesn't stop here anymore."

"But it did bring the town together. When Croy was first founded—"

"All right, all right. What about the middle one?"

Sunny smiled. This was his ace. "All the figures are facing the center, see? And in the center is a figure on a throne, a goddess, with rays of light shooting out of her. She is flanked by The Body Politic and the Spirit of Peace. She is both the source and the outcome of all that surrounds her. She is the Goddess Prosperity." He pulled out his last sheet, his face already shining in triumph. On the other renderings, the faces had been vague washes, and on this one, too, the faces Peace and Polity were mere sketches. But shining on her throne of plenty sat Ada Alquist.

Lerner Alquist rose slowly to his feet. "Where did you get that?" he hissed.

"Get what?"

"Don't screw with me, boy. That!" His finger jabbed at the center figure. "Where did you get it?"

"Ginny—" Sunny started, but Alquist's face twisted and snarled, so he backtracked. "Ginny described her to me some, and . . . and I used her as a model. To prove I could do life studies. She looks a lot like her."

"Bullshit! She doesn't look anything like her mother. She takes after me, worse luck her." He grabbed the sheet from Sunny's hand and laid it on the table and leaned over it. Sunny felt a line of sweat trickle down his side. Alquist absent-mindedly picked up the cup of tea and took a sip. His back stiffened, his whole frame went rigid. In a quiet voice that frightened Sunny more than his rough outburst, the old man asked, "What is this?"

"It's tea, sir, like I said. A specialty of my—"

"I know it's tea, god damn it! What's in it?"

"Spices. Cardamom."

Alquist put the cup down slowly without turning around. Was his hand trembling? Sunny didn't know what to do. Alquist took a deep breath and let out what sounded like a sigh. When he spoke, his voice was flat and calculating. "The faces. Can they be anyone? You can do that?"

"Yes, sir! I even have some ideas. I can put the Mayor here, Hank Tibbits there—perfect for a rancher—Mrs. Gilbert there. And you, sir, over here, as Industry."

Alquist whirled around. "The hell you will. Nobody'd pay for that. But the rest of them, they would. They'd pay plenty to see their faces up there." He smiled unpleasantly. "Let Pautler try and put a stop to that.

Hah!" He slapped the table. "All right, boy, you've got it. See that it gets done and done on time."

"Thank you, sir!"

"And if you can do it under budget, there'll be money in your pocket."

"I can do it, sir. Piece of cake."

Alquist grunted and turned, grabbing his hat. He stopped at the door and said, his back still to Sunny, "That photo had better be back where it belongs the next time I go looking for it or I'll have your skinny black ass nailed to a tree." He fixed his hat on his head and left.

Outside, the sun dazzled Lerner's eyes. He had a hard time making out shapes. He strode swiftly though, lest anyone notice his unsteady gait and read something into it. The color drained away from things. His heart hammered in his chest. A block from the library he had to steady himself against a tree. All around him objects turned to wriggling black outlines. He closed his eyes . . .

. . . and he was there again, at the dinner table, a look of wonder on his face and his hand with the cup in mid-air. He had taken but a tiny sip, and the complex flavors were still dancing in his mouth and filling his head with strange vistas. "What is it?" he asked.

"Do you like it?" she asked, a mysterious look on her face.

"It's the most delicious thing I've ever tasted! How did you do it?"

Ada smiled at him. "Cardamom," she said.

Harry poked his head in. "Is the coast clear?"

"Yeah," Sunny said shakily. Then his good fortune hit him. "Yeah! Yee-haw!" He grabbed Harry and danced around him. "I did it! I did it! I'm a god-damned genius!" He stopped suddenly. "I've got to tell Andy. Can you take me by the church?"

Harry raised his hands and backed away.

"Oh! Right," Sunny said. "What about Stone Face? Is he on site today?"

They located Tucker on a scaffolding and called him down. Sunny herded him into the rusty hulk Tucker called a truck and hopped in beside, all the time talking a mile a minute.

"So," Tucker said. "I take it this is good news?"

"Don't just sit there asking questions. Drive!"

"Maybe you might tell me where?"

"The church! Andy's church! He'll be tickled pink."

But Andy wasn't at the church. Susan was delighted to hear the good news and, yes, she agreed Sunny was a genius. But she hadn't seen Andy all day. They got back into Tucker's rust bucket.

"Where to now, genius?" Tucker asked.

"Do you know where Andy lives?"

"Back o' that old farmhouse, south end of town. Oldfield's."

"Well?!" Sunny demanded.

Tucker ground it into first and they headed off across town. But Andy wasn't there either, no matter how frantically Sunny banged on his door. He came back to the truck pulling his hair and looking wild.

"You could leave a note."

"Brilliant!" Sunny said, all smiles again. "Give me something to write on and a pen or pencil or something."

"Which one? A pen or a pencil?"

"Oh, for God's sake!"

"I got a auto parts receipt here. Do ya think that's the right sorta thing for this sorta note?"

"You're enjoying this, aren't you?"

Tucker handed him the stuff with what—on him—amounted to a broad grin.

Sunny scrawled out, "Come see me at once!" and looked around for something to fix it to Andy's door.

"Ain't cha gonna sign it?"

"He'll know who it's from," Sunny said, rummaging through Tucker's glove box and coming up with a bent thumb tack. The note fixed, they drove off, heading for Sunny's trailer.

"We're going to celebrate tonight," Sunny said cheerily.

"You want me bring something?" Tucker said.

"Huh? Oh, no," Sunny said. "I've got everything me and Andy'll need."

They drove two miles in silence before Sunny noticed how complete the silence was. "What's gotten into you?" he asked.

"Nothin'."

"Great." Sunny stared at him. "You're always like this. Anytime something good happens."

"Or someone new comes along."

"I'm happy. Why can't you just let me be happy?"

Tucker shook his head. "You're happy. That's all that matters."

"Well, yeah."

"What about him?"

"What *about* him?"

"Is he 'happy,' too?"

"What do you mean?"

They pulled off the hard road and onto the packed dirt that led to Sunny's trailer.

"He's different." Tucker said. "He's not like us."

Sunny shrugged. "Harry's not like us and you don't say anything about me hanging around him."

Tucker looked at him. "You know what I mean."

"Well, maybe I don't. Maybe you should spell it out to me."

They had reached the trailer. Tucker stopped the truck and yanked the parking break. "You can't play around with that boy's feelings," he said. "He's not some toy."

"Oh. So now all I'm doing is 'playing around.' And who are you, then, my uncle?"

"Is that what this is about, your uncle?"

"You tell me. Is this about me and Andy, or about me and you? Because if it is, then it's about nothing. You got that? Nothing!"

Tucker looked at him expressionless. Then he turned to look out the windshield. "You're here," he said.

Sunny stared at him a moment, furious. Then he said a voiceless "Fuck!" and slammed out of the truck and ran to the trailer. Inside, he stood panting against the door. Tucker's engine sputtered once, twice, then caught. Through the kitchen curtains, Sunny watched the old heap turn around and roll off down the hill without even raising a cloud of dust.

Damn Jedediah Tucker for making him feel bad! That whole Stone Face act was just that: an act, a way to seem superior. Well, Sunny didn't have time for it. He needed a shower and time to get ready for Andy.

Lerner Alquist sat behind the oak desk in his office above the Kennsing County Savings and Loan. He remembered buying it, proud of its cross-quarter grain and deep finish. He'd promised not to spend too many nights behind it. *Home by supper, home to stay.* That had been the first promise he'd made to her, and one of the first he'd broken. But when you're dealing with land you have to act quickly. Oklahoma land titles were a tricky business. Ada understood. She admired the desk, too, pointing out the dovetailing in the drawers and the delicate runner arch that softened its lines. "You've a fine eye," she'd said.

"I always could spot a beauty," he said to the darkness.

He rubbed his hands along it, raising a faint odor of varnish and sweat. It had darkened over the years through constant contact with his skin, his hands pressed into the wood as he pored over contracts and leases, mortgages and plat maps.

There was blood in its rippling grain, too. Lerner ran his thumb along the left-hand corner, recalling the hapless farmer whose note he held who had blown his brains out right in front of him. How many years ago? Twenty? No, not that long. Virginia had been just a child when it happened, and she wasn't twenty yet. He remembered getting up and walking home immediately afterward, afraid Ada would arrive with his lunch pail. He surprised her in the kitchen and hugged her so fiercely she dropped the sandwich she had been wrapping. Virginia squealed and kicked her legs in the high chair, crying for attention. He didn't tell his wife what had happened, only that he wanted to see her, and that he would make it a practice to walk home for lunch more often. And he did, too, for a while.

He rubbed his thumb over the spot again. Did he imagine it, or was there an unevenness to the finish there? A shallow, thumb-shaped groove? He drew back angrily.

What piece of land was it? Time was, he would have all the facts at his fingertips, every loan and land parcel spelled out in sharp detail in his mind. Had it been the bottom land out past the cemetery? Or the hillside farm near Pesogi? It didn't matter. Lerner knew when he made the loan the land would fail. That was why he'd offered better terms than Brown at the Savings and Loan, outmaneuvering that crafty redskin at his own game. He didn't care about the financial loss when the inevitable foreclosure came; it was the land he was after. So when the farmer, gaunt and dusty, pushed himself past his secretary and interrupted Lerner's study of a land survey, he knew what to expect. He had his answer ready even before the question was asked. No, there would be no reduction in terms. No, there would be no extension. It was too bad the man had gambled his inheritance and his life savings, but what did he expect? Agriculture had been failing in this part of Oklahoma for years. Did he think he could somehow outsmart the odds, the dust storms, the wild gyrations in commodity prices? He should have done his homework before getting in over his head.

Lerner was surprised when the man reached into the potato sack he'd brought with him and pulled out a dark gray pistol. He'd been expecting him to pull out an apple or turnip or some such proof the farm was viable. Lerner shook his head in disbelief. "You won't use that thing."

"You think I won't?"

Lerner looked him in the eye. "If you had the guts to use that, you'd have had the guts to make a go of it."

The man leaned over the desk. "You think I ain't got the guts?" he whispered.

Lerner noted the hand holding the gun did not tremble. Neither did he. "I know you don't."

A smile crept up the side of the man's face. "You don't know shit," he said, and he put the pistol in his mouth and pulled the trigger.

Lerner leapt back, upsetting his chair. He glanced quickly at his shirt and vest. He was unharmed. Not a spatter of blood had reached him. Ellie rushed in, screamed, and rushed out again, hands in the air. He could hear her wailing all the way down the corridor. He walked over to the hat tree and took down his fedora and put it on. Then he followed Ellie down the hall. Just as he reached the stairs, a man came bounding up. Lerner blocked his way. "Call the police," he said. "And see that that mess is cleaned up by the time I get back."

And then he had walked home. He was enjoying a fresh sandwich when the Chief of Police came to the door. "It's just business," he told Ada, and then walked back with him, giving his account of events along the way.

When they got back to the office, the body had been removed and the chair had been righted. There had been some hasty clean-up as well, and the tang of disinfectant hung in the air. "Do you need anything more from me?" Lerner asked the Chief.

"There will be an inquest."

"Of course." Lerner placed his hat on the rack. The Chief was still there, waiting for something. As the seconds ticked by in silence, Lerner grew impatient. "I'd like to get back to work now," he said, crossing behind the desk.

"Don't you think . . . maybe you should close for the day?"

"Why?"

The Chief shrugged. "I was just concerned that . . ." He looked at Lerner, again as though he expected something. Finally Lerner waved his hand in the air as if dispelling lingering smoke. "There's no reason to be concerned," he said. "The man had no relatives." He sat down and took up the land survey he had been reading. He didn't hear the Chief leave, but when he glanced up, he was gone.

He was about to return to the survey when a glistening dollop of red and white caught his eye. It hung on the corner of the desk. "Ellie!" he bellowed, but of course she was gone. He reached out and swiped the gob with his thumb and flung it into the waste can. He took out his handkerchief, walked to the water cooler, dampened it, and rubbed it vigorously over his hand. Then he flung the handkerchief into the waste can as well.

He straightened up and looked around the room. Under the smell of disinfectant lay the odor of rust and burnt sulfur. He picked up the waste can and walked down the hallway to the trash chute and shoved it in. He heard it clatter all the way down the metallic gullet. Returning to the office, he raised the blinds and opened the windows as wide as possible. Sunlight and dust and street sounds poured in, and he sat down to the survey once again. The light was gone from the sky by the time he rose to leave.

Dark then; dark now. *Why is it dark?* he thought. *Why hasn't Ellie turned on the lights?* He was caught for a moment between past and present. Then he remembered. He had let Ellie go some weeks back—an unfortunate scene, full of tears and commotion. But a lean business is a fit business, and these days every penny counts. But why is it dark? He must have forgotten to turn the lights on when he came in. And here was a funny thing: he didn't remember coming in.

"Hello?"

Alquist straightened in his chair. "Who's there?" he demanded. He heard someone walk across the outer office and pause before the door. "If you've got business with me, don't shilly-shally around. Come in, come in!"

The door opened and JayRob Pautler stood there with a comical look. "The door was open, but I wasn't sure anyone was in. The lights weren't on."

"I've been busy. I must have lost track of the time. Flip 'em on and come on in."

JayRob groped for the button and pushed it. They both had a moment to realize Lerner was sitting at an empty desk, then both decided to ignore it.

"Take a seat, Mr. Mayor," Alquist said generously. "What can I do you for?"

"I'm not here as Mayor," JayRob said. "At least, not yet."

"Well then, what are you here for? Make yourself plain."

"I'm here to ask you to halt the construction on the library." He took a sheaf of papers from the inner pocket of his suit coat.

The suit didn't fool Alquist for a moment. He could still smell onions on the man. "Mr. Pautler, I know you don't like this project. I don't know if it's just me or libraries in general that piss you off, but frankly I don't care."

Pautler smirked. "That's not going to work this time, Lerner. This isn't about getting my goat. That goat ain't got."

What the hell is he talking about? Alquist waved his arm dismissively. "I haven't got time for this."

"I think you'll make time for this." JayRob spread out the papers. "You can check the figures—and knowing you, you will—but I think the bottom line is right enough." He pointed to the final figure. "That one right there." Pautler leaned back in his chair and smiled. "I think you'll find you're a little short, there, Lerner."

Alquist leaned back and smiled, too. "And I think you'll find I've got that covered."

When he heard the frantic knocking, Sunny wondered for a moment if Tucker had come back. He raced to the door and opened it.

And there stood Andy, a look of real concern on his face. "I got here as soon as I could," he said, entering. "What's happened? What's wrong?"

"Nothing's wrong!" Sunny said, beaming.

"But your note. I thought— I thought maybe Alquist had come to run you off, or something had happened to you, or—"

"No, no," Sunny said "It's nothing like that. In fact it's good news—"

"Well, what then? Tell me! What?"

"Hey! Slow down. It's great news." He couldn't help laughing. Andy was practically bursting with worry. "I got the commission. Alquist is going to install my sculpture on the library."

"Really?!"

"Really."

Andy swept him into a bear hug. "Oh, man, that's amazing!" he said.

They stayed clenched for a second. Sunny's chest glowed from the heat of their contact. His nipples had gone erect beneath his linen shirt. His cock gave a little twitch. Then they pulled apart.

"Where were you?" Sunny said. "I went all over town looking for you."

"I was in the library."

"You're kidding! I was right there! I could have told you then."

"I was there all afternoon."

"But why?"

"Well, it's a really good library."

"It had better be, after all the money Alquist has poured into it. But why?"

"This," Andy said, and he raised his hand. For the first time, Sunny noticed there was a book in it.

"What is it?" Sunny asked.

"Summaries. Supreme Court rulings." Andy opened the book and started leafing through the pages. "It's not like I doubted you, but I just couldn't believe the things you guys said, that day at Elephant Rock."

"What things?" Andy was still leafing through the book, scanning pages. Sunny frowned. He wanted Andy to be looking at him, not some dusty book. "What things?" he repeated.

Andy stopped suddenly. "Here it is! I wouldn't have believed it, but here it is. This is the decision they based your father's case on, from the Supreme Court of the United States. *The United States v. Bhagat Singh Thind*."

Sunny suddenly felt cold. He was sure no one had ever read that decision except him. "You found it? You actually looked up the ruling?" What if Andy had looked up the ruling against his father as well? What would he think then?

"Listen to this." Andy read from the decision, anger mixing with disbelief in his voice. *"What we now hold is that the words 'free white persons' are words of common speech, to be interpreted in accordance with the understanding of the common man.* 'The common man'! Since when do we base our laws merely on what people think they mean?"

"Appeal to reason and you'll stand alone," Sunny said, "but appeal to common sense and you'll have the whole mob with you, shouting approval."

"The physical group characteristics of the Hindus render them readily distinguishable from the various groups of persons commonly recognized as white. The children of English, French, German, Scandinavian, and other European parentage—" Andy broke off. "Did you get that? 'Other European parentage,' but they only mention northern European countries. Who's next on their list of 'persons not recognized as white'? Italians? Spaniards?"

"Indians," Sunny said quietly, "Mexicans."

Andy was getting more and more worked up. *"Children born in this country of Hindu parents would retain indefinitely the clear evidence of their ancestry.* But children born in this country *are* American citizens, no matter where their parents are from! You're a citizen."

"Yes," Sunny said and took a step toward him.

"They're twisting every which way they can to justify their prejudice and disgust, and disguise it by calling it law. They even say so: *It is very far from our thought to suggest the slightest question of racial inferiority.* Hah! *What we suggest is merely racial difference, and it is of such character and extent that the great body of our people instinctively recognize it and reject the thought of assimilation."*

"Put it down, Andy."

"Instinctively reject! Now we're basing law on instinct!" Andy's eyes were filling with tears. Sunny stepped forward and held him by the hips, looking into his eyes. "Don't you understand? They're saying you can never be accepted because you will always look different—"

"Throw down your books and follow me," Sunny said softly.

"—and as long as you're different, you'll be rejected, and there's nothing you can do about it, you'll never be—"

Sunny pressed his lips against Andy's. Andy was still talking, words and logic pouring from his mouth, but Sunny held steady, and soon

Andy's lips stopped moving, then relaxed, and then with a muffled cry, Andy started kissing back, clenching him by the shoulders, the book falling to the floor. With a gasp, Andy broke free, only to tighten his embrace again and bury his face in Sunny's shoulder, sobbing.

"Here you are," Sunny murmured in his ear, rocking him in his arms. "Here you are at last."

Chapter 10

Prairie Damascene

Matthew Jacobs looked up from his copy of *Apostolic Faith Bulletin* at the knock on his door. A glance at the clock showed it was late afternoon; Mrs. Oldfield had left for the day and he should be going home himself soon. "Come in," he said.

The door opened and Andy peeked around the edge. "I'm sorry to disturb you, Matthew."

He grinned and put the *Bulletin* aside. "You're a welcome sight anytime, Andy. Take a seat." The young man hung his head, hiding a smile as he entered. "What is it? Trouble in the altos again?"

Andy settled in the chair across from him, laughing. "No, sir, nothing like that. I've spoken to Mrs. George and she said it was all a misunderstanding, and she apologized to Mrs. Littledeer. I hope that that'll put an end to it, but—" He shrugged.

"Yes. Those Littledeers can hold onto a slight like it was a life preserver." Matthew shook his head. "Sometimes the biggest challenge we face as Christians is other Christians. But you handled it well, Andy. I'm pleased."

Andy blushed and looked down again. "Thank you."

"So, if it's not a crisis in the choir, what is it?"

Andy rubbed his hands together, then stuffed them under his legs. "It's . . . well, maybe it's a crisis in the choir master."

"You can always talk to me, Andy. I'm your friend, remember?"

Andy nodded. "I'm wondering if maybe the Holy Spirit has given up on me."

There was that flash of smile again, but Matthew read desperation in his eyes. "Whatever makes you think that?"

"I have never received the gift of tongues."

"There are other gifts, Andy, each taylored to an individual soul."

"But doesn't it say in 1 Corinthians, *Those who are unspirited do not receive the gifts of God's Spirit*? There must be some inner flaw that has rendered me unfit."

"The Holy Spirit is not so easily put off. If God waited until we were fit, we would none of us receive His Spirit." Matthew leaned forward, steepling his fingers. "But I think I know what you mean. You want the feel of God in your bones, under your skin, shooting out of your fingers and toes. A God who grabs you by the belly and pulls you through life, so that every step you take you know is His will, not yours."

"Yes!"

"And I am here to tell you, He already has."

"But—"

Matthew raised a palm. "I can see it in you, Andy. I can see the change."

Andy's hands flew through transformations worthy of a magician. Finally he blurted out, "But what if the gift of the Spirit is offered in a manner too terrifying to accept?"

Matthew smiled gently. "So, it *has* been offered."

Andy squeezed his eyes shut.

"What did you feel, Andy?"

"Joy." He shook his head. "And terror."

Matthew nodded. "Sounds about right."

"I thought it would be a comfort. Instead, it's . . ." He opened his eyes. "It's like my heart's cracked open and there's no protection for the wound."

"The gift of the Spirit doesn't make life easier. It makes it more meaningful."

"But it was so *physical*."

"Of course it was. *We* are physical. God made us that way. That is how He wants us, as we are."

"I don't see how He could possibly want me as I am."

"You said it was physical. I think I know what you mean."

Andy looked down. "I don't think—"

"Andy, you light up whenever Susan enters the room."

Andy laughed and looked away. "No, that isn't— That can't be—"

"Do you think the material world is an accident? It isn't. God manifests the world to manifest His love, materially. And the terrible thing, the thing that we cannot face, the thing we cannot *know*—which frightens the Devil out of us—is that God wants *all* of us: mind, soul, *and* body. Not part. All."

"That just sounds so . . . simple."

Matthew rose from his chair. "Oh, dear Lord, it is far from simple! Paul's life did not get simpler when he returned from Damascus. My own Damascene conversion shook me to my very core." He folded his arms and looked out the window. "It was not at all what I expected, not what I wanted. When it came, it made me very angry."

"Angry? At who?"

"At God." He shook his head. "I had my training, my beliefs. I had faith as solid as a rock. And I had, I thought, a calling." He turned and faced him. "And then I fell in love."

He took the chair next to Andy. "You did not know my wife, Amelia. She was a lovely woman, gracious, kind, soft-spoken. Many people thought her a saint. But to me . . ." He smiled. "To me, she was simply the most beautiful creature on God's green earth. I was well past the age most men marry before I even spoke to her. That she spoke back was a miracle.

"But there were difficulties. She was Roman Catholic. If I continued seeing her, I would have to leave my church. They would not accept a pastor with a Roman wife. It looked like my ministry, the thing I was so sure I wanted, was about to end.

"Amelia was in a similar predicament. Marriage in my church would mean nothing in hers. She would be living in sin and forbidden the sacraments. It seemed hopeless. Rather than force her to choose, I resolved to break it off."

Andy sat still. "She wouldn't let you, would she?"

"No. I was the weak one, she, the strong. She gave up her church, her community, even her family. Her parents disowned her and moved to Oklahoma City to escape the scandal."

Andy shook his head. "I don't know if I could have done that. I don't know if I have that kind of courage."

"There are many gifts, Andy, and that is when I saw perhaps the greatest of them all. It is not prophecy, or speaking in tongues, or healing. It is recognizing the stamp of God's love in another human being. Those who are unspirited are those who cannot love. That is what shuts out the Holy Spirit; failing to honor that love, turning our backs on it, raising our hands against it, or simply not having the courage to see it."

"Did they accept her here, the people at Mt. Hermon?"

He smiled wryly. "Once they saw she wasn't a Papist spy, yes. Her beautiful soul won them over. Well, most of them."

"And that was your Damascus moment? Seeing the stamp of love on someone outside our faith?"

"No." He got up and walked to the window again. "Amelia and I had twelve wonderful years together, blessed with a beautiful daughter—as you've noticed—and a growing church. But then Amelia was stricken with cancer. Insidious, implacable, painful, ugly. I got down on my knees and prayed for healing, for relief, for insight into what God wanted of me. And when no answers came, I blamed everyone I could lay my hands on. God, the doctors, myself. I even went back to her parish and asked the priest to give her last rites. He refused."

He turned around. "Everyone gets angry at God, Andy. But when a man of the cloth gets angry at God, it is a fearsome fire. But it was nothing like Amelia's. Hers could burn continents."

"She got angry at God, too?"

"Not at God. At me. For going to the priest. On her last day on earth, she took what little strength she had and let me have it! She told me I was a fool to try to 'fix things.' She told me God would not have gone through all the trouble of bringing the two of us together if He meant to keep us apart in the hereafter. 'God is bigger than that,' she said. 'We all want a sure path. That's what doctrine promises. But God sees in all directions at once. He'll see us all home, no matter which path we take.' And then she left me."

Andy nodded. "He'll see us all home."

Matthew Jacobs sat behind his desk. "Let your heart crack, Andy. I think you'll find Christ is already inside. Give Him the whole full mess of you. Parts of you may drop away like dead limbs, and that's terrifying because you cannot know which parts they'll be. But when God carves you, He leaves you whole."

Andy turned off the county highway at the dirt road that followed Little Bushy Creek, but he didn't follow it all the way to its end. Instead, he turned in at the trail that lead uphill and parked. He stepped around a gate and into the swaying bunched grass and started climbing, startling clouds of grasshoppers into ever-widening circles around him. When he reached the crest, he saw the small abandoned farmhouse he had seen from the highway. There was little paint left on the siding, and strips of curtain flapped in the broken windows. The roof showed patches of tarpaper where the wind had ripped away shingles, and the small porch drooped like the ruined spine of a horse.

He took a deep breath and looked down the hill at the town. Croy lay nestled in the valley of the White Horse like a green oasis. On all sides, the ironwood and blackjack oak claimed land that had not been cleared for farming or ranching, and marched along fence lines that quartered the township. On this hill, he could feel the dry pull of the prairie to the west. It rose up in the dust, breathed out through the bluestem grass, and hung in the heated air as the sun dropped in amber glory toward the horizon. He sat beneath an apple tree whose twisted trunk and branches spoke of hard decades in Oklahoma weather. Stumps of felled trees formed a ruined orchard that spread in rows down the hill.

He hadn't been honest with Matthew. He had wanted to talk about Sunny's kiss, how it had filled his whole body with light and torn his heart away from everything he knew and believed. But instead he had let Matthew's assumptions take over, knowing they were false. When the story of Amelia began to unspool, he let it, giving up his own story, happy to follow any narrative that kept others from seeing the raw flesh of his. It was a familiar relief, a comfortable trap.

Andy leaned against the revenant tree. Before him lay the valley of the White Horse, containing all the expectations of his life: his meager house, his church with its pastor and daughter, the community where he would bring the water of the Holy Spirit to thirsting souls through music. Behind him, over the hill, lay Sunny's trailer.

He looked at the ground beside him. A withered apple lay in the dried leaves and grass, a few small bites taken out of one side. *Probably some prairie dog*, Andy thought, *maybe sometime last year*. He stood up.

"A more meaningful life." His life had no meaning. Instead, it was full of other people's meaning.

If God wanted all of him, then that's what He would get. Not just nibbles; the whole core. If the Spirit thrust Its gifts on him, he would seize them and take them into his heart.

The sun was setting, tinting the rooftops and steeples in town with gold. The water tower shone like a burnished trophy. Andy's shadow reached down the hill toward them. He turned and walked back to the car. He started the engine and headed up the twisting ravine to Sunny's trailer.

Part 2

Fortunati ambo! si quid mea carmina possunt,
Nulla dies umquam memori uos eximet aeuo. . . .

Fortunate pair! If there be any power in my song,
The day shall never dawn that fails to honor your renown.

—Virgil, *Aeneid,* Book IX

Chapter 11

NISUS AND EURYALUS

Virginia reached for a cigarette and lit it without even thinking, clenching the phone to her ear with a shoulder. The pack was too light when she put it down. It was empty. "Shit!" she said, expelling smoke.

"What?" Susan sounded alarmed.

"Nothing." She should stub this out, save it for tonight. She sought the marble ash tray on the other side of the sofa, tottering as she reached for it, then stopped. *What the hell?* she thought and leaned back. "Why me?" she asked.

"Well, she tried talking to her mom, but she just told her to pray and follow her husband's guidance."

Virginia snorted. She could imagine just how much guidance John Tibbits could provide. "Don't you have marital counseling or something at your church?"

"You mean my father?" Susan asked.

"Well, yeah." There was dead silence on the other end of the line. "I see your point," Virginia said. "But why me?"

"Well," Virginia could practically hear Susan blushing, "you were so helpful when it came to me. Once I got you talking."

"Don't remind me. Never chase cheap wine with sloe gin." She took longer to inhale this time, savoring the metallic tang of the smoke on her tongue. "So, why not just pass the wisdom on yourself?"

"Well, I'm technically still . . ." There was a long pause.

Huh, thought Virginia. So, what does that make me?

"Whereas you—"

Susan was the only person in Croy who knew about her and Harry. "You didn't tell her, did you?" If she had blabbed to Ruth, Virginia would break both her thumbs.

"No, no," Susan assured her. "But she and John have been trying awfully hard since they got married, and maybe . . . well, maybe there's just something they've missed."

Trying awfully hard? Virginia thought. *Some girls have all the luck.* Others, a guy just has to walk across a plowed field and they wind up pregnant. And what was she supposed to do, anyway, draw pictures? "Okay," she said without really knowing why, "I'll do it."

"Oh, thanks, Ginny! That's a load off my mind."

"But I want something in return."

"Name it."

"I want your boyfriend to take me down to Rosen's for a pack of cigs."

"Andy? Well, I guess so."

"You 'guess so'? You're still seeing each other, aren't you?"

Susan laughed, but even over the phone it sounded hollow. "Well, if you count rehearsals. He's taking this Service of Thanks awfully seriously. Half the time he's over at Mt. Zion rehearsing Ethan's choir."

Virginia almost said something but took a vigorous tug on her cigarette instead. *Harry would know if there was anything going on. Best not say anything hurtful.*

Susan was prattling on. "I mean, first he's all passionate kisses in the middle of the night—"

"Suzie-Q! And here I thought you were pure."

"Oh, buzz off. And then I practically don't see him for weeks. I mean really, do you understand boys at all?"

"Oh, boys ain't so bad." She took another drag. "It's when they think they're men that the trouble starts."

A corner of her mind noted that she'd gone from wanting to break Susan's thumbs to wanting to keep her from making a fool of herself. She smiled. She'd ask Harry about it. She had a whole list of things she wanted to straighten out with him.

"Do you need that ride anytime soon?" Susan asked.

Virginia looked at the fag end of her smoke. It was hard to believe it was almost gone. She'd only taken, what, five drags? "Yep," she said, "pretty soon."

Andy lay on his back and stretched out his arms. The fingers of one hand touched the wall to his right, while the others dangled in the air not two feet from the opposite wall He crossed his feet and pointed his toes and felt them touch the air conditioner cord that snaked down to the wall socket out of sight beyond the mattress.

He sighed. Light flickered through the trees outside and danced on the window shade. Without a doubt, Sunny's bedroom was smaller than his, but it felt larger, connected somehow to the dancing blackjacks, the birdsong that marked the silence, and the endless breeze making spirals in the dust. In here, he was anywhere and everywhere.

The toilet flushed and Andy heard the door open. He kept his arms out-stretched, knowing his left hand would brush Sunny's thigh as he came back to bed. But instead Sunny stopped short and looked down at him.

"Are you trying to look like Christ crucified or is that just your natural state?"

Andy gave a half laugh and pulled in his arms. Sunny crawled over him, making sure the hairs of his chest grazed his as he got into bed. It raised gooseflesh all along Andy's torso and made exclamation points of his nipples. He sighed.

Sunny raised himself on one elbow and idly played with Andy's left tit. "Why so glum?" he asked.

Andy's eyes roamed around the room. "This place," he said.

"Yeah. Damned small, isn't it? But all that's about to change."

"No, I like it here."

"You'll like the studio even more. I'm going to decide today. The apartment above Rosen's has ideal light for life modeling and sketching, but I can't fire the maquettes there. The brickworks has a full-scale easel and kilns, but the heat! People would melt before I could even sketch them."

"Does it have to be in town?"

"Well, I can't have people trekking out here, can I? There's a space behind Pautler's, a kind of yard with a shed. I hate to give that old wind-bag the business, but I suppose I could build a small kiln there." He shook his head. "Nah. Rosen's."

Andy put his hand on top of Sunny's to stop the circling finger. "What happens to us?"

"Us?"

"In town. It'll be a bit obvious with my car parked outside Rosen's all the time. Nobody needs that much aspirin."

Sunny grinned at him. "I've got that covered. You're going to be one of my life models."

"What?"

Sunny slapped him on the stomach, making it ring like a drum. "Let me show you!" he said and dove for the edge of the bed.

Andy looked at the funnel of hair in the small of Sunny's back and the swirling patterns on his butt. His balls hung between his thighs, swinging from side to side as he dug for something under the bed. Every once in a while, his cock would heave into view, the brown foreskin allowing just the tip of a rosy head to show. "I am truly on the giddy road to hell," Andy said.

"What?"

"Nothing."

"Here it is!" Sunny hauled an enormous art book onto the bed between them. He opened to a marked page and turned it so Andy could see. "It's Nisus and Euryalus, by Jean-Baptiste Roman. It's my next commission. For the war memorial."

Andy studied the color plate. It was obviously the scene of some disaster. Two male figures posed on a low mound, sculpted in creamy white marble that looked as flexible and translucent as skin. One figure was clearly dead, draped bonelessly across the mound, his left breast pierced by a wound that still oozed marbleized gouts of blood. The other figure, too, was doomed, the point of a lance buried deep in his side. Yet he supported his dead friend with one arm and thrust the other fiercely upward, devotion and defiance fused in one grand gesture.

But there was nothing in the out-thrust hand to justify the stance, nothing but a small mallet, all out of proportion to the heroic tableau. "What is going on here?" he asked.

"Aw, it's tragic, really. You don't want to know. But you can see the problem, right?" Sunny said.

"Well, yes," Andy said. Both figures were nude, hardly the sort of thing for a public sculpture in a town like Croy.

"Unless you know the story, you can't really tell what Nisus is doing here. I'm not even sure they still teach *The Aeneid* anymore."

"Virgil," Andy nodded. "I remember reading it in Latin class. But I don't remember these two."

"They probably cut it. They were lovers."

Andy swallowed. "That wasn't in my book."

"Big surprise," Sunny said. "Nisus was the crafty one. He was older. He helped Euryalus win a race by cheating. But when the two of them snuck off to plunder enemy camp, Euryalus, the younger one, got caught. Nisus rushes back to save him, but he's too late. Virgil says Nisus fights on, pierced by lances on every side, striving to avenge his beloved friend, and with his last dying thrust, kills the enemy king." His restless eyes scanned the print, eating up every detail. "In their sacrifice, these two made possible the founding of Rome." He frowned and shook his head. "Jean-Baptiste was brilliant, but limited by his approach and materials. See?" He tapped the picture on Nisus's outstretched arm. "The stone won't support the full weight of a Trojan sword, so he just shows the grip. The yokels around here would probably think that's some kind of hammer."

"Yesss," Andy agreed.

"But in bas-relief, I can show the whole thing. Then this town will have something to talk about besides that monstrous lump to General Longstreet."

"Well if they're nude like that, they'll do more than just talk."

Sunny's eyes flashed at him. "I'm not just going to copy it! I'm going to rework the theme, say something new about the nature of war and the nature of courage—its true roots in the dear love of comrades."

Whitman? Andy wondered. He's going to base a war memorial on a quotation from Whitman?

Sunny ran on. "That's why I need life-models. To pose for it. That's where you come in."

Andy's Whitman thoughts abruptly vanished. "Not on your life!"

"Why not?"

"Well, first of all," Andy pointed to the Trojan warriors, "I'm not built like that."

Sunny waved that aside. "True, you don't get barrel-chested from hefting hymnals. But I don't want perfect."

"Gee, thanks."

"I want real. That's who our soldiers are today. Real people. Not heroes-with-a-thousand-biceps."

"Still, isn't there somebody else in Croy who could do it?"

"Like who?"

A sun-drenched figure on a rock flashed in Andy's mind. "Like Harry Edom."

Sunny's face froze and his eyes, dancing and challenging moments before, suddenly became opaque. After a moment, he looked down at the book and closed it. "He would say no," he said.

Andy sensed he had touched a nerve, one he shouldn't irritate further. "Okay, but can't you, you know, extrapolate from other works of art?"

"If you don't want to come to my studio, just say so."

"Hey, it's not that . . ." he reached out to touch him, but Sunny dodged his hand—a neat trick, Andy thought, in a space so small—leaning over the side of the bed and fishing up a small stack of magazines.

"Here you go," he said, flinging them at Andy. "Here are my 'other works of art.'"

Andy stared in amazement. The magazines bore titles like *Strength and Health*, *Physique Pictorial*, and *Vim*. But their real purpose was obvious at a glance: they were devoted to pictures of muscular young men, naked or nearly so, in classical poses and outdoor settings. Some lounged on romantic ruins, others posed in dynamic but frozen athletics. Their eyes rarely looked at the camera. This allowed the reader to stare in private at what he could not enjoy in public. Even the ads held erotic promise. One for a picture history of the West featured an Indian dressed in breechclout preparing to torture a stripped-down cowboy tied to a wagon wheel. The table of contents listed "Bunkhouse Scene," "Campfire Buddies," and "Bath Day"—all, Andy felt, having little to do with history. "Where did you get this?" he whispered.

"Behind the counter at Rosen's. I guess that's another reason to pick his place. I'm already a steady customer."

"He lets you buy them?"

"He lets anybody buy them. He runs a drugstore, it's a business. Besides, I'm not the only one."

Andy looked up in surprise.

"What? You think we're the only two in Oklahoma?"

Andy shook his head. "Now I'm really scared. I don't even dare go in that place anymore. What would people think?"

"Oh, come on!" Sunny said. He grabbed one of the magazines and read from its cover. "They'd think you were 'dedicated to the radiant health of body, mind, and spirit which frees man from the vulgar and base and inspires him to noble ideals and endeavors.'"

"Horse crap."

"'Tis not. It's the Creed of the Grecian Guild. Says so right here: 'Our goal is the development of a sound mind in a sound body, that we may best serve our God, our fellow man, and our country.'"

"Nobody believes that."

Sunny threw the magazine aside. "Oh, I don't know. I'm kinda fond of serving my fellow man." He leaned on top of him. "Especially this fellow man."

"That's nothing more than *Look* magazine for perverts."

The smile dropped from Sunny's face. "Is that what you think we are? Perverts?"

Andy could hardly speak, ideas tumbling over each other in his head. "In the sight of God—" he started.

"We're in the sight of God now."

"But to other people . . ." Andy looked around the room. "How would I explain this?"

"With this," Sunny said and leaned forward and kissed him.

Andy was still at once, all trace of agitation gone. He looked deep into the gold in Sunny's eyes, lost in the patterns of his irises. Then he raised his head a bit, inviting further kisses. He still felt the pressure of them on his lips when Sunny pulled away.

"Where does your heart go when I do that?" he asked.

"All the way around the world."

"And where does your head go?"

Andy laughed. "Away."

"And your soul?"

Andy turned away, unable to look him in the eye.

Sunny sighed and rolled off him. "Look," he said, "I know what you're going through. When my father was gone for good, that was the worst time for us. We ping-ponged between his folks in Stockton and Mama's folks in Queens. I didn't know what to do. There was no one I could turn to. I had these feelings but I certainly couldn't discuss them with Uncle Bhavjeet, who was even stricter than my dad. So I looked everywhere, I tried every-thing. Sikhism, Christianity, read up on Buddhism, went to sweat lodges and on spirit walks. My family didn't know what to make of me."

"Mine didn't either."

Sunny grinned. "You too?"

"I always had questions. Too many questions. The whole notion of hell, for instance. It just didn't make sense to me. But there wasn't much room for 'dismal doubt' where I came from. Once I got to Wheaton, at least I could ask questions."

"And get answers?"

"Well, *learn* answers. But learning and believing are different things. But what about *your* family? Questioning tradition is—well, it *is* your tradition, all the way back to Guru Nanak Dev."

Sunny threw back his head and laughed.

"What?"

"That's what I said to Uncle Bhavjeet!"

Andy laughed along. "And what did he say?"

Sunny suddenly straddled Andy and pointed his finger at his face, his eyes blazing. "You are no guru!" he bellowed. "You study and you read and you learn nothing! You turn your back on true Gurus and study at Christian and Jew, Hopi and Sufi, Jesus and Any Simple MacPerson."

"Mac*Pherson*."

"Shut up, I'm on a rant. You are half-cooked Sikh! No! Less than half. Sikh from the neck up, Christian round the middle, and God knows what from the waist down!"

Sunny tumbled off him, laughing. Andy was laughing, too. "What did you do?"

"I said, 'Why even from the neck up, then?' and I started to unwind my *dastaar*."

"Wow."

"Yeah. Wow. I think it affected me even more than it affected him. You'd be surprised how much pressure gets released when you take yards and yards of muslin off your head. Anyway, Uncle Bhavjeet threw me out, of course. I came back here and stayed with Tucker for a while, but that didn't work out, either."

"Why not?"

Sunny shrugged. "I'm better off alone. Anyway, I ended up here, pretty much where it all started, on my father's farm."

"Which you're leaving."

Sunny turned to him. "All things change. I think that's something every religion agrees on."

"All things but God. And God's word."

"And which word is that?" Andy didn't answer him. "Look. I went to every church in this town, looking for a place to put my soul. I even talked to old Avril Rosen, who was surprisingly frank. I guess you don't get to be a druggist in a town this small without learning a lot about your fellow man—and learning to keep it to yourself."

"What'd he say?"

Sunny got a puzzled look on his face. "He talked about Jacob doing *puja* in Bethel."

"What?"

"I have no idea. But it doesn't matter. In the end, it was all scholarly this and rabbinical that. Theory and commentary and comments on the commentary. All head, no heart, nothing you could lay your hands on. And the others, the Christian churches, they were the worst. What I called joy they called sin, what I called truth they called heresy. The eastern mystics were no better. The body is dirt, pleasure is a snare, and beauty and joy merely Maya throwing her net of deception over all."

"Vanity of vanities. All is vanity."

"Exactly! From the East or West, it all comes down to the same thing. To save your soul, you have to throw away your body. Everything that brings your heart delight! Turn out your senses and fill them with holy emptiness. But I don't feel that emptiness. I see God in all directions, in the sunset, in the stars, in flowers." He looked at Andy. "In you."

Andy shook his head. "You're confusing the Creator with His creation."

"If God is not in the flesh, then why do we feel the divine when we see beauty? I cannot deny what I see or how I feel when I see it. I can't live like that. I couldn't as a Sikh, and I wouldn't as a Christian. You can't live your life according to some words in a book somewhere."

"They're not just any words," Andy said. "It's not just any book. If I believe as I believe—and I do—then I must believe that, too. God gave us commandments, not a menu."

"You'd rather believe that than what your own body tells you?"

"The body is just corruption." He stroked Sunny's abdomen. "Beautiful, delicious corruption."

Sunny was quiet a moment, staring at the window and the shadows dancing on the shade. The room was full of golden light from the late afternoon. Then he said, "We have a book, too. A beautiful book. So beautiful, in fact, that we give it a golden place to live. It is the wisdom of our gurus. And it says this: If you believe in pollution, there is pollution everywhere, but what has been given to us by divine will to eat and drink is pure. Pollution pollutes only the ignorant."

Something in Andy slipped into place. It happened with such force that a small sound escaped him: "Hah!"

Sunny turned to him. "What?"

"Our book says something similar. 'What God has cleansed you cannot make unclean.' It's a powerful vision, straight from God to St. Peter. He sees it three times, but he doesn't get it. He refuses it. And then it hits him: God manifests the world, the *entire* world, to manifest His love *to everyone*. Everyone has a right to that love. No one is cut off, not even by the law."

"Where is your heart now?"

Andy looked at him. "Here."

"And where is your head?"

"Here."

"And your soul?"

Andy leaned upwards. "Here," he said and pressed his lips to Sunny's. He leaned back and placed his hand over Sunny's heart. "It all works fine when it's just you and me. That's why I never want to leave this place. But we have to, don't we?"

Sunny smiled. "Do you trust me?"

"Yes."

"Then let me show you a way we can always be together, no matter where we are."

Sunny drew him into a sitting position, facing him, then drew closer. Their legs intertwined, and when Sunny drew close enough that their genitals touched, Andy was instantly hard. Sunny smiled at him as his own cock rose to meet his. Andy's heart was beating so hard he could feel it in his face and throat, all along his chest and deep in his bowels. When Sunny grasped their two cocks tightly in his hand, he gasped. He would have climaxed at once, but Sunny kept his hand perfectly still. When Andy's heart rate had slowed, Sunny locked his legs together behind him. Following his lead, Andy locked his own behind Sunny, looking into his eyes. His heart felt completely open and full of a wild freedom. Sunny's hand was still completely motionless.

"Now," Sunny said, "breathe with me . . ."

Chapter 12

Bonae Voluntatis

All those who long for a witness
All those who wait all alone
All those who hope for forgiveness
We are standing, standing
Standing in God's Love.

All those whose hearts never soften
All those the righteous have shunned
Those who are lost and forgotten
We are standing, standing,
Standing in God's Love.

> *Come unto me.*
> *Call out my name.*
> *I carried the cross for you,*
> *My blood will cover your shame.*

All those whose faith has been broken
All those whose dreams are undone
All those whose love is unspoken
We are standing, standing,
Standing in God's Love.

Matthew Jacobs listened from his office, smiling as he heard Susan take the solo. He'd been wondering how Andy was going to make it up to her for not having a more prominent part in the Service of Thanks. "Standing in God's Love" wouldn't be part of that service, of course—it was an altar call, not worship and praise—but he was sure the hymn would show up at Mt. Hermon soon enough. *What a remarkable young man*, he thought. *We are blessed by his gifts.*

He looked down at the letters spread on his desk. *And on the other hand, this.* JayRob Pautler had dropped them off earlier, spouting his usual convoluted syntax and vapid vocabulary.

"If people are really this concerned," Matthew had said, "why haven't they just come to me?"

"Pastor," Pautler had replied, "sometimes it is difficult for people to tell just where your feet touch the ground. Or if."

I suppose vexing your pastor is a gift, too, Matthew thought. *A way of teaching humility.*

Mrs. Oldfield knocked and peeked around his door.

"Yes?" he said, trying to sound cheerful.

"The Mt. Zion choir has arrived, Brother Matthew. And Ethan Jameson."

"Good." Mrs. Oldfield hovered at the door. "Was there something else?"

She came in, closing the door behind her, muffling the hubbub in the church outside. She held a piece of paper in her hand. "I wanted to show you this," she said.

He dreaded another letter, but what she handed him was something else, a seating chart of sorts. He looked at it a moment not comprehending, but when he did he let out a sigh of disappointment. "Do you really think this is necessary?"

Mrs. Oldfield was twisting a handkerchief in her hands. Matthew took note. It was rare that Clara Oldfield betrayed the slightest uncertainty.

"I am aware that Andy is the choir director—"

"Indeed, he is. This should be his decision."

"But he is young and foolish! And he's not from here. He's unaware of certain conventions and sensibilities, certain protocols that ought to be observed."

"Such as?"

"The congregation should be focused on the music, and the Spirit moving through it. They should not be distracted by—other concerns, earthly concerns."

Matthew Jacobs looked down at the letters on his desk. *That train has already left the station*, he thought. "*Bonae voluntatis*," he said.

Mrs. Oldfield blinked. "What?"

"Luke 2:14. Glory to God in the highest, and on Earth, peace, good will towards men."

He knew Mrs. Oldfield didn't need the verse recited to her, but he supposed she wondered what on Earth that had to do with her seating chart.

"That's the King James version, of course, translated from the Latin Vulgate," he said. "But they got it wrong, you see. It is not 'peace on Earth and good will towards men' but 'peace on Earth to men of good will.' But whose good will? In one received text, it could be read as 'peace on Earth to those who have good will,' but in another, it could be 'peace on Earth to those who are in God's good will.' You see the difference?"

Mrs. Oldfield stopped fidgeting. "Frankly, no."

"Just so. Peace either comes from within, or it comes from God's grace. If seeing a black man standing next to a white woman while singing God's praises closes people off from their own good will or from God's holy Spirit, then even a choir of angels won't bring them peace, let alone a seating chart." He handed the paper back to her. "Andy is the choir director. I am confident he is a man of good will."

Mrs. Oldfield opened her mouth but someone entered behind her before she could speak.

"Oh, I'm so sorry," said a short man dressed in black with a white collar. "They said you were in here, Matthew, and I . . . well, I should have knocked."

"It's quite all right, Francis," Jacobs said, "come in, come in. Mrs. Oldfield, you know Father Herron, don't you?"

"No, I— Pleased to meet you," she said, looking everywhere but directly at him.

"Was there anything else, Mrs. Oldfield?"

She shook her head and smiled tightly. "No." She picked up the sheet of paper. "No, thank you, that was all." She closed the door as she left.

Mrs. Oldfield stood outside the office door, wavering. *Was there anything else? Of course there was!* But not with a Roman Catholic priest standing right there. Her mind was racing in all directions. The Pastor had dismissed her plan to avert disaster, mixing it up with Scriptures he had come at every which way but sideways. He must not be thinking clearly.

She looked around. The risers were set up in front of the altar rail and

Ethan Jameson stood on a podium before them, looking over his notes. Choir members milled around, chatting, but some already stood in their places and more were drifting that way. Andy was nowhere to be seen.

Pastor hadn't actually said no. He had said it was Andy's decision. But Andy wasn't here.

She walked up to Ethan and handed him the paper. "I thought—" she said, but didn't know what else to say.

Ethan looked at her, then at the paper. He studied it, looked up at her, then at the combined choirs gradually massing before him. "Yes," he said. "Yes, thank you Mrs. Oldfield. As usual, your thoughtfulness and attention to detail puts us all to shame. People," he said loudly, "your attention, please. A few minor seating changes in the tenor and alto sections . . ."

Mrs. Oldfield walked to the back of the church, coloring deeply from head to foot.

Andy wrestled with the lock on the storage cabinet in the room that ran behind the sanctuary and baptismal well. You entered it from the larger store room to the right of the sanctuary, where the risers were usually kept. The storeroom wasn't much wider than a hallway. A wooden wardrobe held old choir robes, a metal shelving unit rattled with ancient coffee percolators, cleaning supplies, and plastic Christmas decorations. It always smelled damp in here, even after the repairs. Andy was certain he had once seen a rat scurry out the door when he turned on the lights.

Bare bulbs on the ceiling at either end of the room intensified the shadows, making the numbers on the music cabinet's combination lock difficult to read. He would have cursed at the thing but Scott Pritchard was right behind him, holding the sheet music for "Standing in God's Love." Scotty's tagging along on every little task usually didn't bother him, but anxiety was clouding his mind tonight, making him forget the combination. *There's too few rehearsals left!* he thought.

"Maybe I can get it," Scotty said.

"No, I'm sure it—" The lock suddenly sprang open and clattered to the floor. "There," Andy said. "Now just hand me the—"

"I'll help you with those, Andy," a new voice said.

Andy nearly jumped out of his skin. It took him a while to focus on the man standing behind them. Scott was looking none too pleased at his arrival.

"Scotty, they're beginning to set up for the combined choir," the man said.

"So?"

"So maybe you should get along and find your place. There's some changes in how the tenors line up."

"Changes?" Andy said. He had talked to Ethan about voice balancing, but he had thought they would work that out together. He suddenly remembered this man's name. "John, is the combined choir starting already?"

"Oh, no," John Tibbits said. "We've still got time." He gave Scotty a brief glare. Scotty glared back. John turned to Andy. "I'd like to talk to you about something, if you don't mind." He took the sheet music from Scotty and maneuvered himself between them.

"Sure," Andy said, pulling out folders. "What's up?"

"Maybe we can talk later," John said, "when you have some time. Alone." He gave Scotty another look.

Scotty turned on his heel and walked off. "See ya later, Mr. Simms," he called out.

Andy pulled his head from inside the cabinet, the hostility in the boy's voice unmistakable. "What?" But Scotty didn't stop on his way out. "Thanks, Scott," he called out. He turned apologetically to John. "He's just, you know. Boys."

"Yeah," John Tibbits smiled. "I been there. *When I was a child, I spoke as a child.*" He laughed nervously. "Say, I really like this new altar call. Will it be part of the service?"

"Uh, no," Andy said. "We've—that is, Ethan and I—we've pretty much settled on the program."

"Well, that's a shame. But that creation hymn you wrote, that's in, right?"

The choir started running scales out in the church.

"Yes, we're going to announce the final order at the end of rehearsal. Which it sounds like they're starting without us." Andy gave John a big smile but put an edge of urgency on it.

John licked his lips, not looking Andy in the eye. "Look," he said, "you and I are about the same age and . . ." He trailed off.

Andy wanted to see what this "new line up in the tenors" was all about, but he sensed there was something important here. "You can talk to me, John. Anytime."

John let out a big gust of relief. "It's about me and Ruth. You know we're trying to have a kid and . . . and . . . And it's just not working!"

Holy crap, thought Andy. He covered his sudden panic by slamming the cabinet shut and jamming the lock in place. Unable to come up with anything useful, he said, "I've always found Pastor Jacobs to be very helpful."

John looked at him agog. "You mean, for you and Susan—?"

"Oh, no!" *Good Christ, this was how gossip got started!* He was a complete idiot. "I mean, he's always given me excellent advice. On manly . . . things. Fatherly advice."

"Yeah, yeah. I know. The Reverend Mr. J is always . . . fatherly. But you and I, we're about the same age. I mean, it should work, shouldn't it? Unless there's something wrong."

"Wrong?" Andy gulped.

"With the marriage," John said.

Andy wanted to fly out of that narrow little room and right into the middle of rehearsal. He wanted to be running those scales on the piano, those simple, mechanical notes, to be singing them, just a part of the chorus, not a person at all, lost in the sound, one with the music. But he was here instead, in a disused room smelling of damp concrete and rat urine, facing a man who might as well be drowning. And the only way Andy knew how to swim was one he couldn't talk about.

"We'll talk later," he said.

Susan glowed with happiness after the rehearsal. "Standing in God's Love" wasn't on the list of hymns for the Service of Thanks, but Andy had written a superb part for her. She was eager to thank to him, but he and John Tibbits were engaged in intense conversation as they broke down the risers. She could guess what that was about, and feeling a bit embarrassed that she should know so much about someone else's business, she started for the office.

Her father hadn't come out during the rehearsal, which puzzled her. She began threading her way through the dissolving crowd, saying good-bye to a clutch of sopranos from Mt. Zion, complimenting Lila Armbruster on her solo in "When I Think about Jesus," giving a wordless, noncommittal smile when Cleda George, an alto known for gossip, commented on Mrs. Littledeer's unsteady gait, and so made her way to the office without breach of etiquette or occasion for scandal.

When she opened the door, she was ready to toss off a quip about hens and pecking order, but the look on her father's face dried up her cheer. "Daddy, what's wrong?"

The Reverend Jacobs looked up from a list on his desk. "We've lost the hall."

"What?" She closed the door behind her.

"Saint Elizabeth's has backed out. We've lost the hall for the Service."

"But they can't! It's less than two weeks!"

"Father Francis didn't have a choice. Someone got word to the Bishop, and the Bishop got on the phone to Francis and let him have it in no uncertain terms. No use of church facilities by any congregation they are not in communion with."

"But that's absurd!"

"I'm certain Father Francis agrees with you."

"Well then, why doesn't he do something? God damn it all to hell!"

"Susan!"

"Who are they to say who's in communion and who's not? Half this town doesn't even think Catholics are Christians!"

Matthew Jacobs stood up. "You will settle down, young lady, and you will settle down right now."

She crossed her arms and paced up and down, fuming, then finally slammed herself into a chair. "This will kill Andy," she said.

"I doubt it. But before you say another word, I want to hear you apologize for taking the Lord's name in vain."

She wanted to say it wasn't in vain, she had meant every word. But instead she took a deep breath and uncrossed her arms. "I'm sorry. I truly am. But what are we going to tell Mt. Zion and the other churches? Andy's been working on this night and day for weeks. How can we tell him?"

"Tell me what?" Andy asked from the doorway.

"Come in, Andy. Close the door."

"Tell me what, Matthew?" Andy asked again when he'd closed the door.

"Saint Liz's got cold feet," Susan said.

"The Bishop has forbidden them the use of the hall," Matthew said.

"Has he forbidden them to come?"

"Well, no, not exactly. Their choir seems doubtful, though."

"But folks from St. Elizabeth could still come. Maybe not participate fully, but come."

"Yes," Matthew said. "And some would."

"There are other halls, right? The Baptists—"

"I've been calling around," Matthew said, turning back to his list. "There's a wedding and reception at First Baptist. Assembly of God has a hall, but it's no larger than ours. Disciples of Christ, even smaller. Mt. Zion—well, we know the story there. The First Church of the Nazarene never did commit to participate in the first place, and I haven't heard back from the Episcopalians."

"What about the library?" Susan asked. The two men looked at her in surprise. "It's an ecumenical service. It doesn't have to take place in any particular church, or even any church at all."

"She has a point," Andy said hopefully. "And the new rotunda has great acoustics."

"It does indeed," Matthew said. "Let me put in a call . . ."

Andy gave Susan a hug as they left the church. It was a one-armed hug since they were walking side-by-side, but his arm lingered on her shoulder as they headed down the street.

"You were brilliant in there," he said.

"Why, thank you, kind sir."

"I think you may have saved the day. I don't know how to thank you."

"Well," she said, "a kiss would be nice." She liked the way he colored and looked around to see if anyone was watching. *Not like a darkened porch at night, is it?* she thought. But once he saw the coast was clear he leaned in and gave her a very nice kiss.

A very nice kiss. Don't over-think it, Susan.

"You're welcome," she said cheerily, and they continued toward the parsonage, sunlight slanting through the elms. "You know," she said, "when I said, 'Let's back up and start over,' I didn't mean from the very beginning."

He laughed. "I'm sorry. I've been a bit preoccupied lately."

"I'll say. Three new hymns in as many weeks. I just love the latest one. And thanks for the solo."

He beamed at her. "You're perfect for it. Your voice is clear as a bell. Even through closed doors."

She stopped and covered her face. "Oh, no! You didn't hear that, did you?"

"Well, I heard something."

"Did anyone else? Did John Tibbits?"

"No, he'd left already. Something about an appointment at Rosen's—"

"Oh, good God!" Andy turned, scowling. "I mean, 'Good gracious me!' Rosen's! You can't walk me home. You've got to take Ginny to Rosen's."

"What? Why?"

"Well, I promised, and—well— Are you good at keeping secrets?"

He froze suddenly. "Why do you ask?"

His mood change threw her off, but she didn't have time to parse it. Ginny was expecting him right after rehearsal. "Never mind. Just do me a favor, would you please? Take your car and pick Ginny up at her house and drive her to Rosen's."

"Can't she just meet me in the parking lot?"

"No. Pick her up. Please. I'll explain later."

"Well, okay." He turned and started walking back to the church, then turned and called out, "You two like these little games, don't you?"

"Yes," she said cheerily. "Girls. You know."

"Yeah," he said, clearly without a clue.

Well, she thought, *he's about to get one.*

Chapter 13

SEEN AND UNSEEN

Virginia entered the drugstore and walked straight through to the store-room. Harry was there as arranged, slouched against a stack of cigarette boxes. She took off her sunglasses and scarf but kept the raincoat on. "I'm tired of this," she said.

"I can't say as I blame you."

"Oh, don't get all homey on me," she said. "Look at me. I'm as big as a house."

"People see what they want to see around here."

"Oh, really?" Virginia said. "Well, let them try and ignore this." She threw off the raincoat. She got a certain satisfaction from the way Harry's eyes widened.

"Jesus, Ginny," he breathed. "How do you hold it all in?"

"Don't worry. Little Harry Junior's got a ways to go yet."

"Junior? You can tell it's a boy?"

"Well, of course it's a boy," Virginia said. "No girl would give me this much trouble. But what good does waiting do? It won't matter how long we've been married if everyone in town thinks he's a bastard."

"He's not a bastard. You know it and I know it. To hell with everyone else."

"Oh, Harry," she said, touching his face. "You and your pride. I don't care what kind of house we get. A three-room shack is fine with me. Anything at all. But I will not deliver our son while still living under that man's roof."

Harry nodded. "Soon, then. I promise."

Virginia looked him in the eye. "Why not now? The job doesn't matter any more, it's almost done. You've got your payments." He turned away from her and Virginia felt a chill in her stomach. "You have been paid, haven't you?"

"There's . . . a little bit of a hitch," he said.

She crossed her arms. "Out with it. Harry Edom, if you have done something stupid with that money—"

He turned on her with a look so fierce she backed up.

"Something stupid?" he repeated. "If *I* have done something stupid with the money? Oh, that's just great. Yeah, sure, if there's something wrong with the money, it must be something stupid *I've* done!"

"Sorry," she said. "Okay, so, why don't you just—"

"It's your god-damned father, that's what!" He ran his fingers through his hair. "Payments? All I've gotten from him is paper and promises. I didn't want to tell you, didn't want to give you one more thing to worry about."

She steeled herself. "Tell me," she said.

And he told her. Told her how every time he got paid the amount on the check was off, always lower than it should have been for the hours, the men, and materials. How sometimes the checks were returned for insufficient funds. How he had used what should have been his own salary to pay his workers. How every time he brought it up, there was some song-and-dance about the Foundation and the discrepancies would be made up for in the next check. But whenever he tried to get a straight answer, he ran into a brick wall. A brick wall named Lerner Alquist.

When he was done, he stood looking at her. "I had to pay them," he said. "I've known those guys all my life. Most of them have families."

She should have blown up at that—they were a family, too—but all she said was, "Sure." Then, "You got your books, right?"

"Yeah. You mean, the general contracting books? Yeah, I got them."

"Bring them to me."

"What for?"

But then Andy Simms burst into the room.

Andy had trailed into the store in Virginia's wake, fascinated by the pent-up fury in the woman. It had been a strange trip. For one, Virginia had met him at the front door and insisted he pull up to the carriage entrance on the side. Then she had dashed out in a raincoat, sunglasses, and head scarf. The sunglasses he could understand since the late summer day was bright and cloudless, but the rest of the garb was inexplicable. "Rosen's" was all she said. The entire trip he kept stealing glances at her. He found himself gripping the wheel and leaning forward as if he expected her to jump him, but she wasn't paying any attention to him. When he finally took a full look at her, he noticed how the raincoat bulged and put two and two together.

So he trailed after her into the store almost without thinking, wondering what was going to happen next. He was midway down the aisle before her momentum faded away and he realized where he was. He hadn't been in Rosen's since he and Sunny had talked in the trailer. In fact, he hadn't been to see Sunny since. He looked up at the ceiling. He was probably up there now, in his studio. Andy's cheeks burned. A voice jerked his head around to the counter, where Mr. Rosen was talking to John Tibbits. He ducked behind a display of comics, suddenly ashamed to be seen.

"Ordinarily, Rachel would be here now," Rosen was saying, "but you know teenagers. Suddenly, it's beneath her dignity to play at Poppa's little helper."

"Sure, sure," John said. "I understand. *When I was a child . . .*"

Good Lord, Andy thought, *is that the only verse he knows?* He peered around the revolving stand. Was that the counter where Rosen kept the magazines? What was John Tibbits doing there? Then he realized how foolish he was. John had said he had an appointment with Rosen. Besides, he was married; he wouldn't be needing any extra *Vim*.

"Think about it, John," Mr. Rosen was saying. "Do you want to be a grocery clerk all your life?"

"No, sir, I surely do not," John Tibbits replied.

This is silly, Andy thought. There was no reason for him to cower behind a rack of DC comics. Glancing up, he saw John and Mr. Rosen come to some sort of agreement and shake hands. When John turned to leave, Andy quickly picked up a Batman and held it to his face. He kept it there until he heard the bell above the door jingle. When he lowered it, he saw Mr. Rosen turn the volume up on the radio behind the counter and disappear into the pharmacy stacks.

A news program was airing. As Andy crept forward, its words became more distinct.

<pre>
Announcer: . . . While many applaud the hearings,
    Senator Lester C. Hunt of Wyoming believes both
    Senator McCarthy and the House Un-American Ac-
    tivities Committee have gone too far.
Sen. Hunt: The very act of accusation marks these
</pre>

> men, many of them tireless diplomats and Fed-
> eral workers, as security risks, ruining their
> careers. There have even been suicides due to
> the smearing they received, either in Committee
> hearings or from remarks made in the United
> States Congress.
> Announcer: Senator Hunt is proposing legislation
> that would allow lawsuits by those defamed by
> members of Congress.

The counter held a display of toothpaste and shaving supplies. He reached out and picked up a carton of toothpaste, then leaned over the glass, trying to catch a glimpse of what lay behind. The next words from radio nailed him in place:

> Announcer: Senator Clyde R. Hoey of North Carolina
> opposes the measure.
> Sen. Hoey: The employment of homosexuals in the
> Federal workforce constitutes a grave security
> risk. They seek control of our academic insti-
> tutions and the government itself. They are a
> disease, an invasion that corrupts the nation's
> moral fiber and threatens to subvert the Ameri-
> can way of life.
> Announcer: In the upcoming elections . . .

"Mr. Simms, what are you doing here?" called a voice behind him.

He whirled around to see Scotty Pritchard. He laughed and waggled the carton in his fingers. "Buying toothpaste," he said. Scotty looked dumbfounded. He laughed again. "I do brush my teeth, you know. But don't tell anyone."

Scotty laughed then, too. "Why, sure, sure you do. Gosh, Mr. Simms, of course you do."

"And you? What are you doing here? I thought there was no one else in the store."

"I was waiting to talk to Mr. Rosen," Scotty said, looking around nervously.

"I was just looking for him myself. He seems to have stepped out."

"Mr. Simms, I'm glad I ran into you. I didn't get to say, today, earlier, I didn't get to say thanks. For listening."

Andy refocused. Scotty Pritchard wasn't spying on him. Whatever the radio was nattering on about wouldn't mean a thing to him. He had other questions on his mind, questions they had talked about. "It was my pleasure, Scott. Any time."

"It's just that, other people can be hard to talk to. And what you said made sense."

"I didn't tell you anything you didn't already know in your heart."

"Yeah, but my heart can be a kinda noisy place, what with so many other things—and other people, what they say."

"What they say doesn't matter if you know what's right."

They both turned as Avril Rosen came out from the stacks and headed in their direction. Scotty wiped his mouth nervously. "Well, thanks again." He grinned. "And don't worry. I won't let on."

Andy's heart skipped a beat. "About what?"

"About brushing your teeth."

Andy laughed. "Thanks. Wouldn't want to cause a scandal, now, would we?"

Just then the bell over the front door jingled and a tall man in a fedora walked briskly up to the counter and confronted Rosen. "Is he here?" he demanded.

Andy ducked quickly into the storeroom. He wasn't surprised to find Harry Edom standing there with Virginia. "It's your father," he told her. "Out front. I think he's looking for Harry."

"Christ," Virginia said, grabbing her raincoat, glasses and scarf.

"Side door," Harry said. "This way."

Virginia sat quietly on the ride home, her mind clicking away. It wasn't a whirling cloud of emotions anymore; she knew what she had to do.

Andy broke the silence. "It won't work," he said.

Virginia snorted. "You mean my Hollywood-starlet-on-the-run get up?"

"Anyone can tell it's you."

"I know." She took off the sunglasses. "I feel like a fool. But at least this way they can deny they saw anything." She looked at him. "But you wouldn't, would you?"

He shrugged. "I wouldn't lie about it, but I wouldn't say anything, either. Even if you'd told me about it in the first place—Mrs. Edom."

Virginia looked out the window. "Suzie-Q was right. You're a sharp one."

"No, actually, I've been pretty thick. You and Harry and Susan have had me in the middle of it right from the beginning, and it's taken me all this time to figure out."

"Yeah, I'm sorry about that. It's just that, sometimes, you know, someone who hasn't lived here all his life, who doesn't have someone to run and blab to—"

"A stranger."

"Well, an outsider. An outsider has certain advantages."

"Certain uses, you mean."

"Well, yeah, that too." She felt ashamed of herself. The guy had been on their side all along, for Christ's sake. What right did she have to have doubts about him? "Look, I'm sorry," she said, apologizing for one thing but meaning another. "And thanks. I could use a few friends right now. Or strangers. Or strange friends." Great Christ, couldn't she just shut up? She covered her face with her hands. "Oh, I don't know what I'm saying!"

He gave her a moment, then said, "A marriage should be something to celebrate, not hide."

Virginia scoffed. "We didn't even do it in Oklahoma. Drove to Texas. Stopped at the first wide place in the road with a justice of the peace. Some celebration, huh?"

"Not a church ceremony, then?"

She laughed. "Harry? In a church? Not likely. And I'm not likely either, anymore. Not as far as The Church is concerned."

Andy reached out and touched her hand. She stared down at it resting on hers. They drove the last few blocks to her house that way.

He drove up to the carriage entrance again, but before he could turn off the engine, she put her other hand on top of his. "You could do it," she said.

"Do what?"

"Anybody could. It doesn't take a priest. They taught us that in catechism. You could do it. Harry won't of course. It's all nonsense to him. Limbo and hell and all that. I suppose I have The Indian to thank for that." She bit her lip, keeping back the words she didn't want to say, the question she didn't want to ask. So much depended on Andy being a friend right now. "And I can't ask Father Herron. He'd say no, anyways.

He'd have to. But you could do it."

He was quiet a moment. "We don't believe in infant baptism in my faith."

"We do in mine," she said. The dust hung in the air in the car, turning and glinting in the sun. "Will you do it?" she asked.

He nodded. "I'd be honored to," he said. It was the right thing to do. His heart told him so.

But then, as he was helping her up the stairs to her house, she pointed to something sticking out of his pocket.

"What's that?" she asked.

Sunny Sohi sat on the floor in his studio, legs crossed in a lotus, posture erect. I am at peace, he thought. There is peace all around me. Peace comes down from above, it wells up from beneath. Peace flows out from within and streams in from without. The town is awash in tranquility. There is no one I fear. There is no one I hate. All sentient beings are free of anxiety.

Like hell they are. Alquist had come marching up the stairs and blown up the whole afternoon. It wasn't enough that the man had no soul, but he expected no one else to have one either. He had come to argue about the terra cotta. He insisted on using that crap from the brickworks instead of the fine California clay Sunny specified. He had even hinted there would be "spillage" for Sunny to use on his war memorial. It was all implication and innuendo, collusion without commitment. Sunny suspected a kickback was involved, but didn't say so. Their mouths were full of what they were not saying to each other.

Okay, then, let's start again, he told himself. I am centered and whole. There is no one I hate. May I be at peace, may I be of good will. May I forgive any harm done me, intended or not. May I forgive Alquist, intended or not, for pulling me into his schemes. May I forgive Andy, intended or not, for finking out on our sessions. May I forgive myself, intended or—

That was the problem, wasn't it? He had intended it. When he and Andy had started the Tantric breathing, he meant to ease Andy's anxiety. And it did, he could tell. Though charged with energy, Andy had grown still. Sunny had never seen anything like it. It had taken him months to achieve such focus, but in his hands, Andy slid into it like quicksilver into a cup. And then their mouths touched. And then they were breathing as one, Andy opening the back of his throat without even being told to, so the air Sunny drew into his lungs came through Andy's nostrils, and the air Andy drew into his lungs came through his. They began rising slightly on each intake, sinking on each exhale, causing the slightest friction in his hand as they rubbed against each other. Each breath was a step up the mountain. And when they got to the summit, Sunny felt Andy's cock grow suddenly thicker and stiffer. It pulsed and seethed and left their bodies frothed in seed and sweat.

And that was when he felt Andy's soul leap from the core of his being and fly between them and lodge in Sunny's heart. And now, with the real work of the sculpture about to begin, he found he could not move an inch forward without him. He needed Andy's calming presence. He was the still center Sunny could not find on his own. He had fallen in love. How could he forgive himself that?

You start where you cannot start; you begin by beginning. I am at peace, and the world is at peace. May all sentient beings—

Damn it all to hell! Who was ringing the buzzer? He leapt up and strode furiously to the door, yanking it open with a curse.

And there stood Andy, a carton of toothpaste in his hand, frozen like a statue. Sunny caught his breath. "Did you . . . ? Do you want to work on the sculpture? I can—"

"No," Andy said and grabbed him. He pushed himself into the studio, pulling fiercely on Sunny's clothes. The door swung to behind him.

Sunny was startled and delighted, riding the surge of emotions pouring off his lover. He backed into the studio, upsetting the easel and scattering pencils and carving tools. Andy kept coming at him, backing him into the bedroom, tripping as his pants dropped around his ankles.

Before he was fully aware of what he was doing, Sunny was on top of Andy, who lay face down on the mattress, breathing hoarsely and thrusting his hips upward. It was only as he was mounting toward climax that his senses cleared and he saw Andy's eyes shut tight. "What is it?" he asked. "Are you all right? I can pull out—"

"No!" Andy hissed and reached behind, pulling him tighter against him.

Sunny felt a torrent surging through his abdomen as deep muscles began to contract. Then he could not have stopped if the world had come to an end. He lunged and lunged, calling out as he emptied himself into Andy. Andy's eyes flew open and with a deep growl he spent himself in the bedding. Sunny collapsed on top of him.

For a while, the only sound was their ragged panting. The neon of Rosen's sign filtered through the thin curtains and reddened the walls. Their breathing slowed and became one. Sunny softened, and with an involuntary shudder, he slid out.

Andy gasped, his eyes open wide.

"Sorry," Sunny said. "You didn't give me much time. I should have warmed you up some."

"No," Andy said. "That's not what I wanted."

Sunny kissed him on the ear. "There's more," he said. He rolled onto his side and pressed his back against Andy's torso.

"What's that?" Ginny asked

"What?" He pulled the carton of toothpaste from his jacket. "Oh gosh! I left the store without paying for it!"

"You'd better watch that kind of thing," she'd said with a smirk. "Reputations have been ruined in this town for a lot less."

And he'd suddenly thought, *She knows!*

He raced back to the drugstore and paid for it, but the damage was done. *She knows!* He had to explain it Sunny. This just couldn't work, it was far too risky, and the unconscious shoplifting showed just how stupid and careless he'd become. There were just too many people depending on him. He ran up the studio stairs to tell him.

That's what he'd meant to do, but that wasn't what happened. Instead, he'd stood there, arms flapping in agitation until the door opened and Sunny stood before him. He saw the man's face transform from midnight fury to dawn breaking at the sight of him, and the words he had meant to say flew out of his head. Then Sunny had pulled him inside the apartment and the world spun away, their path through the studio littered with sheets of paper and tumbling books and Rapido pens spilling from a cup as they stumbled and groped their way into the bedroom. And there he was, pinned and panting on the mattress and wanting nothing more than to fill every pore and cell of himself with this other man, the man with rays of sun in his eyes.

Andy thought it would hurt. It was an abomination; there should be a price to pay. But there wasn't. Pleasure radiated from deep inside him where Sunny was building a rhythm. It spread to the tips of his fingers, his toes; his lips became like tongues of fire, his eyes flew open and light streamed in, piercing the air and reflecting from every surface. There was nothing between the two of them, nothing but the touch of every atom to every other atom.

Afterward, with Sunny lying on top of him, he wondered if they had closed the door behind them. He shuddered at their recklessness and gave a little gasp. Sunny kissed him on the ear and said something, but Andy's head was spinning with recriminations. Had they been loud enough to be heard downstairs? Then Sunny rolled over. With his back to Andy, he reached around and pulled their bodies together. Their climax should have left Andy spent, but his cock was as hard and hot as a rock in the sun. Sunny arched his back and Andy, slick with his own semen, slid into him.

It was like nothing Andy had ever felt before. His sense of his own body vanished, the boundary between his and Sunny's erased. The two of them climaxed again and the walls and ceiling flew away. A voice as deep as the night came from everywhere at once, more quiet than the bottom of the sea, farther away than the moon, and as close as his own tongue.

Andy did not recall driving back to Mrs. Oldfield's afterward. Turning the water on in the narrow shower of his bathroom brought him back to himself. The head spat and coughed like an invalid and started yielding up a thin spray of warm water. He backed out of the narrow room, pulling his shirt off without unbuttoning it. He kicked off his shoes and unbuckled his belt. His pants slid to the floor and he distractedly kicked them into the bedroom, pulled down his briefs, and stared into the gathering steam, trying to get his thoughts to follow a simple line. He stepped into the stall.

"Shit!" he exclaimed as his socks soaked through. He tugged them off and flung them against the hallway door. A fetid odor wafted up from his groin. He must tell Mrs. Oldfield there was something wrong with the drains. He began to soap himself. He should hurry. The hot water would be gone soon. But he stopped and stared through the roiling mist, trying to remember that moment just before the room and the bed and the body he clung to became real again, and he was still rocking with the sound of that voice, of that word, its echo bouncing from bone to bone within him—

But trying to think about it only made it recede, changing its shape from wonder to recollection, from fire to ashes. Every pore of his soul had opened and been soaked through with Sunny: Sunny's smell, Sunny's heat, Sunny's sweat, Sunny's bucking hips. He would go back to him again, he knew: falling, failing. Would the voice return? What if it did not? He must go back. He must hear that voice again. For try as he might, as the cooling water poured over his shoulders, he could not remember what it said.

Chapter 14

DEADLINES

Lerner Alquist walked briskly across the county courthouse square, his legs scissoring the lawn. He could have walked around the square from his office to the studio above Rosen's, but he was in a hurry. There were a few things he wanted to go over with that boy before they presented their progress report to the City Council.

He reviewed what he knew of his opponents. Pautler, of course. The man had an instinct for business, but fortunately neither the intellectual curiosity nor the mental discipline to follow up on his hunches. The man could smell a rat, but couldn't put his hands on one unless someone led him right to it. He'd have accusations, but no facts.

Bill Sullivan. Upstart, newcomer to the Council. You could still smell the engine grease from his years running an auto body shop. A shifty character, now owner of an automobile dealership and used car lot. Although a fellow Catholic, Lerner knew he could not count on his help. Sullivan was too busy playing holy-rollier-than-thou with his fellow Board members, all Baptists and Evangelicals. Lerner smiled grimly. Sullivan would have no luck there, he knew. They'd abandon him at the drop of a hat, and from what Lerner knew of Sullivan's philandering habits, he knew just what hat to drop if push came to shove. No, he'd have no trouble handling Sullivan.

Marcus W. Gilbert, former high school math and science teacher, now Superintendent of Schools. Lerner knew the type. Thought he would have more power and less work if he rose through the ranks to administrator. Swamped now with every little detail of running Croy's two school systems and facing the very real possibility that they would have to be consolidated. Just because you have your fingers on the purse strings doesn't mean you control them. Lerner could have told him that. He would be too distracted with his own troubles to propose anything, but he might just go along with whatever nonsense Pautler proposed just to clear his plate. Someone to watch, then.

Cyrus Daniel Brown, President of the Savings and Loan and Chairman of the Library Board. Now this was someone to watch out for. Lerner trusted him less than anyone else on the Council because there was no way of knowing what he thought. The man was a cipher, with no apparent personal foibles or weaknesses (other than an allergy to eggs) to use as leverage. He would sit through an entire Council meeting like a large iron cannon ball, not saying a word, and then at the very end make a single remark that would change everybody's vote. He didn't form coalitions, so he was unlikely to be in cahoots with Pautler, but he made Lerner nervous. Among other things, Brown owned the building where Lerner had his Foundation's office. He might know about Ellie's departure and put two and two together.

He'd arrived at the side door to Rosen's. That Simms boy's car was parked around the corner. He hesitated, wondering for an angry instant if his daughter were inside planning yet another way to embarrass him, but there wasn't time. He dismissed the thought with a curse and began climbing the stairs to the apartment.

No, there was one more council member to account for. He'd forgotten Lisle Armbruster. Of course he'd forgotten him. The man was silent as a ghost and about as substantial, held together by loose hairs and baggy pants. If you undid his bow tie, the whole figure would probably collapse in a heap of bones and dandruff. Why he was still on the Council after all these years Lerner had no idea.

He got to the landing just as the Sohi boy came out, pulling the door shut tightly behind him and running his hand through his long black hair. Still wet from a shower, apparently. Sunny smiled at him, white teeth flashing against his dark skin. Lerner frowned. "Haven't you got a comb?" he demanded.

Sunny looked abashed and raked his hand through his hair again. "Um, somewhere, maybe," he said.

"That's all we need, the Council thinking you're some kind of long-haired beatnik."

Sunny glanced at the door to his apartment. "Should I put on my *dastaar*?"

"What's that?"

"My turban."

"Great hopping Christ, no! That's all we need. Come on. There's a couple of things I need to explain to you on the way over."

"Are we taking your car?" Sunny asked as they clattered down the stairs.

"Waste of gas. Keep up," and Lerner strode out into the bright sun. Sunny Sohi did his best, but the difference in their strides meant he was practically trotting to keep up. Alquist began summarizing the members of the Council, careful not to be as blunt as he had been in his own mind, but when he came to Gilbert, Sunny broke in with, "Really? Mr. Gilbert's on the Council? He's my old geometry teacher." He giggled.

"What's so funny about geometry?"

"It's not that. You've got Gilbert and Sullivan on the City Council. Maybe I should brush up on my *H.M.S. Pinafore*!"

The boy was daft. Lerner cut short his briefing. "Let me do all the talking," he said. They finished their quick march to the council chambers in silence.

There were two additional people in the City Council Chambers Lerner hadn't mentioned in his summary. There was Miss Ida Laine Lancaster, the librarian. Croy being as small as it was (and the librarian's salary being as small as it was), Miss Lancaster doubled as secretary during Council meetings. He paid her no mind. And then there was the other person. Sitting in the back of the empty rows of chairs lined up before the Council was Dale Pritchard. That was a surprise. City Council meetings were open to the public, of course, but the public was supposed to mind their own business and stay away. Lerner had no idea why Pritchard was there and that made him wary.

So he was ready when the first salvo was fired. The building plans were spread out before the council and the final report on the dome was presented. Sunny put the front elevations of the sculpture on a tripod and sat down next to him, waiting to be recognized by the mayor. Instead, Sullivan spoke up.

"I have to say, and I think I speak for a number of people when I say it, I have some grave concerns about that sculpture there, Lerner."

"What concerns, Bill?"

"Well, take that center figure. The Goddess of Prosperity."

Lerner grew very still. "Yes?"

"I don't know about you, but as a church-going Christian, I am more than a little troubled at the presence of anything called a 'goddess' on city property."

"But—" Sunny started. Lerner cut him off. "It's just a title, Bill. A working title. It's not," he smiled, "carved in stone."

"But it's finished!" Sunny said. "The design for the center tableau is finished."

"But not," Lerner glared at him, "titled. We can call the figure something else. What would you like?"

"What do you have in mind?"

Lerner shrugged. "The Mother of Prosperity, perhaps? You don't have anything against motherhood, do you?"

"There's no need for sarcasm, Lerner," Mayor Pautler said. "I'm less concerned about the wording than what your young artist friend there just said. It's finished, you say?"

Sunny gulped. "Yes. Well, almost. The maquettes are done. The center panel, that is, and the left panel. The maquette for the right panel is still wet. But I should start on the full-sized molds immediately."

"Lerner," Pautler said, "I thought we'd agreed the Council had final say in all decisions?"

Lerner spread his hands. "I thought you'd had your final say. You set the deadline for completion, you decided on the date for the dedication ceremony. You did all that without consulting me, so I took it as a green light. Work has to proceed if we are going to make that deadline. Thanks to Mr. Sohi's hard work, we'll make it—and under budget as well."

"I'm still uncomfortable with this," Sullivan said. "The entire project is not representative of the community's values."

"Meaning what?"

"It's not just the undue influence of non-Christian values—"

"What?" Sunny said.

"—but our own local people have had no input whatsoever on the design or the figures or what they represent or anything."

"I think the people have expressed their support very solidly in their subscriptions to the project," Lerner said.

"Pledges ain't cash," Pautler interjected. "You say you've *raised* the money, but you don't *have* the money. You've got promises. If I ran my store like you've run your Foundation, I'd be out of business in a week."

"If I ran the Foundation like you run your store, the library would look like a can of peas."

Mr. Gilbert cleared his throat. "I think we've gotten off track here."

"You can eat a can of peas," said Pautler. "At least you know what you've paid for. Peas is peas. What we're getting is a pig in a poke."

"The truth is," said Sullivan, "there has been no input from our local native Americans about that right-hand panel, the panel that shows our Territory heritage. What we have is some foreign, pagan conception of America."

Sunny stood up. "I was born right here in Croy, sir," he said. "I'm as American as you are."

"I've been out East," Sullivan said. "I've seen what they call 'sculpture' out there."

"Oh, for Christ's sake, Bill," Lerner said. "You've been to New York and seen the Metropolitan. That doesn't make you an expert."

"I've seen it. It's lewd and indecent and there will be none of it in Croy!"

"There *is* none of it in Croy! There's no art whatsoever in Croy. Most people in this town wouldn't know art it if came up and bit them in the ass."

"That's just the point, Mr. Alquist," Mayor Pautler said. "Most people don't want to get bit in the ass, not by art nor anything else. So let's just take the whole ass-biting thing off the table. That panel with the Indians has got to go."

"And be replaced by what? A grocery cart?"

"We think something reflecting the contributions of our veterans would be appropriate, celebrating the 45th Infantry, perhaps, and the Battle of Anzio. Pork Chop Hill. That sort of thing. Something more indicative of our community values, our belief in God and country."

"And our eternal vigilance against godless Communism," Sullivan added.

"Fine," Lerner said.

"What?" Sunny exclaimed. "No! I got to start on the molds!"

Lerner gripped his arm. "Mr. Sohi had the foresight to order extra clay in case one of the designs should prove flawed. He can start work on the new design at once. Provided we have your go-ahead."

Pautler's expression soured. "There's still the question of where the money's going. Our local clay is good enough for the bricks that build our buildings and pave our streets. But your artist here has specified out-of-state materials."

"You can't sculpt brick," Sunny started. "You need a much finer—" He looked around the table and at Alquist. Now he understood why Alquist had come to see him. It wasn't about the quality or price of the terra cotta. There was war on. He felt the coolness of the silver bracelet on his right wrist. "Gentlemen," he said quietly, "may I ask what is going on here? What you are doing?"

Pautler looked at him quizzically. "Mr. So-high?"

"Is every little jot and tittle of this library going to be picked over? If what you want is a shoebox with windows, then just say so and be done with it."

"Mr. So-high—"

Anyone who knew Sundar Singh Sohi would know that look in his eyes. Even Lerner Alquist recognized it. He touched the young man's sleeve. "It's Sohi, Mr. Mayor," Lerner said. All he got from Pautler was a blank stare, so he repeated it, "It's pronounced Sohi. I believe Mr. Gilbert may remember his name from high school."

"I surely do. Sundar, good to see you, son. You've grown some."

"Thank you, sir," Sunny said tightly.

Pautler sensed the issue slipping from his fingers. "Nevertheless, Mr. So-hee, you are out of order."

"I apologize, Mr. Mayor, but I thought I was brought here to report on the progress of the sculpture, not take it apart piece by piece."

"There are very good reasons to question every dot and tiddle, as you say."

"And even better reasons to keep them just as they are."

"When we are ready to hear your report—"

"I'm ready," rumbled a voice at the far end of the table. It was Cyrus Brown. "Let's hear it." He looked at JayRob Pautler, who looked startled, then shrugged and gestured at Sunny to start speaking.

"I'm certain all of you have good reasons to examine each line and item in the library construction budget," Sunny began. "You have, after all, a certain fiduciary duty to the citizens of Croy to see that their money is wisely spent, though I gather," he glanced at Lerner, "that the bulk of the funds have been raised privately."

"Those good people deserve our oversight as well," said Pautler. "The Council has final say over how the Foundation spends its funds. That was in the original resolution approving construction."

Sunny looked to Alquist, who nodded. "But in all those details, gentlemen, have you ever had a chance to stand back and look at the whole picture? And in this case, I mean the whole building." He felt a rush of confidence. "I don't think you realize what a gem, a veritable temple of learning you are building here in Croy." Sullivan coughed at the word "temple," but he ignored it. "It begins in the smallest details—the leading in the glass of the clerestory windows for the dome, the designs in the terrazzo flooring—but it carries through to the proportions of the rotunda and the reading rooms, the curve of the dome in relation to the front elevation, the shape and proportions of the pediment, even down to the sculpture in the tympanum. It is all of a piece. Remove one part, and the harmony is destroyed."

Sullivan laughed. "Do you mean to say that we can't replace, say, a banister without the whole building collapsing?"

"No." Sunny looked around. There was outright scorn on Sullivan and Pautler's faces. Gilbert looked puzzled. The large gentleman on the end, Brown, was unreadable. The thin elderly man at the other end of the table was asleep. "I'm not making myself clear. We—that is, Mr. Alquist—had to fight to get the window leading done as described in the blueprints, to get it done right. But look at that design: an inner rectangle surrounded by triangles to form an outer rectangle. The inner rectangle has sides in proportion of 3 to 5, the outer in proportions of 8 to 13. Do those proportions mean nothing to you? You remember them, don't you Mr. Gilbert? You taught them to me."

A slow smile spread across Gilbert's face. "Fibonacci series. Well, it seems not all my days in the classroom were wasted. You're a good student."

"You were a good teacher, sir. Now look at the proportions of the foundation." Gilbert nodded. "And the spiral staircases leading to the mezzanine." Gilbert frowned. "Draw a line from the top of the dome to any side of the rotunda beneath it. I think you can guess what that angle is."

"Good Lord," Gilbert said. "Has that been there all along?"

"Has what been where all along?" Pautler demanded.

"It's phi."

"Fi? Like in *Semper Fi?*"

"No," said Gilbert. "Phi. It's a number, like pi. It's the Golden Mean. The perfect proportion. This whole plan is based on mathematics!"

"It's the same angle the Egyptians used in constructing the great pyramids at Giza," Sunny said, his eyes shining. "It's the same proportion the Greeks used in building the Parthenon."

"More heathen mumbo-jumbo," Sullivan muttered.

"It is not heathen! It's not Christian, it is not Jewish. Nor is it Hindu or Muslim. It is universal. Leonardo da Vinci used it in his art. Great composers have used it in their music. You find it in the patterns of leaves, ears of corn, the spiral of seeds in the head of a sunflower. It is God speaking to us in every detail. And the architect of this building had the insight, the genius to capture it. This building is not just a memorial to the past, it is not a mere repository of books and magazines. It is a link between man and Wisdom, a manifestation of God's promise of a peaceable harmonious kingdom, the embodiment of all people's accomplishments and hopes."

"An ark."

Everyone turned to look at the frail man at the far end of the table. Lisle Armbruster had not, apparently, been asleep after all.

"You know," he said in the sudden stillness, "Lila has been after me for years to give up this Council seat. Foolishness, she calls it. She says people only vote for me because, well, because they always have. Says I'm a fool to run year after year. It's a waste of time, she says, a bunch of nonsense. And with meetings like this, I'm inclined to agree with her."

"With all due respect, Lisle," Pautler said, "the people's business is not a bunch of nonsense."

"Well then, with all due respect, JayRob, let's cut the crap and get on with it. I've been Mayor once or twice myself, you may recall, so I know the people's business when I see it, and this ain't it. I was here, on this City Council, probably in this same butt-busting chair, when we took the vote to build that library, and I am by God not leaving until it is done one way or t'other. So let's cut the crap and get to a vote. Are we pulling the plug on this thing after all these years or not?"

Pautler looked around and did a quick head-count. Sullivan was still with him. Gilbert, no; Armbruster, no; Brown—no eye contact. He swallowed. "Not," he said.

"Then let's approve the damned plans and get out of these people's way. As your late Daddy used to say, we got bigger fish to fry." Lisle gestured towards Dale Pritchard, who shifted uncomfortably in his seat.

The Council gave its approval, provided the right-hand panel was replaced with something suitably anti-Communist, and Lerner and Sunny turned to go. Just then, Miss Ida Laine Lancaster leaned in and whispered something to Cyrus Brown. "Oh, yes," rumbled Brown. "Mr. Alquist, while you're here, a request has come before the Library Board to use the rotunda to hold a Service of Thanks. Do you think it advisable?"

It took Lerner a beat to realize this was not some sort of trap. "No," he said. "It's not advisable. There's still construction equipment in there. Scaffolding. I wouldn't think it safe."

"Thank you," Brown said and nodded briefly to Miss Lancaster, who made a note in her pad.

Out on the street, Lerner and Sunny took long slow breaths. In the eastern sky a huge anvil-headed thundercloud reflected the golden light of the setting sun, its mammata pendulous with shadow. The whole town appeared lit from within, as if even the lowest building or homestead burned with a secret color.

"Do you see now why I had to use their clay?" the older man said. "Local money stays local."

"I'll never finish in time. I don't even know what they want."

"You have plenty of time. You'll think of something. Move out of Rosen's and over to the brickworks. That'll take the Jew out of the question. No more 'anti-Christian influence.'"

"I can't move out of Rosen's!" Sunny said fiercely. The old man looked at him. "I— I have a lease," he added lamely.

Alquist turned away. "Leave Rosen to me. I'll make him see sense." He shaped his fedora on his head and strode off.

Sunny stood alone on the sidewalk, despair wrapping around him and shutting out the light. His design was in ruins and the one tangible symbol of his new life as an artist, his studio, was being yanked away. But in the midst of his self-pity, an idea came to him. It grew slowly as he walked toward the square in the orange afternoon.

The crepuscular light from the passing storm had all but left the sky by the time Lerner Alquist walked home. An occasional flash of lightning cut the darkness, but no thunder spoke in response. Cicadas and crickets sang their separate choruses, practicing the endless spiral of their lives.

The house was dark except for a light in the living room. From the hall, he could see Virginia seated on the sofa, wreathed in smoke.

"I thought I told you not to smoke in the house," he said.

"I'm fine, Daddy," she said, "and how was your day?"

He hung his hat on the coat rack without answering. Looking down the hall, he saw no light in the kitchen. "I don't suppose there's any supper cooked."

"There was. And I ate it. Around suppertime, I think that was."

He walked into the living room. "Do you think you could get yourself out of that sofa and heat it up, then? Or is that too much to ask?"

"Oh, I could do it, all right. But whether or not it's too much to ask," she frowned, "that's a question."

"Oh, for Christ's sake!" He started for the kitchen. "You know, you could do your share around here, more. You can't have people take care of you all your life. Not everyone's your servant."

"I don't need people to take care of me. I take care of myself just fine."

"Oh, yeah, sure you do." He turned around. "That's why that Simms kid drives you everywhere, I suppose. The D.Q. The drugstore. Sure. What the hell. Who needs a chauffeur when you can get some kid to do it for free?"

She brushed the hair from her face. "If you'd let me use the Studebaker, I wouldn't need some kid to drive me around."

"You got two legs. You can walk. Look at me. I'm three times your age and I walk everywhere I please. You're just getting lazy. Fat and lazy."

"Oh," Virginia said. "Fat." She leaned forward and crushed out her cigarette. "How kind of you to notice. Finally." And then she stood up.

He refused to see it at first. All he saw was his little girl, grown up now but chubby again, like she'd been as a baby. But it was more than that. It was much more than that. His face began to burn and his hands clenched. "Who— who—"

"Oh, come on, Lerner," she said with her hands on her hips. "Who do you think?"

"I'll kill him!"

"No you won't," Virginia said calmly. "Not unless you want to make me a widow and your grandson an orphan." She held up her left hand. "You might recognize this. It was Momma's. At least, I think it was. It was all I could find in that drawer you always keep locked so tight. I haven't worn it except the once, when Harry and I exchanged our vows." She gave a brief laugh. "Vows. They sounded more like the pledge of allegiance in front of that JP. Strangers for witnesses. A scratchy record instead of a fine church organ. But it was all legal. And it was all done months ago."

He stumbled towards her. "And you kept this from me!"

"Well, Harry and me, we thought we'd wait for just the right moment. But I reckon that's never coming, so I'm telling you now."

"I'll have it annulled!"

"The hell you will." She walked right up to his face. "I was of legal age. And it's pretty obvious the marriage has been consummated, don't you think?"

"No! You will never—" He whirled away from her. "There are ways. There are ways." He turned back around. "We can get rid—"

"Don't!" Her hand came up so suddenly that he fell backward into a chair. "Don't! Don't you say another word! Don't you dare, not if you ever expect me to call you father again! Do you hear me?"

"I will not be spoken to like this in my own house!"

"Well, your worries are short there, old man, 'cause Harry and me are getting our own place soon. As soon as you pay him."

"That red nigger isn't getting another cent out of me! And neither are you!"

"Oh, no?" Virginia said. She walked back to the sofa and picked up two notebooks. "Guess what these are? This one is Harry's accounts. He keeps pretty good accounts, you know, for a 'red nigger.' And this one? This one's your accounts. You keep pretty good accounts, too. Too bad they don't match the Foundation's."

"How did you get those?"

"I'm not as fat and lazy as you think. Now, either you square it up with Harry, or suddenly these books show up somewhere, and I don't mean the library."

"You can't show those to anyone! You wouldn't dare!"

She smiled at him then and her face became one he didn't recognize, though there were many in town and on county roads nearby who would have recognized it. "You have no idea what I can do," she said.

Chapter 15

Behold How Good

People see what they wish to see and forget what they need to forget. And having forgotten a turn of events that would be too painful to recall—a personal failure, the bearing of false witness, a vow, a disaster—they will deny there was ever a history behind it to begin with. "I would never do such a thing." "That never happened."

When the TriCounty Twister roared through the valley of the White Horse, nothing withstood its hunger to unite earth and sky. Farmhouses and barns, livestock and automobiles, granges and schoolhouses, respectable homes and their hapless inhabitants—all were sucked into its maw, dismembered, and converted into raking claws that whirled yet more land and works and living beings into its core. The hunger knew no end, but its reach was capricious. In the northwest quadrant of town there were striking examples of its gruesome whimsy. The Reverend David Worley and his wife rode out the storm in their one-story home unscathed, though the entire structure was lifted, translated three and a half inches to the east, and slightly rotated. Then it was set down intact, leaving the Reverend to be nick-named ever after "Whirly Worley." The Ardmores, on the other hand, returning from a visit with their Elk City in-laws, found nothing left of their solid, two-story home—not a stick of furniture or a roof shingle— save a commemorative Wedgewood plate hammered into a tree outside where their bedroom had been. The Snepps were all dead: mother, father, and two children, jumbled together in their flattened car, which sat on its roof in the front yard of their untouched home.

There was no tree without a broken limb, and many succumbed in the years that followed to disease, ordinary winds, and the cruel ice storms of April. People wanted no reminder of what those trees had witnessed. They cut down the survivors and replanted the streets with eastern elms that sheltered the neighborhood from its shattered past. In spring, the honey-colored green of the leafing out warmed the air ahead of the season. In summer, a fine sappy mist drizzled down on any car foolishly left uncovered. And in autumn, the streets turned into lofty aisles and transepts in a bright golden cathedral.

And so it became the home of the settled and comfortable: prosperous merchants such as the Rosens and Pautlers; ranchers grown rich enough to leave the harsh rangeland and move into town; bankers and school superintendents; farmers whose farms were worked by tenants and whose closest contact now with the soil was the annual garden show. And so the old center of town, where the Alquist mansion stood, was gradually depopulated of its patrician families as their offspring moved to this newer, less ostentatious and at least superficially more democratic neighborhood. They were joined by newer members of the respectable classes, such as the Sullivans, grudgingly admitted since they had opened Croy's first automobile dealership, and the Pritchards, Dale and Arlene, who had risen through Dale's management of the town's only oil concern and Arlene's remarkable skills as an organizer of church bazaars and charity functions.

It was the sort of neighborhood that considered the police a necessary tool for keeping people (other people, not themselves) from wandering the streets and accosting the children. It was the sort of neighborhood that never really expected to need a policeman or even speak to one face-to-face. It was all supposed to work quietly and out of sight, leaving them to enjoy their lawns, their gardens, their automobiles, and their new television sets.

So you can well imagine Dale Pritchard's indignation when, awakened at half-past midnight by a loud rapping on his front door, he descended the staircase in his bathrobe and slippers and, opening the door, discovered Police Chief Clay Buchholtz on his front stoop, his heavy boots nearly obliterating the rattan welcome mat, with officer Percy Owen fidgeting nervously behind him.

"What the hell is this?" Dale Pritchard demanded.

"Mr. Pritchard," Chief Buchholtz said, "do you have a moment?"

"At this hour? What the hell d'ya think?"

"May we come in?"

Dale Pritchard considered it. A glance up and down the street betrayed no lights on in any of the neighboring houses, but if they continued chatting like this in the still of the night, that wouldn't last for long. Dale was in the middle of an important real estate deal for a development he was planning on the southwest side of town. A police car parked outside his house was bad enough, but to be seen discussing some matter in the middle of the night would raise eyebrows he didn't want raised. "Make it quick," he said and gestured the men inside.

"What is it, Dale?" his wife Arlene said halfway down the stairs, a robe wrapped around her rayon negligee.

"Go back to bed, Arlene," Dale said. He wasn't so much concerned with Clay Buchholtz seeing his wife like that—they had all gone to school together, after all—but it burned him that Percy Owen should get a glimpse, and he was certain he had seen the furtive little fucker cast a glance up the stairs before throwing his eyes to the floor. "What is this, Clay? You got me out of bed and now you've upset the wife. This had better be good."

"Dale," Chief Buchholtz said, "can you tell me where Scotty is?"

"Scotty? What's he got to do with this?"

"Scotty?" his wife asked from the stairs, hysteria tinging her voice.

"Arlene, git!" Dale called over his shoulder. "Get to the point, Clay."

"There's been an accident, Dale. Out at the railroad crossing north of town. Does Scotty drive a Nash Rambler?"

"What do you mean, an accident?" Arlene let out a whimper but Dale couldn't take his eyes off Chief Buchholtz, who was looking at him with a peculiar intensity. "Scotty's home," Dale declared. "Been home for hours. Him and Jink Swofford and that Refior kid drove over to the drive-in at Tyrola. They come back eleven, eleven-thirty at the latest."

"Did you see him come in?"

Arlene let out a cry and ran upstairs.

"What the hell is going on?" Dale demanded. "Cut this bullshit. Tell me what the hell's going on!"

Chief Buchholtz took a deep breath and for the first time broke eye contact with him. "There was a report of an incident, north side of town. Officer Owen responded. The suspects, three of them, fled in a Rambler. Percy here gave chase," here the Chief cast a glare in Percy's direction, "and, well," Clay looked him in the eye again. "The car, the Rambler, ran into the side of a train."

"What do you mean, 'ran into the side of a train'?"

"The Santa Fe, Dale."

Percy Owen stepped forward, his eyes bugging out. "They're all dead, Mr. Pritchard! They're all three of them dead!"

There was a piercing scream from upstairs. Dale froze in place, torn between rushing upstairs to his wife and punching Percy Owen or Clay Buchholtz in the face.

"He's not there!" Arlene screamed from the top of the hall. She climbed down the carpeted stairs clutching the maple banister. Halfway down, she collapsed, her hands slipping down the rails like the bars of a cell. "He's not there!" she sobbed, "He's not there!"

The door at the kitchen end of the downstairs hall swung outward and a figure emerged, walking slowly into the light. He was fully dressed but sleepy looking. He stopped, looking at the three men standing stock still before him and the woman staring down at him from the stairs.

"What's going on?" asked Scotty Pritchard.

His mother gave a cry and came rushing down the stairs, but Dale Pritchard blocked her so roughly he nearly knocked her down. He took two steps toward his son and then struck him across the face so hard the boy ricocheted off the wall and fell in a heap on the polished oak floor.

It turned out the three boys were Darrel John "Jink" Swofford, Paul Hammond "Hammy" Refior, both of Croy, Oklahoma, and Aaron Kyle Wynn, of Dibble City, Jink's cousin on his mother's side. The Refior boy had lived long enough to say, over and over again, "We was just joking, Scotty, we was just joking." That plus the fact that the car was the Pritchards' Rambler and the driver too mangled to be identified had led to the Chief's visit in the middle of the night. It still took a while to figure out who the driver was, but once they could get Scotty away from the house and out of reach of his father, he admitted to lending the car to his friends that Friday night. Where he had been until 12:30 AM Saturday morning he wouldn't say.

The delay in identifying the driver meant it wasn't until Sunday morning that the body was properly identified by his father, John Wayne "Jake" Swofford, co-owner of Swofford Brothers Lumber Seed and Supply and part-time deputy sheriff of Kennsing County. By then, it was too late to notify the Swoffords' pastor, the Reverend Matthew Jacobs, of a death in his congregation, and he didn't find out about it until later that evening as he and a few of his parishioners were cleaning up the sanctuary after Croy's first ecumenical Service of Thanks.

It had been a mad scramble to get the service set up at Mt. Hermon. When the Library Board turned them down, Matthew, Susan, and Andy had hit the phones again, but with the same results. They even tried St. John's Wesleyan out on the county road south of town, but, as Matthew had predicted, they declined.

"There wasn't much hope there, anyway," he told Andy. "If the choir so much as sways, they'd think we were dancing the hoochie-kootch in the sanctuary." A look of sudden inspiration lit up his face. "Say," he said, "why not?"

"Why not what?" Susan asked. "Dance the hootchie-kooch in the sanctuary?"

"No, daughter," Matthew Jacobs said. "We needn't go to such extremes. But we could put the choirs in the sanctuary, couldn't we?"

They turned to look at him. "Andy," Susan asked, "could we? We've been rehearsing with the risers out front, but—"

"Yes," he said. "Yes, they'd fit." With extra chairs in the aisles, plus three extra rows of pews where the risers had been, it would work. He and Ethan would have to conduct standing in the aisle, but that was no problem. They began calling all the participating churches, spreading the good word. Everyone was excited. When St. Mark's Episcopal finally called back on Wednesday to say their hall was available after all, they thanked them kindly and invited them to join them on Sunday evening at Mt. Hermon Bible Church.

The church filled slowly with people, but the more people came, the more people seemed to arrive. Soon the church was bubbling with chatter and talk as neighbors who had never seen each other inside the same church before greeted each other and laughed—a bit nervously, perhaps, but good-naturedly. The choirs had to line up outside because there was no room at the back of the church. Susan peeked in through the side door where they would make their entrance. She called Andy over to her. "Look," she said, pointing inside.

In the middle of the church Mrs. Oldfield was turning this way and that, greeting people, pointing out where there were two or more seats together, encouraging people to skootch together to make room. She wore an expression Andy had never seen on her before. "I think," he said, "I think she's . . . happy."

"I know," Susan said. "Spooky, isn't it?"

And then the service began. Reverend Jacobs gave a welcoming speech and led the opening prayer. There was a hymn from the Assembly of God choir, then Reverend Jameson from Mr. Zion A.M.E. read from Psalm 133:

> *Behold, how good and how pleasant it is for brethren to dwell to-gether in unity!*
> *It is like the precious ointment upon the head, that ran down upon the beard, even Aaron's beard: that went down to the skirts of his garments;*
> *As the dew of Hermon, and as the dew that descended upon the mountains of Zion: for there the LORD commanded the blessing, even life for evermore.*

There was an instrumental piece by the St. Andrew's Methodist Trombone Choir, followed by a soprano from St. Elizabeth's accompanied by Andy on the piano. Reverend Jacobs gave the homily, noting the many trials the people of Croy had endured, and how a steadfast people would never be deserted by their God. The Mt. Zion choir underscored this theme with "I Shall Not Be Moved," and there wasn't a single body in the church that wasn't moved. Dr. Ronald C. Early, the organist at St. Mark's, performed Bach's *Schmücke dich, o leibe Seele* on a portable harmonium, the twinkling of his spectacles in the sanctuary lights matched only by the highlights glancing off his bald head. Then Reverend Hank Stillwater from Spring Valley Baptist led the assembly in a community prayer of thanksgiving, making special mention of the recent storm and its damage and the grace by which no lives were lost. Fr. Herron, in an officially unofficial capacity, introduced the next number with a reading from Psalm 96, "Sing to the Lord a new song," and Andy led the Mt. Hermon choir in his creation hymn, which left the pews and rafters humming with joy. Then Andy gave the signal for the joined choirs to assemble and stepped off the podium.

But his way to the back of the church, where he meant to watch, was blocked by Ethan Jameson. "I think this one is yours, brother," Ethan said, and motioned him back onto the podium.

Andy was bewildered but delighted. He looked at the choirs assembled before him. The radiant colors of their different robes was like looking head-on into a rainbow.

There was just one thing that needed adjusting: Ethan's voice balancing. Mrs. Littledeer, who always sang sharp, should not be standing next to Mrs. Johnson, one of Ethan's best belters. And there were other, minor difficulties. With a few deft hand motions, he got the various parties to swap places, and then he began "When I Think about Jesus."

From the first down beat to the last note, it was pure ecstasy. The choir performed dynamics they had never performed before, following his every lead, mindful of their parts and each other. It wasn't like he was trying to pull or tug them into shape, it was like the shape of the music itself was pouring through them. He wasn't conducting, he was playing an enormous instrument, and not playing it with a mind to how he wanted it to sound, but how the music wanted to sound. When the final chorus with its syncopated clapping kicked in, he was aware of a third element in the music: the audience. It wasn't just listening, it was there with them, shouting and singing along. And when Lila Armbruster hit that perfect high C at the end, it was as if the roof sailed away, borne aloft by every voice in the church.

Andy could hardly believe it was over. The way hearing slowly returns when you wake from a deep sleep, he slowly became aware of the roar of the congregation behind him and the beaming faces of the choir before him. He stepped off the podium and joined them in the sanctuary and, on his signal, led them in a group bow.

It was only when he came up from the bow that he saw Sunny standing in the front row with the rest of the congregation, all of them standing and applauding, but Sunny applauding loudest of all, dazzling in a white linen suit, his eyes gleaming with pride and his smile out-shouting the saints.

Cecil Jameson walked up to Matthew Jacobs as the people began to make their way in casual eddies towards the doors, most of them still aglow from the service.

"I want to thank you, Brother Matthew. It's been a pleasure doing this great work with you."

"It's been an honor, Brother Cecil." Matthew Jacobs scanned the happy crowd. "Look at them. Look at what the Spirit can do."

"It can work wonders. We see it every day, yet we forget." Cecil Jameson turned to him. "I want to thank you as well for providing shelter for my flock. I think I've finally found them safe pasture."

"Oh?" said Matthew. "Has Mt. Zion got its new roof, then?"

"No. I'm afraid that's a lost cause. No, we found a fine, intact, and unused church just t'other side of Napier Corners. We'll be moving there directly."

"The Corners?" Matthew said. "But isn't that quite a distance from Croy?"

"It will be a distance for some, but others have already moved. And it will be closer for some of our rural brothers and sisters."

"But, will we see you again?"

The Reverend Cecil Jameson took his hand. "From time to time, my brother in Christ, from time to time." He shook his hand warmly and left.

The news that the Mt. Zion congregation was leaving Croy clouded Matthew's euphoria. He looked around for Susan or Andy or somebody to talk this news over with. He didn't see either of them, but he saw Mrs. Oldfield at the back of the church talking to someone who looked to be Clay Buchholtz, but the police chief hadn't been at the service. He couldn't imagine what he was doing here now.

John Tibbits helped Andy slide the last of the risers back into storage and then started to excuse himself. "How about the risers from Mt. Zion?" Andy asked. "Are they loaded onto the truck?"

"Ethan and his boys have it taken care of. I, uh, I'm taking off for home, now, Andy." John smiled down at the floor. "Ruth was, she was really something tonight, wasn't she?"

Truth be told, Andy hadn't noticed Ruth Tibbits at all. "Yes," he said, "yes, she was wonderful."

"She was, wasn't she?" John grinned. "Well, good night."

Andy smiled as John strode out of the room. There was still sheet music to put away, and with some reluctance, he opened the door to the long storeroom that ran behind the sanctuary and flicked on the lights. No rats. He was glad of that.

"He's a cutie."

Andy turned around to see Sunny smiling at him. He glanced around. "Don't talk like that. He's one of my parishioners."

"He's still a cutie."

Andy could see through the open door that there were still people in the church. He grabbed Sunny's arm. "Come on," he said, pulling him into the damp room.

"Ooo," Sunny said. "I think I'm liking this church more and more."

Andy fumed under his breath. He got the combination lock open and started sorting the sheet music. "What are you doing here?" he asked.

"You didn't think I would miss it, did you? It's practically all you've talked about for weeks. Happy to see me?"

"I wasn't expecting it." He was stuffing the music into folders without really looking where it was going.

Sunny grabbed his arms. "Hey," he said. Andy turned around. "You were terrific. Your music was terrific."

"Thanks," Andy said, not looking in his eyes, which he knew would be dancing with light.

"No, I mean it. I think I get it now. That Spirit you talk about, moving through the music. I think I felt it."

He looked up. "Really?"

"I'm not kidding. I know what it means. I feel it, too, only for me, it's visual. For you, it's music. But it surrounds you and fills you. It feeds your soul."

"Yes! That's exactly what it's like for me. I'd starve without it."

"Tonight, you fed a lot of souls. You fed mine. Thank you." Sunny cradled Andy's face in his hands, drew him close, and kissed him.

"Mr. Simms!" a voice shouted from the end of the storeroom. The two of them sprang apart so abruptly Sunny was knocked against a cabinet. Mrs. Oldfield was standing under the light at the end of the room, a furious expression on her face. "Mr. Simms!" she repeated. "Have you taken leave of your senses?" She marched towards them down the length of the room.

"It's . . . It's not what it looks like, Mrs. Oldfield," Andy stammered.

Mrs. Oldfield walked right up to Sunny. "What are you doing here? What right have you to come in here?"

Sunny laughed in her face. He gave an elaborate bow and said, "It is an old Punjabi custom, Mrs. Oldfield. Vast felicitations on your splendid triumph. All Croy is a hubbub of delight." He looked quickly from her to Andy and back again. "I leave you so." He walked briskly to the door and left.

Mrs. Oldfield made certain he was gone then turned her sharp eyes on Andy. "Have you any idea what you're doing? Have you any idea at all?"

"Really, Mrs. Oldfield, Sunny didn't mean—"

She seized him hard by the arm.

"I will not have it!" she shouted. "You will not test God in his own house! Nor in mine. You break it off with that boy or you can pack your things and leave tonight."

"Mrs. Oldfield!"

"I will not have it! I will not wake up one morning to find the two of you stripped and mutilated, hanging from a tree!"

"Andy?" Susan's voice called from the doorway.

Mrs. Oldfield turned quickly at the sound, then spun back to him, her voice a tight whisper. "I want your answer, Mr. Simms. I want it tonight. I will wait up for it." She turned on her heel and left.

Susan had been talking with her father at the back of the church about the awful news from Chief Buchholtz when she saw Sunny Sohi hustle out of the storeroom as if pursued by demons. Something had gone on in there. She excused herself and went to the door. She heard Mrs. Oldfield's angry voice inside, hissing at Andy.

"Andy?" she called out. She had to flatten herself against the wall as Mrs. Oldfield sped past without a word. She entered and saw Andy leaning against a cabinet, a hand to his head. "What's with Mrs. Oldfield?"

Andy straightened up. "She's very upset," he said, thrusting folders into shelves and avoiding her eyes.

"I could just about guess that. What about?"

Andy slammed the cabinet shut. "I don't know! Something stupid. Some Klan atrocity she keeps imagining."

"Oh," Susan said, "then you haven't heard."

"Heard what?"

"Someone tried to burn a cross in the Rosens' front yard."

"What? A cross burning? In Croy?"

"Well, no, not exactly. I should have said, someone tried to burn a cross *into* the Rosens' front yard, into their lawn. There's a big cross-like shape on their front yard where someone poured gasoline or lighter fluid or something and tried to set it on fire. The grass is dying all around it. Isn't it awful?"

"Awful. Yes. No wonder she's upset. Do they know who did it?"

"Kids, probably. Trying to be cute. Oh, that's the other awful news. Some kids got killed trying to beat the train at the railroad crossing Saturday night. Jink Swofford was one of them."

"Jink? Scott's friend?" The color drained from his face and he looked at her at last. "Is Scott all right?"

"Yes, he's fine. But the Swoffords, they're tore up something fierce. Daddy's going to see if he can do something to comfort them."

"I . . ." Andy started. "I should help."

She could tell he was really shaken by the news. "Maybe not tonight. You've done an awful lot tonight." She took his arm and started to lead him out of the long room. "Look, why don't you come over to the parsonage. I can make us some tea or coffee. You seem pretty wound up."

Andy was nodding, but when they reached the door to the sanctuary, he pulled himself free of her arm. "No," he said. "No. Thanks, but there's something I've got to do first."

"Tonight? Can't it wait?"

"No." He headed for the door, then turned around. "I'm sorry, Susan. I'll come back later. I don't know when, but—" He flapped his hands and ran out the doors.

"You've said that before," Susan said to the empty church. She looked around. Everyone was gone. Even her father had left, probably to comfort the Swoffords. All the lights were still on. Susan began walking up the side aisle, flipping light switches as she went. *I want your answer tonight.* That's what Mrs. Oldfield had said. And it had not been a pleasant request. Answer about what? She finished one aisle and came back down the other. Whatever it was, she had a hunch it had to do with Sunny Sohi. She reached the front and only the lights above the sanctuary were left. She took one last look across the silent pews, then turned the lights off on her way out, letting the darkness back into the church.

Andy pulled into the space beside the granny house and stopped, turning off the engine. There were no lights on inside. She was not waiting for him in there this time.

He looked up the slope to the back porch. There were lights on in the kitchen. He did not want to go up there. He looked again at the small house he had called home since arriving in Croy. He did not want to go there, either. On a hot night like this, it would be like stepping into a tomb. He wanted to stay right here in the car, his hands gripping the wheel, all the sounds of late summer shut out by the rolled-up windows.

He remained there as still as the dead for he didn't know how long, half an hour maybe. Then as if some tumbler in some mechanical device had slid into place, he opened the car door and stepped into the night. The songs of cicadas thrummed in his ears. Two mockingbirds contested their territories high above, throwing strings of bird-call from tree to tree. A light breeze ruffled the cosmos and dahlias. He ignored it all, focusing on the light in the kitchen, walking in a straight line toward the back door. As he passed the mimosa, something sticky pulled on his ear and then at his face. Suddenly, it was all over him, in his hair, over his mouth, across his eyes. With horror, he realized he had walked into a spider web slung between the tree and some distant anchor. He swiped at the threads tugging at him from every direction, the scent of mimosa filling his nostrils. He was still wiping the sticky residue from his mouth when he knocked on the door.

Chapter 16

YOUR ENEMY LIKE A ROARING LION

Mrs. Oldfield was placing a second batch of Mason jars in their sterilizing bath when she heard the knock at her back door. "Come in, Andy," she called out. Her tenant entered the humid kitchen and stood beside the table, where half a dozen jars of canned tomatoes sat cooling. "It's warm, I know," she said, "but it's even warmer during the day. And you have to get them in when they're ripe or they'll just rot on the vine." She turned around, wiping her hands on her apron and smoothing it. "Won't you sit down?"

Andy stood still beside the table. "I don't know what you think you saw—"

"You and Sunny Sohi. Kissing. And more to it than that, by the look of it."

He laughed nervously. "Sunny's just exuberant. He likes to play pranks. He's a child, really—"

"Do you take me for a fool, Andy? I know what I saw. You gave me your word you would be careful, but instead you give me this *display*. Supposing Matthew had walked in instead of me? Or Susan? Or, God help us, one of the children?" She shook her head and sat at the table, indicating the chair opposite. Andy stiffly lowered himself into it. "How serious is it?"

He swallowed. "Serious."

"How long has it been going on?"

"Since early summer." He shuddered. "Please don't tell Matthew. Don't tell Susan."

"That's not my place. But I won't sit idly by and watch you throw your life away. You are far too valuable."

He gave a short laugh. "Valuable."

Here it comes, she thought, *the self-pity, the self-loathing.* It was all so familiar. "Has this happened before?"

"No." He closed his eyes "Yes. In my heart, yes. But I've never actually—" He looked at her. "This is the first time it's been . . . serious."

"Nothing is ever serious with Sunny Sohi. You'll find that out soon enough."

"What do you intend to do?"

She shook her head. "That's up to you. But if you continue in this fashion, I shall rise to my very feet and call you on it."

"I'll break it off, then."

She nodded.

"Tonight. I'll tell him tonight. If that's what you want."

She looked out the window. Dark summer pressed in on all sides. "What *I* want is not important. What do *you* want?"

Andy pursed his lips. "I don't want to upset Matthew. I don't want to hurt Susan. You say I'm valuable. I don't want to be valuable. I want to be *useful*. I can't do that if I'm cut off from my ministry. This thing with Sunny, it has to end."

"Good. The sooner the better."

"Yes." He nodded. "I'll go there tonight and tell him."

She sucked in her breath. "No. Not tonight. Not *any* night."

He frowned. "I've got to tell him something. I can't just break it off without telling him."

"Why not?"

"Because we're— We mean a lot to each other. We're very close."

She shook her head. "That's exactly the problem. It has got to be a clean break."

"But it won't be!" His eyes grew wide. "If I just cut him off, leave him hanging, he'll want to know why. He'll come around, asking."

"Not around here! I want to be very clear about that, Andy. He is not to come around here, ever. That boy has done enough mischief in this town."

The look on his face tugged at her heart. She read fear there,. but it wasn't the right kind of fear. There were laws, laws with serious consequences, and there was scripture. But it wasn't the law he was afraid of, nor was it the sin. It was its absence, being empty, abandoned. *Well, it's a start*, she thought. Her duty was to charity, not the law. She straightened her shoulders. "A letter, then."

He grimaced. "A letter? That seems kind of cold-blooded."

"I think cold-blooded is exactly what you want. Hot-blooded has not been your friend."

He looked at her for several breaths, then dropped his head and nodded.

"You'll write it, then?"

"Yes."

"Tonight?"

"Yes."

"Good. And what will you do next?"

"Next?" Andy shrugged. "There is no next. Sunny and I are over, done with. I swear to God."

"Yes, and I believe you. You have the resolve of the moment. But what about tomorrow? And the next day?"

"Everything will be back the way it was. My work, the church. Like always."

Mrs. Oldfield shook her head. "Andy, I know you to be sincere and I know you are honest. But you can also be surpassing arrogant. I don't think you understand what you are up against. But I do."

Andy's eyes flashed. "How? How could you possibly know what I'm going through?"

"My husband," she said simply.

He sat back in his chair. "You mean, he—?"

"Oh, no," she said quickly. "Gerald was not— His trial was not the same as yours. With Gerald, it was the bottle."

She saw his jaw clench. "I do not have a drinking problem, Mrs. Oldfield."

"No, but you think the same way, the way a drunkard does." She shook her head. "You think because today, tonight, your resolve is firm, you can keep that resolve."

"I promise you—"

"Of course you promise me. But don't you see? Your very sincerity is a trap." She felt the jars with the back of her hand. They would take a long time to cool on a night like this. "A drunkard will promise anything. So will an addict. So will men like Sunny. They can't be honest with you because they can't be honest with themselves. They aren't whole people. They're broken."

Andy shook his head. "I thought I was the broken one."

"Oh, you are. But that is beside the point."

"I pray to God to make me whole again. Every night and every day."

"You'll need more than that!"

She saw the shock on his face. "It's a weakness, Andy, a sickness. There is a hole in your heart, and you will clutch at anything to fill it. This *behavior* just happened to be the thing at hand. But now it has filled you up, and you will do anything to keep the pain of that emptiness from coming back. You think you are the weakest, lowest, most undeserving creature in the world. But that is just the emptiness calling you."

"I yearn in my heart for God's grace."

"Yes, and God may hear your prayers, and He may see how deep and true your repentance is." She saw tears pooling in his eyes, but she had to press on. "But it is not enough. Try as you might, you will do anything to keep that hole from opening up again."

"Then I'm lost."

"No more than any of us. We are all weak, Andy. God made us that way."

He shook his head. "Not like me. When God made me, He made a mistake."

She stood and turned away to keep her anger from pouring out in front of him. "God does not make mistakes," she said tightly. "Your mistake is in thinking you can do it all by yourself. Through prayer. Prayer is not enough. It will never be enough."

She went to the stove and turned off the burner beneath the Mason jars. They bubbled and hopped for a few seconds then settled down. Her tone softened. "We are all of us weak. We were meant to be. But we were not meant to fail."

She turned and faced him. "When I met Gerald, I was as lost as he was, though in a different way. I had no charity in my heart, though I burned for a man. With my sharp tongue and stiff bearing, most men took flight at the sight of me with nary a howdy-do. It looked as though I would drag on through life barren, as unloved as I was unloving.

"But God threw Gerald and me together—it doesn't matter how—and I realized, here was a soul that could be the water in the desert of my life, and I could be the rock in the roaring river that was his."

She straightened her spine. "It was a struggle. My need for reassurance of his love was great, demanding, selfish. I needed it every day.

Some days, every hour. But his need was great, too. He'd taken the pledge many times, been saved, declared Jesus his personal savior in revivals and services up one side the state and down t'other, but in the end he knew it wasn't enough. It was never enough. He needed a helpmate. He needed me. He was weak, and I was weak—maybe even weaker than he—but together, with Christ at the center, we were something much stronger. We were a family."

She returned to the table. "He never tired in his love. And I never tired in my duty."

"Your duty? What was that?"

She smoothed the unwrinkled tablecloth before her. "Every morning, before Gerald got up, I went through the house—and the shed, the garden, the root cellar, the granny house—and removed every bottle of liquor I found, and poured its contents down the drain and smashed the bottles in the rubbish bin. And every night, after he had gone to bed, I did it again." She looked at him. "And I did it every day till the day he died. As time went on, my search usually came up empty. But not always. And every day till the day he died, Gerald woke up sober and went to bed sober. And he did so knowing I was there, *because* I was there. That is what you need, someone to be there every moment from now on."

Andy frowned. "Do you think Matthew could be my anchor?" he offered weakly.

"No, of course not. Two men can't check each other. They're too much alike. You need a woman for your anchor, a helpmate."

She saw a look of horror cross his face and knew immediately he'd misunderstood.

"Oh, no, not me. That'd be foolish. There's too much distance in our years. But there is someone else, someone who cares for you very much, who would be more than happy to be your anchor."

"Who?"

"I think you know who."

He stared at her blankly.

"Susan!" She nearly barked the name. His obtuseness was trying her nerves.

"I couldn't ask Susan—"

"I don't think you'll have to ask. Once she knows—"

He sprang from his chair. "I could never tell her! What would she think of me?"

He's being stubborn, she thought. *He wants to keep the sin all to himself. Just like Gerald.* "I don't think you'll need to tell her anything. Once she knows you need her help, it won't matter to her what help you need. In her heart, she already knows."

He sat down slowly. "I couldn't bear it if she knew. I couldn't look her in the face."

"You need to trust her, Andy. She is stronger than she looks. And a lot less frivolous than she pretends."

Andy shook his head.

Mrs. Oldfield decided she'd said enough. "One more thing." She rose and retrieved a shiny brass knob from beneath the counter. "I want you to install this on your front door." She placed it on the table in front of him. "It's a deadbolt. I should have done it myself months ago, but Gerald was the handyman around here."

Andy hefted the lock in one hand. He laughed. "What's this, to keep me locked in?"

"Oh, for heaven sakes, no! Don't you pay attention to anything? Haven't you any idea what's been going on around here? There's no lock on that door. Anyone could come waltzing in there in the middle of the night. They take special delight in lynching queers. They'd sell postcards of it. Do you understand?"

Andy swallowed and nodded. She reached out and folded his hands in hers. *"Be sober-minded and alert. Your adversary, the Devil, prowls around like a roaring lion, seeking whom he would devour. Resist him, standing firm in your faith, and in the knowledge that your brethren throughout the world are undergoing the same kind of suffering."*

He pulled his hands free and nodded. "I'll install it tomorrow."

Mrs. Oldfield gave a small smile and withdrew her hands. *The boy is finally beginning to see sense*, she thought.

Andy gave the mimosa tree a wide berth as he walked back down the lawn. The deadbolt lay heavy in his hand. He turned at the door to the granny house and looked up at the bright kitchen windows. For a moment, he imagined hurtling the deadbolt through them, smashing the jars of tomatoes and spraying the walls with his declaration. *How's that for your roaring lion!* Then he took a deep breath and stepped inside. He turned on the light and stood staring at his living room. He stood for several minutes. Then he put the lock on the kitchen counter and went into the bedroom and turned on the light. He returned to the living room and stood a few minutes more. Then he turned off the living room light, went to the bedroom, turned off the light there, and looked out the window. The lights were still on in Mrs. Oldfield's kitchen. When he saw her silhouette turn away, he crept out the door and down the alley, keeping the little house between him and her windows. It was just a few minutes walk from there to Sunny's studio.

Chapter 17

THE MAN WHO WASN'T THERE

Sunny looked around the studio and sighed. It had been a fine work-space, easy for people to get to. Hitching a ride to town with Tucker once a week and then back out to the trailer on weekends, accompanied by Jed's usual tight-lipped silence, had been a strain. But the one-on-one life sessions with the townsfolk were worth it. For once, the people he had grown up around took him seriously. And why shouldn't they? Their faces would gaze down upon the citizens of Croy for generations to come.

And the studio had been more than a workspace. He took one last tour of the small bedroom. He checked the three-drawer dresser and peered under the bed. Then he sat on it. He and Andy had explored continents of desire here, stopping time and erasing boundaries. The glowing Rexall sign outside had enveloped them like a heart and closed out the world.

But now the maquettes were all done, including the redesigned right panel. It was time to move to the brickworks and begin the molds. The work had to be timed perfectly, back-figured from the dedication ceremony in October. Cooling the panels after they were fired would take weeks. There wasn't any room for slip-ups, delays, or distractions. He would transform himself from the smiling, social persona he had assumed to coax farmers and ranchers, merchants and housewives into dropping their native reticence and pose for him unselfconsciously; he would become the furious artist working alone with a single purpose in the heat and noise of the town's biggest employer, a bright locus of creation in a dull sea of commerce. He grinned. He was looking forward to it.

A noise from below broke his reverie. He listened for footsteps in the stairwell but heard none. He got up and crossed the studio and listened at the door. Still nothing. He opened it and peered down the stairs. There was someone at the bottom, leaning against the wall, looking out into the street through the etched glass panes. "Hello?" he called. The figure turned his head and he instantly recognized the profile.

"You didn't tell me they fixed the streetlight," Andy said.

"What streetlight?" Sunny stepped out onto the landing. The door began to swing lazily shut behind him. He stayed it with his hand.

Andy backed deeper into the shadow at the foot of the stairs. "Just outside. It's been out all summer. They fixed it."

"Huh. I never noticed. Are you coming up?"

"No, I can't. I— I don't have time."

"I'll come down, then." But as he started, the door to the apartment swung shut. In the darkness, he tripped and slid down several steps with a yelp, one hand flailing wildly for the railing. He landed on his butt halfway down. "Damn!"

Andy was immediately at his side, crouching on the stair below, grabbing him by the shoulders. "Are you okay?"

"I am such a klutz! Old New York won't have to wring my scrawny black neck if I break it for him." He loosened his death-grip on the railing and relaxed. Pain immediately shot up his tailbone. "Ow!"

"What! Are you hurt?"

"It's just my ass. It's not used to taking a pounding. Not this kind, at any rate." Andy's hands withdrew. Sunny tried to make out his eyes, but his face was an indistinct oval in front of him, barely lit by the gleam from under the studio door. Andy probably couldn't see him, either. "This is ridiculous. Let's go upstairs." He started to rise, but Andy took his hand and pulled him down.

"No. I really can't stay."

Sunny looked up at the closed door and sighed. "There's really nothing up there anymore anyway. Just a few boxes." He turned to look in Andy's direction and grinned. "And the bed."

Andy turned away and drew his knees to his chest. He stared down the stairwell. "I won't be able to come here anymore."

"Oh, so you already heard."

"Heard what?"

"I'm moving."

"What? Out of town?"

Sunny thought he heard panic in Andy's voice. He scooted down a step and put an arm around him. "No, silly. Not out of town. Not far, anyways. But it's time to move the work out to the kilns. I'm moving out of here and back to the trailer."

"You should have told me."

"I was going to tell you. At the church."

Sunny felt Andy's shoulders contract under his arm.

"You can't just come around like that. People will notice."

"People?" He dropped his arm. "Oh, yeah. Like Mrs. Oldfield. Did you calm the old biddy down?"

"Don't talk like that. She means well."

"She means to make everyone as tight and dried up as she is."

"She's my landlady. I have to respect her wishes."

"Why?"

"Don't be an ass, Sunny. I have to live in this town. You do, too."

"Maybe. But not for long. Once the sculpture is up, I'll shake the dust of this town from my feet. I'm not going to end up a collection of stunted dreams. I'm ready to make my mark on the world."

"Did you ever think the world might make its mark on you?" Andy stood. "There are plenty of people out there willing to cut you down, and happily, too."

He stared up at him. "What's gotten into you?"

"People say there was a cross burning in town last night."

"Who?"

Andy's silhouette shrugged. "Klan, Mrs. Oldfield thinks."

"You mean Swofford and his bunch of good ol' boys?" He scoffed. "They couldn't find a match if it was sticking out their butts, let alone light it. The Invisible Empire is visible only to each other, and then only when they're drunk."

"They aren't the only ones. Are you paying attention to the news? It's not just here, but all around the country. Up in Washington—"

"Washington? What's that got to do with us?"

"They're ruining people's lives, hounding them from office. They may as well be lynching them. Do you think folks around here don't notice that? Don't approve? Good Christian people who'd lynch us for real and think it righteous. All because of . . . this." He grabbed Sunny's hand and brought it to his lips. He kissed it and pressed it to his cheek.

Sunny felt tears there, hot on his flushed face. He tugged on the hand. "Hey." Andy stood in the dark, swaying. "Hey," he said again, and with a gentle pull he got Andy to sit down. He wrapped an arm around his waist. "Your good Christian people are wrong if they believe that. Love is bigger than that. Larger than God, even. Their God, at any rate."

Andy squirmed. "Don't be so . . ."

"So what?"

"So *Sunny*."

There was a silence, then they both laughed, the sound echoing up the stairs. Andy sighed and leaned his head on his shoulder. "Seriously, though," he said, "nothing is larger than God."

"Okay, so we are not larger than God. But Love is, it has to be. It's the biggest thing there is."

"God is love."

"Sure. And that includes us."

They were quiet for a while, all talked out. Andy broke the silence first. "Maybe lynching isn't the worst people could do. Maybe the ones that aren't killed outright will wish they had been."

"How do you mean?"

"Is Love larger than Art? If you had to choose between love, between what we have, and never working again—not another sculpture, not another drawing or painting—would you?"

"Would I what?"

"Would you choose us?"

"And never work again?" Sunny laughed. "I'd probably starve to death before we found out."

"But would it be enough? Just us?"

"I'm not giving up Art and I'm not giving up you. The two are the same to me. I can't go a day without thinking about you. Sometimes, I can't go an hour."

Andy stared at the light at the bottom of the stairs. "I can't come back here."

"I'll take a .22 to that god-damned streetlight. But hell, Andy, we don't have to worry about that. The trailer's out in the country, miles away."

He sighed. "Your trailer's the only place I've felt safe since coming here."

"Come on out, then."

"Will you do that chicken again?"

"The masala? Sure."

Andy shook his head. "I don't have an excuse anymore."

"An excuse for what?"

"To be gone. The service is over. No more joint rehearsals."

Sunny pulled him close. "We'll find a way. There's always a way. When Mama and me came back after Dadi left, I thought I would curl up and die. Everyone was so cold, and I was so . . . strange. Jed was the only one who would even talk to me." He chuckled. "And you can just about guess how much comfort *that* was."

Andy gave a short laugh like a puff of air and nodded.

"But we made it through, Mama and me. *The* Indians."

Andy laughed for real this time, quietly. "Where is she now, your mama?"

Sunny took a long, slow breath. "Queens, I think. New York. Back to her people. She couldn't go back to my father's folks again, not after he left her."

Andy was quiet for a while. "Your father left you?"

"Yeah. The s.o.b. had some crazy idea about an independent Punjab. He met up with some loonies out in Stockton and went off to make holy war."

Andy stirred in his arms. "I though you said he was deported."

Sunny shrugged. "That's just what I tell people. It's short, easy to understand. Beats saying he ran out on us. Sounds more tragic, too, don't it? More dramatic. But it amounts to the same thing. In the end, it didn't matter. Partition came along, and," he shrugged again, "he died."

"That's awful."

"Yeah. Folks around here, all they remember is the court case, how he lost the farm, how he wasn't a real American, could never be. When they started saying he was deported, I didn't argue. It's just easier to let them believe what they want to believe."

They sat on the stairs in silence a while longer, holding each other. Then Andy said softly, "I've got to go."

"Yeah," Sunny sighed. He leaned in and kissed Andy on the lips. He started to pull away but Andy took his face in his hands and pulled him into a deeper kiss. When he leaned back, Sunny could finally see his eyes. Maybe his own had adjusted to the dim light, but Andy's face was fully visible now, his eyes shining in the dark. "You know, after my father died, I thought I'd never feel whole again. When I'm with you, I do. You know what I'm saying?"

"I do," Andy said. "I've got to go."

Sunny didn't usually watch Andy leave. When the Rexall sign clicked off at midnight, it was time to part. By 12:04, when the train thundered through town, Andy would be across the tracks, and by the time it blew its final whistle, he would be in his own bed. But tonight Andy left early, stopping for a minute at the open door, glancing up at the light and checking the street before slipping away, his head down. Sunny entered his studio, squinted at the bulb dangling from the ceiling, and pulled the chain. He stood watching at the window. There might be some tick in Percy Owen's patrol that would bring him suddenly around the corner and catch Andy like a thief in his headlights. He held his breath as Andy crossed the street at the corner and disappeared beneath the heart-shaped catalpa leaves. No squad car appeared, nor any other traffic. Croy was asleep. The streetlight flooded the darkened studio, and a deep fury welled up inside Sunny that such a mean simple thing could cut the world in two. He cursed every light and every shadow and every unholy fear that turned the one into the other.

Still, his lover had braved the divide and they had spent the night sitting on the stairs, talking. As Sunny settled into his final night in the studio, a realization struck him. This was the first time, since that day at Elephant Rock, that he and Andy had been alone together without desperately spilling into each other. Instead, they had explored something deeper: their wounds, their fears. And it had been wonderful. He smiled. *Damn*, he thought, *I'm getting good at this.*

The repaired streetlight had almost made him turn back. Maybe it would have been better if he had.

He rehearsed the words he had to say on the way over, but once there, he couldn't bring himself to say them. Not the direct words, the words that would end it. He kept leading up to them and they kept slipping away. *Stand firm in your faith and in the knowledge that your brethren throughout the world are undergoing the same kind of suffering.* But neither he nor his faith were firm, not with Sunny sitting next to him, holding him. Sunny was the firm one, Sunny was what kept him from feeling broken. Would his brothers throughout the world understand the suffering letting go of that would bring?

But just as he was about to give in, just as he was certain he wanted nothing more than to be devoured by this roaring lion, Sunny had confessed his lie. All the way home along the deep summer streets, the words kept ringing in his ears: "That's just what I tell people. It sounds more dramatic, don't it?"

How can you believe someone who makes things up just to sound dramatic? Maybe "You make me feel whole" sounds dramatic, too. What had Mrs. Oldfield said? "That boy has done enough mischief in this town." Sunny was no boy, but if he was a man, he was a man not to be trusted, broken, incomplete. A boy who wouldn't grow up. Andy had no business being with him. He had a responsibility to his church, to Matthew, to Susan, to the children and adults in his music ministry. And to Ginny, too, and her baby to come. A disgraced deacon could seal no souls for the kingdom.

Andy had never felt more alone than those last minutes on the stairs. Sunny couldn't hold him or comfort him or keep him safe anymore because Sunny couldn't really see him or the role he had to play in all these lives. Though sitting right beside him, Sunny may as well not have been there. A sad smile folded Andy's lips. *"Yesterday upon the stair . . ."*

All the windows were dark in the main house when he got home. He opened his door carefully, ashamed to have put himself in such a position, worried about disturbing the sleep of an elderly widow.

He picked up the deadbolt from the kitchen counter, its weight a solid promise in his hand. He knew what Mrs. Oldfield wanted. She thought of ruffians, the likes of John Swofford and his fellow klansmen, or even simple people like Percy Owen who could be driven to any wild action if there were enough of them and some red-faced idiot to egg them on. But it wasn't night riders he imagined storming his room at night. It was Sunny Sohi. He laid the lock back on the counter and stood in the unmoving air, breathing the heat that pressed in all around.

From across the river, sounding closer in the deepening night, the 12:04 shrilled its warning at the edge of town. There would be nothing to impede it. The wreckage from the previous night had been cleared away.

Part 3

Should I not care about Nineveh, that great city, in which there are more than a hundred and twenty thousand people who cannot tell their right hand from their left?—and many cattle as well.

—Book of Jonah

Chapter 18

GOOD PEOPLE

Avril Rosen watched Sunny Sohi carry his last box of belongings to a waiting truck. He sighed. Sunny had been so apologetic about breaking the lease. Truth was, Lerner Alquist had offered Avril a sizable incentive to let him go. Despite his affection for the boy and admiration for his moxie, you had to live delicately in a town like this. You had to keep a certain balance—or rather, help the town keep *its* balance. He had acquiesced, thinking it for the best.

Avril had always taken the middle way, making space for everyone, even the odd ones like Sunny, welcoming all, listening, keeping confidences. In this way, he wove his family into the fabric of the community as deftly as his father had and his father before him. But the incident at his home had opened his eyes. The thread of their lives was loose. It could be pulled out with a single tug.

He brought himself out of these dark musings to pay attention to the young man standing before him, talking. A sharp young man, he'd always thought. Avril had no sons to pass the business on to. There was only Rachel. It was her future he had to safeguard now.

"I just want you to know," John Tibbits was saying, "that I was very excited by your proposal."

"Was?" Avril said. He had meant to say, "Yes?" to encourage him. Instead, his voice had come out like a challenge.

"Oh, don't get me wrong," John said at once. "I'm still very excited, and I intend to take you up on it. That is, if it's still on offer?"

A sharp young man, indeed. Sensitive enough to have picked up a change in the wind. "And why would it not?" Avril asked.

"I know what happened, Mr. Rosen. Last Saturday. And I know that might make you—reluctant to bring someone, a stranger, into your business."

This man can bargain, Avril thought. *Bargain and not even know he's bargaining.* His estimation of John Tibbits went up a notch, but so did his wariness. "I do not make an offer just to take it back a week later," Avril Rosen said.

John Tibbits smiled and wiped his hands on his trousers and grinned broadly. "Great!" Then his face turned serious. "I just want you to know, most people here are pretty upset. This is a good town, these are good people. And most people, everyone I know, everyone I've talked to, thinks it's wrong, just plain wrong. Lots of us, many of us, think that. Ruth does. And we'd like to make it up to you, somehow."

So, it was talked about then, that hard-edged shape burning its way into his family's front lawn. "Thank you, John. But that shouldn't be your reason for taking the job. You should want it."

"Oh, I do! But I wanted you to know. Know how I and many others feel."

"Oh yes, I know. But still, I thank you."

"For what?"

"For being the first person in this town of good people to say so to my face." He put his hands in the pockets of his lab coat. "Now, when can you start?"

Robert S. "Tremblin' Bob" Grenville, pastor at Divine Word Church in Dibble City and host of "The Trembling Hour" radio show (recorded live at 9:00 am Sundays and broadcast at 3:00 pm Central Time), understood why Mr. and Mrs. Swofford wanted their son buried out of his church rather than Mt. Hermon. They wanted the comfort of sharing their grief with the parents of his cousin, Kyle, who had also perished. The father was in a tight rage, and the mother, the very pit of despair. Their only son gone, so suddenly, so horribly. His heart went out to them.

"The two boys was real close," Mrs. Swofford said in a toneless mutter. "And I still got family here in Dibble. We started out here."

"I see," he said. "Happier days."

She nodded.

But then real reason erupted from Jake Swofford. "I ain't burying my boy out of no church where them niggers been jigging," he spat.

Bob Grenville sucked in his breath but said nothing. Grief was grief and there was no sense in trying to school it.

Tremblin' Bob had met Reverend Jacobs a few times before. A good man, certainly, but the whole ecumenical thing had sounded muddled to him. There was something bloodless about Jacobs's preaching, something that had the hollow, dusty smell of books about it. How could mere learning, no matter how refined, face up to the shattered bones and mangled mess of Darrell Swofford's passing? (They called him "Jink," he noted.)

Jake Swofford's rage was born of fear, and fear could be an all-consuming force. But fear could also serve. A preacher with his feet planted firmly in the Word could turn unfocused fear into fear of the Lord, turn anger into righteousness, and hate into hatred of sin. The Swoffords were good people; he could help them be better.

"Yes," he said, "we would be honored to hold the service for Jink and Kyle here, together, as they were in life and at the end. We shall pray them both into heaven, so their souls may slide peacefully and smoothly into the bosom of our Lord, and never know nor feel the torment or sorrow they've left behind."

Susan was reliving every moment of the Special Service in her telling of it: how people were awkward at first as they got used to being in the same church together, the expectation on her father's face, the sense of something growing right there in the room with them as the evening drew on. And then the music! The bond that had suddenly appeared among them all, tugging at their hearts, pulling them together, lifting them up and setting them safe in a new world. "It was like," Susan said, her face shining, "it was like—well, like being born again!"

Virginia looked at her over the curling smoke of her cigarette.

Susan laughed. "Oh, yes, yes, I know how that sounds. And you know how I feel about that sort of thing. But really, no other words come close. It was that . . . grand."

"Well," Virginia said, "it certainly sounded grand. Even from here."

"I wish you'd've come over. You can go out now, right? Now that everything's—" she gestured at Virginia's swollen abdomen "—out in the open."

Virginia shifted on the sofa. "Thanks, sweetie. You sure know how to turn a phrase. And a stomach."

"Oh, now, don't be cross."

"I'm not." She took another drag on her cigarette. "Yeah, I'd'a liked to've been there. But Lerner and me, we have a kind of understanding. A truce, you might say. No public viewing till the happy day."

"That doesn't sound like a truce to me. That sounds like surrender."

"Trust me," Virginia said, spouting a plume in the direction of the lamp, "it ain't." She shifted again on the cushions. "But let's not get into it. You're here to take my mind off that crap. So tell me more. I'll bet your father was happy."

"Oh, yes!" Susan said. "At least at first."

"Only at first?"

"Oh, you know him. Always carries the worries of the whole world on his shoulders. Something happened right after the service that sort of broke the spell. That's when he found out that little hooligan Jink Swofford had got himself killed."

"Yeah, I heard about that. Him and two other boys, ain't it? News like that surely kills the joy."

Susan shook her head. "That's not it. When you're a minister, you live with that kind of thing all the time. You get used to it. No, what really brought him down was, when he went out there that night to comfort the Swoffords, they wouldn't let him in."

"You're shittin' me."

Susan shook her head. "And that's not all. They're having the funeral over in Dibble City, where the Wynn boy was from—you know, his cousin?—and nothing at all at our church. They won't hear of it. And there's Swoffords all over this town. None of them have been back to church since."

"Oh, for Christ's sake," Virginia said. "You'd think something like that would straighten folks out instead of getting them all bent out of shape." She crushed her cigarette in the ashtray. A curl of smoke rose from the mangled end.

Susan felt the silence grow. There was more she wanted to say, but they had gotten off track. Finally she ventured, "There was something else, after the service. Something odd."

"What," Virginia said abstractly, knocking another cigarette from her pack.

Susan bit her lip. "Remember Sunny Sohi?"

"Sure."

"Well, he was there."

The cigarette stopped, arrested on its journey to her lips. "Sunny? In your church? Will wonders never cease!"

"I know!"

"Now I wish I had come. God, we haven't hung out together since, what, high school?"

Susan laughed. "Remember how he used to moon around after Harry?"

"Oh brother, do I. What a dope."

"Oh I don't know. It was kinda sweet."

"Mmm-hmm," Virginia said. "Up to a point."

"So, he was there that night." Virginia looked at her, still holding the unlit cigarette. "And I think he was there to see Andy. I think— You know, I think there might be something going on between them." She gave a nervous laugh.

Virginia placed the cigarette carefully on the edge of the ashtray. "What makes you think that?"

"Well, the two of them were in the storeroom quite a while. And then Mrs. Oldfield went in. And Sunny shot out of there like a rabbit."

Virginia looked at her. "That's it?"

"Well, then I came up and I heard Andy and Mrs. Oldfield arguing. And she said something about profaning God's house."

Virginia snorted. "Oh, come on! You're not all tied into knots because of something that old biddy said, are you?" She grabbed Susan's hand. "That woman sees devils in her undies. Probably because no one else can get in there."

"True enough," Susan said, half laughing. "But there's been, well, other things. And I was wondering—maybe—you could ask Harry?"

"Harry? Hah! Harry hasn't said two words to me in a fortnight. I think this whole Poppa-Daddy thing has got him scared shitless." She saw the look in Susan's eyes and decided to change her tone. "Why ask Harry?"

"Well," Susan said, twisting her hand free, "he and Sunny are still friends, I know, and they go out to that little trailer and the pond and stuff, and drink, and I thought maybe they'd—talk, and . . ." She trailed off. "I sound ridiculous, don't I."

Virginia thought for a moment. "No, Suzie-Q. Harry hasn't said a thing to me. And he would have, if there was anything to say."

Susan relaxed. "So, you think there's nothing to it? You don't think Andy and Sunny are—"

"No, I don't." Virginia leaned back in the sofa. "But Suzie, honey, that ain't what matters. What do *you* think? That's what matters."

Susan laughed nervously and looked away. "Oh, I'm just a worry-wart. All this is over nothing."

"And if it isn't?" Susan looked back at her, panic in her eyes. "Honey," Virginia said as gently as she could, "if you have your doubts, you've got to ask him. Not Harry. Not Sunny. Him."

Susan got up quickly. "Oh, no. No, I could never do that. He'd be mortified. *I'd* be mortified!"

Virginia looked at her friend closely. "Then you've got to decide right now whether or not a thing like that matters. It doesn't to me. I decided that long ago with Sunny. He's a bit of a jerk sometimes, but he's okay. And Andy—I like him just the way he is. He's honest, sincere, kind, and that God stuff he spouts, he believes it just enough to keep me interested, and that's saying something."

Her back was to her. "Do you trust him?" she asked.

"Hell, he's baptizing my kid, so, yeah, I trust him. But Suzie-Q, that's not important. Not do *I* trust him, but do *you*. That's all that matters." There was silence in the room. "You do trust him, don't you?"

Susan turned around and faced her, tears running down her cheeks, her lips tight across her face. *Aw, shit,* Virginia thought, *she doesn't know one way or the other.* She was going to have to have a talk with Sunny Sohi.

Chapter 19

The Mind of God

All those who lie for convenience,
All those who lie to be kind,
All those who lie with their silence,
We are standing, . . .

The window over the sink glowed pale blue with predawn light. Andy had not been to bed. Outside, the birds were tuning up the morning chorus, but he sat at the kitchen table, a scrap of paper before him, clenching and unclenching the deadbolt in his hand. He looked down. There were red grooves in his skin. He closed his fist again.

He could not go to bed until he finished the hymn. He had tried five revisions already and cast them all away. He could not go to bed because he'd dream the dream again: the risen Christ, burial windings streaming away as he rose from the tomb, his dark skin glowing as if a layer of gold lay just beneath. He closed his eyes. The deadbolt cut into his palm. He placed it on the countertop and walked into the living room.

There would be no one at the church at this hour. He had the keys. Maybe he should go there.

Or to Sunny's trailer.

We cannot know the mind of God. We can not know it. Oh, we can try. We can pray and we can cry out to the heavens. And we may even think we deserve an answer. Why would God afflict the just? Why create a moment of happiness, a day of delight, and wrap all that promise and joy up in a child, only to snatch it away so suddenly, so cruelly? And we cry out, "Why, Lord? How have I offended thee? Have I not lived according to Thy laws? Have I not kept Thy name in reverence, given Thee honor above all others?

Have I once cheated, or stolen from a neighbor, or coveted another man's wife?" Surely we deserve an answer. Because it is not fair. And we know, if we are just and fear God, God will answer faith with divine justice, divine mercy, divine love.

And He does. I assure you, my dear and suffering sisters, weeping for the loss of your boys. I assure you, my sorrowing brothers, raging with anger and shame at the way your sons were ripped from your arms, so full of life, so full of promise, so full of the future that was their birthright. I assure you, God does feel your suffering, and knows your despair, and hears your cries of "Why? Why?"

And He sends you His divine love. That is His answer. His divine love, His divine justice, His divine mercy.

But how can this be? What is merciful, or just, or loving about how we are left, bereft and undone by these terrible events? These boys, their lives cut short, no more than blades of grass mown down by the single stroke of a terrible scythe!

And I say to you again, it is His divine love, it is His divine justice, it is His divine mercy.

God is God, and we are not. We cannot know the mind of the Lord. For the Lord created all—the oceans and the beasts therein, the sky and its tremendous tumbling clouds, the land, raising up mountains and rolling out prairies and fields, forests and hills. We may cry till our hearts break, but would all our tears fill a single river? We may shout to the heavens, all of us together, everyone in this church, even in this town, but could we be heard above a single thunderclap? The Lord created all these things—mountains and seas, thunderheads and rivers, the spangled majesty of the stars, the snail and the elephant, the hurricane, the breeze, the continents and all the creatures that roam its far ranges, the blazing sun and the glowing moon, the oak and each and every blade of grass—created He them all in a matter of days, in a matter of hours, in the twinkling of an eye, with the uttering of a single word. And as great as all these things are, who can doubt that the Lord is greater than them all? For He created them, and they are for Him to do with as He pleases. It is His purpose, not ours, that the planets follow.

We cannot know the mind of God. And that, dear brothers, humble sisters, is His great mercy. For would you wish to know what great calculus keeps the world from spinning apart in chaos and darkness? If you could, would you care to count each individual and separate act of goodness or evil, comfort or terror, honor or betrayal, and could you then add them up, each in its own ledger, one shining like the dawn and the other blacker than the night, and know how and when they balance? When the Devil cries, "Skin for skin!", would you know how to answer him? The Lord knows, and the Lord makes certain of it, for that is His justice.

The Lord giveth, and the Lord taketh away. I will not tell you to place your hands upon your lips and stifle your sorrow. I will not tell you to hush your pleading, your prayers, your cries for justice. We are, after all, only human.

But I can tell you, God has answered you. He, too, had a Son. And He lost Him. He lost Him for you, so that you might not be lost. And that is His love. It is here, right now, in this church. It embraces you, it holds you up, and it will be there always, until all sorrows cease and all questions fall silent. That is His divine love. And nothing—not even death—can take it from you.

Families gathered in the home of Mr. and Mrs. Daryl Wynn after the double funeral. They shared comfort and covered dishes and the odd bits of gossip that demonstrate how life goes on with its miracles and irritations despite the weight of loss. Pastor Grenville was standing in the archway between the dining room and the front room balancing a remarkably heavy piece of Bundt cake (which he would not eat) on a wobbling paper plate. He was looking at John Swofford, who sat next to his wife on a sofa across the room. Their positions now seemed reversed from when he first met them. She was looking up and speaking occasionally to the women who would come to drop a word of comfort in her ear. But John Swofford sat in that sofa as though at the bottom of a well. The afternoon light poured in from the porch and the side windows facing the Wynns' driveway, but that corner of the room where John

Swofford sat remained unlit and unwarmed. Tremblin' Bob had noticed the man flinch when he'd come to the line in the eulogy about coveting another man's wife. Maybe that's where the root of this man's darkness lay, the guilty spring for all that anger. There was work to do there, healing to perform.

"A fine afternoon, don't you think, Reverend?" said a little man at his elbow.

He was taken aback by the cheery tone. The man wasn't a member of his congregation. One of the Swoffords' kin, then, come over from Croy. "Quite fine for this time of year," Grenville said, "but I doubt it'll do much to lift the spirits in this house."

"Oh, yeah, sure," the man said. "Yeah, my wife's sister, she knows the Swoffords. And of course, I know them through the lumber yard."

"Of course." Grenville smiled. The man wasn't making any sense, but then people rarely did at these affairs.

"I'm JayRob Pautler," the man said, extending his hand, "from Croy. Pautler's Grocery and Dry Goods."

That was a name Tremblin' Bob knew. "And much more than that, I believe. Mayor, too, aren't you?"

"Well, that." The man made a gesture with his hand. "That's more like babysitting."

"I imagine the mayor of a town has quite a lot of responsibilities, much more than babysitting."

"Well, you do have to watch the purse strings pretty tight. And make a speech or two at high school graduations and such."

"And be someone people can look up to."

"Yeah." The man cleared his throat. "I'm also a deacon at Mt. Hermon Bible Church."

Grenville went momentarily on alert. He knew there might be some bad feelings about moving Jink's funeral, but surely Matthew Jacobs hadn't sent a spy. The man wasn't up for that sort of thing.

Pautler went rattling on. "We get some fine sermons up there, but nothing like that eulogy of yours today. I'd like to hear you preach some day."

"Come to our church any Wednesday night or Sunday. You'll be most welcome."

"I'm not over this way much. Wife's folks, mainly, like I said."

"And of course there's the broadcast at 3, 'The Trembling Hour.'"

"Ha. Yeah. Listen, Reverend, I have a proposition to make. I realize this might not be the best time, but I'd like to strike it while the iron is hot, so to speak."

The man was clearly, if clumsily, leading up to something. "Speak what's on your mind, Brother JayRob."

"I'd like to hear you preach in my church some day."

The Reverend Bob Grenville looked at the man. He was about a foot shorter than him, slightly balding, and perspiring a little, though that might be from wearing a suit indoors in this weather. There was nothing sly or hesitant about his manner. Tremblin' Bob decided to take a gamble. "Mt. Hermon has quite a reputation," he said. "I'm not sure I would measure up. That was quite a to-do y'all had there a while back."

"Yep," Pautler said, "'twas."

"Though not, I 'spect, to everyone's liking."

"No. 'Tweren't."

The two men eyed each other a moment in silence, then Grenville nodded. "Yes, I would be most honored to preach at Mt. Hermon. At Pastor Jacobs' invitation, of course."

JayRob Pautler smiled. "Of course," he said.

Chapter 20

Ninevah

John Tibbits made another circuit of the floor, hoping there might be someone down one of the aisles he could help. But there was no one except little Scotty Pritchard asking after Mr. Rosen, so he sent him away. Still, it gave him a thrill to be in charge. He couldn't do anything pharmaceutical, of course, and there were some things he just wouldn't do. He'd been shocked at what he'd found behind the pharmacy counter. *Playboy* and *Photoshoot* and other "magazines." Rosen had only stepped out for a minute, but if the store were John's, there wouldn't be any of that filth lying around, that's for sure. He should start a list of the things he'd change.

The bell over the door rang and a lovely woman in a yellow and white sun dress stepped in. John's smile broadened as he stepped behind the pharmacy counter. "Good afternoon, Mrs. Tibbits," he said.

"Good afternoon, Mr. Tibbits," Ruth said, smiling broadly.

"Is there anything I can get for you, ma'am?"

"Oh, nothing, really," she said, lightly fingering the toothbrush display. "I just come by to admire a man who's moving up in the world."

John's professional demeanor dissolved. "It's something, isn't it? My second week on the job and I'm already running the store. The whole store! All by myself! Pautler would never let me do that, and I been there more'n two years."

"You're all by yourself?"

"Yes indeedy!"

"Not even Rachel?"

John shrugged. "Haven't seen her in days."

"Well, I am proud of you, John."

She beamed at him, then blushed and looked down. A shadow of worry crossed John's heart. "What is it?"

"Well," she said, still not looking up, "I actually could use something. Something medicinal."

John swallowed. "I— I can't do prescriptions, you know."

"Oh, no, it's nothing like that." She smiled and looked up. "Just a little Kaopectate, maybe."

"Honey, is there something wrong?"

Ruth adored her husband. She even adored the look of panic that swept across his face. She was glad she'd had that little talk with Virginia Alquist (Edom now, wasn't it?) so she was prepared for this reaction. "Oh, it's nothing, really. Just a little queasiness now and then. In the morning." She continued smiling up at him, letting it sink in, and loving him all the more when it didn't. Virginia had been right. Most men are as dumb as a box of nuts.

Across the square, JayRob Pautler stood behind the counter and surveyed rows of groceries, canned goods, hardware, and kitchen supplies. He'd forgotten how much he enjoyed this view, watching the seasonal ebb and flow of customer demand. Gardening and picnic supplies would soon give way to pencil boxes, erasers, and crisp spiral-bound notebooks. He could practically smell them.

The door opened and Avril Rosen walked in. "Howdy, Abe," he bellowed. "What can I do you for?" JayRob always called Avril "Abe." Avril didn't seem to mind and never corrected him. Avril always called him "Robert." Likewise and ditto.

"It's our local artist I've come looking for," Avril said. "I thought I saw him stop by."

"Huh. Jed Tucker was just in here asking the same. Popular guy. Nope. He's out to the brick works most days, firing up the kilns. And getting in everybody's hair, I hear. If he ain't at the library, or out at the kilns, he's squirreled away at his trailer."

"Ah."

The man looked disappointed so JayRob thought to cheer him up. "I think I got the better end of that swap."

"Pardon?"

"I lost a grocery clerk and you got one, but you lost a tenant to boot. Less income, more expense! I think I got the better end o' that deal, Abe."

Avril smiled. "You did at that, Robert. I never could put one over on you."

JayRob beamed. Now they were all nice and cozy. "Anything else, Abe?"

"Yes. I know it's past the season, but I was wondering if you might have some grass seed."

"Seed?" JayRob paused. "I don't think you'll have much luck with seed this time of year. What you want is sod. Over at Swofford's."

Avril smiled. "I don't think I'll need all that much."

JayRob did some quick calculations. *Yes,* he admitted to himself, *for the amount of lawn being replaced, seed might actually be the way to go. If you wanted to cut costs, that is.* He smiled. That Abe. Always a shrewd one with the numbers. "Seed it is, then. You'll find it in aisle five, Abe. Fertilizer, too. Just in time, by the way. That stuff will all be gone next week."

Abe found and fetched a packet of Bermuda blue (no fertilizer, though) and paid for it in coins. He waved away the receipt and headed for the door. JayRob was dropping the coins into the register when he heard someone call out, "Mr. Rosen!" He looked up and saw Scotty Pritchard tugging on Abe's sleeve.

"I've been meaning to talk to you, Mr. Rosen," Scotty said.

"There's no need, young man."

That's a mighty cold tone coming from old Abe, thought JayRob.

"Please, Mr. Rosen. I've got to talk to you. It wasn't me. I wasn't there. I wasn't with them that night."

Rosen took a step toward the door.

"I wasn't there, Mr. Rosen!" Scotty said. "I swear to you!"

Avril Rosen turned around. JayRob had never seen such a look on him before. He wouldn't have thought the man capable.

"Do not swear to me!" Avril Rosen said. "I know where you were that night. And with whom! And that is why you will not see or speak to her again. Not ever."

"Please, Mr. Rosen. I've got to! I—"

"Not ever!" Avril Rosen dismissed Scotty with a gesture and left.

The boy stood trembling just inside the door. He was crying, blubbering something, though JayRob couldn't make out what. That annoyed him. He sure didn't want the kid hanging around in such a state. He shoved the cash drawer shut, letting its sharp ring put an end to the whole sorry episode.

At the Kennsing County Savings and Loan next door, Cyrus Brown watched his Vice President, Henry Otis, use his charm to fill the silences with amiable palaver into which the occasional "Sign here" could be slipped as easily as a razor into a peach.

"It's a great day for Croy," Otis was saying. "This will bring employment, growth, a new neighborhood. Sign here."

The woman seated before them paused briefly before signing yet another document. To Cyrus Brown, Clara Oldfield looked tired, as if the pen were a shovelful of dirt she had been lifting all day.

"And growth is good, change is good," Henry Otis said.

The woman sniffed. "Change is change. It depends on what's growing."

"And one last one, Mrs. Oldfield, here. This makes it final."

Cyrus thought she aged visibly as she lifted the pen. Then she stopped. Was she wavering again? She'd been tough enough to deal with already. He didn't want any accusations afterward. "Are you having second thoughts?" he asked.

Henry Otis looked at Brown as if he'd lost his mind. Cyrus ignored him. Henry turned back. "You've made the right decision, Clara," he said.

She eyed him hard. "I'd prefer if you didn't use my Christian name, Mr. Otis."

"Of course, Mrs. Oldfield. But by signing these properties over to the Development Trust, you have secured your future."

"I've given up my future, you mean."

"You could back out," Cyrus said. He ignored Henry's muffled yelp.

She looked at him steadily for a moment. "No," she said and leaned forward and signed the last document. "You'll make sure the right sort of people move in there."

She was talking to him, ignoring Otis entirely. "We'll look out after you, Mrs. Oldfield," he said.

"You can trust us," his Vice President added.

She didn't appear as though she did, but then she gave a short, quick nod, dropped the pen she had brought herself back into her purse and snapped it shut. "We can send you the originals and a copy or—" Henry Otis started.

"Just put them in my safe deposit box. I don't want to look at them."

"Ah, I don't think we—"

"We'll take care of it, Mrs. Oldfield," Cyrus said. "Do you need a ride home?"

"I have my own car. Thank you." There was a brief silence that even Henry Otis didn't interrupt. "Good afternoon," she said and rose.

They did, too, and Henry Otis showed her to the door. Once he had closed it behind her, he exhaled and shook his head. "I just don't get it."

"Get what?"

"That Oldfield tract makes up nearly all the prime real estate south and west of town. She's never farmed it, never ranched it, still holds the mineral rights. By selling, she's made enough money to set herself up for life."

"So?"

"*So*? She's acting like it's the end of the world! I've never seen someone so tore up over making a fortune."

"She's not 'tore up.' She got us to take on those two sharecropper shacks as well, and got our word we'd sell them to 'the right people' so she won't have to worry about colored folks moving in from across the river. She knows what she's doing."

"Yeah, the old girl can bargain, I'll give her that. But still she's not happy! I just don't understand it."

"There's nothing to understand," Cyrus said settling back into his chair. "Call Pritchard. Tell him he can go ahead."

"There's still the other party—"

"You let me take care of him. Call Pritchard." He reached for a cigar from the bodark box on his desk. There was a soft knock on the frosted glass of the door. "Come in," he said as he snipped off the end.

"I beg your pardon, Mr. Brown, Mr. Otis."

"What is it, Emily?"

"Mr. Edom is here again, sir. About the checks. He insists on talking to you."

Cyrus smiled at Henry Otis. "You see?" he said. Henry Otis smiled back and turned to Emily. "Tell Mr. Edom we'll see him directly," he said.

Outside on the sidewalk, the sunlight dazzled Clara Oldfield. Why was the sun so bright today? Why did the trees look so sharp-edged and dangerous, and the cars go tearing by at breakneck speeds? She got into her car, but it was impossibly warm, having sat in the mid-day sun for an hour. She rolled down the window on her side and would have rolled down the passenger side if she could have reached it. She should get and tend to it, but that would take time. People were depending on her. She turned the key in the ignition and pulled away from the curb.

Two blocks later, she had to pull over, her eyes flooded with tears. "Oh, I don't have time for this!" she said, pressing a handkerchief to her eyes. She took several deep breaths and stared out the windshield, not seeing the elms or the patterned shadows they cast on the street. "You understand, don't you Gerald?" she said. "I just can't look after them anymore. I can't hold them if I can't care for them. I had to let them go." Her mind was perfectly calm. She knew her reasons were good ones, and they sounded even better when she said them aloud. But her tears weren't listening. They had reasons of their own.

Three miles from town, Jedediah Tucker's Ford rattled to a stop outside Sunny's trailer. The billow of summer dust he'd been trailing caught up and swept past him. He expected Sunny to appear when he opened his door, but only cicadas and red-winged blackbirds greeted him. "Sunny?" he called. No answer.

He climbed the metal stoop to the trailer, nearly losing his balance as it tottered under him. "Sunny?" he called again, his voice rising. He tried the door. It was unlocked.

He stepped in and looked around. The place was a mess. It had always been a mess, but this was a granddaddy of a mess, like a backhoe had gone berserk inside, digging up layers of books, papers, art supplies, crockery, and flinging them any which way. "Jesus smacking Christ," he muttered.

"What?" said a figure rising from behind the easel.

It was Sunny all right, but unlike Tucker had ever seen him. He looked like a madman. Hair down nearly to his shoulders, unshaven, shirt filthy, and dark pouches under his eyes that made them glow like coals. "What the hell happened to you?" he asked.

"I'm busy," Sunny said, raking his hand through his hair. It got caught. "What do you want?"

Tucker frowned. There were a dozen petty reasons he'd come out here, including delivering the paychecks Sunny hadn't picked up. But the truth was all he had, so he offered that. "I'm leaving. OU renewed their scholarship offer, so I signed up."

"Congratulations." Sunny's eyes weren't on him. They scurried around the top of the easel, searching the open books and magazines for something.

Tucker watched him and a strange feeling crept over him. It was like looking at one of those lizards that climbs up on a rock and does push-ups, vigilant, quick, but oblivious to the giant standing next to it. "He really got to you, didn't he?"

"Who?"

"That's why you hang around here all weekend. You expect him to come back."

"I don't know what you're talking about."

Tucker nodded. "Yeah. Like usual." He dropped the paychecks on a folding table, briefly noting at least three others, all unopened. He turned and opened the trailer door. Brass-colored light burst into the room. He squinted warily at the stoop. "Ain't you ever gonna fix these god-damned steps?"

"Gophers," Sunny said. He was on the other side of the room now, waving distractedly.

Tucker shook his head and stepped carefully down to the parched earth. Just walking puffed up little cyclones of red dust. He climbed into the truck and backed into a Y-turn. He stopped for a moment, the rattling transmission adding its voice to the comments of red-winged blackbirds in the bushes. Maybe there was something more he should do. But then again, maybe there wasn't. *Aw, to hell with it*, he thought. He ground the gears shifting into first and rattled down the hill to the hard road.

Chapter 21

A Woman's Place

"Now, then, what's to be the size of this beast?" Tremblin' Bob said, rubbing his hands together as he settled into the padded leather chair. His threw his famous smile around the room, pausing at each individual in the pastor's office: Pastor Jacobs himself; Brother JayRob Pautler, the deacon whose invitation brought him here; Andy Simms, the music minister; and Jacobs's daughter, Susan. "I thought seven nights. Seven is usually enough to bring even the most sin-sick to the rail."

"We could open with 'There Is a Balm in Gilead,'" Simms offered, scrounging through a folder in his lap.

"Splendid!"

Pautler coughed. "Perhaps we could settle the matter of the stipend, first?"

"Andy's got this terrific new hymn—" Susan added.

"But first—" Pautler threw in.

The Reverend Grenville held up his hands and grinned again. Andy closed his folder and the others stopped talking. When he had their attention, he looked at Jacobs. "Is there any coffee, I wonder? This weather has left me a tad droopy."

Jacobs looked embarrassed. "Mrs. Oldfield usually makes the coffee and takes the notes. Susan?"

Susan shrugged. "I don't know where she is. She's left everything set up in the kitchen. It's not like her to miss out."

"Miss out?"

Jacobs smiled.

"She's much more than the church secretary, Brother Bob. Mrs. Oldfield keeps this outfit running."

"Then who will take notes?" Grenville turned up his hands as if confessing. "I'm hopeless at it, I'm afraid. Can't make out my own handwriting more than two hours after I jot things down. My dear wife, Birdine, has earned her place in Paradise if for nothing else than she types them up right there on the spot."

"It's a shame she could not be with us."

"Duties elsewhere," Tremblin' Bob said with a grin, imagining his steely-eyed beauty sizing up the town as she casually shopped around the square. But this meeting would set the tone for the next two weeks and notes had to be taken. He turned to the pastor's daughter. "How about you, my dear?"

She turned pink from neck to ear-tip. "I've— I don't . . . take short-hand."

"Oh. Well." He turned away. "Brother Andy? Surely they taught you something practical at that northern academy?"

"I'd be happy to," Simms said. "Just As I Am" slid onto the floor as he fumbled for his notebook.

"Still, Mrs. Oldfield will be sadly missed," Grenville said. "She was to be my ride to the Claremont. Not to mention the coffee. Sister Susan, would you be a treasure and make some for us? Isn't it funny how coffee can cool you down on a hot day?"

Miss Jacobs looked like she had something to say, but Reverend Jacobs stepped in. "It's all right, Susan," he said calmly. She looked from her father to the music director, then left with a "Hmph!"

Grenville smiled. "Now," he said as if nothing at all had happened, "I thought I'd like to start our endeavor with a prayer." In a fluid motion he raised his large frame from the chair and knelt on the carpet with hands clasped and head bowed. Even with his eyes closed, he could hear Pastor Jacobs quickly follow, coming from behind his desk to kneel beside him. The whisper of music sheets sliding to the floor meant Simms had joined them. He assumed the grunt and creak was Pautler going down on his knees.

"Lord," Grenville prayed, "we are grateful to be here today, to under-take this great work. Clear our minds of mundane clutter, open our hearts to all good intention, open a way for Your Holy Spirit, and allow us to surrender to Your inspiration, not vying for stature nor stretching for vain glory. Make us pure vessels of Thy Holy Will, which dispels all strife, relieves all sorrow, and brings health, prosperity, and peace to those in whom You find favor. Bless us, Lord, that we may bring this church back to full health, that we may bring its people back to full faith, and install Thy Son, Thy Spirit, and Thy Word in the hearts of all men. Restore Thy people, O Lord, in Jesus' name we ask it. Amen."

Pautler's and Jacobs's *Amen*s sounded clearly, but there was a breathiness to Simms's, which he noted. They all rose and took their seats except Pautler, who remained standing. "About the stipend . . ." he said.

Grenville shrugged. "Of course, I will accept nothing for myself but a love offering. Whatever the Spirit moves people to give, that is all I need." Pautler relaxed. "There are other considerations, of course," he continued, "but my wife generally takes care of those."

"Perhaps we should wait until she joins us," Jacobs suggested.

Pautler twitched. "Well, that's all well and good, but I do have a store to tend to—"

"Oh, forgive us, Brother JayRob," Grenville said, turning his smile on the man. "I didn't realize you were pressed for time. I'll have Birdine call on you at your store. How's that?"

"Well, if it's all right with Pastor."

"I'll leave the details up to you, Brother JayRob," Jacobs said.

"Okay, fine. Sure. I just wanted to make sure we, uh, that we all agreed, that is, that we render unto Caesar, you know." He smiled tightly. "Right?"

Grenville frowned. "Well, in this case, actually, no."

"I leave it in your hands, brother. You'll do fine. You always do."

"I'm sure Mt. Hermon can depend on your diligence. Don't let us keep you from your obligations, brother." Grenville turned the searchlight of his gaze on the music director. "Now, Brother Andy, do you have a copy of that hymn Susan mentioned? Just to see where it might fit in most beautifully."

The young man blushed. "It's . . . it's not ready."

Susan was in the kitchen scrubbing the inside of the percolator with a vengeance when Andy emerged. His hands trembled and a handful of hymns threatened to escape his grasp and sort themselves on the floor. "Are they still in there?" she asked.

"Yes," Andy said. "It's amazing. He has these themes—"

Tremblin' Bob came out of the office and hurried across the kitchen to the restroom without giving either of them a glance.

Susan threw her brush into the sink. "He's insufferable!"

Andy looked shocked. "What do you mean? He knows what he's doing."

"Did you see how he practically threw me out?"

"He just asked you for some coffee."

"And then found something else for me to do when I brought it in. You'd think this was his church, not Daddy's."

"Well, it's his revival, after all."

"His show, you mean."

"Don't say that. He really does heal people."

She shrugged. "Some people, I guess."

"Why are you talking this way?"

"Andy, it's just a revival. A way to get some money back into the church."

"It's more than that! It's real. It's his gift. We're lucky to get him."

"You're not taking his side, are you?"

"There are no sides in this, young lady," her father's voice said from the doorway. "And it's not my church. It's God's. We're all equals here."

She looked down but didn't give up. "Yeah, well, some are more equal than others."

Her father came up beside her. "Don't quote Orwell, dear. It's boastful. Besides," he kissed her on the forehead, "we do need the money."

"I'm sorry I'm late," Mrs. Oldfield said, standing in the kitchen doorway. "I—"

"Mrs. Oldfield!" Tremblin' Bob boomed from across the room. He crossed briskly and took her hand. "How we've missed you. Susan here did a splendid job—" a look of incredulity passed between Susan and Mrs. Oldfield "—but no one can replace the true handmaiden of Mt. Hermon. Do you know your blackberry pie, famous as it is at your own church bazaars, is even more famous in Dibble City?"

"Well, I—"

"Are you hungry, Brother Bob?" Pastor Jacobs said.

"I am never hungry, Brother Matthew. But I am a great fan of blackberry pie."

"I— I have some at home," Mrs. Oldfield stammered.

"Do you indeed? Wonderful, wonderful! You see? The Lord doth provide!"

Harry knew what Virginia would say. He toyed with using Lerner's restraining order as a reason to put off telling her, but no one, not even Percy Owen, took that seriously now. Everyone knew they were hitched. Still, he paused under the forbidding sandstone arch of the porch before knocking. He ran through a hundred excuses, including blaming everything on Tucker. Hell, that was half true. If Old Stone Face hadn't up and quit to chase some fool notion of a football scholarship at OU, the business might have made a go of it. But in the end, he had to admit selling it was his own decision. He squared his shoulders and, a condemned man, stepped up and knocked.

"Come in!"

Virginia's voice carried clearly from deep inside the house.

Great, he thought. *They'll be able to hear her blow up clear across the county.*

At least the stone walls of the Alquist mansion kept the inside cool on an August afternoon. Virginia was seated on a couch in the parlor. A cigarette had burned to ash in the tray on the table beside her, apparently abandoned after being lit.

"Hey, lover!" Virginia said.

Harry beamed and leaned in to kiss her. "A bit more than that, now."

She returned his kiss. "You'll never be more than that to me 'cuz that's all I need."

He sighed and sat down beside her. "Welp, much as I'd like to agree with you, I reckon I need to be a bit more. For you and young whatsis there."

"Speaking of, I've been thinking about names. What do you think about—"

Harry held up his hands. "I, uh— I want to talk about that, yeah. But I want to talk about something else first."

"Ooo, the strong type," Virginia said. "I like that." But her eyes had gotten sharp as arrows and she was tapping out another cigarette.

"Ginny." He took a breath. "Ginny, I know what you've said and I know what we've planned, but it looks like we, like you, are just going to have to keep living here for a while longer."

She went rock-still. "Longer."

"A while longer."

"How much longer?"

"I've just about got things lined up—"

"How much longer, Harry."

He steeled himself. "Three months."

"Fucking shit!"

"Ginny—"

"I am god-damn fucking *not* bringing a baby into this house!"

"Ginny, listen!"

"No, numb nuts, you listen! You have no idea what my father is like, what he's said about me, about this baby! He is not getting his twisted hateful claws anywhere near my kid!"

"Our kid."

"Yes! *Yes.*" She grabbed his hands in hers. There were tears in her eyes. He had expected lots of things, but he hadn't expected tears. "Our kid." She moved one of his hands to her belly. "In our house, under our roof. Safe, quiet, clean, bright."

"I don't have anything like that."

"Then get one, Harry. Get anything. Anything at all. I can't raise a kid here. Not in this mausoleum full of ghosts."

"You can't raise him in a construction foreman's trailer, either."

"You think not? Try me. Move me in there. Do it now. Do it today."

He looked at her. This was not Ginny: goading, joking Ginny. This was a woman fighting for her family. God in heaven, he loved her. And that made it all the harder. "I can't," he said. "I can't even do that."

"Give me one good reason."

He swallowed. "Because I don't have a trailer. I sold it. I sold it, and I took the money and I invested it."

She dropped his hands. "Get it back."

"I can't. I can't for three months. By then it will be worth almost twice as much. It's a short-term loan, you see—"

"Fuck you."

"Ginny, don't."

"You did all this, this bargaining away of our life, our home, our family, and you didn't even once come to me about it? You didn't once ask me what I thought? What I felt? What I wanted? Fuck you."

Harry stood up. "No," he said. "I'm not your lover, Ginny. I'm your husband. And there are some decisions I get to make. And I've made one. I didn't need to ask because I didn't need your permission and I already knew your answer I want that home as much as you do, and I swear to God we are going to get it. But we're going to get it my way. And if you can't trust my judgment on that, then you can't trust me. And, baby, that's all I want, that's all I ask. Trust me." He looked at her. She was looking up at him like she was trying to see right through his skin into the future of his soul. He got down on one knee and took her hands. "All the love in the world falls to pieces if you don't trust me."

She held his gaze for what seemed like forever, then she nodded and looked away. He got up and brushed off his jeans. "I'll be back later," he said, "and maybe we can talk about them names." She nodded, still not looking at him, and he let himself out.

Virginia reached for her forgotten cigarettes but doubled up when she felt a fierce kick from inside. She clutched her side. "Who's side are you on, anyway?" she said, rubbing a spot below her liver. She looked down the hallway where Harry had gone. "I bet I can guess."

Birdine Grenville knocked softly on the door to their rooms at the Claremont before entering. Her husband didn't like people walking in on him. He was sitting on the bed, an open Bible and a glucose test kit beside him. He had on his reading glasses and held a pen in his left hand. Another pen, forgotten, was tucked behind his ear, and in his right hand he clutched a legal pad covered in scrawls she would be turning into English on her Smith Corona.

"Ah, Birdie," he greeted her. "Did you get what we needed?"

"Yes. No trouble at all."

"You got it from the Jew, right? That other one, the Tibbits boy, he's a member at Mt. Hermon."

She raised both eyebrows at him. "I'm not a fool, Robert. I know who to talk to." She laid the glass syringes out on the table by the bed. "I picked up a little something else while I was there, too."

Robert examined the syringes with indifference. "Oh?" He got a test strip from the kit.

"You might be surprised by what's available behind the counter."

He looked at her and smiled. "Really? My dear Birdie!"

"And Rosen's daughter, Rachel? Whisked off to Chicago, apparently, to remove her from the clutches of a local boy—who just happens to go to Mt. Hermon."

"Better and better." He pricked his finger and squeezed out a drop of blood. "I've had some luck, myself. The Widow Oldfield is quite a gold mine of information. You'd be surprised what treasures can be dug up in a simple country kitchen over blackberry pie." He looked up to see her reaction.

She smiled. "Well, a woman's place is in the home."

Chapter 22

A Matter of Perspective

JayRob Pautler was pleased with himself. As he had predicted, the revival meetings brought people back to Mt. Hermon. The immediate benefit was to the church, of course, but if Grenville permanently moved "The Trembling Hour" to the local radio station, the whole town would benefit. His own store had already seen an uptick. Not a bad day's work for a shopkeeper, a church deacon, and a mayor all rolled into one!

The sight of Lerner Alquist bearing down on him tore him from reverie. *What's got a bee in his bonnet?* he wondered, coming out from behind the counter.

"What the hell are you playing at, Pautler?" Alquist demanded.

"Good to see you, too, Lerner. Is there something I can get you?"

"You brought that damned preacher here, didn't you?"

JayRob smiled proudly. "I did indeed. And a fine day's work—"

"Are you deliberately trying to sabotage my project, or is that just a convenient side effect?"

"Well, you've got me stumped there, Lerner. I don't know what in God's green heaven you—"

"The pledges, Pautler! They've dried up. People aren't meeting their pledges. They're saying it's a sin to spend money on statues to themselves, that it's idolatry or some such bullshit. And it's that damned preacher who's feeding it to them!"

JayRob frowned. "Well, I'm sure that isn't what he—"

"Get him to stop, you hear? Get him to stop or I'll slap a libel suit on him so fast it'll make his fat-lipped head spin!"

JayRob drew himself up and took a step forward. Lerner towered over him by almost a foot, but at that moment, JayRob felt the bigger man. "Now just one minute, there, Mr. Alquist. You may own half the county, but you do not own people's souls. You may tell them where and when they can work, but you cannot tell them how to pray. Nobody can tell them that. Not even New York Alquist! Because God has the final say. *He* does, not New York!"

Lerner drew back, anger and bafflement at war on his face. Then he snarled and left the store.

JayRob looked around. There were people in the aisles, but each turned to inspect some bin or canned goods when his gaze fell on them. He gave his apron a sharp tug and slapped the cash register.

Lerner Alquist cut across the courthouse lawn, his mind clicking away. *Own half the county?* Well, at least Pautler still thought so. If Pautler was fooled, so were most people. But "most people" was not "all," and one person in particular worried him. And sure enough, as he approached his offices, there was Cyrus Brown's lackey, Henry Otis, lying in wait.

"A word, Mr. Alquist?" was his opening. Not even "Good afternoon."

"I'm a busy man, Mr. Otis." Lerner brushed past him and started up the stairs. "If this is business, I'm headed for my office. You can join me there as you please."

Henry Otis's steps echoed behind him up the stairwell, neither of them saying a word. Lerner turned the key in the lock and strode past the empty receptionist's desk and into his office. He left the door open and stood looking out the window as Otis settled into a chair behind him. He could just imagine the smug smile on the man's face. It made his blood boil. But you didn't show that to people like Henry Otis. Lerner turned around with as bland an expression as possible and said, "So?"

"Where's Ellie?"

None of your damned business is what he wanted to say. Instead he let a smile creep up the side of his face. "If she's the one you came to see, you needn't have waited. You have my full permission to see her in my absence."

"That's all right." The man brushed an imaginary scrap of lint from his trousers. "I think I know where to find her."

Enough of this. "I have a trip to prepare for, Mr. Otis, so I'd appreciate it if you'd get about your business so I can get about mine."

"Very well, if we're being candid."

Lerner sat behind his desk. "As candid as the day is long. Which is not to say we've got all day. Get to the point."

"Okay. The point is this. We that is, the Savings and Loan—have been honoring your drafts for the past few months. Drafts for which there have not always been sufficient funds in the account against which they were drawn."

"Cyrus is well aware of the cash flow into and out of that account. There has always been sufficient cash backed by collateral to balance by the end of each quarter. That has been our agreement."

"Yes, that has been our agreement. But we cannot continue it beyond the end of this quarter."

"That's the end of the month. Less than a week!"

"If the new terms—"

"If Cyrus Brown wants a new note, he can damned well hammer it out in person."

"It is not just Mr. Brown—"

"I'll bet your ass it isn't! It's the new development, isn't it? Pritchard and that crowd. They're calling the shots now, are they?"

The man shrugged. "I am not at liberty to—"

"Oh, get the hell out of here, Henry. If Brown has something to say to me, he knows the way to the stairs. Or if that's too taxing, he can try the god-damned elevator. He had it installed in the first place so he wouldn't have to break wind hauling his guts up here." He looked Brown's man in the eye. "He does know how to use an Otis, doesn't he?"

Lerner enjoyed seeing how much effort it took for Henry to keep his temper. The man rose slowly. "If, as you say, you are leaving town on 'business,' then when might Mr. Brown expect to find you in?"

Lerner stood, pretending to consult a calendar. "Tuesday."

Henry nodded. "Tuesday then."

They stood staring at each other, then Lerner cocked his head and raised his eyebrows. "Well?" he said smiling. "I'm sure you have other 'business,' too, Mr. Otis?"

Henry's face slipped and his anger flashed through for a second, then he left.

The smile left Lerner's face as soon as the outer door closed. Something had to be done to get cash flowing into the Foundation again, but selling out to that upstart Pritchard was out of the question. He wouldn't get one damned square inch! But if the Foundation went belly-up, there'd be nothing of his legacy left.

A grin that would have chilled even a banker's heart broke on his face. The Alquist Legacy? Hah! Ada's books were safe and sound in the Library, untouchable. But there were other things: a few deeds, some equities, some ruined land not worth mortgaging. They were crap, but he would not let Cyrus Brown get his hands on them. Or Harry, and that meant Virginia, too. That left . . .

He was going to have to take a business trip after all. He'd been bluffing Henry, but now he knew what he had to do. And there wasn't a lawyer in town he trusted to keep his mouth shut about it. He gathered his papers.

Sunny slammed his fist against the easel, sending clay powder flying from its frame. "What do you mean, 'not ready'?"

Harry looked at Tucker, Tucker looked back. "I mean the mountings have been there for years, decades really, and, well, we haven't tested them and—"

"Son of a fucking bitch!" Sunny threw a hammer across the shop floor. The heat from the twenty-foot furnaces penetrated even here. Sunny had stripped to the waist and tied his hair back. The finished panels, finally cooled after their turn in the ovens, sat in wooden frames draped in canvas, waiting to be secured with thick hemp rope for transport to the library.

"Well, what do you want us to do? Install them only to have them crash down on some hapless shmoe?"

"How the hell should I know? I'm not a construction engineer! I'm not even the architect! Nobody knows who the hell the architect is!"

"Well, don't blame me, for Christ's sake!"

Sunny yanked off his kerchief and hair tumbled to his shoulders. "And how are people supposed to view this marvel, huh? Have them come in here, trouping through this hell-hole?"

"It'll be cooler soon," Tucker offered.

"You may think this is all very funny," Sunny said, "but this is not just some plaster job in a church. This is my *life*."

"Oh, come on. This ain't the Sistine Chapel. It's a library, for Christ's sake."

"I poured everything I have into this sculpture. Everything I am, everything I want is riding on it."

Harry nodded, red-faced. "I have a lot riding on it, too. I face penalties if we don't finish on time. But safety comes first. Think of the people."

"The people?" Sunny pointed to the panels. "*There* are the people! But they'll never know it if they never see it!"

"They'll see it, just later."

"The dedication is Monday!"

"I have a notion," Tucker said. He nodded at the wooden frames. "The panels are done. The frames are solid enough to transport them. They're also solid enough to display them. We'll set them up behind the speaker's stand on the library steps."

"*Behind* the speaker's stand?"

"That might work."

"It sure as hell won't! They were made to be seen *above* the entrance, not head on."

"In front, behind, above. What's the difference?"

Sunny let out a howl and crouched into a ball, his hands on his head.

"What?" Harry looked at Tucker, who shook his head. "Sunny, they'll still get to see it."

There was a small cough behind them. Harry and Tucker turned to see Miss Ida Laine Lancaster in a calf-length dress with matching gloves, purse, and hat standing in the doorway. "I think," Miss Lancaster said, "what Mr. Sohi objects to is the matter of perspective." She regarded Sunny in his crouch a moment, then entered addressing the other two. "The tympanum is above the heads of people entering the library. They must look up to see the figures. So Mr. Sohi has skillfully crafted the proportions to be seen from below. Is that not so, Mr. Sohi?" Sunny peered up at her suspiciously. She smiled. "It is the art of perspective employed since the Renaissance; Michelangelo, for instance. So you see, Mr. Edom, comparisons to the Sistine Chapel are not out of order."

There was silence. Sunny rose and reached for his shirt.

"Hoist 'em," Tucker said.

"What?" Sunny's eyes flashed again, but Miss Lancaster raised a gloved hand.

Tucker cleared his throat. "We still have the cranes we used for the dome. We could hoist the panels in their frames behind the speakers' platform. They won't be as high as the, um—"

"Tympanum," Sunny said through clenched teeth.

"Yeah. But they'll be up there, you know, for folks to see. From perspective."

Miss Lancaster looked at Sunny, who nodded and turned away, shrugging on his shirt.

"Great," Harry said, rubbing his hands together. "We'll get some trucks, and—"

"I'll tell Ethan to get the cranes ready," Tucker said.

"Fine," Sunny muttered.

"Well," Harry said, "we've got work to do. Ma'am." He tipped his head to her and left with Tucker.

Miss Ida Laine Lancaster studied Sunny Sohi's back for a while. Finally, he turned and said, "Thanks. I don't think I could have explained it to those blockheads."

"Explanations are what librarians are for."

"Still, thanks. You showed up in the nick of time." He looked at her puzzled. "Why did you show up, anyway?"

Miss Lancaster stepped up to the shrouded panels and examined them. "No doubt you've heard of Mr. Armbruster's condition?"

"Yes. How is the old gent?"

"As good as can be expected for a man of his age. Mrs. Armbruster is hopeful. But it appears increasingly unlikely that he will be able to speak at the dedication."

"Oh. That's a shame. He was always a champion of the project. Who will speak?"

Miss Lancaster looked away. "Perhaps now you won't be so thankful. Mayor Pautler will be the speaker. He has asked me to prepare some . . . notes for him to use at the dedication."

"Notes. About the sculpture."

Miss Lancaster nodded.

He shook his head. "I saw this coming. It's one last check, isn't it? A final screening for idolatry and obscenity. Why doesn't he come out here and look for himself? Ask me to plaster over some genitals, or chisel flat an exposed breast, or coat the whole damned thing in whitewash."

Miss Lancaster smiled. "Would you?"

"Like hell I would!"

"I think Mayor Pautler is enough of a politician to sense that, Mr. Sohi. Even Pope Gregory relented at last. Besides, it's not that kind of sculpture, is it? I've spoken to most of the folks you've had sit for the figures. They're not the sort I would expect to see strutting around town in a loin cloth or baring their breasts on their way to the five and dime."

"So, what, then?"

"Well, he really does want to say something pertinent, and he is—you might not believe this, but—he is perceptive enough—"

Sunny barked a laugh.

"He is fully aware of the effect he has on your temper, and so has sent someone else to do the research."

Sunny looked her in the eye. "No one has seen the finished panels."

"If that is the way you would like it to stay, Mr. Sohi, then I bid you good-day."

Sunny strode over to the first panel and flung back the tarp. He instantly saw a change in Miss Lancaster's expression. The genteel Southern lady fell away and a sharp-eyed explorer took over. *My God*, he thought, *that's a look I should have captured!* He went to the other panels and revealed them.

She examined them all. She took off her gloves, but Sunny didn't think for a moment she would touch the figures. It was, he thought, so she could feel the space around them, the air they shared with the viewer.

Examining the panel depicting the 1935 tornado, she said, "I see you've studied John Steuart Curry."

"Curry understood how this land shapes people, for better or worse."

"Yet this moves beyond Regionalism. Neither Robert Garrison nor Donald De Lue."

Sunny snorted. "De Lue's a vulgarian."

She regarded the veterans panel next. One soldier, nearly naked, was dead; the other, stripped to the waist, held his comrade with one arm while the other raised a rifle with fixed bayonet. She raised her eyebrows. "Nisus and Euryalus?"

"You know a lot about art for a small town librarian, Miss Lancaster."

"It's a very good library, Mr. Sohi. And I owe a lot to my studies under Dr. Robinson at the University of Tulsa." She looked again at the figures. "Where did you matriculate?"

"I studied at the University of Oklahoma, under Bruce Goff."

"Their collaboration on the Boston Avenue Methodist Church is one of the jewels of American architecture. Did you finish your degree?"

He shrugged. "I audited, mostly. Mr. Goff was very generous with his time." *Among other things*, he thought.

She leaned closer to examine the face of the fallen soldier. "Ah," she said, straightening up. "You have more in common with Michelangelo than I supposed. You've included your own 'face of St. Bartholomew.' Of course, from below, no one will see it."

"Just so."

She smiled. She looked back and forth between the veterans panel and the center panel with its civic figures. The face of Mayor Paulter flanked one side of the Goddess of Prosperity, Mrs. Armbruster the other. A rancher who resembled John Tibbitts leaned against a wagon wheel beneath them "You say no one has seen all three panels assembled side-by-side?"

"No."

"But if I'm not mistaken, the soldier's bayonet will be pointing directly at—"

"Precisely."

She smiled. "Thank you, Mr. Sohi. I think I have all I need. You have drawn the fragments of our history together, a sum greater than its parts. Perhaps we will learn to look at each other in a new way. You ask much of us, Mr. Sohi."

"If you wish to draw down fire, you reach for the stars."

"Yes," Miss Lancaster said, pulling on her gloves, "but Prometheus paid a price."

Sunny began replacing the tarps. He heard Miss Lancaster say, "Virginia," on her way out. "Miss Lancaster," came the reply. He turned.

Virginia stepped onto the shop floor. "So it's done, then?"

"Ginny! For weeks I work alone, and today I'm flooded with visitors."

"Harry brought me out. He's waiting in the truck." Sunny looked her up and down. "I'm not one of your life models, Sunny. You can stop studying me."

"Sorry. It's just that you— You're kind of . . . obvious."

"Well, there's no call for subtlety anymore."

"Do you need a chair? Or some water? It's hellish in here."

"I'm not an invalid. And I don't plan on being here long." She sighed. "But, yeah, a chair would be good."

He fetched one and she sat, exhaling. He hovered near, a finger to his mouth. "How does it feel?" he asked.

"Honestly? Like I haven't taken a shit in three months." She fanned herself. "It really is hellish in here."

"But you and Harry can relax now, right? Everything's out in the open."

She looked up at him. "Not everything."

"Huh?"

"What's going on between you and Andy?"

He walked off, idly picking up a hammer from the floor. "I don't know what you're talking about."

"Don't kid a kidder. We grew up together."

"So?"

"So give me a straight answer."

His eyes sparked. "You have no idea how funny that is."

"You could get him sacked, you know. Excommunicated, or whatever the hell they do."

"And what happens to me doesn't matter."

"Sunny—"

"Because I've always been a screwup."

"Sunny, everyone's used to you."

"Oh, I see. They're *used* to me. That's nice."

"You know what I mean."

"Boy, do I." He smacked the hammer against his palm. "It's all fun and games with Sunny Sohi. Secret meetings, frisky rendezvous, everything done in the dark and dirty and over in a spurt. But you don't have to take him seriously. There's no real feelings there. In the end, it's back to the *real* world, back to the *real* job, back to the church or the wife or the people who really matter."

She sat very still. "The wife? That better not mean what I think it means."

"Oh, don't wind yourself up. That died years ago, when we stopped being kids."

"Good. 'Cuz I know where Lerner keeps his guns, as well as his books and old photographs."

"Spare me the Annie Oakley routine. This ain't Miss Burdell's Theater Arts class."

"You reckon?" She waited, but he still wouldn't answer. She got up. "There's other people involved, Sunny. Real people. There *is* a real world, and it has real consequences. The two of you can't hide forever."

"Says the woman who traipsed around town in a raincoat and sunglasses all summer."

She shook her head and walked away. He yelled at her back, "Why are you putting all this on me, anyway? Do you really think I'm the one in charge?"

She looked at him and clucked her teeth. "If you're not, whose fault is that?"

Chapter 23

OUT ON A SPREE

Susan hummed cheerily as she collected music folders. "We are going to wow them tonight!" She looked at Andy, but he was scribbling something on the sheet music spread across the piano. She tried again. "And it won't be just Mt. Hermon we'll be wowing. It'll be the whole five-county area."

Andy shook his head, still not looking up. "I have no idea what you're talking about."

"Well, maybe I shouldn't tell you. It's supposed to be a surprise. But Mr. Hancock from the radio station is going to be here. Isn't that exciting?"

Andy shrugged. "I don't know. Is it?"

She gave him her best exasperated smile. "Don't be so thick. Grenville's very popular. Mr. Hancock is going to see if maybe they can broadcast the meeting."

The color drained from Andy's face. "On KROY? They can't!"

Susan shrugged. "Daddy's already given them permission."

"But, we're not ready! I haven't finished rewriting 'Standing.'"

"It's fine the way it is."

"Reverend Grenville doesn't like it. The verse about broken faith—"

"Reverend Grenville isn't the only star in the heavens. It's your time to shine." *My time as well*, she thought. "Your music is wonderful. It deserves to be heard the way you wrote it. Everything's ready, the soloists, the choir. You heard them just now. Even Mrs. Littledeer was on pitch. You really are—"

Andy moaned and leaned over, his hands over his ears.

Susan stopped her patter and looked at him, crouched in a ball on the piano bench, small and thin. "Did you eat anything today?" He shook his head. "Well, no wonder you're a bundle of nerves." She stroked his back.

He relaxed a little and his hands dropped to his lap. "Hey." He didn't look up. She leaned in and kissed him on the cheek. "Hey," she said again, softer.

Andy leaned his head on her shoulder. "It all has to be perfect."

"No, it doesn't. Daddy always says God doesn't expect prayers to be perfect. Just pray, that's all. And that's all a service is, really, a prayer."

Andy spoke into his chest. "That's what Matthew says?"

"Yes indeedy."

"What do you say?"

Her mind raced through the scene she had conjured, of her standing before the microphone in rapt joy, faces lifted to her voice, and of one distant listener snapping his fingers and turning to his colleagues and saying, "That's the one! That's the voice we need!" Then she erased it all. "It doesn't have to be perfect. It just has to be—what it is. An offering. A prayer."

Andy straightened up. He leaned over and kissed her. "You're my prayer."

She blushed. "Yes, well, there will be plenty of prayer tonight, but not if you faint from hunger." She got up. "Come on. Let's get you some good old-fashioned home cooking."

"Herman's?"

"None other."

The afternoon crowd at the drive-in was thin. A late summer intensity hung in the air, not at all like the indolence of a few weeks ago, with all the time in the world to kill. A person might not consciously know it, but the body did. The sun was still warm, but slanted lower; the evenings still drew out like taffy, but began sooner; nights, soft and hushed, were now also damp and chill. Tickseed along the roadside began to lose its brash colors and earn its name; dust and insects hovered in a golden haze close to the ground. Cicadas droned endlessly in the trees, making one last bid for generation before seed and husk disappeared together into the ground.

Andy brought Susan her "Coke" of 7-Up and a real one for himself. She insisted he eat something, and unable to face one of Herman's infamous burgers (consisting of equal parts hamburger, Italian sausage, and onion ground together and grilled in a patty), he settled on a hot dog.

They sat at a picnic table under the trees and talked quietly about the revival meeting that night. Andy was just beginning to relax when he bit down on a piece of gristle in the frankfurter. Susan immediately noticed the change in his color. "What is it?"

"I think I'm going to throw up."

She looked around. "The john's around back," she said matter-of-factly. "Or there's the bushes if you don't think you'll make it."

"I think I'd—" he started, then just got up and headed for the back side of the drive-in. He nearly bumped into a couple walking arm-in-arm.

"Hey there, Music Man," Virginia greeted him. "What's the rush?"

"Um . . ." was all Andy got out before hurrying off.

The couple joined Susan. "What's with him?" Virginia asked.

"Herman's fine cuisine," Susan said ruefully.

"Oh, yeah. It takes a lifetime."

Harry chuckled. "I don't think even a lifetime is long enough."

"Oh, I don't mean to get used to it," Virginia said. "I mean to digest it."

They laughed, but Susan's heart wasn't in it. She had meant for Andy to be relaxing under the trees, not throwing up in the dingy bathroom behind Herman's. "I shouldn't have brought him. He's been taking this whole revival thing too seriously. He needs to relax."

"*He* needs to relax?" Virginia pointed to Susan's hands. They were balled into fists and working their way up and down her thighs. Susan laughed at the sight and quickly tucked them behind herself and changed the subject. "So, what brings the two of you out to Croy's finest eatery? And together, I see."

"Yes sirree!" Virginia threw her hands wide and spun in an ungainly circle, her belly orbiting the rest of her body like a small moon. "For all the world to see!"

"New York's out of town," Harry added. "And the job is done. Stone Face and the rest of the boys just finished installing the panels." A racket announced Tucker's truck pulling into the parking lot. "Here they are now."

Susan watched Tucker unwind himself from the driver's seat and head for the take-out window. She smiled and waved, but the smile froze on her face when she saw Sunny get out and head toward the rear of Herman's. "So, the sculpture's installed," she said, trying to keep up the conversation.

"Well, sort of. You'll see at the dedication."

"The great unveiling!" Virginia crowed. "And just in time, if you know what I mean." She rubbed her abdomen.

Susan's attention finally settled on her old friend. Her eyes grew wide. "Is it that close?"

"Yeppers."

"Oh, Ginny, I'm so sorry."

"I'm not. Can't wait to get rid of the little baggage."

"Not so little." Harry touched her belly.

"Watch yourself, buster."

"No, I don't mean I'm sorry about the arrival of the, um, the little . . ."

"We don't know what it is," Harry said.

"It's a boy, for the umpteenth time. I keep telling ya."

Tucker walked up to them then, a soft-serve ice cream cone dripping from his left hand. He muttered something to Harry, who excused himself and the two of them walked off a bit and talked low.

"What I meant to say before," Susan sputtered, "was, well, I mean, I'm sorry I haven't been there. I've been so out of touch lately. I've been busy. At church, I mean."

Virginia squeezed her hand. "I know what you mean." She looked around. "So, where is he?"

"He'll be back," Susan said. "Soon." She didn't notice she was clenching her fists again.

Andy splashed water on his face, trying not to notice the crushed bugs on the walls and sink, or wonder what else might be included in the rinse-up he hoped would revive him. The graffiti on the walls of the single stall were primitive but explicit. They had driven him out before he could actually throw up. He hoped cold water would dispel his nausea, but only a lukewarm trickle came from either tap. He looked in the mirror and saw a man older than he remembered staring back through scratches that maybe spelled a word or maybe were just mayhem.

He had nearly run smack into Harry and Ginny Edom in the parking lot. Funny to see them again. He thought back to that warm spring evening when they all met. It seemed like it had happened to some other generation, some golden era he had read about once.

The door to the restroom swung open with a bang. "I'm sorry," he said loudly, rubbing water into his face with one hand and reaching for the cloth dispenser with the other. "I'm just washing up. I'll be done in a minute."

"No hurry," the voice behind him said.

He spun around, his face still dripping wet. "Sunny. What are you doing here?"

Sunny shrugged. "It's the best place in town to meet old friends. And make new ones. Not to mention the artwork." He nodded at the stall.

Andy stared at him.

"Seriously, I just came in to take a leak." He reached up and Andy jumped back. Sunny froze a moment, his arm extended, regarding him with those gold-flecked eyes. Then he reached past him to the dispenser and gave the roll a tug. "You'll want a fresh one," he said.

"I can get it myself," he said and tugged the roll again. It wouldn't budge.

"So, where have you been?"

Andy kept his back to him, rubbing his hands on the rough cloth. "Extra rehearsals for the choir."

"I thought the extra rehearsals were over."

He turned. They were only three feet apart. "This is something new. A revival."

"Oh, right. Because life isn't lively enough. We've got to pretend we're dead first so we can enjoy being revived."

Sunny's face was all smiles, his eyes teasing. Perspiration began wicking through his shirt, making it cling to his chest. He moved closer and his voice dropped. "I wondered what happened to you, why you stopped coming around. I can't stop thinking about you."

Andy swallowed. "I can't, either. Every time I try, I see Him."

"Who?"

"Him."

Sunny laughed. "How am I supposed to compete with that?"

"This isn't a joke, Sunny. I thought I had finally found my way. A true way to a tangible relationship with the Divine. Through you."

Sunny's face fell. "*Through* me? What am I, a culvert?"

"But I was wrong. It's a dead end." He wiped his hands on his trousers. "You wouldn't understand."

"You're damned right I wouldn't."

The room was heating up. He had to get out of there. "Look, just get out of my way."

Sunny stepped back. "I'm not in your way. You're in mine." He pointed at the stall again.

Andy gritted his teeth and left.

Susan could hear Tucker from across the asphalt even though it was obvious he and Harry were trying to keep their voices down. "He hasn't cashed them," Tucker was saying. "Not a one!"

"Keep it down, Jed," Harry said, glancing around nervously. "Where's that old Stone Face when I need him?"

"But what's going to happen when—"

"Here comes Andy now," Virginia said rather loudly, as if sounding an alarm. Harry hitched up his belt and rejoined them, leaving Tucker behind.

Susan wanted to run up to Andy and encircle him with her arms. He'd been back there with Sunny for a while. For too long? She waved and he ruefully waved back. "All better," he said.

"Good to see you again, Miracle Man," Harry called out.

Susan looked for a cringe from Andy, but his face held a steady smile. "Well," he said, "here we all are again."

"Why, so we are." Virginia beamed. "Remember, Suzie-Q? And no cranky old Lerner this time to break up the party."

"There's a party?" Andy smiled. "What's the occasion?"

"Ada's Memorial, signed, sealed, and delivered!"

"The work's all done." Harry tossed his head in Tucker's direction. "Thanks to Jedediah Tucker and his gang. So we decided to celebrate, go out to dinner. And I'm buying."

Susan arched an eyebrow. "Dinner? Here?"

"Well," Harry shrugged, "I'm buying."

"Not just dinner," Virginia added. "Dinner and a movie."

"Oh, a *real* date." Andy looked at Susan. "I've heard of those."

"Me, too." She smiled. He was beginning to sound like his old self again.

"Maybe we should try it sometime."

"Why, Mr. Simms. What a forward proposal!"

"Watch yourself there, buddy. She's talking proposals." Harry nodded at Virginia. "You can see what kind of trouble that leads to."

Tucker joined them, "Movie's in twenty minutes."

Virginia grabbed Susan's arm. "Why don't the two of you join us?"

"Oh, no," Susan said. "We couldn't. We've got—"

"What's the movie?" Andy interrupted. She looked at him, stunned. Surely he wasn't thinking of ditching the meeting?

"*A Place in the Sun*," Harry said.

"'A love that paid the severest of all penalties!'" Virginia added in a salacious whisper.

"I don't know about that—" Susan began.

"Me, neither," Harry said. "But at the rate we get new shows around here, I'll be old and gray before that Pearl Harbor movie comes out. I can't wait to see the battle of Schofield Barracks." He mimed an anti-aircraft gun, complete with sound effects. "Ack-ack-ack-ack!"

Virginia swatted him. "You and your guns!" She turned to Andy and Susan. "Harry still thinks he was personally gypped out of World War II."

"If it had been just one year longer—" Harry began.

"You'd be dead," Virginia finished, "along with a million others. Dead or cracked in the head."

Andy laughed sharply and pointed at Tucker. "Like your uncle, right?" Everyone stopped talking and looked at him. Andy's smile froze on his face. "Old Crazy Head, right?"

There was a shift in Tucker's stance. A wall seemed to come down across his face. "No," Tucker said and turned and walked off a few paces.

Andy looked at Harry, Ginny, and Susan. "What? That's his name, isn't it?"

"No," Susan said.

Harry shook his head. "Jed can call him that, but you better not."

Andy was bewildered. "I'm sorry, I— I thought that was his family name. Like Crazy Horse."

Harry set his shoulders. "We don't all have quaint and colorful names."

"Harry—" Virginia said, touching his sleeve.

"What's this I hear about a movie?" Sunny boomed, bouncing across the parking lot.

Susan hitched her arm around Andy's. Now they were two couples—

Harry and Virginia, Andy and Susan—facing Sunny and Tucker on the outside. "I don't think so," Susan said. "Andy and I have church."

"Aw, Suzie-Q," Virginia pleaded.

"Some other time, then," Harry said.

"Hey! Maybe we can make it a triple date," Sunny said. "The Sanctified Duo there in the orchestra seats, holding hands, chastely. You and the Missus, canoodling in the back row. Me and Jed up in the balcony. We'll have a gay old time!"

"Shut up!" Andy exploded.

Susan turned, startled. "Andy?"

He tore loose from her grip. "That's enough! We've had enough of you." He practically charged Sunny. "Who asked you to butt in? Why don't you go bother someone else for a change?"

Sunny looked like he'd been punched in the stomach. Over Sunny's shoulder, Susan could see Tucker turn and watch.

"Butt in?" Sunny's eyes darted back and forth across Andy's face, looking for something, looking lost. "*Me* butt in? This is *our* time. This is *our* night!"

"Sunny," Tucker said warningly.

"Fuck you!" Sunny shouted suddenly in Andy's face.

Susan saw heads turn at the take-out window and inside Herman's. She tugged on Andy's arm but he wouldn't budge.

"This is for *me*!" Sunny said bitterly. "I've been working my ass off all damned summer. So has Harry. So has Jed. Where have you been? You're the one who's butting in. You're the one who doesn't fit. You think you can just join in any old time you want, just blend in with all these nice, normal, Christian people? Just be one of the guys, one of their pals?"

Tucker came up behind him and touched his arm. "Sunny, come on."

"Fuck off, Jed!" He turned back to Andy. "You think you're safe. You think you've got it made. Because you're the right color and you go to the right church and you latch onto some nice girl at the first sign of trouble. Well, here's a news flash, Miracle Man. You'll never fit in. You'll never be one of them. No matter how hard you try. No matter how many layers of normal and nice and 'sanctification' you pile on top of yourself. Never! No matter what! To them, you'll always be just another kind of nigger."

There was a sudden silence. Even the cicadas stopped.

"Come on, Sunny," Tucker said. "I'll take you home."

Sunny wheeled on him. "I'll find my own way home, god damn it!" Tucker's stony expression cracked briefly, a flicker of hurt. Sunny was blind to it. "I don't need you. I don't need any of you. Someone's always willing to take me home. So long as it's dark. So long as nobody sees." He furiously waved away Tucker's hand and stalked off.

"We'll be late, Susan," Andy said calmly. "We should be going." He turned and headed for the car, not waiting for her answer. Susan glanced desperately at Virginia, who shrugged and shook her head, then she turned and followed Andy to the car.

Harry walked up to Tucker. "He didn't mean it," he said softly.

Tucker shook his head, watching Sunny's figure flicker down the sidewalk, one moment struck by the golden slanting light, the next disappearing in deep shadows. "No," he said. "He meant it."

Part 4

Then he took a glance at the stars
And said, "I am sick."

—Surah as-Saffat

Chapter 24

CORINTHIANS

Andy's car hummed along the brick pavement of Main Street, but inside there was a silence Susan was afraid to breach. As they approached the Rialto theater, the car slowed to a stop. Susan looked behind them. There was no traffic. You could toss a bowling ball down Main Street on a late afternoon without hitting anyone, but stopping in the middle of the street felt queer. She felt the eyes of shopkeepers peering at them from behind their plate glass storefronts.

Andy looked at the movie house, the mess of his hair framed by the marquee above and posters on either side. "Young people asking so much of Life! Taking so much of Love!!" they declared. "Andy?" she asked.

"He's a liar," he said. He turned to face her. "Don't you believe a thing he tells you. He's a liar." He put the car in gear and they turned off Main Street, crossed the tracks, and headed south. "I've got to change my shirt," Andy said flatly. He was soaked through with sweat. An acrid smell filled the car. "Good idea," she said, keeping her voice casual. "I could use some freshening up myself."

Andy stiffened. "You can't come in."

"Excuse me?"

"I mean, it wouldn't be proper."

She laughed.

"Well, it wouldn't, Susan. Not the two of us, alone, in my place."

"Oh, Andy. Nobody's going to see. Nobody's going to care."

"Mrs. Oldfield might."

"See? Or care?"

Andy grunted. "Yeah, I guess you're right. In fact, she might even approve."

"Do what?" She tried sounding shocked, but it was laughable.

"Never mind. You can come in, if you want."

Then it hit her. "Has she been playing match-maker?" Andy turned red, which was confirmation enough. "I think I'll just wait outside till you're done."

Andy's car rolled carefully down the alley, raising no dust at all. "No, really," he said, setting the brake, "you can come in."

"No, I'll wait for you on the lawn." She got out and walked up the slope to the mimosa tree. Andy stood at the entrance to the little house and smiled at her, gave a half-shrug, and fumbled through the door.

Susan turned and looked up at the back porch of the Oldfield house. She had half a mind to march up there and have a word with that woman, but then she sighed and sank down on the grass. She ran her hand through the heavy blades, already cool to the touch though the sun was not yet down. She glanced at the sharecropper shacks across the alley. They looked more run-down than she remembered, and there were For Sale signs out front. Those hadn't been there before, had they? When was the last time she was out here? Gerald Oldfield's funeral? But she'd barely been in junior high then, and now she was . . .

She smiled at herself. Oh, yes, she was *so* grown up now. A young woman, ready to make her way in the world. Ready to start that shining career on the stage which Miss Burdell, her high school drama coach, had painted for her. "You were born to change the world!" Miss Burdell had said. "All true artists change the world, for they change the way we see. They are revolutionaries. They are born to fight the world, to over-turn the commonplace, to open our hearts, our minds, our souls. Never forget, my dears: you are warriors!"

Miss Burdell never got in trouble for her incendiary talk. The Board of Education concluded long ago there was no real powder behind the fuse. But when the torch was passed to Susan, she grabbed it. She fell in love with that dream of herself and her place in the world. One bright day, all this mundane small-town drama—the clumsy high school plays, the awful Hill-Billy musicals, the years of singing in her father's church—would fall away and she would fly.

But what have I done, actually? she thought. *What steps had I taken to see if my wings really work?* Instead of going to college, she had stayed in Croy. Instead of seeking fame and fortune, she had waited for them to find her. *And instead of following the path of the warrior artist, I have fallen in love with a boy who might never get past the first kiss.*

She sat up abruptly, flushed and chilled at the same time. The thought had snuck up on her, catching her unawares. And now Andy was coming out of the granny house, a glass of water in his hand, grinning. He had at least four years on her and had been to college, but it was starkly clear to her that she was the older of the two. Older in ways he would never be able to talk about, and in ways she could never tell him.

Tell him, no. But maybe I can show him.

"I'm sorry about blowing up back there." Andy sat beside her, handing her the glass. "It's just that he shouldn't say things like that."

"Who? Sunny? Things like what?"

Andy shrugged and looked around. "You know. Like what he said about a 'date.' 'Have a gay old time.' That kind of stuff."

Susan waved her hand. "Nobody pays attention to Sunny. He's always spouting off."

"Well, he shouldn't. People will talk."

He was getting worked up again. "It's nothing. Forget it."

"It's not nothing, Susan. It's people's lives. And their souls."

"You're worried about Sunny's soul?"

"Well, of course. Aren't you? Haven't you been listening to Reverend Grenville's preaching?"

She put the glass down and took his nearest, flightiest hand in hers. He flinched. "Look, Andy, there's no need to worry about Sunny."

"Words have consequences," he persisted. "Don't you believe in judgment, in Heaven and Hell?"

She shrugged. "Heaven, yeah. I'm pretty sure about Heaven. But Hell?" She shook her head. "I asked Daddy about it once. He told me, 'A man would be a fool to think God had neglected to create Hell, and crazy to think He would ever use it.'"

Andy looked away from her, the light of the setting sun touching his eyelashes with fire. "That's not what I was taught," he said. "That's not what Scripture says."

She smoothed the lap of her dress. "Either way, they're both a long way off. In the meantime . . ." She leaned in and kissed him on the mouth. He pulled back and looked at her, his eyes searching hers. Then he leaned in and kissed her back. She could hear his breath coming in short inhalations, the sound carried away by the touch of a breeze. A cicada wound up its oscillating buzz nearby and they pulled apart. He stared at her as she stood. She reached out her hand. "It's time to go," she said. "Church."

Sunny furiously paced the streets of Croy as twilight darkened around him. When he finally stopped, he found himself under the marquee of the Rialto. No doubt the others hadn't waited for him and were already inside. He snuck in the side door, like they'd done when they were kids, and made his way to the balcony. There was no sign of Jed, and that fed his bitterness. An elegantly dressed gent everyone called Curly sat alone in the back row. He didn't move a muscle or even flick his eyes in Sunny's direction as he hunkered down into the musty seat beside him. Neither spoke a word into the fuming darkness, but in the end, after the show, it was Curly who gave him a ride home.

There was a wordless caress on the way. Then after the turnoff from the county road, Curly stopped the car and turned off the lights. He leaned over and stroked Sunny's long, black hair, sighing as the gibbous moon struck blue highlights from his locks. Sunny was used to this kind of sentimentality, but he realized now there was something else in the sigh. Sunny had never grown his hair this long before, not since coming back from California. A wave of sympathy washed over him, and he slid his hips forward a little to make it easier. A line from the movie came back to him, "Love me for as long as I have left. Then forget me." Maybe it was that, or maybe it was the moonlight glinting off Curly's head as it bobbed up and down in his lap that brought tears to his eyes.

1 Corinthians, dear brothers and sisters, Chapter 6, verses 9-11:

Do you not know that the wicked will not inherit the kingdom of God? Do not be deceived: Neither the immoral nor idolaters nor adulterers nor homosexuals nor thieves nor the greedy nor drunkards nor revilers nor robbers will inherit the kingdom of God. And such were some of you.

It's an odd jumble, isn't it? A kind of yard-sale of sin. There's something for everyone! Some real bargains, there, if damnation is what you seek. All the way from such trifles as reviling—what's that, "reviling"? Slander, isn't it? And gossip? Who hasn't shared some really good gossip? Yet there it is. It makes the list, right up there with the abomination that has been unspeakable since the time of Lot. The wretched vice that brought Sodom and her sister cities to ruin, tumbled them from their peak of shining pride to a shattered plain of burning pitch—scoured from the earth in a hail of brimstone and a whirlwind of wrath.

We, too, can reduce our cities to cinders. We hold that power in our hands. We *invented* that power. And we're proud of it. And instead of trembling at our arrogance and error, we lust for more. Unsatisfied that we could annihilate a single city, we sought greater destruction. Unhappy that we might match the destruction of Sodom and Gomorrah, we sought the power to destroy the whole world. Why? Because we thought it was right? Or good? Or that is was God's will? No. We did it because we *could*. Because we believed we were in charge.

The Son of God appeared to destroy the Devil's work, and yet we pursue it! That is what every one of those sins so neatly listed in Corinthians has at its heart: the overwhelming lust to place the satisfaction of our own will and desires at the center of our lives, where instead should lodge the King of Kings. We worship creation instead of the Creator. We glorify our power instead of giving all power and glory to Him.

Where will it lead? My brothers and sisters, where can it lead? You need look no further than the news of the day to see where we are headed. We pried into the soul of creation to find the Mind of God, and what did we find instead? Weapons of unspeakable horror, the very fires of Armageddon. And did we blanch? Did we pause? Did we place our hands over our mouths and say, as Job did, in all humility, "I cannot do what God has done, I dare not to undo it"?

No. A-bombs were not enough. We wanted H-bombs. And we by God built them!

How foolish. Is there a single impulse in our hearts that does not have, at its root, the foul decay of this world? Do you not know that all things of this world are under the Devil's thumb?

And the Devil showed his hand this summer, did he not? Good Ol' Uncle Joe detonated his own thermonuclear device. That sort of blew the lid off things, didn't it? What of our grand designs now, now that Godless Communism has all the power and pride that we thought was ours alone? The fires of creation—did we really think we could hold them in our hands and not get scorched?

I have been there, friends. I have seen what we can do. I visited, with Reverend Tanimoto, the burn hospitals of Hiroshima, the dying wards of Nagasaki. I have seen what modern man can do with all the wisdom and wonders he has acquired. I have seen modern science at its best.

The eyes of those who looked upon Hiroshima's blast melted in their sockets. That was but a fore-taste, my brothers and sisters. This sin-soaked world will be torn from our greedy grasp and cleansed, yea, cleansed as in a refiner's fire, purified and made whole again! Modern man with his lust-driven life will be blasted away.

And where will you be, my friends? Will you be standing with them, as your homes, your televisions, your cars, the very eyes with which you eat the world melt and run down your cheeks?

Or will you be in the Kingdom of God?

Do not be deceived. It does not matter if your idol is power or the flesh, wealth or the pursuit of so-called knowledge. Neither idolaters, nor adulterers, nor homosexuals, nor thieves, nor the greedy, nor drunkards, nor revilers, nor robbers shall enter the Kingdom of God. For such were some of you. For such are *all* of us.

The Spirit certainly descended that night. The altar call was particularly fruitful. A great many souls were healed of the chief sickness of this world, pulled away from that seam of pride and independence, of scientism and modern humanism that ran through the American character like dry-rot. Faced with the real character of this world, they had snapped like twigs. Tremblin' Bob glowed with the fire he had lit in their hearts.

A shame that fellow from the radio had missed it. Birdine had delivered that disappointing news just before the meeting started. He had waved her away. "Now is no time for such things," he'd said, perhaps a bit too curtly. He owed her one, as he often did.

Tonight's catch had been easy. He had seen them falling toward the rail before they even left their pews. He was particularly pleased to see a number of young people from the choir clustered in the prayer circles. There were still holdouts, however; those whose voices sang the hymns but whose hearts were still as stones. A couple of them he had pegged. That Swofford fellow, for instance. If he clenched his jaw much tighter his teeth would shatter. *That nut's about to crack*, he thought. *And what shall we find inside?*

JayRob Pautler approached him, one hand outstretched, the other holding an envelope. "Will you come to the dedication Monday, Brother Bob?"

Tremblin' Bob ignored the envelope. "I confess I am a little uncertain whether I should. Monuments of such a secular nature . . ." He looked over his shoulder to his wife, who came up and relieved Pautler of the envelope.

"I just thought, what with the subject of your sermon and all, it would be the perfect opportunity."

"I'm afraid I don't follow you, Brother JayRob."

"You know, new-culer war and the Ruskies and all."

The Reverend Grenville smiled and wiped a handkerchief across his forehead. He had the giddy urge to rip someone's eyeballs out, and he knew that meant his blood sugar was dropping. He needed a moment in private, and soon.

"My husband's a little tired, Mr. Pautler," Birdine said, taking his arm. They turned away.

"Yes, yes, of course." The little man rubbed his hands together. "I just mean, it'd be a shame, what with the radio and all."

"Radio?" Grenville turned back.

"Yes! That's why Hancock wasn't here tonight. They were delayed setting up, some sort of last minute construction on the library site. But we're all set, now! Good to go! And it won't be just local. What with the shelter and the Civil Defense people and all, and, well, of course, your sermon. You could nail it right there! So I just thought it would be a shame for us to miss the opportunity—for you to, you know, hammer it home. To a wider audience."

Grenville smiled. "Birdine, my dear, do you think Brother JayRob might want to join us for a bite to eat?"

Andy's fingers flick across the keyboard but evoke no sound, no music, just the sound of his fingers clicking against the keys. The rhythm of it ripples up his arms, tunnels into his brain. It keeps getting faster and faster and he cannot stop. The ivory keys start sticking to the pads of his fingers. If he can just hit them harder, hit them faster, they will come loose and the rhythm will stop. If they loosen and drop from his hands the silence will stop and the music will bloom. But the keys keep sticking and sticking, and they pull out of the keyboard and cling, welded to his fingers like bars of iron, and he cannot get rid of them. He shakes his hands and he flings out his arms, but the piano keys knock against the soundboard and clatter on the bench and there's no place he can hide them. He sits on his hands and still he can feel the stiff ivory and wood tapping out their rhythm under his thighs.

The piano is gone and he's alone in the room, a small room with walls that are far away but confining since he cannot move from the bench. A figure appears in the air above him, dressed in the robes of the Holy Land. It is Montgomery Clift and he's wearing a crown of thorns. His face is scarred. "But why?" this Jesus asks him. "Why?" And slowly the robe opens, not like the gowns in the Sunday school books he stared at as a boy, but like the curtain of a theater, pulled by velvet cords, and the man's full nakedness unveils before him. "No!" Andy cries out and tries to draw the curtain closed, but his fingers are clumsy and fat and still have piano keys growing out of them. "Why do you persecute me?" Jesus asks. "Why?"

Andy sat bolt upright in his bed, tears pouring from his eyes. His sheet was soaked with sweat. He groped his way out of the bedroom to the front door and opened it, but could not take a step outside. He sank to his knees, using the doorframe for support. *"Oh Lord,"* he prayed, *"by night and day I cry to you. You have put my friends far from me; you have made me abhorrent to them.* Cut this sickness from my heart. Tear it from my brain. *Do not utterly forsake me.* I will do anything to gain Your love again. I would do anything to make this stop."

He looked up at the sky and a wave of nausea overtook him. He ran for the bathroom.

The stars and the night rode on.

Chapter 25

EARTH HAS NO SORROW

Susan went pew by pew down her side of the church, making sure the hymnals were ready for tonight's meeting, the last in Reverend Grenville's revival. Mrs. Oldfield and Mr. Pautler did the same on their side. She could see Pautler's constant chatter was distracting Mrs. Oldfield, who was doing her best to affect deafness. Susan felt a pang of sympathy for her and smiled.

Ordinarily, Lisle Armbruster would be helping them, but Mr. Armbruster had just been discharged from the hospital that morning. Her father, returning from a home visit, told Susan not to expect Mrs. Armbruster either, so the altar committee was down by two. Susan finished her side of the church and looked around to see what she could do next.

The choir needed tending to. They were milling around waiting for the risers to be set up. Andy hadn't shown yet and she was beginning to worry. Scotty Pritchard asked her if he could help. "I'll open the storeroom," she said. She started for the office for the key when Andy came in through the side door. She switched directions and headed for him. He looked like he hadn't slept, but before she could ask, he said, "Why aren't they warming up?"

"The risers are still in the—"

"The piano is right there!" Andy flung his music on it. "Do I have to do everything? John!" he yelled. Two heads in the choir turned. Andy dug in his pocket and tossed a ring of keys at John Tibbits. "Get the risers out."

"I can help," Scotty said. When no one answered, he headed to the storeroom anyway.

"Is everything all right?" Susan asked.

"They're coming,"

"Who's coming?"

"Hancock and the rest of them. Radio people."

"Oh." Her solo had been last night. It would not be part of the broadcast. She shook the disappointment from her head. "Well, we're ready for them."

"Not yet we aren't. Choir!" Andy called. "Let's stop lollygagging around. Those of you not helping set up, let's get started." He began banging out scales on the piano, not even sitting down. Susan stood beside him, stunned by his abruptness. He turned and jerked his head toward the group of sopranos and she took her place.

JayRob Pautler stood in the foyer, greeting his fellow congregants as they entered. He kept a sharp eye out for Grenville and Hancock, wanting to make sure their entrance was noticed. He stepped outside and scanned the street for their car. There was the smell of rain in the air. He scowled at the sky, darkened by clouds that had put an early end to the sunset. He hoped to impress the visiting preacher and the radio man, but a downpour would put a crimp in attendance. Hancock's car pulled up then and Mrs. Grenville stepped out accompanied by a man JayRob hadn't seen before. The car pulled away and the couple approached.

"Where's Reverend Grenville?" JayRob asked with a tight smile.

"Mr. Pautler," Mrs. Grenville said, "I'd like you to meet Reverend Joshua Mathers." The strange man reached out his hand. JayRob grasped it but kept his eyes on Mrs. Grenville. "Reverend Mathers is one of our associate pastors," she said. "He will start the meeting if my husband is unable to make it on time."

"Not make it? But—"

"Very pleased to meet you, Brother JayRob," the man said with loud enthusiasm. He gripped JayRob's hand with both of his and didn't seem inclined to let go. "I hear you have been doing marvelous work here. Just marvelous. A great many souls healed and brought to the light."

"But—" JayRob was having difficulty nodding, smiling, and arguing all at the same time. "Mrs. Grenville, I thought we agreed that Brother Bob, that is, Reverend Grenville would be preaching all of the—"

"We do have an agreement, Brother JayRob. It is between Mt. Hermon Bible Church and The Trembling Hour Ministries. Reverend Mathers is one of our finest. I'm sure you will find him perfectly suitable until my husband arrives."

"I'm just the warm-up act, you might say." Mathers laughed and released JayRob's hand. "Shall we go in?"

JayRob looked over their shoulders for some sign of Reverend Grenville or Harvey Hancock or any of the radio people, but none of them appeared. He turned and let Mrs. Grenville and this second-string preacher into the church, escorting them up to the sanctuary with his disappointment in tow.

> *Come, ye disconsolate, where'er ye languish,*
> *Come to the mercy seat, fervently kneel.*
> *Here bring your wounded hearts, here tell your anguish;*
> *Earth has no sorrow that heaven cannot heal.*

Andy led the chorus in the opening hymn but felt like he was on automatic. His mind raced through the music he anticipated needing this evening, wondering how he would balance the sopranos without Lila Armbruster. He barely heard Pastor Jacobs's opening prayer or the introduction of Reverend Mathers or his invocation. Midway through the following hymn, Andy saw Reverend Grenville and Harvey Hancock enter through the side door. Grenville shook hands with Mathers, who smilingly shifted down a chair in the row of seats in the sanctuary. Hancock slid into the outside end of the first pew, right across from the choir. Andy breathed a sigh of relief when he noticed no sign of recording or broadcasting equipment. Just then, there was a flash of light, and for a heart-stopping moment he thought a reporter had taken a photograph. But a gentle rumble of thunder reassured him it was just lightning. A light rain began to fall.

Tremblin' Bob had chosen Jesus the Physician as the theme for his final sermon. He was happy for the late summer rain pattering outside and worked it into the imagery of washing away sins and bringing healing to the land. "We cannot earn our way to heaven, for the rain falls upon the just and the unjust alike," he said. "We are saved by grace alone, through faith alone, by the redeeming power of Christ's sacrifice on the Cross alone."

The electricity in the air charged the congregation as well. A storm of redemption was about to break in this very church. "But what does that sacrifice matter if we do not accept Him who made it into our hearts?

Brothers and sisters, the stone that was rolled away from the tomb as our Lord rose from the dead was but a trifle, a pebble, a grain of sand compared to the stone that lies on our hearts. And what is that stone? Pride. How can we admit to our sins before God if we will not admit to our sins before each other? Come to the railing! Lift that stone from your hearts! Come to the fountain of life! Drink deep of God's everlasting mercy."

There were already two prayer groups at the railing, sinners in the center of each, surrounded by deacons with their hands on their shoulders, praying with them. Tremblin' Bob's voice deepened and swelled, drowning out the sound of the rain outside. "If we do not bend, if we do not break, if we heed not the call, we shall never be whole. Say it with me, say it aloud: I am a sinner! I am alone! I need my God to save me from the horrors of eternal fire! Save me, Lord Jesus!" A propitious peal of thunder rolled overhead. "He is here, brothers and sisters, He is here! Listen to the might of his answer. He has heard your cry and He is waiting just a few short steps away. O Lord, I am not worthy that thou shouldst enter under my roof! Say but the word! Say but the word! He has spoken, my brothers. He has spoken! And the word is, Come!"

The hairs on the back of Andy's neck rose up. Something very odd was happening. He had been playing "Come Ye Disconsolate," but as the Reverend Grenville's sermon wound higher and higher, something else started coming out of his fingers, a song of tremendous passion and luminance. He rose slowly from the bench, his fingers still playing this new, harmonious, triumphant song, his eyes barely able to see the keys or follow his hands as they flew across the keyboard.

Tremblin' Bob's eyes were fixed on the air above the congregation. His upraised arms began to tremble. A pair of teen-aged boys knelt at the railing, one of them from the choir. Pastor Jacobs gathered a prayer circle around them. Tremblin' Bob continued to pour out his heart. A jerking movement in the pews drew his eye. John Swofford had stumbled getting out of his pew. It looked like his legs were trying to pull him back toward the door while his face drew him forward. He gripped the ends of the pews, pulling himself along. Grenville stepped away from the lectern in the center of the sanctuary. He intended to lead this healing circle himself. But then . . .

Andy's hands floated off the keyboard. He had time to throw a desperate glance at Susan, who rushed in to take over at the piano. Then the room spun around and he found himself on his knees at the railing, eyes wide and hands in the air. "I have sinned!" he cried. "My heart is full of darkness!" He shook so hard he would have fallen over if so many hands hadn't held him up, hands on his head, hands on his shoulders.

"Forgive this sinner, O Lord! Heal him!" Reverend Grenville boomed as his large hands landed on Andy's head. "Show him Your mercy!" He leaned in, but Andy couldn't see him. Waves of sound rushed over him. Several men prayed over him, their voices overlapping. There was crying and shouting in the groups beside them as well. Reverand Grenville's voice cut through: "Do you accept Jesus into your heart!" His hand trembled, making Andy's head shake. Andy wailed, almost crushed under the weight of that hand. "Jesus cannot want me," he said. "My heart is a sewer."

"No sin is so foul it cannot be forgiven. No soul so sick it cannot be healed."

"I burn with unnatural lust! I have lain with a man as with a woman!"

The voices around Andy dropped. One set of hands sprang back and he nearly toppled in that direction. "Fetch Pastor Jacobs," Grenville said in a tight whisper, then raised his voice and proclaimed, "We thank you, O Lord, for bringing this soul back to Your kingdom. We bless and praise Your name . . ." Andy lost track of the words. The others prayed as well, but not the spontaneous words that surrounded him earlier. They all echoed Grenville, repeating him nearly word-for-word, as if they could think of nothing else to say.

Susan saw her father leave the circle he was leading and join the tight group around Andy. She could not hear what he or Andy was saying, only Grenville's booming voice over all. Something was wrong. She saw Reverend Grenville pass a signal to Reverend Mathers, and then Grenville, JayRob Pautler, and her father hustled Andy off into the church office. A moment later, JayRob came out and closed the door behind him. He stood in front like a sentinel, his face unmoving. *What is going on?* she worried. But Reverend Mathers moved the revival along the course the Spirit had laid out, and she could not leave the choir unattended. She cursed to herself. What good were her gifts if they kept her from Andy when he needed her most? She continued to pound out the hymns, but the music was meaningless. Her fingers slammed against the keys but there was no joy in them. *What is going on in there? What's wrong?*

She knows, but she refuses to know she knows.

Chapter 26

HEAVEN CANNOT HEAL

Andy sat with his head bowed, hands clenched and thrust between his legs. "I am so sorry, Matthew. I am so sorry to have brought this disgrace to your church. I have tried to be rid of it. I have prayed, I have wept, I have sought guidance from the Scriptures. But nothing works. It returns again and again to my mind and my heart. I cannot undo what I have done, and I cannot get rid of it." He covered his face. "God has abandoned me."

Matthew Jacobs put his hand on Andy's shoulder. "No, Andy, God has not abandoned you. Listen to me. *Neither life nor death, nor angel nor prince, nothing that exists, nothing yet to come, no power nor height nor depth, nor any created thing, can ever come between you and the love of God.*"

"*The love of God made visible through our Lord Jesus Christ,*" Grenville added. He put his hand on Andy's other shoulder. "Brother Andrew, God puts up with everyone—even those who sicken Him. And why? Because scattered among the wicked are those particular people in whom He has found favor, to whom He desires to show mercy, and by showing mercy, reveal His glory. You have to choose, son. Are you among those people in whom God has found favor? Or do you take your place among the ranks and legions of those who will be destroyed?"

Andy looked from one face to the other, searching for guidance. "I cannot *choose* to be among the elect. Surely, I have proven that again and again! I cannot shake this thing. If I could, I would. But I haven't the strength."

Grenville moved in front and took his trembling hands in his large, warm palms. "God does not want your strength. We are saved through faith, not works. Faith alone, in Christ alone, through the Cross alone. His blood is sufficient for all sins, for all men, but effective for only a few. Do you wish to be among those few?"

Andy nodded.

"You must accept Jesus as the center of your life—not your desires, not your appetites, not the will of your body, but only Him. The Holy Spirit must overwhelm your will and burn away everything until nothing else remains."

Andy moaned, shaking his head. Grenville looked in alarm at Pastor Jacobs. "Andy," Matthew said, "you have already taken the first step, the hardest step. You have admitted your sin. We are brothers in that, Andy. You and I and Brother Bob, here. We are all sinners. All have fallen short of the glory of God. Your sin is no greater than any of ours."

Grenville frowned and turned to Andy. "Brother Andrew, we know how earnestly you wish to be rid of this abomination, how it bears down upon you, how it crushes your soul. All that can be lifted now."

Andy's face shone with sweat and tears. "Please forgive me!"

Grenville's hands moved to Andy's head. Andy's arms rose in the air light as balloons. "Yes, brother," Grenville said, "God hears you. And His forgiveness is waiting, waiting to fall like a sweet rain on parched earth. Say but the word and your soul shall be healed."

Andy hesitated. "What word? What must I say?"

Grenville took a deep breath. "The names, brother."

"What?"

"Who else has been tainted with this sin?"

Matthew Jacobs cleared his throat. "Brother Bob—"

"Brother Matthew, I have seen this evil before. And believe me, nothing can tear apart a church faster than this."

"Andy has already confessed his sin."

"But not fully! We need to know how far this infection has spread. It must not be hidden! It is a cancer on the body of Christ, and it has to be cut out. At once and completely!"

Andy's arms dropped and he doubled over in his chair. "Why did God make me like this?"

Grenville drew himself up. "The pot has no right to ask the potter, 'Why did you make me this shape?'"

Matthew knelt beside Andy, putting an arm around his shoulder. "I think what Reverend Grenville is trying to say, Andy, is that your salvation might give hope to others who are similarly afflicted."

"There are others, aren't there, son?" Grenville said, his hands clasped.

"I—" Andy looked up and shook his head. "I have no right to say."

"Who is it?"

Andy's eyes squeezed shut and his head rocked from side to side.

Grenville suddenly bent down and whispered harshly, "Is it Scotty?"

Andy's eyes flew open. "Who?"

Matthew sprang to his feet. "*What?*"

"Is it Scotty, Andy?" Grenville pressed. "Is it the Pritchard boy?"

"Brother Robert—!"

Andy looked wildly from one to the other. "Scott? My God, no! I'm not a monster! There's only one man. Just one man. I love him. I wish to God I didn't, but I do." Grenville drew back, his face red. "When I'm with him, I feel whole. When I'm not, I feel like God has torn out my soul. Why would God do that?"

Grenville's backhand nearly knocked Andy to the floor. Pastor Jacobs seized his arm, shouting "Brother Robert!" but Tremblin' Bob was shaking from head to foot. "How dare you mock God in His own house!"

Jacobs seized the larger man by the shoulders. "Robert!"

"You have *sex* with men. Sex! Filthy, disgusting, unnatural sex. To call it love is to blaspheme against the Holy Spirit. God did not create love to be abused by men such as you. It is sick, it is vile, it is worthy of death!"

"Stop this at once!" With an effort, Pastor Jacobs turned Reverend Grenville away from Andy. "Reverend Grenville, this is my church, this is my parishioner. I will take it from here."

Grenville looked startled, as if awakened from a dream. "You have no idea what you're dealing with here, Matthew. The power of this sickness—"

"Thank you, brother." Pastor Jacobs loosened his grip on the man but stayed between him and Andy. "You have done enough. I will take it from here."

Grenville took out a handkerchief and mopped his brow. "You are in error. This is an error. Brother Andy, God has not given anyone permission to sin. He has placed before you fire and water. Stretch out your hand! Choose!" He looked from one to the other. "I will pray for you," he said. "I will pray for you both." He put the handkerchief away and left.

Andy sat slumped in the chair, the side of his face beginning to swell. Matthew sat beside him.

"I am truly sorry, Andy. Brother Robert is ardent, but for your soul's sake. As am I. Yours alone. Whoever else is involved is no concern of mine."

"What am I to do, Matthew? He's in my bones, he's in my blood, he's in my brain."

"Scour him out. Take every image of him from your mind and replace him with Jesus."

Andy closed his eyes. "I can't. I've tried. It only makes it worse."

Matthew rose and walked behind his desk. "Take it slowly, Andy. One step at a time. You've acknowledged the sin. You've confessed it before God and your neighbors."

Andy inhaled sharply. "Oh, God. Susan!"

Matthew closed his eyes and prayed, "Dear Father, give us the strength of Your love, and lead us in the ways of Your mercy. We may not see the path before us yet, but we know You are with us always. You will see us safe to Your kingdom." He opened his eyes. "All of us. Amen." There was silence. "Amen, Andy?"

Andy nodded. "Amen."

Metthew cleared his throat. "I think it best you go home now and rest."

"I am so sorry, Matthew."

"Don't worry about me. Or Susan. Or the choir. You have been through the fire, and there may be more to come. But for now, rest."

Susan couldn't bear the wait. The revival was over and the congregation dispersing, but no one had emerged from the office. When she heard raised voices, she headed for the door. A tug on her arm stopped her.

"You can't go in there," Mrs. Oldfield said.

Susan yanked her arm free. "Who are you to tell me where I can and cannot go in my own church?"

"This is not your church! This is the Lord's church. And the Lord's work is being done in there."

"What do you know about it?"

"No more than you!"

Susan's heart went cold and she glanced at the closed door.

"And I know my place," Mrs. Oldfield added, "which is something you need to learn, young lady, sooner or later."

Just then, Reverend Gronville burst from the office and nearly knocked Mr. Pautler over heading for the kitchen. Susan went after him.

JayRob didn't know if he should go after Susan or check on how things stood in the office. He was distracted when Harvey Hancock came up and shook his hand. "That was terrific, JayRob! " he said. "Is Reverend Grenville available now?"

He had forgotten about the radio man. "Brother Bob likes to recover in private after such a powerful amount of witnessing," he extemporized.

"Well, I can imagine. He was terrific! He'll be great at the dedication tomorrow."

Tomorrow? He had forgotten all about the library dedication! "Yes, uh . . ."

"He will be speaking, won't he?"

"Well, I imagine—"

"Great!" Hancock clapped him on the shoulder. "See you there, pal." Hancock joined Mrs. Grenville and Reverend Mathers, and the three of them appeared to be engaged in cheerful congress as they headed for the door.

JayRob's mind kept churning, his role as deacon, his role as Mayor, his role as businessman chasing each other to no end. When Pastor Jacobs came out of the office, JayRob caught him by the arm. "Where's Simms?" he asked.

Jacobs gave him a hard look. "I've sent Brother Andrew home. He has had quite an ordeal tonight." He started for the kitchen.

"Brother Matthew," JayRob called out, stopping him. "About the dedication." Jacobs looked at him, puzzled. "The children's choir." Jacobs shook his head, still not understanding. "Simms is to conduct the children's choir in 'God Bless America' at the dedication tomorrow. Don't you think, in light of his *ordeal . . .*"

Matthew Jacobs took a deep breath and closed his eyes. "Yes, of course."

"Everyone thought he did such a splendid job at the Special Service. But now—"

"Yes, yes, Brother JayRob. I have already given Andy a leave of absence from his duties here."

"But we're kinda on the hook for—"

"Yes, all right! I'll find somebody. There's a favor I can call in. Now—"

There was shouting from the kitchen. Pastor Jacobs left without finishing.

Susan surprised Grenville by the refrigerator. All she wanted was to ask about Andy, but he was immediately belligerent.

"What are you doing in here?" he demanded.

"What are *you* doing in here?"

"Young lady, I have no time for your nonsense." He yanked open the refrigerator door.

"You won't find your coffee in there."

"Get out of my way!"

"I'm not in your way. I'm standing way over here. What are you looking for, anyway?"

Grenville slammed the door shut. "It is time you learned a little respect for your elders, child." He held one hand behind his back.

"I am not your child and my elders get all the respect they deserve. What has gotten into you? And what have you done to Andy?"

"Susan!" her father's voice shouted from the door. "Apologize at once to Brother Robert."

"What is going on, Father? Where is Andy?"

"That's none of your concern. Now, I'm waiting for that apology."

She saw a look pass between her father and Grenville. That was all she needed. "I want to see Andy."

Her father blocked the door. "I've sent him home, Susan."

"Well, then, lend me the car and—"

"No. Leave him be. Andy needs some time by himself tonight. Go home. I'll be there directly."

"But—"

"Directly. I am not of a mind to discuss it, Susan. Go home. We'll talk about your disrespect and your disobedience later."

Susan stared at her father, speechless, then left, blinking back tears.

As soon as she was out of the kitchen, Grenville brought his hand out from behind his back. It held an apple. He bit into it viciously. "She's a wild one, Matthew. She needs a lot of work."

Matthew Jacobs stepped up to his fellow pastor. "I won't argue the point, Robert, but it's not her wildness that concerns me just now."

Grenville chewed two more bites of apple before speaking. "You think I was too hard on the boy."

"Yes, frankly, I do. Confessing the act was hard enough. It would be for anyone. But pressing him to name names was uncalled for."

Grenville eyed Jacobs as he finished the apple, then he placed the ravaged core carefully on the counter top. "Ezekiel, Chapter 37, Brother Matthew. The watchman who sees the enemy and fails to sound the alarm bears the guilt of every iniquity he could have prevented." He looked up. "If we do not call the sinner to atone for his sins, his corruption is on our hands. If we do not publicly accuse these men, rout them from their dark and fetid holes, God will call us to account as surely as He will them." He walked to the sink and rinsed his hands. "I have seen it, Brother Matthew. I have seen it rip through a church like a tornado. Even the merest whisper is ruinous! Have you forgotten how much damage was done to our church?"

"Those charges were never proved."

"But the damage was done! Parham never preached again. It nearly snapped the Pentecostal movement off at its root."

"I am well aware of church history, Brother Robert. But the times we live in have also made me aware of how much damage a witch hunt can do."

"A witch hunt? Very well, a witch hunt! And what is a witch but evil living among us unexposed? Evil that must be excised, cut away, cast out and burnt!" Grenville's face was not red and his forehead did not bead with sweat as before. There was cold fire in his eyes. "The question is, are you the man to do it?"

Pastor Jacobs took a deep breath. He was struck at how clear his mind was, how certain the path before him lay and where it would lead. *So, this is what it looks like,* he thought, *the Invitation.* "Thank you for your service to our church and our congregation, Reverend Grenville. Deacon Pautler will present you with the proceeds of this evening's love offering. At your hotel room, if you prefer."

Grenville's expression changed. A great tension left his body. It was not the release of defeat, however, but the settling of cold conviction. "If that is what you wish, Brother Matthew."

"That is what I wish, Brother Robert."

Grenville walked to the door and turned. "In all Christian charity, and in the spirit of love, I must tell you: you are letting your own uncertainties and compassion cloud your heart. You are making a grave error."

"No, Brother Robert. I may be, as you say, beset by uncertainties. But this is not one of them. Good evening."

"God be with you, Brother Matthew." Grenville paused at the door, waiting for a reply. When none came, he left.

On his way to the front door, Reverend Grenville was presented with an envelope by JayRob Pautler.

"The rain has stopped," JayRob said cheerily.

Grenville nodded. "For now."

JayRob smiled. "I think your wife and the others are waiting in the car."

"Thank you, Brother JayRob." Grenville paused, looking into the night. "I think I will speak at the dedication tomorrow after all, if that is still possible?"

JayRob broke into a huge grin. "Will you, really? Wonderful! Absolutely! We will be honored to have you."

Grenville tucked the envelope into his suit coat. "Not in the least. I am but the servant of a higher purpose."

Chapter 27

A Latter Rain

Susan hugged her knees to her chest in the darkness of her room. She was dressed in her father's old clothes, a pair of ragged sweat pants and a work shirt. As a teenager, she had often retreated into the comfort of this outfit whenever her mother's absence suddenly manifested as a painful hole in her heart. Now the clothes only mocked her. She had tried to appear contrite, hoping a pair of well-performed apologies would soften her father, but he had been unyielding. He had forbidden her from "disturbing" Andy and sent her to bed.

Sent her to bed! As if she were still a teenager. Her angry tears were as much at herself as at him. She had locked herself in this box, living here under his roof when she should have struck out on her own long ago.

She sniffed back her runny nose and straightened up. She shouldn't just sit here feeling sorry for herself. She should be thinking of Andy. And just because her father was treating her like a seventeen-year-old didn't mean she had to play the part. Besides, she recalled, that seventeen-year-old had been rather clever. Daring, even.

She got up and put on her sneakers.

Harry Edom gave a start when he heard the rapping on the etched glass of the front door. He calmed himself as he walked to it. *It can't be Lerner*, he told himself. *The old goat won't be back till tomorrow. Besides, he wouldn't knock on his own front door.* Nevertheless, when he opened it, both parties were startled. "Susie!"

"Harry!" she said at the same time. They laughed nervously, and both started to say, "What are you doing here?" and broke up again. Harry held up a hand and stepped onto the porch, closing the door softly behind him. "Okay," he said, "you first."

"I was hoping Ginny would still be up."

Harry took a deep breath and passed his hand over his brow. "No, thank goodness, she's finally asleep."

"Is something wrong?"

He shrugged, wide-eyed. "How would I know? I've never been pregnant."

Susan shifted from foot to foot. "Maybe I should come in. Maybe there's something I can do."

He shook his head. "She's just tired. And who can blame her? She's carrying around enough for two babies."

Susan put her hand to her mouth. "Oh, Harry, do you think—?"

"No, no! We checked. That is, the doctor checked. Just one. He guaranteed it. And he'd better be right or I'll knock his block off."

Susan laughed softly, and then took his hands in hers. "I'm really glad for you, you know."

"Yeah. Thanks." They stood for a moment, then Harry pulled his hands away. "So, Suzie-Q, what brings you out in the middle of the night?"

She sighed and looked away. "It's Andy. I think he's in trouble. I can't call him because there's no phone there. I could go over, but . . ."

"Yeah, that's quite a get-up you're wearing."

Susan looked down at her sweatpants and untucked shirt tails. "No, it's not that, it's . . . Well, my father won't let me use the car, and it feels like it might rain again, and I thought Ginny could let me borrow her dad's—"

Harry shook his head. "Nope. New York has taken the Studebaker to Oklahoma City on some lark or other and won't be back till morning." He saw her shoulders slump. Her brow furrowed and her mouth drew down in a tight frown. He'd seen that look on Virginia. He knew you didn't argue or try to reason with a woman once she got that look. "Look," he said, "why don't you take my truck? It's around back."

She lit up immediately. "You sure?"

"Sure. You know how to drive a stick, don't you?" Susan gave him a look. "Yeah, I thought so." He fished his key ring out of his pocket and detached the car key.

"Thanks," Susan said, grabbing it eagerly and starting down the porch steps. She stopped at the bottom and looked up. "You didn't say when you wanted it back."

He shrugged. "Take your time." Susan continued to stare at him. "I don't need it till morning. It'd be a good idea if I was gone when Lerner comes back."

Susan hesitated a moment, then dashed up the stairs, hugged him, and dashed back down and around the house. He heard the engine start, and moments later the truck backed out of the drive, turned around, and headed down the street. Though he listened for it, he didn't hear the gears grind once. *Well*, he thought, *that's* two *things to tell Ginny.*

The rain started again as Susan drove to Andy's house. She knew the way even though she'd been there only once, but when she pulled into the alley, she saw no lights on, either in the granny house or in Mrs. Oldfield's. She stopped and thought. Maybe her father had been right all along; Andy just needed a rest, some quiet time by himself. She felt foolish. Then she noticed Andy's car was gone. *Where could he be at this hour?* she wondered. And then she worried.

She started the truck again and rolled slowly down the alley, trying to think. She would just have to return Harry's truck and go home. Now she really felt dumb. She'd been gone only ten minutes, and the rain was starting to pick up. She'd have to ask Harry for a ride home or she'd be drenched. Getting back in without notice would be hard enough without wet sneakers squeaking up the stairs.

The rain poured down as she approached the Alquist mansion a second time, but a movement across the street by the church caused her to pull over and stop. There was someone crouching against the front doors. She opened the door and called out, "Andy?"

The figure didn't move but she was certain it was him. She got out and ran to the shelter of the doors, one hand shielding her eyes from the rain. It was Andy. He was hunkered down, rocking. "Andy," she said gently, kneeling down beside him. He flinched at her touch. "You're soaking wet." Andy sobbed and she put her arm around him. "Why aren't you inside?"

He looked up. "They took my keys. They won't let me in."

Susan was suddenly furious. "I'll get Father—"

"No!" Andy stood up abruptly, almost knocking her over. "You shouldn't be here. You shouldn't be with me."

"But I want to be."

"I am cast out."

Susan shook her head. "Not to me." He stared at her, then turned and walked off into the rain. "Andy?" She stood. He didn't answer. He moved in a straight line toward his car, as if the rain weren't even there. He got in and drove off. *What can I do?* she thought. *What's right?* She didn't know how to figure it out, but she knew almost for certain that she didn't have much time. She got into the truck and followed him.

Mrs. Oldfield stood in her kitchen, looking over the dark sloping lawn. She'd been awakened twice that night by the sound of a truck rolling down the alley. The first time, she had gotten up warily and crept to the back door, her heart pounding. But the truck had stopped only briefly, then moved on. Nevertheless, she had turned on the hall light and looked up the sheriff's number. Memorizing it calmed her, and she turned off the light and went back to bed.

When the unfamiliar engine woke her a second time, she went directly to the back door and stood watch, ready for anything. The truck had stopped, its lights still on. There were no lights on in the granny house. Mrs. Oldfield *tsk*'d in disgust when she saw that Andy had left his door open. *I gave him that lock! Has he no sense?* The truck turned off its lights and a man stepped out. Only one man. She thought she knew who, too, from the long black hair, and she opened the back door and swung the screen door open. *One sharp word should do it.* But something about the way the man moved was not right. The figure stopped just outside Andy's door. "Andy?" a woman's voice called.

Clara Oldfield backed swiftly into her house, barely catching the screen door in time to keep it from slamming. It wasn't him after all. It was . . .

Both her hands covered her mouth. What should she do? She couldn't breathe. Should she call Pastor Jacobs? Should she pray? For what? She stood there watching as the young woman entered Andy's house. Clara backed all the way into the kitchen, her eyes on the open door to the granny house, her mind a blank. Her legs brushed the edge of a chair and she sat down, unable to look away.

She was still there when the rain clouds loosened their grip and pale blue light slid through ever-widening sky to disclose the dawn.

Chapter 28

DEDICATION

Susan dropped Harry's truck off at the Alquists' before the sun touched the top of the water tower. Andy, following in his car, drove her the short distance to her house and returned home, reversing the back-and-forth of last night's chase. It was all done in silence. Susan's clothes were dry except for her sneakers, so she took them off and entered her home barefoot. At the foot of the stairs leading to the bedrooms, she could hear her father's gentle snore and was overwhelmed with shame. She sat down on the stairs and started to cry, but then her instincts kicked in and she managed to creep into her room undetected before the floodgates really opened.

She thought of all the little ways she had betrayed her father's trust. The sneaking out at night, the cigarettes, Ginny's flask of hooch. And she remembered the really big betrayal, the summer after high school, when she and Ginny had vowed to lose their virginities, and the two of them had plotted, almost like it was a game, which boy would be "the one." Ginny had chosen John Tibbits because, as she put it, he'd be a pushover. Susan had been less direct, saying only that it couldn't be anyone in town, all the while having in mind a certain preacher's son from Ardmore she'd met at last year's Summer Bible Camp. She and Ginny had felt wicked and powerful, at times taking their dreams seriously, at other times being deliberately crass, each ridiculing the other for the slightest trace of "mush." They were alternately hysterical and solemn, talking about boys the way they were certain boys were talking about them.

In the end, it was Harry Edom who had been Ginny's first, and he had been no push-over at all. She really fell for him, his rough independence and the way he carried himself without a trace of shame about his lack of connections, his mixed blood, or his decision to drop out of high school. Ginny's whole heart had gone out to her working class roughneck. She

rebuffed any warning from Susan and grew livid at her father's ultima-
tums. In the end, she had gambled all on Harry, and the two of them had
gotten married in secret. By comparison, Susan's "first love" had been a
betrayal not only of her father, but of her own secret hopes. Once she and
the boy had completed their assignment, the relationship lost its thin
veneer of high purpose. A month later, when they formally broke it off,
she felt as if nothing at all had really happened. That, and nothing else,
made her sad.

She wondered at the time why God hadn't punished her for the mis-
use of His gifts. But last night, standing outside Andy's door, she thought
she knew why. He had been preparing her for this moment when another
soul needed her and the knowledge she had gained but could not bring
himself to ask for it.

But in her room, last night's flimsy excuses showed themselves for
what they were: self-serving vainglory, taking the role of heroine in her
own story. "Stupid!" she yelled into her pillow, striking it with her fist.
"Stupid, stupid, stupid!" She cried for herself and her father and her
Andy, the Andy that never was and the Andy she now knew could never
be. She hoped in the darkest canyons of her soul that each of them would
forgive her.

She heard her father stirring and stifled the rest of her grief. There
was a ceremony at the library today. She and her father and Andy would
all be there. If her father found out what happened last night, it would
crush him. And could she face Andy again? Could she even live in the
same town with him?

She wiped her tears away with her hand. That wouldn't be decided
today. For today, everything must be as it was, or at least as it seemed.
She had her role to play. She could do that.

Sunny stepped out of the shower and looked at himself in the mirror that
hung on the bedroom door. His hair neared shoulder length, and his beard
was soft to the touch. "You are not to blend in!" his uncle Bhavjeet had
roared back in Stockton when he announced his intention to be a "normal
person." In answer, he had undone his *dastaar*—not simply taking the
turban off, but slowly and quietly unwinding it before the old man's eyes.
With each pass of his hands around his head, his uncle's voice rose and his
face darkened. "We are special! We are a people apart!"

And who was this in the mirror, then, but some long-haired artist try-ing to play the role of local bohemian? When had he ever fit in? When had he ever been "normal"? The clothes, the speech were Western, but the East poured out of his skin and eyes. "Singh," he said softly. "Lion."

Well, then. He had the comb, somewhere; and the *kirpan*—kept, he'd told himself, for the fine craftsmanship on the handle; and he had never given up wearing the silver *kara*, enjoying its bright flash on his wrist with each bold gesture. But the ridiculous *kachhera* was long gone, glee-fully chucked with the rest of his underwear the first day he slid into a pair of jeans. He opened the bottom drawer of his dresser quietly so as not to disturb the man sleeping in his bed. Moving aside a jumble of t-shirts, he found the length of *dhamala* neatly folded on the bottom. He took it out and laid it on the dresser.

He found his linen suit and the iron and moved out to the kitchen. A towel on the easel provided a level surface to crisp up the trousers and sleeves. When he put the suit on and stood before the mirror again, he had to admit he was impressed. The white of the linen made his skin seem both darker and more lustrous. He smiled. There was no fitting in now!

He picked up the *dhamala* in both hands like a prayer shawl and calmed himself. Done right, wrapping his hair would be a kind of medi-tation. He clamped one end in his teeth and began winding the rest around his head.

The first try didn't work. It looked like some kind of lumpy cloth pudding. He muttered a curse, shook out the *dastaar*, and started again

"It seems a shame to hide it," said the man in the bed. He would be Sunny's ride into town today. "A sin, really."

"You hide some things to show off others," Sunny said. This time he pulled more tightly at each pass over his head, his hands and arms re-membering without effort. He laughed to himself. Of course. "Like falling off a bicycle," as Uncle Bhavjeet would say.

Andy stood outside the church. He was supposed to run the children's choir through "America the Beautiful" one more time before the dedica-tion ceremony. He no longer had keys to the building, but if anyone showed up, he'd think of something. The kids weren't bad, really. The tune was simple enough, and volume and enthusiasm would not be a problem. It was mostly a matter of getting them to pay attention to him as he waved his hands and mouthed the words so they could all keep in tempo and sing in unison.

But nobody showed up.

Against Harry's better judgment, Virginia insisted they wait until her father returned before leaving for the ceremony. "The deal is over," she said. "I've kept out of sight while he raised money for mom's memorial. Now everything is out in the open and he needs to know it." She gave him a sharp look. "Don't roll your eyes at me, buster."

"I'm not—" Harry stopped before he made matters worse. He stood in the front hall, ruining the hat he meant to wear by wadding it up in his large hands and slapping it out against his thigh. Virginia looked perfectly calm.

When Lerner came through the front door, Harry straightened up, ready for anything. For the first time since Harry had known him, he looked actually old. His shoulders were stooped, and he wasn't wearing his signature fedora, revealing a surprisingly sparse and fragile-looking shock of silver hair. The minute he saw Harry, though, the old Lerner came back, spine ram-rod straight and fire burning in his eyes. But he said nothing.

"Good morning, sir," Harry said.

"Daddy," Virginia said, "I just wanted to remind you what we agreed."

"I don't need reminding," Lerner said in a low voice.

"Harry and I are husband and wife, and we will be living together."

"But not here."

"No. But you need to get used to seeing us together. It's not just Harry and me, anymore—or at least, it won't be soon. We're a family, and a family has to get along."

"Does it?"

Harry thought for sure he'd be caught in the crossfire between his wife and her father, but Lerner's shoulders slumped again and he said, "Yes, I suppose it does," and started slowly up the stairs.

Harry glanced at Virginia, who shot him a confused—almost disappointed—look.

Lerner stopped a few stairs up and spoke without turning around.

"Mister . . . Edom. I wonder if I might have a word with my daughter. Alone, please."

"Certainly, sir." He managed to get out the front door despite Virginia's hissing at him and trying to catch his arm. He left the porch and went a safe distance down the walk, cramming his destroyed hat onto his head and thanking God for a narrow escape.

When Virginia came out moments later, he asked sheepishly, "What did he say?"

She looked back at the front door, frowning. "He apologized."

"What?" He didn't believe it. "For what? You mean, about us?"

Virginia shook her head. "No. I don't think he'll ever change his mind about that. But— He said it was for something he said once, about the baby."

"What was that? What did he say?"

She searched his face, came to a conclusion. "It doesn't matter. But he asked me to forgive him."

He gave a low whistle. "And did you?"

Virginia looked back at the mansion. "Yes," she said, her voice full of wonder. "I did."

The scene at the site of the dedication was middling chaos. The street in front of the library had been blocked off, and people stood in chatting groups, most of them in the street since the walk in front of the library steps was taken up with the speaker's platform. Bunting was draped across the entrance and colored ribbon wound around the lamp posts for a block in either direction.

The ropes stabilizing one of the frames hanging from the cranes had loosened in the night and the frame banged authoritatively against the platform. Harry went to work on it while Tucker sat in the cab of the crane in case it needed to be hoisted higher. This provided a point of interest for the gathering populace, who debated the issue of whether rope should tighten or loosen in a rain. Electricians from KROY crabbed across the planking, laying cables and placing mikes and performing their traditional incantations. Lisle Armbruster, in a wheelchair and a patch over his right eye, was wheeled onto the platform by an enthusiastic JayCee, followed by his wife fussing in a flowered hat.

Virginia scanned the crowd, feeling lighthearted. She saw Susan arrive with her father, and, from a different direction, Andy Simms. Susan and Andy made eye contact, but there didn't seem to be the kind of warm recognition she expected from lovers. Maybe what Harry had told her about last night wasn't true. Or maybe it was. How do young lovers of a fundamentalist stripe act toward each other the morning after? She had no idea. She had never been good at keeping her emotions under a hat. She turned her attention to the platform.

Miss Lancaster was tidying papers on the lectern. Mayor Pautler arrived with that pompous preacher from Dibble City. *What is he doing here?* Virginia wondered. Scanning the crowd again, she saw John and Ruth Tibbits and John's father, Henry; a clutch of Littledeers and Longacres; Bill Sullivan and his wife—was she just a tiny bit pregnant? *Well, well. It must be catching.* The Rosens, Mrs. Oldfield, the Swoffords, even old Reverend Cecil Jameson and a few Negro couples she hadn't seen in weeks. A group of children emerged from around the back of the library, chattering and running, followed by Ethan Jameson. Virginia had always found him handsome, even back when they went to separate high schools and she only saw him occasionally at Herman's. It seemed like centuries ago.

But there was someone missing. She searched the crowd and didn't see him, so she sought out Harry. She found him securing a rope behind the speaker's stand. "Harry, where's Sunny?"

"No idea," Harry grunted, pulling on the rope.

Tucker joined them. "All secure," he said.

"Jed, have you seen Sunny?" Tucker shrugged and shook his head. "Well, he's got to be here. It's his sculpture, isn't it? So where is he?"

Tucker frowned. "How the hell should I know?"

"We've been kinda busy, Ginny."

Virginia looked at them in disbelief. "Do you mean to tell me neither of you lunk heads thought to go get him? What is he supposed to do, walk?" Harry and Tucker looked at each other. The men's silence was infuriating. "Oh, come on, guys! You can't be that pissed off at him. They're going to start without him!"

"I'll go," Tucker said reluctantly.

"Wait," Harry said, looking off. "Here he comes." A smile broke across his face.

Virginia turned and saw a figure in a brilliant white suit making his way through the crowd. His linen jacket fell below his knees, his eyes shone, and his teeth gleamed in a smile. His head was topped with a lavender turban. The murmuring crowd parted before him as he strode to the platform and mounted the steps.

"I'll be damned," Virginia said. "*The* Indian."

Out front, Susan and Andy finally had time to get in a few words. "Are you okay?" Susan asked.

"Sure," Andy said. Then, "No. No one showed up for the rehearsal. The kids are all here, but I don't know where they're supposed to go in the program or where I'm supposed to stand or anything."

"Miss Lancaster is handing out programs. I'll ask her."

"No, it's my job. I'll ask her."

They saw her leave the platform and head behind the platform so they followed her. As they rounded the corner they ran into Ethan Jameson looking up at one of the suspended panels. "Brother Andy!" Ethan grinned broadly and shook his hand. "I'm so glad to see you're feeling better. Do you feel up to conducting the children's choir after all?"

Andy looked form Ethan's face to Susan's. "No, I— What?"

"When Susan's father called, we were only too happy to be able to do something for Mt. Hermon." His smile faded as the confusion on Andy's face grew. "You did know I was asked to step in, didn't you?"

Andy took a deep breath. "Yes, yes. Thank you, Ethan. It's a great relief to know it's in your hands. I don't think I would be up to it."

Ethan's smile returned. "Well, I'd best get ready. You know kids. Like herding rabbits!" He wove his way through the backstage crowd to where the children were assembling.

"Andy," Susan said, "I didn't know."

"It's all right. It's better this way."

"It's *not* all right! They have no right." She grabbed his arm, but he gently detached her hand.

"It's done, Susan. Let it go. Let's just enjoy the ceremony."

"Ladies and Gentlemen," announced Mayor Pautler, leaning too closely into the microphone. "Please stand for our national anthem." It was an unnecessary request since everyone was already standing. The anthem was played by the High School Pep Band, and a few people, caught up in the excitement, actually sang. To make bookends of his remarks, Mayor Pautler said, "You may be seated," though only the folks on the platform actually sat, except of course for Mr. Armbruster, who hadn't risen from his wheelchair.

The rest of the platform party consisted of the members of the City Council, the Reverend Robert S. Grenville, Lila Armbruster (next to her husband), Lerner Phillip Alquist, his daughter and her husband, the head of the construction crew, Harry Edom. Sunny sat at the end, his colorful attire matching the bunting much better than the dark suits worn by others. An honor guard of ROTC cadets stood at one rear of the platform. Ethan Jameson sat on the far right, separate from the rest of the party, near the stairs the children would use when they came on stage. The children themselves shuffled and giggled off-stage, kept in line by that air of comportment only a librarian of Miss Ida Laine Lancaster's standing could convey.

Mayor Pautler then introduced Council Member Bill Sullivan, who led everyone in the Pledge of Allegiance. This caused a moment of confusion as the platform party, having just settled in their seats, had to stand once again. Furthermore, the honor guard was actually behind them, so they had to turn their backs on the crowd to face the flag (except for Mr. Armbruster, who continued to stare out at the crowd through his one unblinkered eye). The pledge went off without a hitch—or mostly: Bill Sullivan, being both a Legionnaire and a member of the Knights of Columbus, couldn't resist adding "under God" into the pause right after "one nation," and it rang out in the noontime air like a challenge. People just shook their heads and smiled. Those Catholics. Always trying to be more American than Americans.

Mayor Pautler continued his role as emcee and announced, "Reverend Robert S. Grenville of The Trembling Hour Ministries will now give the invocation."

People bowed their heads, so no one noticed the looks that passed among the platform party as a consensus was quickly reached about whether they should stand for yet a third time. The consensus was "No."

Dear Heavenly Father,

"Don't need no microphone, do he?" muttered a Longacre to a Littledeer. "Shush!" hissed Mrs. Littledeer.

We are gathered on this beautiful day before this beautiful edifice to memorialize the persistence and diligence of Your people in the face of adversity. But we do so not to celebrate ourselves, but to acknowledge Your Grace, for it is through Your Grace that we have been given this land, and through Your Grace that we have prospered. As the prophet Isaiah has said, *The Lord will guide you. Your ancient ruins shall be rebuilt; you shall raise up the foundations of many generations; you shall be called the repairer of the breach, the restorer of streets to live in.*

Almighty God, You have brought us through storm and drought, through war and depression. We acknowledge that it is not the hand of man that creates lasting treasures, but the Hand of God, and it is not in stone and brick that You create it, but in the hearts of the faithful.

When we look upon this work, may it remind us of how fragile and fleeting all works of man truly are. If we admire its beauty, may we be reminded that the beauty of this world is but illusion, a snare to trap the unwary in worldly concerns and fleshly desires. And so, when we lift our eyes to gaze upon this marvelous work, may we lift them even higher, not to gaze upon the image of ourselves, but upon the Image of God the Eternal, Whose light breaks forth like the dawn, forever. Amen.

There was a rumble of *Amen*'s and then a bustling of children as they took the stage. Engineers from KROY moved two more microphones on stage, the clatter and bang of their placement amplified for all. That left no room for Ethan, but he quickly improvised, stepping down from the stage and using the chair he had been sitting on as a make-shift podium. This unusual arrangement plus Ethan's electric expression grabbed all the children's attention, and they started "America the Beautiful" not only in unison but also on pitch, and ended mostly the same.

Their departure was a little less orderly. The lectern was jostled, and the pages of Mayor Pautler's speech went scattering. He made the best of it. "It was too long, anyway," he announced, and the crowd laughed their approval. "We all know how important a day this is, and how long it has taken us to get to it. A library for the general public use was included in the original City Charter at the founding of Croy in 1912." He looked to the side of the stage. "You see, Miss Lancaster, I did remember something from all that research you did." He chuckled and turned front again. "But the town was a busy one, and we didn't always have time for the niceties. If it weren't for the persistence of one man, and the generous contributions of his dear wife, Ada, this library would never have gotten off the ground. Literally. I am referring, of course, to Mr. Lerner Phillip Alquist." The Mayor began the applause and it caught on soon enough. "And let us not forget the workmanship of many hands through the decades since the foundation was first dug, and the work just completed this year, supervised by an able young man—who just happens to be Mr. Alquist's son-in-law—a native of Croy, and a proud citizen of the Chickasaw Nation, Mr. Harry Edom." A pause, filled with smatters of applause. "And now, finally, today, I am happy to dedicate the crowning glory on this Memorial Library, a sculpture to be placed above the entrance, designed and executed by an adopted son of Croy, Mr. Sunder Sing So-High." (Sunny nodded graciously from his seat, not batting an eye.) "Commemorating the many events in our past, both trials and triumphs, as Reverend Grenville has so aptly put it. All the great doings and other stuff that have led us to our current state of peace, prosperity, and good, American government." More applause. "And I am especially happy to see that someone very special has been able to make it today, someone who has been there from the very start, Mr. Lisle Armbruster. Lisle—" The applause caught him by surprise, but he caught on quickly enough and was the last to stop. "Lisle was there when he and Mr. Alquist and my father first came up with the idea of a Memorial Library, and it is only fitting that he do the final act of dedication and unveil the memorial sculpture."

Applause and cheers filled the air. Virginia was thankful for it since it covered her father's muttered comment, "Pompous lying bastard."

There was a brief conference on the platform between Mayor Pautler and Mrs. Armbruster. Mr. Armbruster continued to stare straight ahead, unblinking. Pautler stepped back up to the microphone. "The sculpture will be dedicated by Mrs. Lila Armbruster, who speaks for her husband."

Lila stepped up to the microphone, and a long braided red cord was put in her hands. Harry leaned in and whispered to Virginia, "I hope this works."

"You *hope?*"

Harry shrugged.

Lila Armbruster tilted her face up to the microphone. A breeze ruffled the chintz flowers in her hat. "I hereby dedicate this sculpture and the library it will adorn to the memory of all the pioneers, settlers, and citizens who endured so much to found our city, and to the brave soldiers, sailors, marines, and airmen who have sacrificed so much to preserve it." She pulled the cord, and the wrappings around the sculpture, suspended behind the speaker's stand and six feet above their heads, fell away.

The crowd leaned forward.

Chapter 29

FRAGMENTS

Clara Evangeline Oldfield (née Whitlock)

Clara Oldfield sucked in her breath. There on the left panel, the one that commemorated the victims and survivors of the TriCounty Twister of 1935, was a scene from her own life. It clearly showed her and Gerald Oldfield being helped into a storm shelter whose door was held open against the tearing wind by an adult Negro man. *How did the Sohi boy know that?* she wondered. *I never told a soul.*

There had been no one left to tell: her parents, her sister and her brother-in-law, and their two children had all perished that day. The memories came rushing in, too fast to hold back. She had gone to van-Doozer's to buy a toy for her nephew, whose birthday was coming up. It had looked like it might rain, so she had brought her umbrella. She selected a tin milk delivery truck complete with a set of tiny bottles you could load in and take out. He liked trucks, and she thought this one would be the least likely to make noise and upset her high-strung sister. Opa Mae had been affecting airs since she married Marvin Snepp, and Clara, in a fit of pique, had accused her of worldly pride. The gift was meant to double as a peace offering. By the time she left the shop, a wind had come up, but it was a funny sort of wind, blowing every which way. A block from the store, large rain drops began smacking the wood planks of the sidewalk and she raised her umbrella as she hurried across the street. There was a rumble like continuous thunder behind her.

Suddenly, Gerald Oldfield roared up in his automobile with the top down and came to a skidding stop. Clara ignored him. In a town with few cars, Gerald Oldfield's roadster was an ostentatious stand-out, and it was best not to take notice.

"Clara Whitlock!" he hollered.

She continued walking.

"Clara Whitlock! Get in!"

The effrontery shocked her. She turned to rebuke him. Not only would she not ride in a car at the invitation of some man, but she would definitely not ride with Gerald Oldfield, who had a reputation for driving too fast and too drunk. "I most certainly—"

A roaring gust of wind tore the words from her mouth and the umbrella from her hand. She watched in amazement as the umbrella flew away from her in an arc, then abruptly changed direction and flew back up the street the way she came. Her eyes followed it and widened in terror as she saw the plate glass front of vanDoozer's burst into a thousand shards and the roof disintegrate upwards in a spiral of timber.

"Damn it, woman, take my hand or we're both dead!"

She grabbed his hand and he yanked her aboard and floored the accelerator, heading east. He drove through town like a maniac. It probably saved their lives. Hailstones the size of oranges battered them both as Gerald reached the Oldfields' farmhouse, but he didn't stop. Instead, he drove right through the roses, past the house, and plummeted down the slope of the back lawn, nearly upsetting the car and sending them both flying. He slammed on the brakes, gouging deep troughs in the turf, grabbed Clara's hand and pulled her along to the storm cellar where a portly Negro stood, holding the door open against the ever-rising wind.

"Mister Gerald! Mister Gerald!" he cried. "In here, quick!"

Gerald nearly threw Clara down the stairs. "You, too, Cecil!" he hollered above the wind.

"My family, across the river—"

"You'll never make it! Now!" He grabbed the man and pushed him inside and fell in on top of him, one hand pulling shut the door above him. It vibrated and jumped and hammered, but with a trembling hand he reached up and secured the bolt. A great roaring filled their ears and Clara rolled up in a ball on the floor and began to wail.

She might have lost her mind right then and there, her core hollowed out by terror, if a warm, steady hand had not lain lightly on her shoulder. *"Oluwa mi ni oluso-agutan,"* said a still, calm voice, *"emi ki yio fe."* She looked up into the face of Cecil Jameson. He stared into the far distance as if he could see beyond the dirt walls of the cellar, through the crust of the earth itself to another shore. She did not shrink from his touch but looked deeply into his face. The howling outside grew louder.

Gerald tugged at her dress. "Come away, Clara. He's gone mad."

"No," she said, pulling away, still looking up at Cecil. A stillness seemed to flow down from the man and fill her. "The Lord is my shepherd," she said. "I shall not want."

"*O si mu ki mi dubulẹ ninu papa ewe.*"

"He maketh me to lie down in green pastures."

"*O nyorisi mi lẹba si tun omi.*"

"He leadeth me beside the still waters."

Both hands lay upon her shoulders now. "*O si pada ọkàn mi.*"

"He restoreth my soul," she said. The howling inside her ceased altogether. Gerald took her hand.

She never told anyone about it, how she and Gerald and Cecil recited the rest of the Psalm in unison as the world tore itself apart above them, two of them speaking a language they had heard since birth, the third in a tongue neither had heard before, but which Clara knew as clearly as if she, too, had been born on the banks of that shadow-filled shore. She never told a soul how her second baptism, the Baptism of the Holy Spirit, had come to her through the hands of a colored man.

John Wayne Swofford, Businessman, Part-time Deputy Sheriff

Jake Swofford looked at the tornado panel and snorted in disgust. There it was again, the same old fairy tale about how the niggers saved the poor white folks. In the background, there was even a group of jigaboos handing out lumps of bread to a line of starving women and children. It weren't anything like that. His daddy told him so. They didn't get their bread from the black trash across the river; they got it from the VFW like any self-respecting citizen.

His eyes slid over to the center panel. Nothing there caught his eye or made any sense to him: two stiff figures with idiot expressions standing on either side of a woman in a chair, some guy slouched against a wagon wheel beneath them. Real comic-book stuff.

"Look at that Hindoo," Dale Longacre laughed at his side, pointing out Sunny. "Looks like the circus come back to town."

"This whole shit-show is a circus." Jake spat on the ground.

Dale pointed to the soldiers' panel. "Has he killed that fella?" he asked. The foreground showed two soldiers, one of them obviously dead, the other supporting him with one arm and holding his rifle, bayonet fixed, in the other. Jake Swofford recognized the weapon.

"That's Pork Chop Hill, you dumb-ass."

"Why they got their shirts off, then? Wasn't that in winter?"

"It's a allegory or some such."

"Aw, you're full of it. That ain't Korea. Look there behind them."

Jake was about to tell Dale to shut his trap when his eyes were grabbed by the scene behind the two main figures. It showed a US trooper training a machine gun on a bunch of surrendering Germans while another trooper raised a pistol in the air. Above them was a stylized eagle with a swastika in its talons. Jake smirked at the image: that idiot Hindoo had gotten the Nazi emblem all wrong. The eagle's wings were too square and the swastika wasn't angled like it should be. You should get it right or you shouldn't try.

He felt a fierce stab in his gut that made his eyes smart and he looked down so Dale wouldn't see. That Refior kid may have thought it was all fun and games, but not his boy. He'd brought Jink up right. He was proud of what he'd done. You don't mix pure with polluted. Rosen could spread all the grass seed he wanted but he'd never cover the burning truth.

He looked up again. Wait a minute . . . That wasn't the Reichs eagle, but the 45th Infrantry's insignia: the old swastika and the thunderbird they switched to right before the war. He clenched his fists. That Hindoo bastard had carved a nasty little joke and shoved it right in their faces: Red Indians over the White Race. *I'm going to get that towel-headed little queer for this,* he thought. *One of these nights, I'll make him pay.*

Lerner Phillip Alquist, Businessman

Lerner faced the panels as motionless as if he were a statue himself. He didn't hear the comments ebbing and flowing around him, or feel the sun on his face, or even see the whole of the sculpture. Everything lost its edges and disappeared except for the face at the apex, Ada's face, up there above them all, just as she was twenty years ago. *It's her, it's really her.* Nothing else mattered.

Henry John Crawford Tibbits, Rancher

Hank Tibbits, rancher and father of John Tibbits, head clerk at Rosen's Drug Store, had a dozen things to do out on the ranch but had come into town for the morning anyway to humor his son and his new wife, Ruth. When they told him he was going to be a grandfather, well, he decided to stay in town to celebrate and attend the dedication with them. He stood in the crowd shaking his head—not at the terra cotta panels or the library, fine as they were, but at himself. *A grandfather? Me? Well*, he had to admit, *it was bound to happen sooner or later*.

His son poked him in the ribs. "That rancher fella there on the center panel. Pa, is that you?"

"Naw!" he said automatically, then took a closer look. It was a figure reclining against a wagon wheel beneath the feet of two tall folks and a lady on a throne. He gave a surprised laugh. "Well, I'll be horn swoggled, it is! Look there at his hand, see where the little finger's nipped off? Remember when that happened?" He sure remembered it: the metal gate slamming shut as the bull went wild and lunged against it; the pain, the blood, the cursing; and his sweet and gentle wife, God love her, taking out the shotgun.

His son said, "Ma wanted to kill that bull right then and there. You stopped her."

"It was a good bull. Good stock. Said so then, say so now."

"I remember," John Tibbits said. "I think that's the day I decided to go into retail."

He looked at his son, then broke into a grin and slapped him on the back. He returned to admiring the sculpture. "That Indian fella sure is clever. I couldn't for the life of me figure out why he kept coming out to the ranch. Most days he just wandered around. Couldn't see what he was interested in. Turns out, it was me!" He shook his head. "Sure is a clever fella. Where in heck is he, anyways?"

Lila Louise Armbruster (née Hammond)

Lila Armbruster held her hat on with her left hand and twisted around to see the unveiled sculpture. The sunlight lit up her face. *Why, it's beautiful!* she thought. She turned to beam at her husband, but he sat immobile in his wheelchair, staring out into the crowd. She touched him on the shoulder. "It's beautiful, Lisle," she said. He didn't respond, so she leaned into his ear. "The library, Lisle. It's finally done."

"About fucking time," he said.

She patted his hand and looked up at the panels. "Just beautiful."

Robert S. Grenville, Radio Evangelist, Host of The Trembling Hour

The Reverend Grenville stared in shocked disbelief. In the noon-day sun, he could clearly see the shadow of nipples beneath the stone drapery covering the breasts of the figure on the center panel. He'd heard a lot about that "Goddess of Prosperity." Birdine told him not one of the good women of Croy admitted to posing for it. No wonder! He heard snickering in the crowd behind him. He couldn't bear to look upon that figure further, so his eyes slid over to the soldiers' memorial and he caught his breath. *But that's Andy Simms!* Bare-chested and leaning over another young man whose clothes had been torn from his body. A fierce certainty gripped him. *So, now we see who the other man is!* He swiveled around in his seat and scanned the platform looking for the deviant, but he wasn't among the dignitaries. Turning to the crowd, his eyes lit upon Andy Simms, staring slack-jawed and horrified at the panel. The guilt was as plain as the nose on his face. Grenville looked around. Where's Pautler? He needed to have a word with that man. *This cannot stand! This monument to lust must not stand!*

Jonathan Robert Pautler, Mayor

Mayor Pautler looked out at the crowd. It was clear they enjoyed the ceremony. Folks were pointing and talking, and there were smiles all around. Well, mostly smiles. And some of the pointing was at him.

"Has he killed that fella? Why is he looking like that?"

"Better look out, JayRob. You're next!"

"What?" Pautler called out, smiling.

"He's right behind you, Mayor!"

He turned around and looked up at the sculpture for the first time. It looked fine to him, all proper and to specification. There was Mrs. Gilbert as "Civic Duty" to the left of "Prosperity," and his own figure to the right as "Good Governance." But wait a minute, now. The bayonet on that soldier pointed straight at his neck! He turned and smiled nervously at the crowd. Had anyone else noticed? Was that laughter he heard? He turned back to the soldiers' panel and looked again, hoping the figures had rearranged themselves. Then he noticed who held the rifle. He recognized the other soldier as well, the one the Simms boy was practically swooning over. *It's that So-high boy!* He glanced furiously at Grenville, whose face was a mirror of his own. Pautler shook his head. *I had nothing to do with this!* Grenville directed his attention to the crowd. Pautler looked out and spotted Andy Simms. The look on his face was all the proof he needed. His face a deep red, he marched over to Sunny Sohi, standing and accepting compliments from the crowd. Grenville followed right behind him.

Virginia Helen Edom (née Alquist)

Virginia Edom was unaware she had stood up and her mouth had dropped open.

"That's Jed's uncle!" Harry said beside her

"Huh?"

"Stone Face's crazy uncle, with the pistol, there on the soldiers' panel." Harry looked around. "Where *is* Jed? He should see this."

"Great," Virginia said, but she could not really hear him. She marveled at her mother's face, so serene above the scenes of terror and destruction, strife and crisis gathered like waves on either side of her. But she, calm and secure, was above it all, a guiding and unifying spirit, the golden promise that makes all the sorrow and struggle worthwhile.

Virginia rushed over to her father and flung her arms around his neck. "Daddy, you did it!" she said. "I get it now. It was worth it. I'm so proud of you!" She stretched up and kissed him on the cheek. He recoiled, frightened, as if woken from a dream.

Susan Cassia Jacobs

Susan pulled on Andy's arm, trying to thread her way out of the crowd with him in tow. He was like a drunkard, unable to turn away from the unveiled figures, unable to guide his own feet. "Where are you parked?" she asked. He said nothing. Emerging from the edge of the crowd, she saw his car midway down the block. "Come on. Let's get out of here." She hoped they could make it without anybody noticing them.

When they got to the car, Andy made no move to open the doors, so she fished the keys out of his sports coat, unlocked the door, and stuffed him into the passenger seat. She got in on the driver's side and started the engine. She looked at him. "Just go," he said. They headed west.

Neither saw the ruckus erupting on the speaker's platform.

Sundar Singh Sohi, Artist

Sunny couldn't be prouder. People came to the edge of the platform to congratulate him. At last they had seen and recognized him for who he was. He leaned over the edge and shook a few hands.

Lila Armbruster touched him on the arm, smiling affectionately. "You're the very image of your father," she said. "I remember when he used to come to town like that, all—"

Mayor Pautler pulled his other arm. His face was as red as clay. "What is the meaning of this, this *display* of pornography!" he hissed.

Mrs. Armbruster gasped and pulled back.

"What?" Sunny was confused. What did Pautler want now? He glanced up at the panels. "It's exactly to your specifications."

A large man, Grenville, the preacher who had done the invocation, stepped up, crowding him. "This is not what the good people of this town want. It is not what they deserve," he said.

Sunny saw Mrs. Armbruster backing away, her hand on her heart. "Who the hell are you to say what the good people of this town want?" he said.

Harry stepped between them. "Let's everybody just calm down," he said.

"And you're in this, too, up to your neck!" Pautler barked.

"What's going on there?" the old man in the wheelchair said.

Pautler turned around. The crowd was beginning to take notice. Sunny saw his eyes flick to the KROY crew.

"Let's take this to Lerner. He's the one paid for it."

Sunny was not going to let them ruin his day. Lerner had to back him up. He joined them as they formed a circle around the man, thin hair ruffled by the breeze, a vacant smile on his face. Ginny held his arm. "Daddy?" she was saying. "Daddy, are you all right?"

"Lerner, we've got to talk," Pautler said.

"Don't listen to them, Mr. Alquist," Sunny urged. "This is your crowning achievement, what you've worked for all these years."

"This is how they always operate." Grenville spoke urgently. "Subverting our schools and our libraries and every corner of civic life with their perversions."

"There is nothing perverse about these magnificent people!" Sunny insisted.

"What?" Lerner didn't seem to hear them.

"It needs to be torn down, Lerner," Pautler argued. "Now! At once! Or I'll have Chief Buchholtz arrest the lot of you for public indecency!"

"You're a bunch of barbarians!" Sunny yelled.

Lerner turned away and looked up at the image of his wife. Pautler poked him. "Lerner, are you listening to me?"

Lerner Phillip Alquist turned and smiled at them. "It's Ada," he said and collapsed at their feet. Virginia screamed and fell to her knees beside him.

Chapter 30

ISOLATED EARTH PEOPLE

Jedediah Tucker promised himself to keep his mouth shut. It was none of his damned business anymore. He wouldn't even be driving Sunny back to his trailer now if he hadn't been the only one left. Ginny was hysterical over her father, Harry was wild-eyed over Ginny and the baby, Andy was nowhere to be found (that was probably a good thing), and whoever the hell had driven Sunny to the dedication had vanished.

But Sunny's flaming indignation made it hard to stay quiet. The guy wouldn't shut up, calling Pautler every low name in the lexicon and a few choice words Jed was pretty sure were Punjabi. Then he started in on that preacher from Dibble City. Then on Lerner Alquist.

"The old fart had better not fold on me!" Sunny fumed.

"Maybe you should be concerned he doesn't up and die on you."

"Oh, Lerner's tougher than nails. He just got dizzy. It's nothing."

Jed shook his head. "You're always so sure of everything."

"Oh, blow me." Sunny drummed his fingers on the roof of the cab. "I'm sure of one thing. As soon as I change out of these duds, you're taking me right back to town. I'll stand guard over it with a shotgun if I have to."

"Have you got one?"

Sunny said something else in Punjabi and stared out the window. They pulled to a clattering stop outside the trailer and Sunny opened the door before they even stopped rolling. Jed found he couldn't hold back anymore. "Why'd you do it?"

Sunny was on the ground, the door in his hand. "Do what?"

"Why did you have to make it so . . ."

"Spit it out, Jed. So what?"

"Explicit."

"Explicit? You mean erotic." Sunny shook his head, smiling bitterly.

"The heroic is always erotic. That's what makes it heroic! If they aren't charged with life, if they aren't full of potential, then what do they sacrifice? It's meaningless!" He slammed the cab door and headed for the trailer.

Tucker got out but didn't follow. "They're going to make you do it over."

"The hell they are," he said bounding up the steps.

Then something peculiar happened. It looked to Jed like Sunny did a little jig on the top step, then his legs jutted out one way and his head and arms the other. He disappeared into the jimson weed by the door, the overturned steps settling in a cloud of orange dust.

It was comical. Jed walked around the front of the truck. It was a joke, right? "Sunny?" he called. He started walking, then running toward the trailer. Sunny lay on his side. When he turned him over, a patch of blood the size of a hand showed on the right side of his turban, dark red against the lavender.

Tucker felt for a pulse, found one, and tried to revive Sunny by jostling him and calling his name. Nothing worked. He thought he should get water and splash it on his face. There would be some inside. But the steps had overturned. "God damn you, Sunny! I told you to fix them stairs." He reached the doorknob but found it locked. "Okay!" he said aloud. "Okay!"

He picked Sunny up and carried him to the truck. He hoisted him on one shoulder and slid him into the passenger seat. Then he ran to the other side and got in.

The engine made a single sharp grinding noise and stopped. He tried again. There wasn't any sound at all, not even a solenoid clicking. He broke out in a heavy sweat. He pumped the gas pedal and tried again. Nothing. "Jesus fucking Christ!" he screamed and beat his hands on the wheel. The horn sounded, startling him. He sat still a moment, breathing heavily.

He wiped a sleeve across his forehead to keep the sweat from burning his eyes. Then he got out and looked at the dirt road that wound downhill, following the ravine. It was nearly a mile to the county highway, two miles from there to the nearest telephone in town. Someone might come along, and then again someone might not.

He went back to the truck, opened the door, and lifted Sunny carefully in his arms. He took one more look down the road then started up-hill, taking the path that lead to the settlement at Pesogi and his crazy uncle's house.

The door swung open while he was still twenty yards away. His mother's brother stood there, unmoving.

"I saw two men," he said. "They fight with war clubs."

"Not now, uncle," Tucker said, breathing heavily.

"A third runs from them, frightened, dressed in woman's clothes."

"We don't have time for that, damn it! This man needs your help." Tucker laid Sunny out in the dust before his uncle's house. Sunny flowed from his arms like some heavy liquid. He fought the urge to vomit.

His uncle took a couple of steps forward and looked down at the unmoving figure. "This is beyond me. This needs stronger medicine."

"I know that. Do what you can. Does your car have gas?" His uncle nodded, bending over Sunny. "I'm calling ahead to the hospital," Tucker said. On the phone inside, he spent a nightmare repeating over and over to a succession of idiots that he was bringing in a head injury. "Skull fracture," he shouted at last and hung up. When he got outside, his uncle had brought out his old Army kit, but he was shaking his head, looking at the blood-soaked *dastaar*. "This is not a bandage."

"No."

"It probably saved his life, though. Maybe."

"Will you come with us?"

His uncle looked up. His eyes were clear. "Yes."

Susan gripped the wheel of Andy's car while Andy slumped unmoving on the passenger side. "Where are we going?"

"Anywhere," Andy said. "Just drive."

They headed west. They drove for what seemed like hours. The sun crawled across the sky, baking them inside. Andy didn't seem to notice. Susan rolled down the window on her side, but Andy kept his rolled up. He stared out the windshield but did not seem to be aware of where they were. Susan felt the skin on her left arm begin to tighten and burn.

They passed through Marlow without once having to stop for traffic. Outside of Lawton, they saw a car with a flat by the side of the road. "Stop!" Andy called out.

There was a woman beside the car. Andy got out at once.

"Oh, thank you for stopping," the woman said, embarrassed and relieved.

Susan set the hand brake and got out. The woman came up to her. "I've been here nearly an hour, and there's been no one," she said.

"I can fix this," Andy said. "Do you have a jack?"

"In the trunk, I think."

Andy went to work, and the woman, nervous, kept talking. Susan didn't listen much. She could tell from the woman's clipped speech that she was from out East somewhere. She had followed her husband to Fort Sill when he had been called up and she had taken a job in Lawton. Now there was some sort of difficulty which she was loath to explain to her husband. She actually used the word "loath." "And on top of everything else, I'm late." She shook her head. "Martin will be in such a state. I'm Ruth, by the way."

"Susan," Susan said, distractedly shaking the offered hand. Her attention was on Andy, how calmly and efficiently he went through the motions: jacking up the car, replacing the tire, tightening the bolts, and getting everything back into the trunk. *I should be relieved*, she thought. *He's completely calm. He's acting as if nothing has happened.* But that only worried her more.

The woman spoke again as Andy closed the trunk. "I don't know how to thank you," she said. "I was beginning to worry, with evening coming on."

"I know," Andy said. He turned to Susan. "We should go back. I'll drive."

"If there's anything I can do for you—" the woman started.

"No, thank you, ma'am."

"My husband's just at Fort Sill. He'll gladly pay you."

"No, no. Happy to help. Our pleasure. Come on, Susan. It's time."

The woman watched the young couple get back into their car and head back the way they had come. *How remarkable is that?* she thought. She did not especially believe in Providence, and yet these two—the same age as she and Martin, maybe younger—showed up out of nowhere along a lonely stretch of road at just the right time. They changed her tire, then turned around and went back the way they came, as if they had been sent out here for the sole purpose of helping her. Kindness from strangers so far from home! What is that if not Providence? A *mitzvah*.

She should have at least gotten their names so she could tell her husband. The woman was Susan, wasn't she? But she hadn't gotten the young man's name. She started the car and headed back to town. She wished the best for that other couple, headed in the direction of the rising dark, and vowed to repay their kindness some day. Then they vanished from the details of her life.

Virginia drove her father home in the Studebaker. He had revived enough to insist on being taken home, not to St. Joseph's, but the fact that he let her drive convinced her he was still on shaky ground. Once they got him home, she shooed the mayor and that over-bearing preacher and Harry out, telling them her father needed rest and quiet. When Father Francis telephoned, she reported her father was resting comfortably on the sofa in his study. Where Tucker and Sunny had gone she didn't know and couldn't care less.

She fixed a simple supper of chopped steak, potatoes, and greens. He livened up as he ate. When he finished, he said, "Thank you, Virginia." When she reached for his plate, he said, "Leave it. It's been a long day. You should get some rest." She kissed him on the top of the head and went upstairs and lay down.

She was awakened by angry voices. She crept down the stairs. The voices coming from the study were Mayor Pautler's and her father's.

"It's got to come down!" Pautler insisted.

"You'll stop at nothing, will you? Well, it's done, and that's an end to it. If you don't think your pose is flattering, that's just too bad."

"This is not about my *pose*. My pose don't come into it a-tall! This is an insult to the entire town."

"I couldn't care less if Sohi had given you two noses and a baboon's tail. It's done, and it's going up where it belongs."

"Will you listen for once, you arrogant Yankee? That's not it *at all*! That's not what I'm talking about!"

Virginia entered the room and leaned against the door jamb. "Daddy?"

Lerner looked at her, then wheeled on JayRob. "Now look what you've done, you son of bitch. You've woken my daughter."

JayRob flushed with embarrassment, then pointed an angry finger at her. "Ask her, if you don't believe me. She knows all about them. Ask her!"

The room swam around her. "Ask me what?" She was barely able to get the words out.

"What do you *think*?" Pautler said, practically spitting. "It's an obscenity. Those two half-naked boys in their . . . position. My God, Alquist, can't you see it? It's that Simms boy and his god damned Hindoo. Two god-damned faggots hoisted up for all the town to see!"

"Oh!" Virginia said softly.

The color drained from Lerner's face. He stared at her.

Pautler looked from one of them to the other. Finally he snorted in disgust. "I've thought many things about you, Lerner. I've thought you petty, arrogant, vindictive, and greedy. But I've never thought you a fool." He started for the hall. "Your wife was a fine lady. Refined, elegant, kind. A good Christian woman. And this is the memorial you give her? What would she say, Lerner? What would Ada think?" The panes in the front door rattled as he left.

Her father turned to her. "What do you know about this?"

Virginia headed for the sofa, not looking at him. "You're not going to listen to that old wind bag, are you? You can't take him seriously." When she turned to face him, it felt as if her head lagged a few seconds behind the rest of her body.

"Is this your way of getting back at me? For what I said about Harry, about the baby? Is this some kind of twisted revenge?"

"No, Daddy!"

"Tell me it isn't true, then. You've had that Simms boy at your beck and call all summer."

"I won't say a word against Andy Simms."

"You don't defend him, either, I note. And that heathen little Sambo. What about him? You've been thick as thieves since you were kids."

Virginia clamped her lips shut. Anything she said now would only enrage her father further.

"Was Harry in on it, too? Laughing at me behind my back? Talk to me!"

Virginia shook her head. "Don't, Daddy. Don't think the worst of them."

Lerner paced up and down in front of the fireplace, barely listening. "I thought you were finally showing some sense, some respect. But you were just trying to soften me up! Playing to my weak side. Well, you've still got a thing or two to learn about me. I don't have a weak side!"

Virginia sank to the sofa, clutching her stomach.

"Don't speak, then, damn you. Your silence tells me everything. They're not getting away with it!"

A wave of pain and nausea washed over Virginia. The room contracted to a single blurred circle in front of her. She couldn't see her father and could barely hear his voice, bellowing over the telephone in the hall.

"Percy? Get Longacre and Swofford and meet me at the library. I've got work for you. Yes, now, god damn it! I don't give a rat's ass if you *are* on duty. I'm getting rid of that damned sculpture once and for all. Bring sledge hammers and jacks and, hell, I don't know. Dynamite, if you got it. I can't stand the sight of it. Get trucks. We're pulling it down and dumping it in the Canadian. And send some boys out to the trailer, too. Sohi's, you idiot! That devil has squatted on my land long enough. Burn it down, and I don't care if the black-skinned bastard is in it or not!"

Virginia sucked in huge gasps of air. The circle in front of her relaxed a little, letting in a bit more of the room. She could see the lamp, the carpet, the fireplace across the room. She heard the front door slam as her father left. She had to get to the phone. Leaning on the arm of the sofa, she struggled to her feet. She looked back. The cushion was soaking.

She pulled herself along the mantle and out into the hall to the phone. Taking deep breaths, she was able to calm her trembling hand enough to dial. The voice on the other end flooded her with relief.

"Hello?"

"Harry? Harry, you've got to stop him!"

"Ginny? Ginny, what's wrong?"

"It's Lerner. He's gone crazy. He's going to wreck the sculpture and kill Sunny!"

"Ginny, you're not making sense. He loves the—"

Virginia screamed as another contraction wracked her body.

"Ginny!" Harry's voice sounded desperate. "What is it? Is he there? Is he hurting you?"

"God damn it, Harry! The baby's coming!"

"Jesus Christ! I'll be right there! Hold on, Ginny, hold on!"

"No!" she screamed into the phone, but the line had already gone dead. "God damn you, Harry Edom! The one time in your life you pick to do the right thing, and it's the wrong thing! Fuck, fuck, fuck!" She slid to the floor, toppling the table and dragging the phone with her.

Her father's henchmen would get to the library any minute now. What could she do? Could she remember Tucker's phone number? It swam around in her head but got all jumbled up with the pain ricocheting around her belly. Who could she call?

Miss Ida Laine Lancaster put down the receiver, her mind flipping through plans of action like cards in a Rolodex. She stepped outside, hugging herself though the night was warm. She glanced up and down the street, then up at the sky. The moon slipped in and out of rafts of clouds. Unbidden, two lines of verse came to her:

O guardian of the grove, approve my plan
To save my friend and scatter far the clan.

Byron? she wondered. She shook her head. *There's no time for that now.* She looked up again. "May the moon favor our purpose," she prayed and hurried inside.

Lerner walked blindly through the night, crossing intersections on automatic, heading not for the library, but his office. "A fine tribute to your late wife. A fine memorial for Ada!" He did not see where he was going. Had there been any traffic around the square, he would have stepped right into it, but he did not see the curb as he stepped off, did not see brick-paved Main Street as he crossed, did not see his office as he passed it by. Could he really have been such a fool? Could all the work and sacrifice really have turned out to be nothing but a vulgar joke? All those years, all his plans, the miles of paperwork, the painful, endless negotiations, the hours of meetings. Did they add up to nothing? Had it all been a waste?

The town could shun him, fear him, loathe him, even laugh at him. It did not matter. But what would Ada think?

Part 5

I opened the bolt of my door to my beloved, but he had turned aside, and was gone. . . . I sought him, and found him not: I called, and he did not answer me.

—Song of Solomon

Chapter 31

ADA

"I'm afraid I have to disagree with you, Mr. Alquist," Miss Ada Dowdell said, smiling up at him. "I think numbers can be quite beautiful."

Lerner was captivated and speechless. It was an unfamiliar feeling and he liked it. Miss Dowdell's eyes sparkled with a mixture of mischief and encouragement, and he found it impossible to look away, though he was aware his stammering fascination was drawing notice. *Hang them all*, he thought, *she's worth it!*

In fact, she was the first thing he had thought worth it since coming to Croy. On the whole, his ventures in the new state of Oklahoma had not been productive. The one oil strike in town had proven to be on a very limited field, and not on a parcel he owned the mineral rights to. His partnership in the Oldfield coal pit was coming to an end as surface mining became more and more expensive; he had no interest in extending the life of the mine by extending it underground. But he persevered, feeling in his bones that some day even the least productive of his investments would pay off. He invested in a parcel here and a small farm there, and acquired a sizable lot in the most settled part of town, where he was building his home. He had had the foresight to get out of cotton before the boll weevil struck, so some of the tenant farms were beginning to pay. He felt his grasp of the future was clear-headed enough to start looking for a wife to help populate what promised to be the most splendid home in the county.

But all that concentrated attention on real estate, farming, ranching, and mineral rights had taken a toll on his social skills. Recognizing the deficit, he had accepted Lisle Armbruster's invitation to attend a reception for his niece, Opa Mae Whitlock, whose engagement to another of Lisle's relatives had just been announced. He expected the affair to be filled with the usual vain and silly young women he had encountered in town. The prospects were dim.

However, Lisle Armbruster had recently become station master of the Colorado, Gulf, and Santa Fe Railway and its chief agent in south central Oklahoma. With the convergence of lines from Oklahoma City and Tulsa just north of town and the line's extension south to Dallas, the Santa Fe would be an important engine for commerce and growth. And so, despite personal reservations about the quality of the pickings, he agreed to attend the reception and inspect the goods.

He nearly left the party as soon as he arrived. His first introduction was to Miss Clara Evangeline Whitlock—not the bride-to-be, but her older sister. Granted, she was closer to Lerner's age and temperament, which was probably why Armbruster had introduced them, but Lerner soon discovered why this particular Miss Whitlock was not the one being celebrated tonight. She was as sour as a grapefruit, and managed within the space of a few curt words to convey her opinions on the topics of both temperance and Roman Catholicism. He turned away with a brief word of parting and, setting down his punch, searched the room for Lisle, intending to make his apologies.

Then his eyes lit upon the dark beauty with the dancing eyes. She occupied a settee, dressed in an elegantly trimmed light blue dress. There was no sign of a wedding ring, though it was hard to tell from across the room. Next to her sat another young lady in a pink concoction that made her look like a strawberry phosphate topped with vanilla ice cream. If one of these was the about-to-be-wed Whitlock sister, then the chances were good the other was her maid of honor. It was a question he sought to resolve. When he found Lisle chatting with an elderly woman in a cane wheelchair, he caught his arm and propelled him towards the settee with the determination of a freight train.

Lerner was noticed before he made his approach. Miss Dowdell had turned to her dearest friend from Normal School and was about to make inquiries when Opa Mae unfurled her fan and sighed heavily. "This weather wears on my nerves. I declare I wouldn't be here if it weren't for all these people."

"If it weren't for you, my dear Opa, all these people wouldn't be here."

"I think the weather has gotten to you as well, Ada. You're not usually so short."

In the months since Ada had left college to attend her ailing father in

Whitt, Texas, she had forgotten how easily bruised her friend's feelings were. "I apologize, dear Opa. You deserve your happiness."

Opa Mae smiled shyly and squeezed Ada's hand. "It is a favorable match, is it not?"

"Most favorable, and I think the greater favor has been done to Mr. Marvin Snepp. He is lucky to catch you." Ada saw the blush rise in her friend's cheeks and knew the damage had been repaired. Now she could ask her question. "Who is that tall distinguished gentleman speaking to your sister?"

"Him?" Opa Mae said. "Oh, that's Lerner Alquist. Thinks he's a big to-do around here, but in truth he's just a carpetbagger in a tailored suit. Thinks he can get his way with anything."

"He's not having much luck with Clara," Ada observed.

Opa Mae sniffed. "Who does?"

"If I'm not mistaken, he's about to make his way over here to be introduced."

Opa Mae sat up straighter. "Really?"

Ada thought she detected a note of anticipation in her friend. Her fan certainly fluttered more quickly. "Should I be prepared to defend the honor of Southern womanhood?"

"Oh, Ada!" Opa Mae shot her an exasperated glance. "Can't you be serious for a minute?"

"Well, maybe for a minute, if the weather allows."

Her friend ignored her jibe and tapped Ada with her folded fan. "Here they come. Whatever you do, don't say you're from Whitt. Whitt's nowhere. Say you're from Graford. People have at least heard of there."

"Miss Ada Riley Dowdell," Lisle Armbruster said with a small bow, "may I present to you Mr. Lerner Phillip Alquist. Mr. Alquist, Miss Dowdell." Ada extended her hand. She noticed that Lerner took it with great delicacy and, if she were not mistaken, a bit of a tremble. Lisle withdrew.

"My great pleasure, Miss Dowdell," Lerner said.

"Charmed, Mr. Alquist," Ada replied. She glanced at Opa Mae, who was attentively looking in the other direction. "My dear friend, Opa Mae, informs me that you are among those rapacious Yankees we should be so very careful around."

Lerner gave a nervous laugh. "Hardly that. I'm from Wisconsin, not New England."

"Ah. A difference worth noting."

"I have not seen you around town, Miss Dowdell. Are you from these parts?"

"No, sir, I am from Texas." She peeked again at Opa Mae. "From Whitt."

Lerner shook his head. "I'm afraid I have not heard of it."

Opa Mae turned to look at her, both eyebrows arched, and turned away again. That alone encouraged her. "Have you not heard of the cotton gins at Whitt? The sound alone carries for miles. And the famous grist mill? Steam-driven, no less."

Lerner smiled. "Now you are teasing me."

"Surely the healthful waters of Whitt are spoken of, even here in Croy? It is our principal export: Whitt's Elixir. Bottled and shipped by my brother, and by his brother before him. Have you not heard of it? Or is Whitt completely unknown in these parts?"

Lerner gave a short nod of his head. "Until now, it has been an undiscovered province. But with your arrival, Miss Dowdell, I am certain we shall all become more familiar with Whitt."

"Pardon me," Opa Mae said, rising, "but I believe my mother wishes to introduce me to her Great Aunt Harriet, who has traveled here at considerable inconvenience and no little discomfort. Will you manage by yourself, dear Ada?"

"I shall, dear Opa. The weather has improved considerably."

The comment on the weather baffled Lerner, but he secretly rejoiced at Great Aunt Harriet's discomfort, for it drew the silent and obviously disapproving Miss Whitlock out of their circle. Then he looked into Ada's eyes and found himself dumbstruck. No words of conversation appeared on the blank page of his mind. He felt a rising panic.

Ada smiled. "Since we can rule out rapacious carpet-bagging, Mr. Alquist, may I ask what it is that you do?"

He grasped at the opening like a drowning man at a life preserver but, like a drowning man, succeeded in sputtering out only a few words at a time, ending with a clumsily self-deprecating comment about the amount of time he spent poring over deeds, ledgers, and accounts. "I spend my entire day with numbers. Dull, flat, lifeless numbers. Nothing could be plainer or less appealing."

It was then that she made her remarkable comment about numbers being beautiful, but before he could ask her for an explanation—anything, really, to keep those dancing, teasing eyes on him—Lisle Armbruster came up. "You can't keep our visiting beauty all to yourself, Lerner," Lisle said. "Miss Ada Riley Dowdell, may I introduce to you Mr. Robert Bennett Pautler?"

Lerner felt the glow of the evening quickly fade. Miss Dowdell, a true lady, tried to share the conversation equally between himself and the talkative Pautler, but Lerner had no patience for it. Within the space of a few minutes, he excused himself and left. As soon as he stepped outside the stuffy Armbruster home, he took a deep breath and looked up at the sky and its sparkling stars. "Yes," he said aloud, "beautiful indeed."

There was a surprising amount of shopping to do in the days leading up to the translation of Miss Opa Mae Whitlock into Mrs. Marvin Haley Snepp. However, lit as she was with the glow of approaching matrimony, Opa Mae could not but notice how inevitably each day a question or two about Lerner Phillip Alquist would drop carelessly from her friend's mouth. So one day, on their way back from vanDoozer's, where the hats were not as fashionable as she had hoped, she arranged for the driver to take their carriage past the lot where Mr. Alquist was building his home.

Ada was amazed at the sight. She had been expecting a grand house, of course, but of timber or the local brick. Instead, Alquist was building his home out of native Oklahoma sandstone. Its yellows, tans, and golds glowed in the sun, and rather than the usual ruined landscape one expects around ongoing construction, the home seemed nestled among already mature fruit trees and blooming lilac bushes. Fascinated, Ada descended from the carriage and walked up to the porch.

Lerner found her there, gazing up at the arch framing the entrance. "Miss Dowdell! What a great pleasure to see you again."

"Mr. Alquist." She smiled and then turned to look again at the porch and its arching entrance. "What a remarkable home you are building."

"It is nearly done," he announced proudly.

"How have you managed to preserve the lilacs and trees? They appear to have been here for years."

"They have. I had the lilacs planted before I even broke ground. I wanted them to be in bloom as soon as the project was done. When my wife moves in, she will find the place complete in every detail."

"Oh." Ada turned and looked back at the carriage. Opa Mae waved. "You wife is a very lucky woman to have a husband with such foresight."

"Well, she will be, when I take one."

Ada looked at him. For once, he thought he had the better of her. "Indeed? Then, you are not yet married?"

"Indeed, I am not, Miss Dowdell." A smile spread across her face, but he noticed she did not blush. Then she glanced yet again at the archway. "The design is my own," he added.

"But influenced, if I am not mistaken, by the latest trends. The line of that arch, for instance, is Arts and Crafts."

He felt caught in his own boast. "Yes. Very perceptive of you. You seem to know much, Miss Dowdell. Mathematics, architecture."

Ada made a slight gesture that reminded Lerner of butterflies, of petals opening, of wheat swaying in a summer breeze. "It is only book learning."

"Quite a lot of book learning."

She smiled at him. "Well, I have quite a lot of books."

"That is most refreshing to hear. I myself have a small collection, mostly law and land rights. But I have made provision for more in the design of the house. It will have a study and a library, in addition to the four bedrooms."

"Four bedrooms? You do plan ahead, Mr. Alquist."

"Well . . ." Lerner felt the heat rise in his throat and spread across his face. *Men do not blush*, he told himself sternly. "I live in hope."

"As do we all, Mr. Alquist. But stone walls leave little room for you to change your mind, should the future prove more fruitful than you planned."

Lerner opened his mouth to reply but found himself abandoned by his vocabulary again. All he could do was grin boyishly and look away, stroking the sandstone archway and gleefully imagining tearing it all down.

Opa Mae saved him from further embarrassment. "Yoo-hoo, Ada darling," she called from the carriage. "We mustn't keep the seamstress waiting."

"I'll be there directly," Ada responded. She looked apologetically at Lerner. "Final fittings. One last chance to get everything perfect before the happy day."

"You will outshine the bride," Lerner said, startling them both with his frankness. Ada blushed and Lerner began to stammer an apology, but she held up a hand. "Let us just say good-bye for now."

"If it is just for now, Miss Dowdell, then I will say good-bye."

She nodded and walked to the carriage. Just as she was getting in, Lerner rushed up, lilac blossoms clutched in his hand. "They . . . they pale by comparison," he stuttered.

Ada seemed struck dumb by the gesture. Opa Mae rescued them again. "Thank you, Mr. Alquist. They will look lovely in the hall." She tugged on Ada's sleeve to get her to sit down. "Thank you, Mr. Alquist," Ada murmured.

"Miss Whitlock, Miss Dowdell," Lerner said, touching his hand to his forehead. As they pulled away, he realized he had made the gesture of tipping his hat to them, but he was not wearing a hat. It suddenly seemed absurd to him to be without a hat, and he resolved to remedy that at once.

It would be months before Lerner would have the opportunity to tip his new hat to Ada in person. A telegram awaited her on their return to the Whitlocks'. Ada's father, whose health had rallied in recent months, had suffered a sudden setback. He had collapsed at home and was not expected to revive. Her elder brother urged her immediate return. There was barely time enough to load her trunk on the carriage and make the south-bound train. And just like that, the day turned to ashes. Arriving back home after saying good-bye to Ada at the station, Opa Mae saw the wilting lilacs on the hallway table and burst into tears. "Oh, Momma," she cried, "it's just horrible."

Her mother drew a comforting arm around her. "I know, dear." She stroked her daughter's hair. "Poor Ada. What will she do in that big empty house by herself? And in the middle of nowhere. What will she do for society?"

Opa Mae sniffed. "Oh, she'll manage." She straightened up. "But who's going to be my maid of honor now?"

"My dear, there's always your sister."

Opa Mae looked up at her. "Clara? Oh, no!" and she burst into fresh tears.

Ada arrived too late. Robert Orton Dowdell was interred in the cemetery at Graford after a private service in Whitt. There was some talk of burying him in the family cemetery on Oran Hill, but her brothers and uncle argued for a more central location, and they prevailed.

She soon found out why. The men in the family had no intention of holding onto the large farmhouse and its surrounding land. Her brothers' wives had no interest in such a large, drafty place without modern conveniences. The only reason for holding onto it at all was to provide a place for Ada to live. That this arrangement was temporary was abundantly clear. Ada might be welcome in either of her brothers' homes, but it was clear that neither sister-in-law wanted a live-in relative. Perhaps a smaller house just for her could be built behind one of her brothers' homes. "Smaller" was the key word. Most of her things would have to be sold or left behind, and by "her things," what they meant was her books, which ranged throughout the family homestead from cellar to attic. If one of her brothers did build her a house, there would not be room for a tenth of them. Which brother would build the house was a thorny issue, but it would be settled soon, and Ada would have little say in the matter.

Her brothers were not insensitive men, but they had been fully grown when she was born and spent little time with her. Arley Dean had left home while Ada was an infant to run the family cotton mills in Whitt. The steady decline in revenue from that source probably contributed to her father's decline as the fortune he had accumulated over a hard-lived life withered away under his son's incompetence, just as the cotton harvest withered under assault of the ever-spreading boll weevil. Orton, her younger brother, seemed intent on squandering his portion of the family fortune on bottling and marketing the questionable local spring water. When their mother died, she had taken over running the household for her father, both brothers by then busy raising families of their own. Now that she was the sole occupant of the house, there was no point in keeping it.

She did not anticipate any help from her uncle Colin, either. Colin Dowdell looked on the land around Oran Hill as little more than an asset to be subdivided and sold as quickly as possible. To him, the house on the hill was just a collection of furniture with no value save what could be raised at auction.

In any direction she looked, Ada saw a dismal future.

It was in this frame of mind that she received Lerner's third letter.

The first had been an elegant and sincerely felt expression of sympathy on the passing of her father. She had replied quickly but formally, expecting to hear nothing further. The second letter, arriving two months later, had been longer and announced the completion of the house. She had sat down at once to write a reply, but found she could not. His letter had a distant formality that she feared was all too sincerely felt. It would be selfish of her to speak of her desperation and loneliness, and dishonest of her not to. She carried the letter with her and, whenever she felt certain she was unobserved, took it out and read it. After a week of this, she felt embarrassed for herself and put the letter away.

Then, three weeks later, the third letter arrived. "My Dear Miss Dowdell," it began,

I hope I may address you as 'My Dear Miss Dowdell' without offense, though in truth I wish to address you as 'My Dear Ada.' Since your sudden and sad departure from Croy, the days have been less bright, the evenings without charm of any kind, and the nights an utter blank, as if no stars shone and the moon had been stolen away. The town and my life in it are bereft of anything to commend them, lacking art, lacking life, lacking wit.

I realize it is intemperate and perhaps impertinent of me to speak to you in this manner so soon after your dear father's passing and after so short an acquaintance. I realize and appreciate that you are still in mourning, but if I do not express myself, I feel I will lose forever the one spark of delight I have known since coming to Croy. The house is done, but the house is empty. It has walls of sturdy Oklahoma sandstone, but stones alone do not make a mansion. No fireplace can warm a home that does not already have love at its heart, and no home can have love at its heart if the owner himself has a heart that is empty. For such is the condition of my heart these days. The only thing that fills it is memory of you.

My dear Ada, forgive me, but I must know. May I hope? If I may, then I can wait. If not, then no fire will ever warm these walls, nor any spark brighten the night.

Your faithful servant,
Lerner Phillip Alquist

She had been in the midst of packing up the house when the letter arrived. Most of the furniture had been sold, the few works of art distributed among the disdainful sisters-in-law, and the land already surveyed into parcels. Her books had been packed into crates, but she had no idea where the crates would go. Like her, all that was certain was that they must go.

It took her less than a minute to determine her reply. She entered her father's study, its barren bookshelves staring forlornly down at his great desk. She picked up the silver-framed photo of herself that her father kept there and wrapped it carefully. She interrupted the men loading furniture onto a cart and had them take her into town, where she posted the package back to Lerner. Inside, she had tucked a note with a single word, "Hope."

Three months later—a bit sooner, perhaps, than the usual decorum of mourning required, but none too soon as far as her brothers and uncle were concerned—Ada Riley Dowdell stepped off the Santa Fe onto the platform in Croy. She waited a few moments before alighting. She knew the train would not be pulling out immediately. There were several crates that had to be unloaded first.

She spotted Lerner at once. He was anxiously straining forward, as if by effort alone he could stretch even taller and see further. He clutched a fedora in his hands. When he met her eyes, he suddenly seemed to shed twenty years from his face and frame. He sprang forward to greet her. "Mr. Alquist," she said, offering her hand.

"Dear Ada," he said, kissing it.

The trip had been not only hard and uncomfortable, but also burdened with the knowledge that there was no going back. There was nothing left of the old home. But Lerner's warmth melted away all of Ada's tension and worry. "Phillip," she said, softening her formality with the name she had come to use in her letters to him over the months.

"Where are your bags? I cannot wait to show you the house."

"The bags are . . ." She turned in time to see them being off-loaded behind her, "right here. But we must wait for . . . for the other things."

"Certainly. I'll put them in the carriage. Where are they?"

Ada scanned the platform uncertainly, then looked at him. "Here," she said.

Lerner looked brightly around the platform, stacked with several dozen crates. "Which ones?"

Ada swallowed and tears sprang to her eyes. "All of them."

Lerner stared at her in disbelief. "All of them?"

"Yes. All forty-seven of them." She started crying and buried her head in his shoulder. "I told you I had quite a lot of books."

Lerner patted her on the head and swallowed. "Yes. Quite."

"Oh, Phillip." She pulled away from him. "Tell me and I'll send them back at once. Only, don't send me back. I can't face them, their condescension and their pity. I can't go back."

"Hush! Don't even think of it. Of course you're not going back. And neither are your books. We'll find a place for them. I promise." His head was spinning as he said it. The house had a library, of course, and a study, but two rooms would not be enough. It did not matter. He had his Ada.

Ada pulled out a handkerchief and looked up at him, shaking her head. "Oh, yes it is. Don't spare me, Phillip. I know there's not enough room. Stone walls make it difficult to change your plans."

Lerner shook his head. "I would tear them down and start all over again to make room for you. Think no more of it. I will think of something. I am nothing if not resourceful."

She straightened up and smiled at him, the sparkle returning to her eyes. Here at last was a man who felt no need to diminish her in order to embrace her. She had found a home.

The immediate solution was to move five of the crates to the mansion and store the rest in the courtyard behind Pautler's Dry Goods. There was a kind of lean-to there that would keep the rain off, but Lerner knew enough about small-town curiosity to take additional measures. He added a small shack and hired a colored boy, the son of his carriage driver, to live there and look after the crates and keep prying hands away. All this was temporary. Come winter, the weather would be too harsh for the crates and the shed too cold for the boy.

It was Ada who came up with a permanent solution. One night while he worked at his desk in the study, she came up to him. "Lerner, you said once that Croy would always prosper as long as we had the rail line."

"That's a fact. We are a major shipping point for local agriculture and the brick works. Wood and paper products, too. There will always be work here."

Ada nodded. "Work, yes, but why will people want to live here, raise families here? I've seen what happens when nothing but commerce builds a town: the commerce leaves and the town dries up and withers. I saw it happening to Whitt as the mills closed down."

Lerner put down his pen. "Times are hard now, that's certain. But they won't always be so."

"We should plan that they won't. Phillip, I think I know what I want to do with the books. I want to build a library. And not just for my books, but for the whole town."

Lerner's eyes became inward-looking. Ada sat down quietly, knowing he was going through calculations, coming up with the critical questions she herself had imagined. "The whole town," he said at last. "I know this town. The 1912 Town Charter stipulates the establishment of a library, but one has never been built. There never seems to be enough capital to pull it off, or books enough to start the collection. It has never been a priority." A lopsided smile crept up his face. "The last time I brought up the matter with the council member in charge, he told me what he thought of it—'with embellishment,' as they say around here. But with your books to start it . . ." He looked up. "My dear, they mean so much to you. Could you possibly give them up?"

"They have done what they can for me. It is time they served others."

A light dawned in Lerner's eyes and the smile spread across his face. "Have I ever told you what a remarkable woman you are, and how much I love you for it?"

She got up and kissed him on the head. "Yes, you have. You do every time you get that look in your eyes."

Chapter 32

CHILDREN, GODS, AND ELEPHANTS

Neither of the Alquists were dreamers. They knew there was much work to be done to make their vision a reality. Ada started drawing up plans and elevations, using the resources of her books to start with, and traveling by train to Tulsa to consult with architects and builders to flesh out the details. Lerner drew up a business plan and a fundraising campaign, based in part on securing a grant from a philanthropic society in New York. It meant spending more time at the office, but he promised he'd always be home in time for supper. Most days, Ada would walk a dinner pail down to his office at noon and they would spend the hour together, talking over strategies and practicalities. He was amazed by her ability to turn the simple patterns of nature—the spirals in a sunflower head or the radial beauty of a coreopsis—into architectural details and proportions. She marveled at his savvy assessment of political and economic will in the town and surrounding countryside. He had her plans made into blueprints, but before Ada had a chance to proof them, Lerner got wind that the foundation he hoped to court was about to cease all funding. He rushed the plans off to New York and, eager to prove the town's earnestness and commitment, donated a site to the city and started work immediately on the foundation, using his own funds to pay for the excavation.

It was more than the possibility of losing outside funding that urged Lerner on. Late autumn brought stronger rains, and Ethan, Cecil's boy, had ended his guard duty over the crates when his father insisted he start school. Lerner had been put out with his coachman over that. He thought it a waste of time to give Ethan "book learning" when it was clear his future lay in a strong back and manual skills. But when Lerner hinted at this disappointment to Ada, she raised her eyebrows at him. "A well-trained mind is needed in any job," she remarked. "Otherwise you might as well employ machines."

Lerner took the advice to heart and thought of ways he might replace some of his workers with machines. His first step was to purchase a 1934 Studebaker to replace his carriage, reducing Cecil's role at the Alquist mansion to a part-time position taking care of the one remaining horse and keeping the carriage in good repair for special occasions. Lerner was proud of the Studebaker and drove it the few blocks to his office every morning and back every evening. It expressed his confidence in the future, despite hard times.

His faith was not rewarded. The philanthropic society turned down the library plans. "Too large, too ornate, and too extravagant for a town the size of Croy," the society's secretary had written in a letter to the town council. Lerner returned from the council meeting humiliated and furious.

"Who are they to declare what dreams a town may have?" he bellowed, striding up and down in front of the study's fireplace. "Of all the arrogant, condescending, high-hatted—"

"Phillip," Ada said quietly.

"—Eastern sons of bitches!"

"Mr. Alquist. You are not on one of your farms, now. There is no call for either volume or vulgarity."

Lerner stopped, ashen-faced. "My dear! Please forgive me." He rushed forward and took her hands, kissing them. "I have been so driven these past weeks. I have overlooked our purpose. At least the foundation is finished. It is safe and dry. We can store the crates there over winter. In the spring, we can begin building anew."

"Dear Phillip," Ada said, "plans are just plans. They can always change. And they may well have to, for we are already building something much finer than a library." She moved his hands to her belly, and she saw again that look in his eyes that told her all would be well, no matter what plans may come and go.

Not long after, Ada was shopping in Pautler's for ingredients for a tincture she hoped would ease her discomfort in the mornings. She had gotten the recipe from Opa Mae when Ada paid her a visit. She had seen little of Opa Mae since her marriage to Marvin, and Ada worried their friendship had gone stale.

Opa Mae insisted on setting out a full, formal tea for Ada, although it was scarcely midday and Ada said she was not hungry. It was in how Opa Mae poured the tea that Ada finally saw the truth. Her hostess perched on the edge of her chair, lips pursed, as she elevated the pot in one hand and the cup and saucer in the other. Ada saw that she was not having a friendly visit with her old college chum. Rather, Mrs. Opa Mae Snepp, wife of Marvin Snepp, owner of Snepp's Hardware, was entertaining Mrs. Ada Dowdell Alquist, wife of Lerner Phillip Alquist, local real estate baron and civic philanthropist. So it would appear in the social column of *The Croy Evening Call*. There would be no mention of the considerable trouble Mrs. Alquist had caused Mrs. Snepp by calling on her unannounced, but Ada knew how it would play out among the ladies of the Rebeccah Lodge. She already felt socially isolated by her husband's position, so rather than leaving early, she remained through the entire awkward ceremony.

Eventually, after a tortuous interlude of pleasantries, she brought the topic of conversation around to Opa Mae's children—two of them by now—and hinted at how much she admired her friend for being so wise in the ways of motherhood. That brought the warmth back into Opa's eyes and she relaxed noticeably. "They are such a joy," Opa Mae said. "The Lord has truly blessed us."

"It is a blessing that Phillip—that is, Mr. Alquist—and I hope to share someday as well." When Ada saw a look of confusion cross Opa Mae's brow, she added, "Someday soon."

Then her friend was back in full bloom, fussing over her and asking indelicate questions and finally, without any prompting at all, offering the recipe for the tincture, "for getting through those first few mornings."

However, Pautler's was proving inadequate to the task. She was unable to find two of the ingredients on Opa's ornately penned list. Perhaps they were seasonal or common only in local gardens. She approached the counter to ask the clerk, but stopped when she saw he was tending another woman.

"Card ham?" the clerk was saying. "No, ma'am. We don't have no ham here."

The woman was dark-skinned, but not in the same way as the Chickasaw women Ada knew. There was a layer of warmth in this woman's skin, like trapped sunlight, and she carried herself with a bearing that reminded Ada of a pair of English girls she had known at Normal School.

"Not ham, you foolish man," the woman said crisply. "Cardamom. Cardamom. It is a common enough spice."

The clerk folded his arms and shook his head slowly. "Nope. Not common here. Maybe you might try over 'cross river. Lots of common folks there."

Ada felt her blood rise and she strode up the counter. "Pardon me, Daryll—it is Daryll, isn't it?—but I think you've misunderstood Miss . . ." She turned to the other woman.

"Mrs. Mrs. Balwinder Sohi."

Ada gave her a slight bow, which was returned. "What Mrs. Sohi is asking for is cardamom. I've used it in baking myself for Mr. Alquist's Christmas cake, and I do believe I bought it right here at Pautler's." The clerk didn't budge. "Or should I take my custom across the river as well? I'm certain your invitation to shop elsewhere would interest Mr. Pautler. Not to mention my husband."

That shifted him. "I'll have to check the stockroom. I don't know as we have any t' hand."

"Oh, there's no need for that, Daryll. You'll find it on aisle three, left side, top shelf." Ada turned to Mrs. Sohi. "That's probably why you didn't see it, my dear. Those top shelves can be hard to reach." She turned back to the clerk. "Two, please. One for me and one for my friend." She smiled.

The two women stood shoulder to shoulder, immovable. Outnumbered, Daryll uncoiled from his arrogant slouch. "Won't be a minute," he said and slumped off.

As soon as he was out of sight, Mrs. Sohi let out an audible breath. It occurred to Ada that she, too, had been holding her breath.

"Thank you," Mrs. Sohi said and smiled. Ada was delighted by the difference it made. Mrs. Sohi's face, which had looked stormy enough to shoot lightning, was now as soft as the dawn.

"You sometimes have to put your foot down," Ada said apologetically. "Croy is full of good-hearted people, if you just remind them of it from time to time."

"Oh," Mrs. Sohi waved two brown-creased hands, "I know all about the good people of Croy. My family have been here off and on for many years. But that one," her face darkened again, "he is new to me."

"Well, Mrs. Sohi—"

"Please, call me Kamar."

"And you must call me Ada." She extended a hand, but just as her new friend took it, Ada suffered a rush of lightheadedness. She jerked her hand back to her stomach and reached for the counter with the other. "Oh," she said, seeing the alarm on Kamar's face, "I am so sorry. It's just . . ."

Kamar steadied her with a hand and nodded. "I know. It is always worse in the first months."

Ada looked at her in surprise. "How did you know?"

"Well," Kamar looked down and smiled shyly, "it is why I wanted the cardamom." She looked up, her eyes bright. "My mother always said there was nothing like a good masala chai to ease the mornings."

Ada could hear Daryll approaching with the bottles of spice. She clasped Kamar's hands in hers. "Could you show me how?"

To Kamar's disappointment, the cardamom was ground, not whole, but she agreed to show Ada how to make chai with it anyway. "It is not the same as grinding it fresh ourselves, but it will have to do." So began their friendship. Despite their different backgrounds, they discovered much in common. Both were at home and yet out of place in Croy. Ada's religion was a barrier in some social circles, where Evangelicals turned up their noses at Roman Catholicism as a form of apostate Christianity. But Balwinder Singh Sohi and Kamar Kaur Sohi were Sikhs, which branded them as nothing less than pagans, worse even than the heathen remnants of the Five Civilized Tribes who refused to convert to Christianity.

Ada knew how it felt to be the object of casual condemnation. She saw it in the eyes of certain shopkeepers, a look that said, "You may live in our town and shop in our stores, but when comes The Judgment, there will be a parting of the ways." There was fear sometimes, too, in those looks, which she knew grew from her husband's reputation as a hard-driving businessman and implacable landlord. Reputation can run roughshod over fact in a small town. She tried to soften the name of Alquist in her own dealings with the townspeople and the occasional tenant farmer's wife she encountered in the market, but she could see the mixture of fear and vengeance behind the courteous smiles. She had seen it recently in the face of her own friend, Opa Mae. She vowed Kamar would never see it in hers.

They had another thing common: their dynamic and industrious husbands. Hers worked tirelessly at raising enough money to finish the library, a goal Ada now thought perhaps beyond even his grasp. Kamar's Balwinder was determined to turn an unproductive farm on a hill west of town into an orchard. His determination often meant he and Kamar went days without seeing each other between sun up and sun down.

The first time Ada met Balwinder Singh Sohi was at the Sohis' home. It was six months after both she and Kamar had been delivered of their respective children: a girl, Virginia, to Ada, and a boy, Sundar, to Kamar. Cecil drove Ada out to the farm house in the "special occasion" carriage. Kamar, who had had few visitors and little chance to get into town since "Sunny's" birth, was delighted to see her. Balwinder was equally delighted to see Cecil, not because he had any particular relationship with the Negro driver, but because he was proud of his orchard's progress and needed an audience to appreciate it properly. He greeted Ada with great courtesy and precision and immediately ordered Kamar to serve tea. Kamar, after giving Ada a look that said, "As if he needs to tell me," ushered Ada into the spotless but tiny living room as Balwinder escorted Cecil out to the fields like a visiting dignitary.

Ada settled Virginia in her lap and took in her surroundings. Although the Sohis' farmhouse was less than a fourth the size of her former home on Oran Hill, many aspects of the place tugged at her heart. The quiet of its location, the birdsong and breeze floating in through the windows, the angle and intensity of light in the living room, all reminded her of more contented times tending to her father and long afternoons spent immersed in the solitude and comfort of her books. For the first time in several years, she missed them.

Kamar returned with the tea service, miraculously balancing Sunny on her hip at the same time. The little boy made a giggling noise and reached out to Virginia. Ada noticed her little girl give a twitch and stare in blue-eyed wonder at the other infant. *Does she know she is looking at another human being?* Ada wondered. *Or does she think it's just a brown-skinned version of herself?*

"You see how they greet each other?" Kamar beamed. "I am sure they will be great friends, just as you and I are."

"I am glad they have finally met," Ada said. "I had meant to call earlier, but—"

"You do not need to explain to me, my dear. I know how busy you have been—how busy we both have been."

"I was afraid you might think I was stand-offish."

Kamar showed the palm of one hand and poured chai with the other. "I have no reason to believe you think milk runs in your veins."

Ada laughed. "Oh, I have missed your company! And I am so glad to have finally met your husband. I have seen him in town, of course. I often thought of introducing myself, since you and I are so close, but I didn't know how to proceed."

"Oh, Balwinder would never have spoken! Not without a proper introduction from your husband or brother. But here in our house, you are a guest, so it is easier."

"He looks very distinguished in that turban. Does he always wear it?"

"Always. It is a *dastaar*. It is one of the ways one Sikh recognizes another."

"I have seen pictures of such head coverings in my books about India."

"Those were most probably Hindus, not Sikhs. Unless it was British India. The British preferred Sikhs in their military when it served their purposes."

Ada put down her cup. "There is something I have always wanted to ask, dear Kamar, but I don't wish to pry or offend."

"Speak freely. There can be no offense when friendship is at the heart."

"I don't believe I have ever known any of your people to live in this part of the country. I am sure I would have noticed."

"Oh, you could not miss us," Kamar laughed. "Sikhs make a point of that. We consider it an honor to be 'distinguished,' though here in Croy, it hardly seems worth the trouble. No one would mistake us for Oklahomans! No, Balwinder and I are very probably the only Sikhs in the entire state."

"But then how did the two of you ever meet, and how did you end up here?"

Kamar's eyes went wide with surprise and crinkled in delight, then she laughed so freely Ada was swept into it. Finally, Kamar wiped the tears from her eyes, leaned forward to touch Ada lightly on the knee, and said in a voice of conspiracy and merriment, "The elephant died!" Then she erupted in laughter again, trying to contain it with a hand to her lips.

"Bad news for the elephant!" Kamar said. "Good news for me." And she told Ada the remarkable story of her family and Balwinder's.

Kamar's father, Sachveer Singh, was part of a large and extended family that had immigrated to Queens, New York, from Canada. By the time he was eighteen, Sachveer had grown tired of the traditions and restrictions of his community. By chance, he was in Boston when Longstreet and Bowles, a small traveling circus, lost its elephant handler (whiskey, concussion). Eager to see more of America, he secured the job by showing up for the interview in full Sikh regalia. He rode atop Longstreet and Bowles's prize possession whenever the circus made its entrance into a town. Kamar's mother soon joined him, and they toured the East Coast, the upper Midwest, and the South. Each autumn, the troupe would head for winter quarters. Some larger circuses chose Sarasota, Florida; many smaller concerns chose Hugo, Oklahoma; Longstreet and Bowles chose Croy. It was convenient to rail lines leading east and north for the spring breakout, and being an agricultural and ranching center, had plenty of open land to pasture, feed, and stable the animals. Kamar was born on the road, but every October found her in Croy with her mother, father, and the rest of her circus family, who added color and spice and the occasional fistfight to Croy's otherwise dull winter months.

At about the same time her parents were touring the eastern United States, Balwinder's brother, Bhavjeet Sohi, arrived in California and settled into the Sikh community in California's central valley. Bhavjeet had jumped ship from the ill-fated *Komagata Maru* while it was embargoed in Vancouver. Five years later, when news of the Jallianwala Bagh Massacre reached him, he sent for his younger brother. "The times are drawn like knives, my brother," he had written. "All kings are butchers. Come to where we have no kings. Cross the dreadful ocean, come to America. You will be safe. You will prosper."

Balwinder had come but had not prospered. Where Bhavjeet saw opportunity, Balwinder saw obstacles. Bhavjeet despaired that his brother would ever meet success and saw him retreating into bitterness. He began reading incendiary editorials in *Ghadhar* and talking about returning to India to overthrow the British Raj.

But then, a way opened. Bhavjeet had backed a loan to a second-generation German immigrant who had success in almond and cherry orchards in California's central valley. The German wanted to return to his parent's lost homestead out east and needed a loan to secure the deed. "Out east" turned out to be Oklahoma. Unfortunately, he was unable to recreate in the cross timbers the success he had enjoyed in California's golden valley. He followed a descending line of failures in cotton, then ranching, then vegetables, then fruit trees, as first weevils, then drought, then economic depression slammed into his dreams. When he could not meet the note and faced losing the land his parents had sweated and died for, he took his own life.

Bhavjeet saw a chance to give his brother a new start. "There is opportunity in that land," he told him.

Balwinder scoffed. "If it is so full of opportunity, why are its people coming here?" But in truth he was already convinced there was no future for him in Stockton, especially under the ever-helpful hand and ever-critical eye of his older brother. Within a week he had packed and left for Oklahoma.

The farm was indeed a lost cause. A single small house had been erected and then abandoned on a hill just west of town. An apple tree grew shaggily beside it, dying a slow, twisted death. Balwinder wondered if he, too, might end his days on this god-forsaken plot. But when things had looked darkest, the circus came to town. He immediately leased the land for pasture while the troupe set up their winter homes in Croy and at the settlement of Pesogi.

"Then," Kamar said, her eyes dancing, "the elephant died."

It might have collapsed from exhaustion or despair or just old age. There was no veterinary to determine the cause and no one seemed to care. "I think my father suspected Balwinder. They had argued over where the beast should pasture and how much it ate, and when it dropped dead on his land, it did not bode well."

"That must have made it difficult for you to see each other."

"Oh, not at all! We managed to sneak away from my father and brothers. We were both very much Americans in that regard. But we had to be careful." Kamar smiled. "So to get on my father's good side, Balwinder offered to dispose of the elephant without charge. And that's when our luck changed!" She clapped her hands. "While digging the pit, Balwinder broke through a layer, and suddenly it filled with water. No one was with him, so he kept it secret."

"But what of the elephant? Surely it must have become, well, odious by then."

"But it was winter, you see! Or nearly so. He borrowed a backhoe and buried the beast farther off. But the first pit completely filled with water. So more digging, and then a pond, and then a pump, and then water for the house and field. It changed everything."

That spring, Balwinder saw for himself what the German had dreamed. With water finally in adequate supply, the apple tree bloomed. That autumn, it bore fruit: cheerful yellow globes with a blush of rose that sold as quickly as he could bring bushels of them to Pautler's. He was advised the species was called "Golden Delicious." He ordered seventeen saplings from Stark Brothers plus six kinds of pear and planted them before the circus troupe returned in October.

"But our circus, like our elephant, was on its last legs. I told Balwinder so. He proposed terms to my father, and after enough back-and-forth to appease their pride, it was agreed. His brother paid for the entire wedding. His whole family arrived by train from Stockton. It was more colorful than even the circus."

"I'll bet the town was thrilled!"

"Oh, they were!" She sighed. "If only it had lasted, that good-will."

The following spring, the Longstreet and Bowles Circus decamped, never to return. It was swallowed up by creditors the day it hit the East Coast. Abandoned in Baltimore, Sachveer and his wife returned to the insular community they had escaped twenty years earlier and settled down.

"So you see, my father ran away to join the circus, and then the circus ran away from him!"

Ada sighed. "What colorful lives. Mine is so pale by comparison."

"Oh, do not envy a colorful life, my dear friend," Kamar said, refreshing their tea. "I would gladly have a bit less color and a lot more certainty. Farming is so at the whim of God. But this year, if He wills it, we shall finally have a harvest worthy of our sweat."

This was not the first time Ada had heard Kamar speak of "God" or "the Lord," or say "God is One." It contradicted what she was taught: that all non-Christian faiths were heathen, "a pandemonium of demons and devils masquerading as the Divine." Yet Kamar's "One" sounded much like Ada's Trinity. She meant to ask her about it, but Virginia chose that moment to begin a general fussing that quickly grew into a full-throated bawl. "I'm so sorry," Ada said, trying to settle the infant. "I suspect she is hungry again. She has such an appetite!"

"Say nothing of it," Kamar said. She indicated her own child sleeping in her lap. "This one will barely eat a thing, but sleeps all the time. A born dreamer, Balwinder says. Do you wish to . . . ?"

Ada blushed, embarrassed by her own embarrassment. "I think perhaps we should head home. Could you please call Cecil?"

Kamar nodded. "I shall make Balwinder release him. The poor man has surely had his fill of apple trees by now."

Ada hoped her discomfort had gone unnoticed. Kamar rose as she did, waking Sunny, who again reached out to Virginia. He looked at the other baby's red-faced howling with the sort of wonder evoked by a new toy. Kamar laughed and pulled him back with an apology, and the two friends parted with the promise of visits to come. Ada looked forward to them. There was much she wanted to ask Kamar about children, gods, and elephants.

Chapter 33

FIRE AND ICE

Virginia quieted on the trip back to town, lulled to sleep by the creaking of the carriage springs and the rhythm of the horse's hooves. Ada drank in the countryside, particularly reveling in its scents, each of which had a complex story to tell: the mixture of dust and horse sweat recalling Texas days of bone-hard harvests and lazy nights on hay rides. The scent of drying alfalfa rose in sweet and sour waves from one side of the road, while from the other the lively tang of cow manure offered its own commentary, the two sides telling a wry tale of beginnings and endings. Even the occasional hint of sweat that wafted back from Cecil carried with it an overlay of lavender water, a testimony to his aspirations.

She must have fallen asleep with Virginia in her arms, for the next thing she heard was Cecil saying, "Almost there, Miss Ada, and yonder's Mister Lerner himself to welcome you home."

She brightened at once, her mental haze evaporating in crisp anticipation. She had so much to tell Phillip!

"Where have you been?" he said, smiling up at her and patting the horse on its neck. "I thought I might join you at home for lunch this time."

"Oh, Phillip, I have had the most delightful time." She gathered up Virginia as Lerner helped her down from the carriage. "I have just been out to the Sohis' farm—"

Lerner's smile vanished. "You what?" His jaw flexed in agitation and he turned to Cecil, still sitting in the driver's seat. "Did you do this?"

Virginia squirmed sleepily. "Phillip?" Ada asked, shifting the infant to her shoulder. "What's wrong?"

Lerner ignored her. "Did you?" he shouted at Cecil.

Cecil drew back and his face paled. "Miss Ada asked—"

"Get down from there, you ignorant shit!"

"Phillip, I don't understand—"

"Get down, I say!"

Cecil put the carriage crop slowly in its slot and climbed down from the seat. Lerner towered over him, anger coming off him in waves. "How could you do such a thing? How could you be such a fool? Don't you have a lick of sense?" Cecil stood, wide-eyed and silent, spittle hitting him in the face as Lerner raged. "Well, god damn it, haven't you? Answer to me, boy! I'm talking to you! If you haven't a tongue, I'll whip it out of you!" He reached for the crop.

"Mr. Lerner, I meant no harm!" Cecil hollered, his back against the carriage.

"Phillip, no!" Ada cried, grabbing his arm. The storm of voices woke Virginia and she began to wail.

Lerner turned to Ada, his face red. "Woman, do not interfere!"

"But it's true! I asked him to drive me out there. If there's someone to blame—and I don't see why there should be—"

Lerner wrenched his arm free. "Ada, get in the house."

"But Phillip—"

"I said, get in the house! And take care of that child!"

She hesitated. He still stood next to the carriage, within arm's reach of the whip. "I will not." The two of them stood facing each other, Virginia's wails filling the space between them. "Not if there is the slightest chance any harm will come to Cecil, who was only doing what I told him to."

Lerner took several tense breaths, and then turned to the coachman. "Get out of my sight," he said. "Take your things and go. You are dismissed. If you are still on this property an hour from now, I'll have you arrested for trespassing."

Cecil made as if to lead the horse away but Lerner knocked his arm aside. "I'll take care of the god-damned horse! Now get out of here."

Cecil gave one pleading glance to Ada, then turned and walked off to the carriage house. Lerner turned to her, his face a tight frown, the jittery horse held firmly by its bridle. She turned away and walked into the house.

It took her a while to get Virginia to settle down. She tried feeding her, but the child was too upset to nurse. Eventually, the crying wore the infant out and she fell asleep, her face knotted with unhappiness. Gradually, it smoothed. Ada looked down and wished she could as easily forget the scene she had witnessed, and the worse one she had barely prevented. She heard her husband come in, and she rose from beside the cradle and went downstairs to the study. She intended to confront him, but her heart softened when she saw how upset he was himself.

"My dear," he said, "I am so sorry you had to see that."

"Phillip, I don't understand what just happened. All I did—"

He raised his hands to stop her. "First, let me apologize. I am sorry I raised my voice to you. Please forgive me. It is a side of me you should never have to see."

She smoothed her dress with her hands. "If your apology means I will never see it again, then I accept it."

He smiled, but she could tell there was tension behind it. "Please, sit down."

She sat in the large chair by the unlit fire.

Lerner walked up and down a few paces before turning to face her. In the gentle voice he used when being tender, he said, "Ada, my dear, you cannot interfere when I am disciplining my people. It is essential that you understand this."

She looked at him. His face was the same face as her dear Phillip, the voice was the same, but it wasn't the same person. "Since when is my telling you the truth 'interference'?" she asked.

"Please, Ada. The truth is not at issue. Cecil's impertinence has been growing by the day. It was time to put an end to it."

"I would hardly call taking me for a ride in the country when I ask for one an impertinence." Lerner looked away from her, lips pressed together. "Phillip, what are you not saying?"

"Cecil should have known better than to take you out there by yourself."

"How can he know such a thing when I do not?"

"Perhaps you do not. Indeed, apparently, you don't. But Cecil should."

"He is our servant. He does what we tell him. If there is a fault—and I still have no idea what that fault might be—but whatever it is, it is mine. Do not take it out on Cecil and his family. How will he support them?"

Lerner straightened up and took a deep breath. *He is trying to control himself,* Ada thought, *but why?* She was suddenly as angered by this effort to hide his temper as she had been frightened by its display earlier.

"It is not my concern how that man takes care of his family," he said. "What is my concern is how I take care of mine, and he has put you in jeopardy."

"He has done no such thing!"

"He has compromised your safety and your reputation."

"My . . . ?" Ada felt the color rising in her cheeks. "Do you think my virtue so fragile that it could be shattered by my having tea with a friend?"

Lerner took another long, tense breath. "What friend?"

"Kamar Sohi, of course! Whom did you think?"

"It is not the woman, but her husband I object to."

"And why is that, may I ask? He was the soul of courtesy, and besides he spent the great balance of the time outside, showing Cecil the orchard and talking apples. That is hardly what anyone would call scandalous."

"Ada, you cannot possibly be so naive. There was no one else out there with you, was there? No one but a pagan Hindu and a nigger coachman. Now, how do you think that looks?"

Ada rose. "Phillip, don't you trust me?"

"It isn't a question of trust. It's a question of propriety. Rumors don't need facts to spread."

"Then propriety is just another name for hypocrisy, bigotry, and hatred. No, not even that. It doesn't take hatred to be a bigot. Ignorance and habit will do."

"Am I ignorant, then? Am I a bigot?"

Her mind came to an abrupt halt at the question. The floor on which she stood suddenly felt as if it were made of sand. Who was this man who was speaking to her now? Did she even know him?

Lerner must have seen confusion in her eyes. "Now it is *you* who don't trust *me*," he said. "I know the way of these things, my dear. For your own sake, you must not go out there again."

The sand was slipping out from under her. "I *must* not?" she whispered.

"You have other friends."

Ada raised her chin. "Oh? Name them."

Lerner looked at her blankly a moment, then waved impatiently. "Opa Mae Snepp."

"A woman you yourself describe as 'silly and vain,' a 'froth of vapidity,' 'an expanse of air masquerading as a woman.' Is that whom you want me spending my time with? Shall I invite her to dinner tomorrow so that you may enjoy her company as well?"

Lerner made a low sound and turned away. *Now he* is *angry*, she thought. *Good.*

"I don't care who," he said over his shoulder. "Make others. But not that Sohi woman."

Ada found her footing again and stood erect. "My friends are my friends. No one may take them away from me. I will see them and speak to them whenever I please."

Her husband stiffened. "Then perhaps I have a use for Cecil after all. You may contradict my wishes, my dear, but he certainly will not. If his position in this household is so important to him and his family, then he will not take you out there again."

Ada stared at Lerner in disbelief. Had he forgotten who she was? She knew her way around a horse and carriage better than most men in town. She didn't need Cecil to cart her around! But she kept the retort to herself, lowering her eyes so Lerner would not see how much it cost her to hold her tongue.

He mistook her silence for acquiescence. He moved in and drew an arm around her, kissing her head. "My dear, this is for your protection. Yours and Virginia's. I only want what's best for you."

He left her in the study, saying he would have a word with Cecil first and then return to the office. Alone, Ada braced herself against the mantelpiece, determined not to collapse in a rage of frustrated tears. She took several shaking breaths before she calmed down and straightened up. She looked up at the portrait Lerner had commissioned of her. She was seated on a red velvet chair wearing her blue dress with the white trim, the dress she had been in when they first met. In her left hand was a rolled up sheaf of blueprint paper, and on the table beside her lay another plan, its curling edges kept in place by an artist's compass in one corner and a small blue vase of coreopsis and sunflowers in the other. She reached out and touched the frame and then the mantelpiece again. For the first time since she had moved into this splendid house, it seemed cold.

Ada's reaction had shaken Lerner. The look in her eyes when he asked, "Am I a bigot?" had chilled him to the bone. Up till now, their arguments had been brief and trivial, and ended in pleasant reconciliations. But on this issue he knew there could be no compromise. Bigotry had nothing to do with it; it was pure business. For years, Lerner had cultivated his friendship with the tedious Lisle Armbruster, and now his efforts were finally bearing fruit. Over a recent Rotary luncheon, while others argued the deplorable state of Oklahoma football, Lisle had let slip that the Santa Fe was thinking of running a line west of Croy over to Daggs Valley and then on to Lawton and Fort Sill. There were no east-west lines through that part of Oklahoma, and shipping freight through Croy would easily save the railroad hundreds of thousands annually. Whoever owned land along the right-of-way could name his price, and Lerner intended to be the only man between here and Fort Sill with that advantage.

There was only one logical route for the line through the hills west of town: up Little Bushy Creek and across the relatively flat prairie south and west of Pesogi—exactly where the Sohi's orchard now bloomed. Seizing the farm would not be easy and it could not be quick; it needed some fairly tricky legal maneuvering. So cutting off all communication between his wife and Sohi's was essential; one slip would queer the whole deal.

Lerner's scheme was abetted by Balwinder's pride. As soon as the first lawsuit challenging Sohi's ownership of the land was filed, he demanded that Kamar cease all contact with Ada. An argument between Balwinder and Kamar ensued, as deep and damaging in its fire and fury as the Alquists' had been in its silence and ice. In the end, both husbands had their way, but by enforcing their wills, they tore more important bonds in the heart.

Ada knew nothing of this but had her suspicions. She wrote a letter to Kamar, trying to excuse the broken promise of her return, but when the letter returned unopened, she feared the worst. One day, while approaching Pautler's, she thought she caught a glimpse of Kamar through the window. She quickly veered away, heading for vanDoozer's instead, but arrived at its doors feeling ashamed of her cowardice. What if Kamar had seen? What would she think of her? She turned and went back to Pautler's, but when she entered, she saw only Darryl Longacre leaning against the counter by the cash register. He straightened up at the sight of her but did not smile. Feeling even more shame, she feigned confusion, gave Darryl a weak smile, and left.

A few days later, Ada answered the front doorbell to discover Clara

Whitlock on her doorstep. "Clara!" she exclaimed with relief and surprise.

"Good afternoon," Clara responded without a trace of warmth. "I hope I'm not disturbing you." She glanced behind her.

It was such a curiously furtive gesture. *That's her church across the street*, Ada thought. *Does she think someone might be watching?* "Not in the least. Won't you please come in?" Ada stood aside, fully opening the door to the cool interior. Clara hesitated, her hands working the purse she clasped tightly to her chest. "What is it, Clara?" Ada felt a sudden catch in her throat. "Is it Opa Mae?"

Clara Whitlock looked sharply at her. "No, she's fine. Which you could see for yourself if you were of a mind to." She reached into her purse and produced a small brown envelope. "The postmistress asked me to give this to you."

It was unstamped and unaddressed except for her name. There was no return address. It wasn't actually a letter at all, but a carefully folded piece of butcher paper. It smelled of . . . Her heart skipped a beat. "Who is it from?" she asked.

"I'm sure I don't know. And don't care to. Good day." Clara Whitlock turned on her heel and walked off without another word.

Ada closed the door and went quickly to the study, where she found a letter opener that broke the paste holding the paper together. A small bit of powder escaped the envelope, and she again caught a whiff of that spice that gave her hope. She read the careful cursive script while the house filled with silence:

My dear friend,

These foolish men and their grand plans have put a bar between us that I fear neither of us may cross. My heart would break except that I know it is not of your doing. I knew that at once when I saw the anguish that wrote itself across your face when by accident we nearly met the other day. I left by another route to prevent even one more jot of pain from crossing that face I so long to see.

The times are not good. They are dark, like a night without a moon. But they will not always be so, and we two know they will not always be so, for the moon of truth shines brightly in our hearts. The weak use force, the fearful use fear. We shall use our hearts, and one day they shall bring us together again. Always your friend,

The letter ended without a signature, but the cardamom that floated to the floor was signature enough.

Lerner lost the first case against the Sohis, which his lawyers based on alien land laws that prohibited ownership of real estate by persons ineligible for citizenship. In his decision, Judge Clifford Alford cited Oklahoma State Supreme Court precedence, saying "the prohibition on acquiring title does not apply since any lender, even an alien, may enforce a deed executed as a mortgage." The joy Ada felt at this decision pierced her heart. She knew her happiness was a betrayal of her husband, but she hoped the judgment would bring an end to the enmity between the two families.

But Ada did not know of Lerner's larger plans, and in those he was successful. Much to his delight, no word of the Santa Fe's plans had leaked to the larger community. He hired a Chicago surveying company to map the probable routes, then went methodically about the business of buying key properties along the most likely. He bought up the Edom allotments piece by piece without anyone in that contentious family communicating his interest to anyone else, even their own kin. He bought up foreclosed farms in the west county, operating through an Oklahoma City bank to cover his tracks. He decided against going after the Tucker clan's holdings in Pesogi (though they would be handy if the line took a less obvious route west). Within two years, he owned key properties along any route that would thread its way west of Croy.

Only the Sohi property stood between him and complete dominion over the future right-of-way. In a way, the initial judgment against him actually worked to his advantage. He allowed people to think he had given up and turned his attention elsewhere. He even sold a small parcel or two to speculators to throw further confusion. No one suspected his larger design, not even his wife.

But that larger design would unravel if the rail line did not go up Little Bushy Creek and cross the Sohi farm. If it took another route, all his purchases to the west would become dust bowl worthless. He pressed his lawyers to come up with another angle that would win him the property. Citing *United States v. Thind*, they attacked not only Balwinder's right to property, but his right to reside in the United States. For good measure, they went after his wife and son, bringing their citizenship into question, lest he try to transfer ownership to either one.

The viciousness of the attack horrified Ada. No matter how the second suit played out, she doubted she and Kamar could ever be friends again. The day the decision was to be read from the bench, she insisted on attending. She hoped for a chance to see Kamar one last time and offer a public apology. But she was disappointed. Only Balwinder and his lawyer—a Mr. Hansen imported from California by Balwinder's well-heeled brother—appeared. Balwinder looked neither at her in the public seats nor at her husband at the plaintiff's table.

Judge Alford's decision was succinct. While the previous lawsuit had established Bhavjeet Singh Sohi's right to the property by virtue of the mortgage against it, it did not address the legality of Bhavjeet Sohi's transference of title to his brother, Mr. Balwinder Singh Sohi. Mr. Balwinder Sohi had not established Oklahoma residence, was not a U.S. citizen, and, under *United States v. Thind*, could not become one. In short, the land was not his, but his brother's. Whether his brother could continue to hold it was a question not before the court, but as the property was seized in foreclosure, the court's expectation was that its equity would be converted to capital to satisfy the terms of the loan. In light of this finding, the question of citizenship for Mrs. Kamar Singh Sohi and her minor child was moot.

Balwinder turned to his lawyer, his dark eyes burning. "What does it mean?"

Hansen hung his head. "It means we lost, Mr. Sohi. I am very sorry."

"How can this be?"

"I am sure your brother—"

"My brother can go to the devil! And you, sir, you can go with him."

The judge leaned forward from his bench. "Mr. Hansen, is there a problem?"

"Your Honor—"

Balwinder spread his arms, encompassing the courtroom. "Honor? Where is there honor?"

Judge Alford pressed his lips together and said tightly, "Mr. Hansen, I suggest you advise your client to hold his tongue. This court has ruled, justice has been served, and there's an end of it."

Balwinder looked directly at him. "You call this justice? I worked that land! I planted those trees! I bring the fruits to market! How can you take this from me?"

"Balwinder—" Hansen began.

Alford cut him off. "Mr. Sohi, this court does not take kindly to litigants who cannot buck up to a judgment against them."

Balwinder Singh Sohi pointed a finger at Lerner Alquist like a bright sword. "You judged against him! How can he come back a second time? What buck up did you give him?"

Judge Alford straightened up. Local lawyers knew the look on his face and feared it. "Mr. Hansen, your client is flirting with contempt. I recommend that everybody calm down and go home. And I mean now." The judge slammed down his gavel and rose. He stopped when he saw Balwinder scramble past his lawyer to the plaintiff's table. He signaled the bailiff to go after him, but Balwinder got to Lerner first. Ada shrank in her seat behind the railing, but Lerner did not back down.

"You want my orchards? You want my farm, my hill, my house?" Balwinder hissed, inches from Lerner's face. "Take it! Take everything! May it bring you and your family nothing but sorrow and ruin. May all your hopes and dreams die up there, as surely mine have died." The bailiff had reached him then but Balwinder brushed him aside and stormed out of the court. The bailiff looked questioningly at Judge Alford, but the judge just shook his head and left.

Lerner turned to face Ada, a mocking half-smile creasing the side of his face. His expression changed when he saw hers. "My dear," he said, reaching over the rail to grab her hands. "You're trembling. You look like you've seen a ghost."

She knew she must look terrible. Her heart fluttered and she doubted she could stand without fainting. But worst of all, she knew he had no idea why she felt this way. "Oh, Phillip, Phillip . . ."

"Did he frighten you?" Lerner swiveled around to search the courtroom. "Where'd that bailiff go? I can have him go after him. He shouldn't be allowed loose like that. I'll have him arrested, I—"

"No!"

Lerner turned quickly, concern overcoming the anger in his eyes. She reached up and touched his face. "No, Phillip. There's no need." She steeled herself. "It was just a moment. The feeling's gone, now. You've done enough."

Chapter 34

CRAZY WOMAN WEATHER

The day that would rewrite the history of Croy dawned with a heaviness that was oppressive and restless. The sun rose huge and blood-colored, and its first touch on exposed skin encouraged townsfolk to stay indoors and farmers and field hands to cover up as much as they could despite the heat. The sky turned brassy and its glare kept people's eyes earthbound. When a bruised blue-black patch appeared on the northwestern horizon around mid-morning, many hoped it foretold a summer thunderstorm that would relieve the heat and clear the worried air.

Virginia, now nearly two and a half years old, seemed especially sensitive that day. She woke cross and stayed colicky all morning, fraying Ada's nerves. Though the house remained cool inside, Virginia's wailing filled the rooms with tension. Ada finally took both of them outside to the front porch, where the motion of the swing and Ada's humming of a tune she half remembered quieted the child. From the porch she saw a figure approaching, carrying a child on her hip. The woman was practically to the gate before Ada overcame her disbelief and recognized her. "Kamar!" she called out. Putting the startled Virginia in a basket, she rushed to open the gate.

Kamar's face broke into a grin, but Ada could see at once her happiness didn't travel fully through her. "My dear friend," Kamar said, and the two leaned forward and kissed each other on the cheek. "Eh?" Sunny said from his perch on her hip, reaching for the porch.

"Yes, she is there," Ada told him, gripping his small hand. "My dear Kamar, won't you please come inside? This day is not meant to be spent outdoors." She noticed for the first time the signs of dust and perspiration on her friend. With sudden insight, she realized that Kamar had walked all the way from her farm, and that almost certainly meant she was exhausted, and here without her husband's permission. "I'll have Cecil bring us some lemonade—or perhaps tea?" She guided them up the front steps and onto the porch, where she picked up Virginia.

"That is most kind. Is your husband not at home?" Kamar asked in even tones, but Ada knew what she meant.

"He is at the office and will probably be there until late today. We have all the time in the world."

The two women entered the cool of the hallway. Kamar hesitated when Ada motioned her to the front sitting room. "Perhaps not all that much time, after all," Kamar said. "Balwinder does not know I am here, and I suspect it is the same with your husband as it is with mine."

"At least let me get you some water," Ada said and headed for the kitchen, Kamar following.

As soon as they entered the room, Kamar headed for a chair and sat down heavily. Her face drew down with weariness and she deposited Sunny in the chair beside her with visible effort. Ada soaked a cloth in water, wrung it out, and handed it to her without a word, then poured them both some water from a stone crock in the icebox.

Kamar pressed the cloth to her face and took a long drink. She looked at Ada with eyes so full of sorrow Ada almost broke into tears before she said a word. "It is the end, I fear. I have been a prisoner in my own house since the day of the judgment. Balwinder is consumed by his anger and sense of injustice."

Ada reached across the table and grasped her friend's hand. "But surely you can appeal the decision. Balwinder's brother has connections, resources . . ."

Kamar closed her eyes and shook her head. "A madness has taken hold of him. He would rather be wronged and wounded than take another cent from his brother. He has cursed the land, this country, everything about his life here. He intends us to return to India."

Ada's heart sank. Sunny squirmed in his chair and Kamar let him down. He toddled over to Ada's lap, where Virginia sat watching him in fascination. "It is so simple for them," Ada said. "It should be for us as well."

"If men could be as simple as children, the world would be at peace. But men have lions in their blood, and so it cannot be." Kamar's usual reserve dissolved and she covered her face with her hand and began to cry. Ada set Virginia on the floor beside Sunny and came around the table. The two women rocked each other, tears running down their faces.

"I shall never forget your kindness to me," Kamar said, regaining her composure and looking Ada in the eyes.

"Nor I yours," Ada said. "With every cup of tea, I will think of you." Kamar smiled at her warmly. "And every time I see an elephant." At that, Kamar laughed outright and the golden spark came back to her eyes. It delighted Ada so, she added, "And any time I bite into an apple."

But instead of cheering Kamar further, the remark had the opposite effect. A look of horror crossed her face and she turned away, fresh tears on her cheeks. "Oh, my dear friend!" Kamar said. "How can I tell you?"

"What? Have I said something wrong?"

Kamar turned to her, her face angry through the tears. "He is killing them. He is killing the trees! Balwinder has this horrible machine, all stink and racket, and he is cutting them down, every one of them!"

The blood drained from Ada's face. "No. No, he cannot do that."

"He says he will leave them nothing—nothing! He would burn down the house as well if Sundar and I were not inside."

Ada went to the back door and opened it. "Cecil!" she called. "Cecil, I need your help. At once!" She turned back to Kamar. "I cannot allow it. I cannot lose it a second time."

"Lose what a second time?"

Cecil appeared on the back steps. Ada turned to him. "Cecil, hitch the horse to the carriage."

"Miss Ada—?"

She turned to Kamar. "I will persuade him myself."

"No, my dear friend," Kamar said, rising. "He is not reasonable. He will not listen."

"Miss Ada, Mr. Lerner told me never to let you near that place again. He will not permit it."

The air around Ada crackled. She clenched her fists and felt on the verge of loosing self-control. "*Permit* it?"

Kamar touched her on the arm. "Is this wisdom, dear friend?"

"I have to do this, Kamar. There are lions in my blood as well, and I cannot see that farm destroyed. It means too much to me. It means—oh, I don't know. It means much more than a home."

Kamar looked at her intently. "I have seen that look in your eyes before, when we first met. No argument will change your heart now." She nodded. "Go."

Ada turned to the coachman. "Never mind the carriage, Cecil. I will take the horse alone." He stood unmoving in the doorway, looking from one woman to the other. She stepped forward but he did not back down. "I will saddle it myself, if need be. Don't think I won't!"

Cecil took a deep breath. "No, Miss Ada. I'll help. It may be the last thing I do for you, but I will help."

The selfishness of what she asked suddenly came home to her. "Oh. No, Cecil, no. You must have nothing to do with this. Lerner would—" She stopped in mid-sentence, baffled by her own words. It was the first time in years she had referred to her husband as "Lerner" instead of "Phillip."

Cecil broke in. "Miss Ada, I have known for some time my place here was coming to an end. I feel a different calling, and I may as well begin today. Let me help."

When the horse was saddled and Ada had changed into her riding dress, the three gathered under the porte cochère. "I will look after the little ones until you return," Kamar said.

"If my husband returns . . ." Ada began, but didn't know how to finish.

Kamar shrugged. "It is in God's hands."

"Amen," Cecil said. A peculiar snapping sound crossed the sky from northeast to southwest, like a quick succession of rifle shots. They all looked up, expecting a thunderous boom, but none followed. "I don't know about that sky, Miss Ada," Cecil said. "It looks like a fierce wind coming."

"I shall be back in no time. Balwinder will either listen or he won't. But I must try." She turned the horse and rode down the driveway and disappeared.

Cecil and Kamar watched her go. Two more cracks of thunder ricocheted across the sky above them. In the kitchen one of the children began to cry. "I must see to the children," Kamar said. She looked at Cecil. "What will you do?"

Cecil shook his head slowly. "Mr. Lerner will find out, no doubt about it. I best not be here when he does. I've been packed up for weeks. Now's as good a time as any." He turned to Kamar. "You folks, you look out now, hear? This can be hard country for . . ."

Kamar smiled. "For anyone. We live by faith."

Cecil nodded, and the two of them went their separate ways.

The sky ahead of her was turning a greenish color that made Ada sick to her stomach. The peculiar lightning was more frequent. She could see it now, snaking across the dark clouds like the veins under a taut muscle. She began to wonder if she would make it back home before the storm broke. That might work to her advantage. If she and Balwinder had to sit out a summer downpour she might talk some sense into him. If he would talk to her at all, that is. Kamar had not been hopeful about that.

She heard the sound of the chainsaw before she topped the crest of the hill and her heart fluttered in panic. The saw sputtered, roared to life, then was still, leaving just the sound of a low moaning wind in the background. As she passed the house, she saw with a cry that nearly half the trees were already on their sides, stumps sticking up in forlorn rows across the hill.

She dismounted the skittish horse and hitched it to a bush. "Mr. Sohi!" she called out. The chainsaw started up and she walked toward the sound. "Mr. Sohi!" she called again but doubted her voice could be heard above the rip of the saw's teeth biting into living wood. The wind picked up, carrying her words away along with fat drops of rain that flew sideways.

She located him by seeing a tree shiver and fall. She called his name again.

Balwinder looked up, startled. His face was lined with sweat that trickled from under his *dastaar* and into his beard. "What do you do here?" he shouted.

"You must spare them!" Ada shouted back. A roaring sound surrounded them, persisting even though the saw had stopped. Behind her, the horse whinnied and reared, threatening to tear loose from its hitch.

"Foolish woman!" Balwinder shouted. "Your horse will escape." He dropped the saw and headed toward the animal.

"Forget the horse," Ada yelled, following him. "Let me talk to you!" But he was already several strides ahead of her. He grabbed the horse by the bridle to keep it from rearing again. She started to run after him.

There was a moment of complete stillness that seemed to suck the breath from her, and then all the trees in the orchard, both standing and felled, lurched in one direction.

Ada's feet rose by themselves from beneath her and she was turned upside down. She screamed, the sound torn from her lungs. She saw the ground fly away beneath her and tree limbs rush by on either side. Then something hard and sharp grabbed her by the neck, and that was the last Ada Riley Dowdell knew of this earth.

Balwinder looked up at the shriek. He had but a moment as the horse tore from his grip to see Ada pulled up as if by a giant hand, feet first through the thrashing tree beside her, and snag there. Then an enormous force slammed into him from the left. A tree limb, perhaps one he had cut that morning, knocked the wind from him with a crack that surely meant broken ribs. He tried to keep his eyes on Ada but she disappeared in a swirling, roaring blackness. His sight narrowed to a blurry disc as the storm and his fading consciousness closed in on him. He thought he saw Ada's dress suddenly rip free of the tree and sail upwards, and another, smaller object fly off in the opposite direction. And then he was tumbling, tumbling, cartwheeling head-over-heels down the hill and into the ravine as the horror roared by overhead. He lay there senseless, his *dastaar* half unwound and wrapped around his body, buried under tree limbs, clods of dirt, corrugated tin from a dozen roofs, and dead and dying livestock—but providently face up. He would otherwise have drowned in the mud that poured down the gully of Little Bushy Creek in the storm's wake.

Lerner Alquist thought he would surprise his wife by taking lunch at home for a change. The days when she brought him his dinner in a pail had grown fewer and fewer, and while he told himself it was because she was busy raising the child, he felt an increasing distance between them, and he wished to close it. When the railroad deal went through, they would be able to afford domestics that would free her time and his, and then their real married life would begin.

He stopped by the Santa Fe depot to speak to Lisle, but the little man was not in, so he headed south along Front Street. The sky darkened overhead and he heard the rumble of thunder behind him. *Perhaps I should have taken the car*, he thought. *If a storm breaks now, I'll have to take the carriage back to the office. Then both car and carriage will be downtown and Cecil will have to fetch one back.* He smiled to himself. He knew which one. Nobody touched the Studebaker except him.

Wind stirred the trees as he mounted the steps to the porch. A startling clap of thunder made him look up just as he was about to pass under the arch. The sky looked peculiar, lumpy, like the underside of a pot of boiling water. He looked down the street toward downtown. A black fog seemed to be rolling in from the northeast. There had been dust storms in years past, but this looked different, darker.

"Mr. Alquist!" a woman's voice called from the doorway. He turned around. At first he couldn't place the woman. She was dark-skinned like a Negro and held a black boy in one arm and a blond girl in the other. It was disorienting. The wind pushed him first from one side and then the other. Finally recognizing Sohi's wife, he sputtered, "What in blazes are you doing here, woman?"

"It is Ada!" Kamar said, the whites of her eyes standing out against her dark face.

"What about Ada? Come out of there!" He could not tolerate that woman's presence in his house. And what was she doing with his child? He stepped forward to snatch Virginia from her arms.

"She is out there, in the storm!"

Lerner froze. The sound of an approaching freight train filled his ears. *But there is no train this time of day!* He whirled around. Blackness filled the horizon from side to side. He could barely see the edges of it, but when he did, he saw it was moving, revolving, coming closer. "Jesus God in Heaven!" He took a step away from the house, then turned around. "Take the children! Head for the basement! Go! Now!" He turned without waiting for an answer and started running, running back toward the center of town, straight into the whirling mass. "Ada!" he cried. Dirt flew up and stung his eyes. Tree limbs snapped off and flew at him. He dashed into the street to escape them. A roadster careened past, nearly running him over. "Ada! Ada!" His suit jacket was torn from his back and he fell on his side. The wind pushed him across the brick-cobbled street, scraping his face in the dirt and trash that seemed to come to life and dance before him in a frenzy. "Ada!" His feet were tugged by a mighty hand that he could not resist. The crook of his arm caught on a maple sapling and he hugged it to him, flattening himself against the dirt as best he could. He looked up once and felt his face stung by a thousand wasps. He cried out and buried his face in the earth. The howl of wind was shattered by deafening booms as the houses on either side of him exploded.

The entire town was swallowed in darkness. Every home, business, school, and church west of the White Horse River was in the mouth of the beast.

Chapter 35

REMAINS

Joining the Kennsing County Sheriff's Department was the first step in Marty Jackson's life-long plan. He intended to become an Oklahoma State Trooper, spend a couple of years earning his reputation, then move on to Texas and become a Ranger. He was sworn in as a deputy on a muggy afternoon in 1935. The next day, a twister wiped out most of Croy's police force. The Sheriff's Department stepped in, running a command post from the relatively unscathed county courthouse. Everything for blocks around the building was reduced to kindling. There was a real danger that what was left of the town would catch fire and burn. Marty itched for something to do—rescue trapped survivors, confront looters, distribute food, aid, water—anything but be stationed here behind a desk at the county courthouse, manning a radio and posting lists of the dead on the wall outside. It didn't seem right that there should be so many dead and no one to arrest.

Harlan George, who'd been sworn in only three weeks before, strolled in from the night. A blast of cold air came with him. "New list from the hospital," he announced, slapping the sheet down on the desk. His attitude of indifference was betrayed by the way he chewed his gum. Jaw muscles bulged with each clamp of his teeth.

"I don't give a damn what you say. You will take her name off that list or I will have your guts for garters!" a man shouted from the coroner's office. Harlan twitched.

"Mr. Alquist," came the coroner's weary voice, "we have the body, the dress is almost certainly— "

"You have nothing!" Lerner Alquist bellowed. "A body, and not even that!"

"We're still looking for—"

"Five miles from town! My wife was in town, I tell you, waiting for me at my office. What in the god-damned hell would she be doing five miles from town?"

Harlan shook his head. "That Alquist fella," he said. "I seen him up at the hospital earlier. He's got his head wrapped up tighter'n a tick, but it don't seem to have hindered his jaw none."

Marty glared at him. Harlan was out there where the action was and he was stuck here behind a desk. "Maybe you'd be hollering, too, if all they found was parts and a dress."

Harlan stopped chewing and looked at him. "See ya, Marty," he said and left.

Marty picked up the new list of the dead and started reading through the names. He was from further out in the county toward Liddle, but he still recognized some of them. It made his hand tremble. A cold breeze blew through the office and nearly tore the list from his hand. He was about to yell at Harlan to close the damned door when he looked up and saw it wasn't Harlan standing there at all.

The man was wild-looking, wide-eyed and dark skinned, though not a Negro or any kind of Indian Marty had seen before. His face was caked with mud and dried blood and streaked from what looked like tears. His loose trousers were torn and muddy and his once-white shirt bloused out around his midriff. He wore no shoes and it looked like his feet were bleeding. *Well*, Marty reasoned, *they would be if this guy walked through all that crap out there in the street.* Snapped tree limbs, shattered glass, broken bricks and roof shingles covered everything, making it hard to distinguish street from sidewalk or even where houses and yards had been. It was hazardous even in thick-soled boots. But stranger than the man's bleeding feet was his hair, which hung in tangled black masses clear down to his waist. Marty had never seen hair that long and thick on a man, not even a Navajo.

The man trembled, probably from the cold, and carried something—a melon, maybe—wrapped in a towel.

"Come in, sir," Marty said. "It's warmer inside." It had snowed—actually snowed—the night after the twister, and the temperature had not risen since.

The man staggered forward, eyes locked on his. "He must never know," he said.

"Know what?" The guy was still shivering though the door had swung shut behind him. "Who must never know?" The man was up to the desk now. *He's scared*, thought Marty. *Terrified*. The man held the bundle out in front of him like an offering.

"He must never know it was me." With stiff arms in jerky movements, he placed the package on the desk. "Please," he pleaded. "Do not tell him."

"I don't get your meaning, mister."

"He must never know. He must never know it was I who found her."

"Her?" Marty asked. He stood up suddenly and backed away from the desk, staring at the round thing wrapped in muslin.

The man backed away slowly, toward the door. His eyes were still on Marty's. "Please," he said. "Do not tell. He must never know."

Marty Jackson looked at the bundle then looked at the door. There was no sign of the long-haired man. The room was dead silent; all he could hear was the hammering of his own heart. Then bit by bit other sounds crept in, the ticking of the Regulator clock, the wind against the window, the raised voices in the room next door.

"Well," he said. "Well—"

He knew what he had to do next, but he didn't want to touch the thing. He picked up the bundle as if his arms weren't his own and walked slowly into the coroner's office, where the argument raged. He thought maybe he'd gone deaf again because the room went silent as soon as he entered. But the coroner looked at him, then looked at the bundle, then took it from him and gently, gently placed it on the table beside the stiff and soiled dress. He carefully unwound the long strip of muslin, and when he revealed, at last, what lay beneath, the shriek that tore through Lerner Alquist before he collapsed to the floor—well, Marty Jackson heard that all right. He would take that sound with him to his grave.

Balwinder Sohi found his wife and child in the basement of the VFW along with the other homeless survivors. Kamar gave a shout and ran to him as soon as he entered the hall. She clung to him, crying. The pain of her embrace roused him from his shock. Still caked in mud and stained with his own blood and that of another's, he looked down at her tear-stained face and that of his son and said, "What remains?"

"Remains?" Kamar said, wiping her cheeks with the palm of her hand. "Do you mean, our household things? There is nothing, Balwinder. Nothing remains."

He nodded, not comprehending. "Pack everything. We must leave this place of death at once."

Lerner came home that night a madman. He tore every picture of Ada he could lay his hands on out of its frame and ripped it to pieces—every photograph, every drawing, even the oil painting above the mantel, dismembered, torn asunder, and burned. He could not risk looking at them. If ever he did, he would see not her warm and lively eyes, the promising, teasing smile, but instead that ghastly visage wrapped in a bloody towel. He burned them all, all but one. When he seized the photograph off his desk, intent on smashing it to the floor, he froze. As his arm swung up in an arc, the silver frame flashed in the light and his arm locked tight as if clamped in a vise. He could not tear his eyes away from her. She had given him this portrait, her promise, her answer, all those years ago. "Hope."

He sank to his knees, pressing the photo against his forehead and sobbing. The grief flooded out of him like a river, taking all his strength and all his will with it. The sounds he made filled the room, the house, clawed at every wall. The raw power of it frightened him but he could not make it stop, he did not want it to stop. When it had emptied him, he could barely lift himself from the floor. He staggered over to the desk and opened the center drawer, placed the picture in it face down, and locked it. He never took it out or looked at it again. But it was there. He knew it was always there . . .

Lerner stopped short. The night came slamming back, the trees sharp and black, the crickets scraping endlessly, the syrupy air heavy with life. He stood on a sidewalk in some part of town he did not recognize. Lost. He was lost. The realization yanked him eighteen years forward, into the present.

No! He was not lost. The picture! That black devil Sohi had used Ada's picture to carve her portrait on the memorial. Ginny must have given it to him. Ginny, who had taken Ada's ring. Ginny, who had gotten into his ledger drawer. Ginny, who had . . .

He had to go back. The portrait must be in its drawer in his desk. Sohi must have returned it!

He glanced around, looking for landmarks. His eyes picked out the water tower above the trees. It seemed impossibly far away. He must be clear across town, near the county road. He started running, running back to the house with its fine stone arches and delicate lilac bushes, all of which could go to blazes in dust and ashes as far as he was concerned.

But that photo must still be there!

Chapter 36

DUST AND ASHES

Andy sat erect and still as the car sped eastward into the rising night. The evening wedge, that bruised and solemn shadow of the Earth, broadened, deepened, and drew over them.

He was focused, clear. There must be a cost, and now he knew what it was. The moment he had climaxed inside Susan, a pain sharp as knives had torn through his member, each thrust raking him raw over hot coals. He yelled and pulled out so abruptly Susan had grunted. Grunted, like an animal, and Andy knew immediately his sin had pulled her down with him. They were deep in the void, the silence and emptiness of the absence of God. There was only one way to redeem them. There was only one way back to the heart of God.

Susan tried several times to get Andy to talk, but after one or two single-word responses, she gave up. It was nearing midnight when they passed through Daggs Valley. Susan started recognizing farms by the constellation of their yard lights sliding by, but instead of heading directly into town, Andy headed north. Susan started worrying about her father, who must surely be wondering where she was by now. She looked over at Andy. "Aren't we going back to town?"

He didn't answer. She leaned over and looked at the dashboard. "We're nearly out of gas. I think the nearest pump is outside Swofford Brothers."

At the junction with Tyrola Road, Andy turned south, back toward town. He finally spoke. "I could hear them."

"Who? Hear what?"

"Laughing, pointing."

"That wasn't about you. It couldn't have been."

"Do you really think people are stupid?" His voice was calm but hard.

"No," She slumped in the seat. It was pointless trying to talk him into believing something she didn't herself.

The first lights of town appeared ahead. They passed the cemetery and Andy slowed down. "I can't go back," he said. "Everything's changed. I can't go back to that." He applied the brakes slowly and brought the car to a gentle stop. They were just past the first streetlight on the edge of Croy, where Tyrola Road turns into Post Street, where the Santa Fe tracks leave the thicket of cottonwoods around the White Horse and head into town.

"Andy?" Susan waited for an answer, but there was none. "We can't stop here, it isn't safe."

"I know what has to be done." he said. His voice had lost its edge. He was making simple declarations now. "We need to start over. We need to start again."

She sighed. "It wouldn't work. You know it wouldn't."

"No, I don't know it wouldn't. Can't we at least try?"

She turned to him. "Isn't that what we've been doing all summer?"

He looked at her peculiarly, as if not at her at all, but at some distant point beyond her. "I know I wasn't all I should have been last night. God knows, I didn't mean to hurt you."

"You didn't hurt me," she said. "It's just— I knew the moment I saw the look on your face I shouldn't have . . ." She dropped her eyes. "It was wrong."

"It was a judgment. But we can fix that. We can make it right. Then everything can go back to the way it was, the way it should be." He turned his face away. "I can't go back there the way things are now. I couldn't face your father. Not with the whole town knowing."

"They don't know anything."

"What they're thinking, then."

She felt her temper rise. "Who gives a damn what they think? There's more to life than this small-minded town and its gossips."

"But don't you see? This is my heart, my soul. I don't know what to do with my life without the church, without music."

"Andy, you're talented. You could make a living anywhere. Get out of here. Go to Dallas or Los Angeles or someplace. Don't go back. Go on."

"Matthew—"

"To hell with my father."

"If you loved me—"

She closed her eyes in exasperation. "Oh Andy, don't you see? I do love you. That's why I can't—"

The blast from the train whistle cut her off and drove every other thought from her head. "Andy!" she yelled. "The train! Move the car!"

He shook his head and became very still, as if he didn't even breathe, as if his heart didn't even beat. "Marry me, Susan," he said.

She spun in her seat and saw the Santa Fe bearing down on them, its reflected headlight on the rails forming two gleaming rays that passed directly beneath them. She opened her mouth to answer, but instead her ears were nearly shattered by the blast of the train horn.

"I'm not leaving here until you say you will."

"Are you crazy?" She found the door latch and flung it open. "Get out, Andy!" she screamed. "Get out!"

He shook his head, his lips moving, but she could hear nothing. The whistle was blowing almost constantly now. The locomotive's brakes engaged and their wail became a wall of sound that filled the night. She dashed from the car, not looking back.

To Andy, the night was perfectly still. He was perfectly calm. Susan standing in the ditch, frantic, a few yards away was like a photograph. There was no world outside the car, no time outside this moment. He sang, "All my troubles and worries have no hold upon me. I think about—"

About what? he wonders. Funny, he can't think what the next word is. And then it doesn't matter.

Lerner stared at the drawer. There was no glint of silver beneath the papers. He rifled its contents, tossing ledgers, deeds of trust, and bank statements to the floor without regard. Nothing! He pulled the drawer from the desk and hurled it across the study to smash against the wall.

The house was quiet, empty. Lerner sank into a chair. His mind was scrambled, full of anger and fear and a growing panic. He searched his memory for the face of his wife, but all his mind's eye could dredge up was Virginia's face, angry, defiant. Then Harry's, mocking, sneering. And his own, which seemed like a stranger's. He shook his head and leaned forward, his face pressed into his hands. But once again, when he pulled on the memory of his wife, all he could see were plans and drawings. Her face, like the portrait in the silver frame, was nowhere to be found.

It came to him with cold certainty: *That black bastard never returned it*. He used it to finish the sculpture, the portrait of Ada in terra cotta. He'd kept the photo. And Lerner had sent men out to Sohi's trailer to burn it down, and to the sculpture to smash it to pieces and dump it in the Canadian.

He was running again, out the door without even knowing it, this time headed for the library. *It must be there*, he told himself, *it must still be there!* A train whistle sounded far off, then sounded again. And again. He kept running. Trees, houses, parked cars disappeared as he flashed by. There was but one goal before him, one purpose to his life: to fill his eyes once again with the face of his beloved.

He ran up the middle of the street, feet slamming against the pavement. "Ada! Ada!" his mouth was saying, but no sound came out. There was no breath left in him. He turned the corner, made it to the sidewalk in front of the library, and cut behind the speakers' platform. But went no further. He stared disbelieving at the empty scaffolding. The frames holding the panels were gone, leaving slack ropes swaying in the slight breeze. The strength poured out of him like sand from a sack, and he sank to the pavement just a few steps from the library entrance.

The night air was rent with the shriek of metal wheels on metal rails, the crash and boom of boxcars knocking head to tail, and then a sudden and dreadful silence. A moment later, sirens started to wail, and every dog in town woke to spread the news.

Percy Owen might have seen Lerner stretched along the library steps while on his usual rounds, but Percy was busy prying what was left of Andy Simms from the wreckage of his car. Eddie Littledeer, volunteer fireman racing north along Third Street, might have seen him, but his eyes were on the column of smoke rising from the grass fire sparked by the dying car. Moments later, the ambulance team, flashing by just a block to the east, might have seen something if either of them had looked in Lerner's direction, but neither did. Jake Swofford and Darryl Longacre might have met Lerner on the library steps as planned, but they were engaged elsewhere, having decided it was more fun to burn down Sunny's trailer first.

And so Lerner Alquist lay there, sprawled before the blank, unfinished face of Ada's Memorial. Minutes slid by as the moon hurried in one door and out the other of the heedless clouds.

It was Miss Ida Laine Lancaster who found him; Miss Ida Laine Lancaster who stole quietly from the basement entrance, locking it behind her, looking both ways before rounding the corner of the building to make sure no passing cars saw her. She was almost down the library steps before she stopped, went down on one knee, and touched the body of Lerner Phillip Alquist, known to many hereabouts as "New York," lying crumpled and motionless and, though the night was warm, already cold as stone.

Chapter 37

FINDINGS

The inquest into the circumstances surrounding the death of Andrew Lewis Simms at the Post Street crossing of the Gulf, Colorado, and Santa Fe Railway in the Town of Croy, Kennsing County, State of Oklahoma, was conducted by Dr. Wellborn Hope from the Central District Office of the Oklahoma State Coroner. It was held in Conference Room C of the Kennsing County Courthouse on the Thursday following the tragedy. Barring a finding of suicide, the funeral would be the following Saturday at Mt. Hermon Bible Church with interment at the city cemetery immediately following, Mr. Simms having no surviving relatives in his hometown of Parkman, Illinois.

An unusual number of people turned out for the inquest. Susan found herself in the second of four rows of seats, jammed between Clara Oldfield and Chief of Police Buchholtz. Percy Owen was in the row behind her. Her father, Mayor Pautler, Ruth Tibbits, and a few congregants from Mt. Hermon filled the other seats. Ethan Jameson sat in the back row against the wall; no one asked him to move.

Dr. Hope got down to business quickly.

"On the face of it," he said, "this case appears a suicide." Susan heard a gasp from Mrs. Oldfield and found herself holding her breath. "However," Dr. Hope continued, "we are not here to be satisfied by appearances or rumors. We are here to ascertain what, in fact, actually happened. Although this is not a court of law and I am not a judge, testimony here is still testimony. That is, if you lie, you go to jail. Everybody clear on that?"

He cast his gaze around the room. There were no comments. "Very good. Chief Buchholtz, if you would, please."

The Chief gave a quick description of the scene, stumbling momentarily when he referred to it as "an accident."

"Accident is a judgment, Chief," Dr. Hope interjected. "Please refer to it as the incident."

The Chief amended his report and concluded with the efforts to extract the body from the wreckage, its conveyance to St. Joseph's Hospital, and the pronouncement of death at 12:27 AM on the night in question.

Dr. Hope dismissed the Chief and called the next person to testify, Susan Jacobs. Even though she knew it was coming, she jumped when she heard her name. She was certain everyone could see her hand tremble when she took the oath.

The coroner wasted no time. "Now, Miss Jacobs, as an eyewitness to the event, please tell us what happened."

Her mind went suddenly blank, unable to form words. She balled her hands into fists and dug them into her thighs.

"Miss Jacobs, I know this is difficult, but it is necessary. Just be as brief as possible and you can get through it."

"We were stopped. And the train came." *Is that brief enough?* she thought.

"You mean, Mr. Simms had stopped the car on the tracks?"

Susan shrugged. "Yeah, yes. I guess so."

"Did he say why?"

She looked at them all. "Well, we were . . . We'd been driving all day and I had just remarked that we were out of gas, and—" She shrugged. "The car stopped just about then."

"Stopped? Abruptly, or slowly?"

"Slowly. It just sort of rolled to a stop."

"So, you think the car ran out of gas? Is that what you're saying?"

"I— I don't know."

"Did Mr. Simms say anything? Did he say he had run out of gas?"

"He didn't say anything. He just sat there."

"Just sat there? Not a word?"

Susan shook her head.

"Speak up, Miss Jacobs."

"I don't know why! He wouldn't move!" She burst into tears.

The coroner moved a box of Kleenex closer to her. When Susan regained her composure, he asked, "You said you had been driving all day. Where to?"

Susan shrugged "We were just out, driving. West. We drove west."

"And what was Mr. Simms's state of mind while he was driving?"

He thinks Andy was driving, she thought. She shook her head. "I don't know."

"Well, was he happy, sad, relaxed, tense?"

"He was fine. He— We stopped once. There was a woman, near Lawton, with a flat tire. Andy stopped and changed the tire for her."

"Do you know this woman's name?"

"No." She caught herself. "Wait. Ruth something. I think her name was Ruth. Her husband worked at Fort Sill and she thanked us and said her name was Ruth. She wanted to pay us, but Andy said it was his pleasure, he was happy to help. And then we noticed how late it was getting and we turned around and came . . . home." Susan stared off into the distance, wondering that she had remembered so much.

The coroner excused her and then called Dr. Gaston LeGoff of the State Forensic Laboratory. Dr. LeGoff was tall and wore pince-nez glasses and took the witness seat as if he were a conductor about to lead an orchestra.

"Dr. LeGoff, you performed the autopsy on Andrew Simms?"

"Yes, I did."

"And what did you determine was the cause of death?"

"There was, of course, considerable trauma due to the impact with the train, but that was not the cause of death. The train did not kill Andrew Simms."

There was a buzz throughout the courtroom.

"And if the train did not kill him, Dr. LeGoff, what did?"

"In my opinion, and in the opinion of the State Lab, Mr. Simms died of a heart attack brought on by myocardio sarcoidosis, a form of Boeck's Disease."

"What is the basis of this opinion?"

"Although the body was in problematic condition—" Susan felt her stomach drop. Beside her, Chief Buchholtz cleared his throat. "—we were able to extract the heart. We did a histological examination of tissues taken from the walls of the organ, and it revealed extensive replacement of myocardium by numerous partly confluent granulomata. These granulomata were involuted and showed extensive and dense fibrosis."

"Could you explain that in laymen's terms, please?"

"Certainly. When we examined Mr. Simms' heart under a microscope, we found extensive granulomatous inflammation—that is, small, fleshy swellings—in the heart muscle. Essentially, the heart had become a source of irritation and inflammation, as if it were a foreign object. The body attacked itself. Sarcoidosis can occur in the kidneys or the lungs or other organs, but in those cases it usually presents clear symptoms, leading to treatment. In the heart, it rarely does."

"Untreated, this disease leads to . . . ?"

"A sudden and massive heart attack, what we sometimes call sudden cardiac death. It would have been abrupt, without warning. Startling, perhaps, but not painful. He would have lost consciousness almost at once and been unable to speak or move."

"His father!" Mrs. Oldfield blurted out from her seat.

Dr. LeGoff looked annoyed, but the coroner looked out at the rows of chairs. "Who is speaking, please?"

Mrs. Oldfield rose, though she had not been asked to. "I am, your Honor. Mrs. Clara Oldfield."

"I am not a judge, Mrs. Oldfield, but thanks nonetheless for the honorific. And how did you know the deceased, Mrs. Oldfield?"

"Andy Simms is—was—my tenant. I'm his landlady. I remember he told me, earlier this summer, his father died of a heart attack, quite young."

Dr. LeGoff shook his head. "Evidence of hereditary sarcoidosis is inconclusive."

"Thank you, Mrs. Oldfield," the coroner said, "you may sit down." He made a note, earning a frown from Dr. LeGoff. He turned to him. "What would have been the prognosis of this disease if it had been detected and treated?"

"Dismal. Few people live more than two years with sarcoidosis, regardless of which organ is affected."

"Did Mr. Simms know he had this condition?"

"I doubt it. Myocardial sarcoidosis is almost never diagnosed, except on autopsy. I have surveyed local physicians and none of them have had Mr. Simms as a patient, and even if anyone had, they would have had no reason to suspect the condition. It would have gone undetected. Mr. Simms was, for all outward appearances, a normal, healthy young man."

Susan's heart skipped a beat. Mrs. Oldfield stiffened beside her.

"Can you be certain he had the heart attack before the train struck him?"

"Well, he certainly didn't have it afterwards."

"Nevertheless, are you certain it occurred before?"

"Certain, no, but it seems highly likely. Otherwise, he would have been able to leave the car. He would not have endangered Miss Jacobs."

"But if he had suffered," Dr. Hope checked his notes, "'sudden cardiac death,' would he have been unable to move, unable to speak?"

"Yes."

"Miss Jacobs, does that fit with your experience of the incident?"

Susan simply nodded. The coroner noted her response for the record.

Her father was next. Susan could not bear to watch. She shut her eyes.

"Reverend Jacobs," Dr. Hope began, "you were Mr. Simms' employer?"

"Yes. Well, actually, Mt. Hermon Bible Church, of which I am pastor, was his employer. I was his supervisor. But I was more than that. I was his friend."

"How did Mr. Simms appear to you in the week leading up to the incident?"

Susan heard her father hesitate and she opened her eyes.

"I'm not certain what you mean by the question."

"What was his frame of mind?"

"Andy Simms was the most cheerful, talented, enthusiastic person I have had the pleasure to meet."

Susan saw a look cross Dr. Hope's face. Her father had not directly answered the question. "I have here a note," he said, fingering a piece of paper, "from one of your parishioners stating that Mr. Simms had been suspended from his duties as music minister at Mt. Hermon a day before the incident."

Susan saw her father shoot a look across the small room at JayRob Pautler. Pautler neither moved nor blinked.

"Not suspended," Rev. Jacobs said. "Given a leave. It was intended to be a short one."

"Why was he 'given a leave'?"

"We had just finished a week-long series of revival meetings. He needed a rest. I mentioned he was enthusiastic. Andy was not the sort of person to slack in his duties. He was enthusiastic to a fault."

"So, he had been under considerable strain."

"Considerable *physical* strain, yes. He deserved a well-earned rest. We could do well enough without him for a week. My daughter could stand in as music minister, as she has before," he looked at Susan, "though—and no offense to you, my dear—everyone preferred Andy."

Susan smiled. "So did I," she whispered.

"And do you think he would ever have done anything intentionally to endanger himself or Miss Jacobs?"

Susan's father looked directly at her, his eyes full of care and compassion. She felt at that moment as if his heart and hers were one and the same.

"They were the best of friends. I believe, in fact, that he loved her. Andy would never have done anything to endanger Susan, or anyone else for that matter."

Yes, Susan said. It was the most heartfelt prayer she had ever prayed.

Her father was dismissed and stepped down.

Please let that be all, she prayed again, but her heart caught in her throat when Dr. Hope said, "Chief Buchholtz, please."

The chief rose but the coroner held up his hand. "No need to come up, Chief. Just one or two questions."

Buchholtz stood in place at attention.

"There was a fire along the tracks after the incident, was there not?"

"Yes, sir."

"How would you characterize that fire?"

Buchholtz frowned. "How do you mean?"

"Well, was it a big fire, a small fire, lots of smoke?"

The chief shrugged. "The fire crew had it out right quick. A small fire, I guess you'd say."

"Is that what you'd expect if the car had a full tank of gas?"

Susan saw the chief's back relax. "No, sir. If there'd been much gas at all, I would have expected much worse."

"Thank you. That's all. You may sit down."

There was no more to be said by anyone. Within the hour, the coroner ruled Andrew Lewis Simms had died of natural causes. The collision with the train was an unfortunate sequela, though fortunately involving the driver alone, the passenger having escaped to a safe distance and the locomotive crew escaping injury as well. Importantly, he also ruled the

Gulf, Colorado & Santa Fe Railway Company free of any negligence or responsibility in the unhappy incident. The inquest adjourned.

Susan rose along with the others. "You had a narrow escape," Chief Buchholtz said. She looked up, frightened, but he had walked off.

Clara Oldfield rose beside her, clutching both hands to her chest. "How wonderfully God displays His mercy."

Susan couldn't believe her ears. "Mercy? What is merciful about a train wreck?"

Mrs. Oldfield put a hand on her arm. "He died by God's hand, in God's grace. And you, my dear, it was a miracle you were spared."

She jerked her arm away. "There was nothing miraculous about me. I ran. I ran!" She began to cry.

"Don't blame yourself, Susan. It's God's will."

"What's He got to do with it?"

"He looked down and took pity on him. By His Grace, Andy can be buried in consecrated ground."

"He's *dead,* Mrs. Oldfield. What does it matter what kind of dirt they throw on him now?"

"Susan," her father said behind her. "Let's go home."

Dr. Ronald C. Early, Organist

It was not noted at the time, but on the night of the tragedy on Post Street and the equally shocking death of Lerner Alquist—both occurring so soon after the happy celebration on the steps of the Memorial Library— Dr. Ronald C. Early did not return to his rooms at Mrs. Chisholm's Boarding House. He had not been there the night before, and he did not return by the end of the week. Shortly thereafter, an unstamped envelope appeared in the mail drop at Mrs. Chisholm's containing the balance of that month's rent and a brief note saying that the rooms would no longer be needed. A Bach scholar, musicologist, and splendid organist, Dr. Ronald C. Early—known to some as "Curley"—was much missed by the congregation of St. Mark's Episcopal, especially at Advent.

Chapter 38

A FORMULA FOR MIRACLES

Susan took her hat off as she entered the parsonage, but she didn't put it on the table. She held it in her hands, staring into the hallway that led to the kitchen. She heard her father come in behind her and close the front door. "Did you notice how they all were dressed?" she asked over her shoulder.

"Who?" The light in the hallway was soft. Its reflection off the floor lit the walls in a fading yellow light. A few motes turned in the air.

"The people at the inquest," Susan said. "All dressed up, like they were going to meeting. Even more than that: like it was Easter Sunday. Everyone in their finest."

Her father put a hand on her shoulder but she didn't turn around. "It was important to them," he said. "People are still in shock. Two deaths, so suddenly. And Andy's was so . . . troubling. I think it was their way of paying respect, in case . . ." He didn't finish.

"In case the verdict had been different." Susan shook her head and pulled away from him. "I'm sorry, Daddy, but I don't think I can help you at Andy's service."

"I understand." She heard him hang his hat on the hall tree. "Just being there will be hard enough."

She faced him. "No, I don't think I can be there at all."

He looked at her a moment, then dropped his head. "People will notice your absence."

"Tell them I'm at the hospital, visiting Ginny. God knows Harry needs the help."

"That isn't it, though, is it?"

Her fingers worked their way around the brim of her hat. "I'm carrying too much inside, Daddy. I know how it will be. 'A Celebration of Christ,' is how they'll put it."

"That's how *I* will put it. That is what we believe."

"They'll try to erase him! 'A man who came through many trials to Christ.' Trials we put him through!"

"Susan—"

"I'm sorry, Daddy, but if I don't say it, I'll just explode. It would be a kind of lying, lying with silence. There's been enough of that."

He put his arms around her and hugged her while she cried. He stroked her hair until she stopped shaking, then offered her his handkerchief. "You don't have to bear it alone, you know. There's always someone you can lay it on."

Susan wiped her eyes and shook her head. "I tried that. We both did, Andy and me. It didn't work. I'm sorry, Daddy, but I don't think the Lord was there for us. Not this time."

He dropped his arms. "I meant, you can lay it on me."

Susan looked up but didn't answer.

"Susan." He reached for her again. "Susan, am I losing you as well?"

She shook her head. "I don't know, Daddy. I truly don't know."

"I don't think I could bear it if I did." He stood there in the hall, the door outlining him in quiet light.

She looked at her hat. "I need to go to the hospital, see how Ginny's doing. I promised Harry." She stepped around her father, then turned and kissed him on the cheek. "I do still love you, Daddy. That hasn't changed. It never will."

Harry jostled the wriggling infant in its warmed-up blanket. The baby was bawling, the effort turning his entire tiny body red. Harry leaned in toward Virginia's bed. "Listen to the lungs on this guy! He's a sparkplug, ain't he?" Virginia's eyes remained closed, as they had most of the past two weeks. He turned and addressed the infant. "Hey, who's fighting my baby, huh? Who's fighting my boy?" He grinned at the continuous howling. *At least he's the right color, now*, he thought. *That yellow cast sure was spooky.*

"Andy?" A weak voice rose from the bed. Virginia's eyes were open.

"Hey, baby," he said, "are you with us again?"

"Andy . . ." she said and reached for the squirming bundle. The effort exhausted her and her eyes closed again.

It was the second time this had happened and it worried Harry. Why did she keep asking for Andy? She didn't know about the wreck, of course. She'd been in the hospital that night since before it happened. But why did she keep reaching for the baby and saying "Andy"? Did she want him to name the child Andy? Harry didn't know what he thought about that. *No, that's not true*, he thought. *I know what I think, and it ain't good. I can't name my son after a guy who . . .* He could almost hear Ginny challenging him in his head: Who what? *Spread himself all along the railroad tracks!* he argued back. *Not to mention the whole queer thing with Sunny.* He shook his head. *No. No way a kid of mine is going to be saddled with that name.*

He'd heard about the coroner's verdict—who hadn't?—and he suspected he wasn't the only one having trouble swallowing it. People were making up all sorts of explanations. He certainly wasn't buying the "wondrous story" he heard making the rounds at the hospital. He didn't believe a word of it, even though his "miracle baby" was part of it. He had no truck with miracles. Good doctors were what saved his premature son's life, and good nurses were keeping him alive. Sheer luck had discovered Virginia's tumor before it did more damage. But still, people will tell their stories.

"Mr. Edom?" a gentle voice asked.

"Huh?" He snapped to, confused to find Virginia still unconscious in the bed when he felt like they'd just had another of their arguments, one he was losing.

"It's time we put this little fella back in his special bed," the nurse said, extending her arms.

"Oh, sure." He gave him over awkwardly. There was some special way you were supposed to hold babies, but he couldn't remember what it was.

"Oh, and Mr. Edom? They're asking about the name again."

"Name?"

"Yes. Down in records? For the birth certificate. Now that we know he's going to stay with us, we'd better have a name for him, hadn't we?"

Harry was appalled at the casual way she talked about his son's tenuous start in life. "Uh . . ." he sputtered, "er . . . Andy?"

The nurse smiled. "Randy? Randy Edom?"

"Yeah. Yeah, right. Randy." He grinned with relief. He could blame it on the hospital. Ginny couldn't hold that against him.

"Any middle name?"

"No."

He followed in a blissful fog as the nurse carried little Randy back to the incubator room. "I'll get the paperwork started just as soon as I get him settled," she said.

Harry was still gazing on his boy when Susan came up and touched him on the arm. "Hey, Harry."

"Hey," he said, not turning from the window. The nurse had been right. Now that his son had a name, he seemed more real.

"I was just down to the room. Ginny's still out of it."

"Uh-huh."

Susan looked through the window with him. "Which one?"

It seemed obvious to him, but he pointed out his boy anyway.

"Have you and Ginny picked a name yet?"

Harry nodded. "Randy."

"A family name?"

"No. Just Randy."

Susan shook her head in wonder. "Gosh, he's so small."

"Small but mighty."

"I'm sorry, I didn't mean to be—"

"No, no," Harry said. He was suddenly filled with the joy of bragging. "You should hear the lungs on that guy. A real spark plug! He was just eager to get started, is all. A week or two premature, but, boy, he wanted out."

Susan smiled. "Ginny wanted him out, too."

Harry's eyes went wide. "Yeah. Thank God we won't be going through that again." He felt his throat tighten and he turned to the wall.

She touched his shoulder. "Harry?"

He turned, tears on his cheeks. "I almost lost her, Suzie-Q."

They sat in plastic molded chairs with a planter on either side and he told her about that night at the hospital: the premature birth, the hemorrhage, and Virginia going into surgery just as the city ambulance brought in first Andy then her father. "It was a nightmare," he said. "Everything happening at once. And then they found the mass, and . . ." He came up short and just shook his head.

Susan held his hand. "But they got it, right? They got it all?"

Harry gulped and nodded. "Yeah, but Ginny won't . . . We won't be able to—" He got up and walked over to the maternity window again.

"Let's just say we'd better take good care of this little guy, here. He's all we got."

"Oh, Harry." She gave him a hug. "I'm so sorry."

He shrugged. "No need to be sorry. We got one. That's more than some get."

"If there's anything I can do . . . ?"

Harry ran his hand through his hair. "Well, yeah." He looked down the hall. "It doesn't look like Ginny is going to be out of the hospital before we have to bury the old fart. I mean, Lerner. I mean—"

"I know who you mean."

He shook his head. "This is so weird, Susan! The old bastard could barely stand me living in the same town with him, and now I'm supposed to bury him? It just doesn't feel right. And with Ginny not even there! It's like some kind of bizarre curse, like some kind of vengeance I'm taking on him."

"No, Harry. It's just life. It's just coincidence. Sometimes—"

She stopped as a nurse carrying a clipboard approached them. She smiled familiarly at Susan and asked Harry for a signature. The young woman continued smiling at her while Harry signed the form; Susan had to turn away to escape the unabashed stare.

"Well, that was rude," she said when the nurse left.

"What?"

"Look at them." The young woman had stopped partway down the hall to speak to some other nurses. They all turned and looked at them, smiling. "It's creepy."

"Aw, don't pay them any attention," Harry said. "They treat little Randy the same way."

"What way?"

Harry shrugged. "It's just something they say. Two miracles in one night."

"What miracles?"

"Well, little spark plug there, and you."

"What do you mean, me? What are you talking about?"

Harry shifted uneasily. "Well, they say the Miracle Man performed one more miracle before God snatched him up to heaven. He asked God to see you safe, and you were thrown clear when the train hit the car."

Susan turned pale. "But that's not what happened!" she exclaimed.

"Hey, hey! Quiet. This is a maternity ward, you know?"

Susan glared down the hall. "I've a good mind to slap some sense into that girl!"

"Settle down." He brought them back to the chairs. "It's just people making up stories to help them make sense of things. Two deaths, two lives. Two miracles."

Susan glared at the eternally green plants. "How can lies help any-thing?"

"Would the truth be any better? The real truth?" Susan's hands tightened into fists. "Man, you are wound tighter than a tick."

She shook her head. "This town will drive me crazy."

"Well, if going crazy helps . . ."

She gave him a half-smile and he felt relieved—but only a little. *Useless lunk*, he heard Ginny say in his head.

He felt even more useless when he answered Cyrus Brown's request to meet him in his office the following week. The large man sat behind his desk, not rising or offering his hand, just indicating the polished oak chair for him to sit in. Harry settled but didn't speak, being pretty sure what the meeting was about.

"How did that investment work out for you, Harry?" Cyrus asked, cocking his head a little to one side.

"Not as good as I hoped."

"But you got back more than you put in, didn't you?"

"Barely. You led me to think it would be much more."

Cyrus cocked his head to the other side and looked at an open folder on his desk. "It was an investment, Harry, not a guarantee. Still, one wants to see a brother Chickasaw prosper. We are one nation, after all, even if the connection is somewhat . . . diluted."

Harry bristled but said nothing.

Cyrus looked up. "Any plans?"

Harry shrugged. "The oil fields are hiring. I could roughneck it again. That'll bring money in soon enough."

"It'll bring in money, but not soon enough." Cyrus turned the folder on his desk around so Harry could read it. "I'm calling in the note on the Alquist property."

This was the topic Harry had feared since that day, weeks ago, when he had confronted Lerner about the bad checks and appealed to Brown for remedy. It was then he had found out just how badly extended Lerner Alquist was, and what the old man had put on the line. "You pick a fine time for it, Cyrus. The old man dead, and his only heir lying in the hospital, barely able to spell her name."

"I pick my fights to win them. You chose to pay your men, I chose to extend the terms of the loan. Those terms are now past due."

Harry eyed him steadily. "You have to live in this town as much as I do."

Brown shifted in his chair. He appeared to be considering something, but Harry wasn't taken in. Whatever came next, Harry knew Cyrus Brown had been planning it for some time. "I'll make you an offer," Brown said. "Sell Virginia's deeds to that land west of town to the development corporation and you can keep the house."

Harry smiled. Ginny didn't need to be here at all. He knew exactly what to say. "They aren't mine to sell."

"You're her husband."

"That's right. And she trusts me." He looked at the bookcases lining one wall and shook his head. "You know, I remember a time when, if a white man married a Chickasaw woman and then turned around and sold her land out from under her, why, they'd both of them be kicked outta town." He looked Brown in the eye. "You remember something like that, don't you?"

Brown's gaze didn't waver. "Times change."

"Not that much. But it's clear some things have." He reached over and closed the manila folder. "I'm sorry, Cyrus. You and I don't walk the same path anymore."

Cyrus Brown sat very still. "You and I never walked the same path, Edom. Your family sold that option a long time ago."

Harry stood. The urge to reach across and punch that round, placid visage welled up and washed over him. Then it passed right on through, gone in a breath. "They say blood's thicker than water, but I guess money is thicker still. No deal, Cyrus. What's Ginny's is Ginny's. You wouldn't be trying to get around her if that trust Lerner set up for her and Randy didn't have you tied up in knots. The way I figure it, you tied most of them knots yourself, and I reckon they can just stay that way."

"I'm making one last offer."

"Go suck an egg."

Brown said nothing. He reached across his desk to a bodark box and took out a cigar and lit it. When it got good and smoking he looked up at Harry expressionless. With the slightest nod, he indicated the door.

In the bright afternoon light outside the Savings and Loan, Harry stopped and listened for the sound of Ginny's reproach ringing in his head. When several seconds passed and it didn't come, he headed back to the hospital. For the first time in days, he felt he could tell her the whole awful truth.

Chapter 39

Witness

The memorial service for Andrew Lewis Simms was held several days after his burial in the cemetery north of town. The burial, just two days after the coroner's verdict, was sparsely attended; between the train wreck and the autopsy, there hadn't been much to bury. There had been no viewing, not even of a closed casket. The town had much on its mind: the death of one of its leading citizens and the collapse of his personal empire; the simultaneous disappearance of the Memorial Library sculpture and its artist; the tide of gossip that washed from one side of town to the other. The more interesting rumors—involving miracles, perversion, and financial skullduggery—were quickly displaced by the more alarming one that the Santa Fe was not going to repair the main line through town. It had been twisted into modern sculpture by the derailment of several boxcars during the accident. With Lisle Armbruster no longer fit to act as agent, it was thought the railroad would abandon the route in favor of one further east. With so many targets to choose from, people had difficulty focusing their disapprobation.

But by the time of the memorial service, that toughness inherent in the cross timbers country had begun to reassert itself in the citizens of Croy. The rail line was going to be repaired after all, and with that worry lifted, there were soon other things (and other people) to talk about, and what might have been a source of scandal just a few weeks ago had mellowed into a kind of sentimental regret.

The day of the service itself was especially fine. There was a clarity to the air filled with delicate acuity: the afternoon light noted each blade of grass and articulated leaf, voices carried without effort, and a song sung outdoors could be heard clear across town.

All the windows of Mt. Hermon Bible Church were open to the autumn afternoon. The pews were full. As Pastor Jacobs had predicted, many wanted to pay their respects to Andy and were grateful they could do so with a clear conscience. Without Susan, the preparations had nearly overwhelmed the pastor. It was Clara Oldfield who noticed his sagging energy and suggested calling in someone from their sister church. In a moment of exhaustion and weakness, he agreed. Brother Joshua Mathers would run the service, Brother Matthew Jacobs would give the eulogy.

Flowers were not usual at such a service in their church, there being more pragmatic and missionary uses for the money. Nevertheless, a few garlands and bouquets graced the sanctuary. "From my garden," Clara Oldfield said, depositing her vase beside the pulpit. "We can use them in the service tomorrow." Most surprising was a wreath with a card reading "The Trembling Hour Ministries." Matthew supposed that was Mathers' doing, not Grenville's. The church was otherwise undecorated. Mathers and Jacobs sat in plain chairs in the sanctuary, the choral risers standing mute witness beside them.

Mathers started with an invocation, which was followed by the congregation singing "Come Ye Disconsolate." The singing sent shivers up Matthew's spine. When Andy had led the choir, the hymn had been full of harmony and color. Now it seemed stark and painful. *Perhaps I am truly hearing it for the first time*, he thought.

Then Reverend Mathers rose and stepped up to the pulpit. "We are here to remember our brother, Andy Simms, a man who came to us with many gifts and came to Christ through many trials," he began. "But we are not here to celebrate his life. Andy would not want that. He understood, as all those who come to Christ do, that the gifts we bear are not our own. Andy accepted Jesus Christ as his Lord and Savior, and from that moment on, the Holy Spirit filled the vessel of his life. And once the Spirit fills you, there is no room for anything else. There is no self, no accomplishment, no reaching for favor or acclaim, for it is all the Spirit's doing, not our own. There is nothing to celebrate except the Glory of the Lord. Andy knew that, Andy believed that, Andy lived that. And so this is not a celebration of Andy's life, but a celebration of the Grace of our Lord Jesus Christ as it was so beautifully evident in his life."

Matthew felt as if he were outside himself, looking in. How many times had he said these very words himself? And yet how odd they now sounded. "They'll try to erase him," Susan had said. Is that what he had been doing all these years? *With Christ in the center, we are all equal*, he thought, *but does that make us all the same? Is there nothing to be said about Andy himself?*

Mathers invited members of the congregation to celebrate the Grace of God as reflected in the life of their brother Andy. The church was silent for a while.

John Tibbits was the first to rise and step to the front. He had difficulty talking, opening his mouth more than once before anything came out. Finally he said, "I believe Jesus has touched my life. I believe He has touched it, and He has touched my wife, and our infant child, who God is sending to us. And for this, I . . ." He glanced at Mathers. "I have Andy Simms to thank. He helped me see, to feel the power of the Spirit. To see it come through the music, through the choir, through my own dear wife. He was a window. A window into faith and what it could do for us. And for that, I . . . I thank you, Jesus, for sending us Andy to show us your Glory." He returned to his seat without looking up.

Lila Armbruster stood next before the congregation, her eyes bright with tears. "I just want to say what beautiful, beautiful music came to us through Andy. I always feel closest to God when I'm singing, and now we have these beautiful, beautiful hymns he wrote." She put a handkerchief to her eyes. "Eternal praise. Amen."

There was a moment of silence. Then Scotty Pritchard stood and walked slowly to the front.

"I'm just . . . I want to say . . ." Scotty began, but broke off, crying. Matthew stirred, but Brother Joshua got to him first, holding him to his shoulder as he cried. Then Scotty pulled away, saying, "I'm fine." Mathers looked at him questioningly, then nodded and sat down.

"I just want to say," Scott began again, "I just want to say, I'm young, and I don't understand. Why is he gone? Why was he taken from us, and why like that?" He looked like he was going to break down again, but instead his voice grew stronger. "I lost four friends this summer. Four friends, and someone I really loved." Matthew heard Mathers stir in his seat, but he made a gesture and he settled down. "That's too many!" Scotty declared. "I know God is good, and so good has to come from this, but I just don't see how. Andy Simms was the only person who ever really listened to me, who really heard me. And I'm not the only one he treated like that. He taught me that love starts in the heart. If you listen to your heart, if there is truth there, then there is Christ there, and your heart cannot lead you wrong. Well, I listened to my heart. I still listen. I listen, but I can't hear anything. It's all gone, and I don't know why." He looked up, staring at the ceiling. "Jesus. Jesus, I'm listening." He stood a moment, oblivious to the silence around him. "God must be good. That's what Andy said. God must be good, or nothing in life would be beautiful. There would be no love, there would be no music, there would be no sunset at the end of the day." His hands floated up beside him. "This day is beautiful. Andy would think so. So God must be good." He searched the ceiling as if trying to peer through it. "God must be good. God must be good."

Someone in the congregation said "Amen" and Scotty suddenly seemed to realize where he was. His arms dropped and he looked around. "Amen," he muttered and sat down.

Mathers turned to Matthew. He knew what that look meant. As pastor, it was his duty to take the emotional charge that Scotty had left hanging in the air and turn it towards the Light. But Matthew felt suddenly weary, as if his body were made of sand. He gave a barely perceptible shake of his head and looked down.

Mathers rose and stood before the people. He looked out over their pale and puzzled faces and took a deep breath. "Scotty is right," he said. "It is hard." He cleared his throat and started again.

I knew Andy only briefly, during last month's revival. He was a talented, bright, good-humored young man, full of joy and life. And the death of such a one, so close to so many and so willing to serve the Lord, is hard to bear. Andy was taken from us with such force and violence that we were left unprepared, unready, without even a proper way to mourn. But we should not mourn; we should rather celebrate his return to Jesus' embrace.

The Lord sees all: the flaws we have, the trials we face, and all the trials to come. Andy's trials were not so different from ours, and Andy's capacity to face them no greater. Perhaps that is what Jesus saw when He looked down upon Andy's ruined heart, and spared him.

The Lord spared him a wasting death. He was spared that tribulation. His body, so close to betraying him, as all bodies must, was discarded, but his soul remained intact. The Spirit's timing is impeccable. Andy had come to Jesus just the day before, and he left us still in the sanctity of that Grace, before sin could mar his soul again. And as a sign of the Spirit's will, despite the awful power employed to work it, no harm came to anyone else: not the passenger in Andy's car, nor the engineer on the train, nor any of the brave police and firemen who responded to the carnage and prevented a wider catastrophe.

Andy's death, even the manner of his death, reveals the Glory of God. This is the mark the Spirit has placed upon this town, that all who know it and all who may hear of it will know of God's Power and Glory, and know that those who have entered His Kingdom need fear no corruption, no destruction, no pain in this life or the next, for their God has covered them in His Blood and will bring them safely home.

Mathers sat down, practically vibrating with energy. *He's full of himself,* Matthew thought, surprised by his anger. Why should he be angry at Mathers? What the man had said was perfectly orthodox. Why then did it strike him as a wad of rhetoric, a set-piece? Others spoke afterwards, but Pastor Jacobs lost track, words and images swirling around in his head. Then he realized that the church had grown silent and Mathers was looking at him again. It was time for his eulogy.

He stepped up to the pulpit, the words he had planned to say floating before him. He could see them written out on paper, the carefully chosen phrases, the verses neatly copied like pages in a notebook. "Leave some space for the Spirit to get in," a voice in his head said—and he erased the eulogy from his mind and opened his mouth to hear what might be revealed.

Brother Joshua has invited us to see the Glory of God in the twisted steel and mangled wreckage of that dreadful night. I confess I find this hard to do. In large letters outside our door is a sign that says, "Christ is the answer," but that isn't the whole of it. Christ *has* the answer, but we must go looking for it.

When Jesus walked this Earth, His disciples often turned to Him and asked, "Master, what are we to do?" They looked to Him to turn their dangerous and threatening world into a New and Holy Kingdom. Not some symbolic kingdom in the heart, not some future, far-off kingdom in the sky, but a kingdom right here and now. Jesus tried to tell them they got it wrong. He proved that He *could* do it by rising from the dead. He proved He *would not* do it by ascending into Heaven.

Why? How are we to enter the Kingdom of Heaven when our rabbi, our Master is gone?

One of the last parables of Jesus—Matthew 13—is that the Kingdom of Heaven is like a net thrown into the sea, a net that collects all kinds of fish, good fish and bad fish, and in the end the good fish will be separated from the bad. I can see the scene before me like I was there: Jesus preaching to the crowds gathered along the shore, a crowd so vast he had to stand in a boat to address them all. What was he saying? "The good fish will be separated from the bad." Yes, but who will be doing the separating? It is not the fish caught in the net. It is the Fisherman standing in the boat. So before we say, "Andy was taken before sin could mar his soul," let us think about that image, and about our place in it.

We spend too much of our lives separating who is good from who is bad. We get ahead of ourselves. We separate ourselves from God and each other when we try to stand in that boat in His stead.

I knew Andy Simms less than a year, but I knew him better than I know some of you. I knew him through his music. For that is where Andy truly lived, in his music. That is where the gifts he brought us shined most brightly, and where he is still. Though his face we may not see again, that part of him which filled our hearts with joy is still with us. We have only to open our mouths to sing, and there it is.

Andy's capacity to love was not a common thing. No love is a common thing. It is pride that makes us try to weigh it, to say with certitude that one kind of love is the only kind God will accept. And the minute we do that, we step onto that rocking boat, on those uncertain, stormy seas that only One knows how to still.

If we can but lose our certitude, if we can sometimes doubt, I say that, too, is a gift of the Spirit. Because it makes us listen. It is a silence that bears witness, it is the absent Master who teaches. Having all our questions settled, all our dismal doubts dispelled, is not a sign of faith, but a symptom that our ears are stopped up with doctrine.

Our brother Andy had many gifts, but I think we couldn't bear to receive them all. We wanted only the ones we understood, only the ones we already knew, the ones we were certain of. The good ones. We cut off those gifts we did not understand and we threw them away. I think that is what really put those holes in Andy's heart: the parts of him we threw away. But Jesus knew our brother complete, whole, and perfect as he was, knew him and loved him and snatched him up suddenly, before that awful engine could destroy him. And now those holes are in our hearts. That silence, that absence is Andy's final gift to us. Let those who can, listen.

Chapter 40

PEOPLE OF THE LIGHT

Virginia Edom and Susan Jacobs stood leaning against the passenger fender of Virginia's car across the street from the Santa Fe depot. This was where the Trailways bus would stop on its way through town if anyone were waiting. Virginia held a four-month-old baby cradled in one arm; the other arm transported a cigarette to and from her lips on a regular schedule. Susan clutched a suitcase in both hands, but she grew tired and set it down. When she straightened up, an obvious bulge showed beneath her winter coat. It was cold and the two women held themselves tightly. Neither liked awkward good-byes, so for the longest time neither of them spoke. It was Susan who broke the silence. "Did he really tell him to go suck an egg?" she asked.

Virginia cocked her head and smiled. "You know Harry. Not the most subtle of guys."

Susan shook her head. "Cyrus Brown had some nerve. While you were still in the hospital, too."

Virginia shrugged. "My being in the hospital had nothing to do with it. It was already a done deal. Harry saw it coming, tried to do something about it. I didn't see it at the time, of course. I just thought it was another hare-brained scheme of his. But he was trying to save the house, save our reputations." She exhaled a puff of smoke in a half-laugh. "Can you imagine that? Harry Edom, saving the family name of Alquist from the disgrace of bankruptcy! Lerner must be spinning in his grave."

"It just doesn't seem right, that old toad squatting in your house. And it *is* your house. It will always be the Alquist mansion as far as anyone is concerned."

"Brown can have it. Fat lot of good it'll do him. Fat lot of good it did us. Nope, Harry did the right thing, holding out when Cyrus offered him the swap."

"Those properties must be worth something. Brown wouldn't have offered otherwise."

"I doubt it. Have you taken a look around here lately, Suzie-Q? There's never going to be a rail line west of town. Hell, in ten years, I doubt there'll be a rail line *through* town. No, Lerner sold off all the good stuff to keep afloat. What he left me—me and the kid—is worth squat." Randy twitched in her arms and she smiled down at him. "Hear that pumpkin? You get squat." Randy giggled. "Yes, yes you do. In just eighteen years. Should be a whole lot of squat by then."

She looked at Susan. "Thanks, by the way, for helping while I was out of it."

Susan shook her head and sighed. "I wish I could be here while Harry is away."

"I can manage pretty well by myself. Always have." Virginia gestured at the suitcase with her free hand. "I always knew it would come to this someday. But the way I pictured it, the suitcase would be emblazoned 'Broadway or Bust!'"

Susan smiled. "Funny, in my dreams it always said 'Nashville.'"

"Or, hey, 'Hollywood'!"

"Dear Miss Burdell. What a lot of nonsense she filled our heads with."

"Yeah, God love her." They turned to each other, and then simultaneously struck a pose and declared, "We were born to change the world!" When the laughter subsided, Virginia took a long drag on her cigarette. "Don't come back, Suzie-Q," she said. "What's here for you? I've made my choices, I got what I wanted. Well, what I asked for, anyway."

Susan shook her head. "I can't just give up. I can't let them take my father's church away from him."

"Well, in your state, you're not exactly an argument in his favor." Susan turned away. "Sorry, hon, but you know it's true or you wouldn't be leaving."

"You're right." She exhaled heavily. "Truth is, I don't even know if Daddy wants to hold onto Mt. Hermon anymore. They don't seem to have understood his eulogy any better than—oh, anything he's done." She pushed off from the car and threw her arms open. "Maybe I should keep quiet, but I just can't take it anymore! What they're saying about Daddy, about Andy, about me. They don't care. They march on, the

Army of the Lord, people filled with a Holy Light, trampling everything in their path, including their own wounded." She kicked the car.

"Hey," Virginia said.

Susan smiled wanly. "Sorry. Shouldn't take it out on old Stu, should I?"

"Oh hell, go ahead. It's paid for. It's the one thing that *is* paid for."

"Some warriors we turned out to be, huh?"

Virginia regarded her a moment. "You did. You still are. You've got something, kiddo. Don't throw it away on a place that can't even see it, let alone care about it."

Susan laughed, her eyes wet. "I said the same thing to Andy."

Virginia almost asked, "When?" but thought better of it. She nodded toward Susan's growing belly. "Andy's kid deserves a better chance."

Susan turned and looked down the street. Virginia could tell she didn't want to talk about it anymore. She crushed the cigarette out with her heel.

"Here it comes," Susan said.

The north-bound bus was a silver blob headed their way, a plume of diesel smoke in its wake. "Yep," Virginia said, then added offhandedly, "Hey, while you're up there in Oklahoma City—"

"Yeah?"

"Well, Norman's not so far away. You could, you know—"

"What?"

"Well, see how Sunny and Tucker are doing."

Her friend's face closed up. "Sunny Sohi could have stayed in that coma for all I care. I never want to see him again."

"You blame him, don't you."

The hard look melted. "No. I blame myself."

She made one last effort. "Well, Tucker could use the company. I kinda miss the old Stone Face."

Susan shrugged. "We were never close."

The bus for Oklahoma City rolled to a dusty stop in front of the depot and wheezed open its door. Susan picked up her suitcase and they crossed the street. It was an awkward good-bye after all, Susan bending half-over in the doorway to the bus, Virginia leaning in and juggling Randy. There were quick kisses on the cheek and something unmemorable said, and then the door closed and she was gone.

Well, that's that, Virginia thought. *Harry off to the oil fields, Susan off to her aunt's for the duration, if not longer. My father dead and buried. The rest of the gang scattered.* Her cigarette butt still smoldered on the sidewalk. She kicked it to the gutter and headed for the Studebaker. "Nobody left but you and me, kiddo," she said to Randy as she wedged him between pillows on the passenger seat.

A great heaviness came over her. She tapped a cigarette out of the pack in her purse and paused before lighting it. She looked at the depot across the street. She couldn't remember the last time a passenger train had come through town, but she was sure one had once, when she was a kid. *It's all falling apart*, she thought. She tapped the Pall Mall against the wheel and put it to her lips. *Well*, she told herself, *things have to fall apart if they're ever going to be put together again. Maybe different, maybe better.* She lit up and sucked deeply, then picked a loose flake of tobacco from her tongue. *Maybe not. And that's enough deep thoughts for today. It's moving time.*

Jedediah Tucker felt awkward with the bunch of yellow wildflowers in his hand. It made his whole arm feel useless. He had picked the flowers from around the pond upslope from Sunny's trailer—or rather, upslope from the charred earth where Sunny's trailer had stood. The first time he'd come back looking for his truck, the ruins of Sunny's trailer were still smoldering. His truck was there, but all four tires were slashed. *They should've burned it, too*, Tucker had thought. *Save me the trouble.* This time when he went, even the truck was gone.

He approached the nurses' station where a woman worked diligently on a chart. He was used to the remarkable concentration these woman could evidence, capable of ignoring a six foot four inch, two hundred and fifty pound Indian standing less than three feet away from them for minutes at a time, so he spoke up immediately, asking if Mr. Sohi was taking visitors today. The woman looked up and smiled. "He should be back from physical therapy soon. You can wait in his room if you like. His uncle Bushyhead is in there now."

Tucker scowled, but she had returned to her paperwork and didn't notice. *Sunny's uncle? But his name isn't Bushyhead, it's—* something Indian. India Indian. He sighed and walked down the sterile hallway. When he pushed open the door to Sunny's room, there sat his own uncle, weaving a piece of straw by the window. Tucker almost turned around and left when he saw what his uncle fashioned: a *panicua*, a straw figure to hang on Christmas trees—yet another fragment his crazy uncle had picked up from some tribe or other and claimed as his own.

Tucker stood in the doorway long enough for his presence to be felt. His uncle looked up. "Your friend will be here soon," he said.

Tucker put the wilting bouquet on the bedside table. "You've been telling stories to the nurses again."

"He hears the red-wing blackbird, I think. '*Toke mat'a ni, toke mat'a ni!*'"

Tucker settled into the other chair. "I've heard that story, too, uncle, and it isn't one of ours."

His uncle put aside his straw work. "You didn't let me finish, before. That story when you came with your friend in your arms. It is also not one of ours. Perhaps you will not hear it."

Tucker crossed his arms. His uncle would go on no matter what he did.

"It was a place of chaos and disgust and filth, that place where the two men fought with their war clubs, that place the man in women's clothes fled from in fear. It was there that the Isolated Earth People and the People of the Light met and came to peace. It was there that they were purified. They were both of them purified, the Isolated Earth People and the People of the Light. They became one people there and have not been apart since that time." His uncle nodded toward the bedside table. "Yellow flowers now grow over that place, a place that was once a place of chaos and disgust and filth." He picked up his *panicua* and worked another shaft of wheat into the design.

Tucker stared at him, angry at the easy wisdom. "Will they ever fit together, uncle? Your stories and your bird calls and your straw figures? Or will they always be just a jumble of fragments from different clans?"

Uncle Crazy Head held up the finished figure, a little devil, and twirled it by a long stalk through its center. "As long as we see separate clans, they will be a jumble. We are all crazy heads."

There was shuffling at the door, and Tucker turned to see Sunny walk in. He was using a cane. He was freshly shaved and his hair had been cut, though the part of his scalp that had been shaved for the surgery had yet to catch up. Brad, the physical therapist, walked behind him in that alert posture Tucker knew was ready to grab Sunny by the belt if he should start to slump. But Sunny made it all the way to the bed and sat without assistance.

"Much better!" Brad said. "Tomorrow, then? Same time?"

Sunny smiled. "I'll check my schedule."

Brad laughed. "Squeeze me in, if you can." He turned to Tucker. "Nice to see you again, Mr. Tucker, and Mr. . . . uh . . ."

"Bushyhead," Tucker's uncle said.

Sunny laughed out loud. Brad laughed, too, though he didn't know at what. "Tomorrow, then. See ya!" and he left.

Sunny fell back on the pillows, exhausted. "Squeeze him in? Oh, man, I would love to!"

Tucker glanced nervously at his uncle, but the man just stood and handed the *panicua* to Sunny. "This one is for you."

Sunny took it and examined it closely, admiring the many folds and interwoven stalks. "A little devil, is it?" He smiled. "Got that right."

"I'll wait a while outside," Tucker's uncle said and left the room.

"What do you think of the cane?" Sunny asked brightly.

"Don't you ever stop?"

"I think it makes me look dapper." Sunny tapped the cane on the floor but didn't meet Tucker's eyes. He glanced over at the table, noticed the limp flowers, and reached for them. "You bring these?"

"Yeah. From the hill above the pond."

Sunny nodded. "Was there . . . Did you find anything?"

Tucker shook his head. "It's all gone. They cleaned up the site. Even towed away my truck."

"Doesn't matter," Sunny said. He pulled a sketch pad off the table and flipped it open. "Get me that pencil, will ya?" Sunny indicated a broad-leaded pencil on the window sill.

He fetched it and stood beside the bed, watching Sunny draw, his left arm holding down the pad like a dead weight. "The season's wrapping up."

"I know. I heard the last game on the radio." Sunny smiled. "You were mentioned."

Tucker blushed and looked away. How could Sunny still do that to him? And why did he let him? He took a deep breath. "I could maybe come visit more often."

"You've done enough." He waggled the pencil in his fingers. "The doctor says you probably saved my life. You and Uncle Crazy Head. Thanks."

Tucker clenched his jaw. "I spoke to Miss Lancaster. She says—"

"I don't care."

"Sunny, they can still—"

"It's done," he said firmly. "I made it. They saw it. It's done. They can saw it into bricks or throw it in the river for all I care. I'm done with people who refuse to see themselves."

He started working on the drawing again.

Tucker looked over and saw what filled the pad. It was part of the soldiers' panel, studies and angles and different perspectives. And everywhere, Andy's face: lit from above, lit from below, turned to look at his fallen comrade, staring straight out of the page. "Him again."

Sunny looked up.

"Why is it always him?"

Sunny's whole body became still and his eyes grew deep and distant. "If I remember him, I live. If I forget him, I die."

Tucker knew for certain then who were the Isolated Earth People, and who were the People of the Light.

Virginia stepped out of the Studebaker and hoisted Randy up on her hip. She looked at the small, four-room house that was now hers and sighed. A bush near the front porch threatened to swallow it whole, and multiple colors of mismatched roofing spoke of a long and storied history of leaks. Randy made a quizzical sound beside her. "Yeah, I know," Virginia said. "Think of it as cozy."

The real estate agent had followed her in a car that looked fresh off of Sullivan's lot. He got out and jingled the house keys.

Virginia turned away. "God give me strength," she said in a voice she hoped didn't carry.

"Would you like some help with the boxes?" the agent said, indicating the Studebaker's full back seat.

"No thanks," Virginia said. "Me and kiddo here can manage."

The agent looked relieved. "Well, here you are," he said, dropping the keys into her hand. "I think you'll like it here. Quiet neighborhood, nice people. And you can do a lot with these old sharecropper—homes."

She looked at him sourly. She was sure he had come within an inch of saying "sharecropper shacks." "I'll just bet," she said. He took that as his cue and bid her good day and left.

Virginia crossed the lawn but didn't want to enter the house just yet. She walked around the back, where she found the inverted-umbrella shape of a clothes drying tree minus its clothesline. "All the modern conveniences," she said.

Across the gravel alley, she saw an older woman working in her garden behind a small, low house. Further up the lawn was a large, two-story home, probably the original farmhouse to the three sharecropper's quarters on this side of the alley. The old woman looked up. Virginia smiled and waved. "Hiya!" she called.

The woman rose and scowled and Virginia immediately recognized Mrs. Oldfield. Randy squirmed on her hip and began to bawl. She shifted him to her arms and jiggled him, but his crying only got louder. She smiled helplessly at her new neighbor and shrugged. Mrs. Oldfield's scowl grew deeper.

"Great," Virginia muttered. "Off to a fine start."

Ida Laine Lancaster, Head Librarian, Croy Memorial Library

Miss Ida Laine Lancaster stood in the dim light of the storeroom and lifted the tarp that shrouded a wooden frame. It was one of three stored in and around the city. She took one last look before dropping the canvas and securing the rope. She felt tears pressing into the corners of her eyes but pulled them back, thinking them unprofessional. *Someday*, she said to herself, *this beauty and strength, this work of love, will see the light of day. But not here, not now. The uproar would surely destroy it, like a tornado that rips apart everything in its path.* She must keep it safe until the storm passes, though when that future day might come was anybody's guess. She doubted it would be in her lifetime. But that's what libraries were for: to hold the truth in safekeeping until the world was ready, until it came seeking the answers to questions that had already been answered a hundred times before, though people had forgotten.

She turned out the light and locked the door, taking the key with her.

Acknowledgments

Readers of the early drafts of this novel gave me the encouragement I needed to continue. I am particularly thankful to Rémy Ceci, whose support was unwavering; Maurice McCann, David Worley, and Sara Elward, whose decades of friendship did not blunt their critiques (and, indeed, may have sharpened them); Wade Dowdell, who really did listen to me read the entire thing aloud; and the members of the Palo Alto Gay Book Club, who read the first complete version prior to its many revisions.

I am also indebted to the sharp eyes and sound advice of my fellow authors and editors who helped identify flaws and inconsistencies in the text: Surajit Bose, David Pratt, Lewis DeSimone, Gar McVey-Russell, David Pederson, and Felice Picano. Any shortcomings or errors that remain are mine.

A historical novel needs deep roots. I found them in Ada and Marlow, Oklahoma. I am particularly indebted to the faculty and staff of Oklahoma's East Central University. In particular: Dr. Rich Alford, Department of Sociology (who told me about the buried elephant); Dr. Christine Pappas, Department of Political Science; and Angie Brunk, Reference Librarian at Linscheid Library. Christopher Clark and the library staff at Ada Public Library guided my search on the history of Ada, and Debbe Ridley of the Marlow Chamber of Commerce opened the Marlow Area Museum for me on a Sunday and provided commentary on the exhibits and photocopies of many archived newspaper articles.

Additional resources include the web site on Oklahoma Carnegie Libraries created by Susan Booker of the University of Oklahoma and Tanya Finchman of Oklahoma State University ("Historical Architecture in Oklahoma," http://geog_arch.okstate.edu; select "Oklahoma Cities with Carnegie Libraries"). This historical survey is a treasure trove of documents about the struggles many towns faced trying to build and maintain their libraries, including this detail about the one in El Reno: "the flat areas along the projecting portal roofline once held a sculpture." Billy Jim Crawford, Ed Russar, and Jeff Bowles provided personal histories about growing up gay in Oklahoma in the 1950s and 1960s.

Clark-Ann Haas helped me recover photos and eye-witness accounts of the TriState Tornado of 1925; we both grew up in communities where the events of that dreadful day were part of living memory. Tamara Linse's article, "A Senator's Suicide," in the *Casper Star-Tribute* (November 1, 2004), offered insights into Senator Lester Hunt's tragic death following threats by McCarthy-era Republicans to expose his son's homosexuality.

I have always been close to people with deep spiritual convictions, first and foremost among them my partner, Vivekan Don Flint, of blessed memory. I have listened to, read, and marked the words of Rev. Canon Christopher Seal (Ret.), Rev. Brad Helmuth, Rev. Ricardo Avila, and Jeremiah Aja, and have had long conversations with my friends Rev. David Worley, Stephen Riddle, and William Bonnell. They have helped shape my understanding of the function of faith in being human. (Mr. Bonnell also assisted in translating the lines from Virgil's *Aeneid*.) However, the religious views expressed by the characters in this story and the characters themselves are entirely my own invention.

About the Author

Louis Flint Ceci has been a high school teacher of English and drama in Benton, Illinois; an assistant professor of Journalism and Mass Communication and department chair at the University of Northern Colorado, Greeley; a commercial actor and freelance science journalist in the Denver-Boulder area; and a senior software engineer for several Silicon Valley companies, lastly at Skype, where he helped design and develop a user interface for the blind and visually impaired.

His poetry has been published in *Colorado North Review* and *Impossible Archetype*. His scholarly articles on linguistics and poetics have appeared in *College English* and *Literature in Performance*. He won the Gold Medal in the Poetic Justice Poetry Slam at the 2002 Gay Games in Sydney, Australia.

His short stories have appeared in *Jonathan* and *Trikone Magazine*, and in the anthologies *Queer and Catholic*, *Best Gay Erotica*, and *At Second Glance: Gay City Volume 4*. He has twice been a finalist in the *Saints+Sinners: New Stories from the Festival* short story contest, and was inducted into the Saints+Sinners Hall of Fame in 2017.

He is an avid U.S. Masters swimmer and won two gold and three silver medals at the 2020 International Gay and Lesbian Aquatics World Championships in Melbourne, Australia.

He lives in Nevada City, California.